FLYING FOX ACROSS THE MOON

BEN LAFFRA

BRICK, NEW JERSEY
2020

FLYING FOX ACROSS THE MOON
©2020 Ben Laffra
First Edition
Cover art by Jeffrey Kosh Graphics
Published by Optimus Maximus Publishing, LLC

This book is a work of fiction. Names, characters, businesses, organizations, places, events, and incidents either are the product of the author's imagination or are used fictitiously. Any resemblance to actual persons living, dead, or otherwise, events, or locales is entirely coincidental.

This book is protected under the copyright laws of the United States of America. Any reproduction or unauthorized use of the material or artwork contained herein is prohibited without the express written permission of the author.

ISBN: 978-1-944732-52-3

Ben Laffra has surprised me and will perhaps startle many of his followers with his new release of "Flying Fox across the Moon". He has stepped away from his usually serious genre of Historical Fiction to write a thoroughly entertaining light hearted book of a family with the name of Loots in India. Its written style is a classic example of a first person protagonist narrator. While the story is "represented" as a fictional account, Ben Laffra's whimsical description of the idiosyncrasies of the many characters strewn across the pages appear very real. His version of the British Raj of India is revealed as a fascinating, hypnotic and eccentric era and the individuals in the Loots Clan of Cantonment Bangalore are delightfully described as equally strange; if not a bit wacky! And when you read about the impish behaviour, capers and life of Tom Loots it smacks once more of a real life character. Frankly that makes it all the more interesting and leads one on to delightful conjecture of whether it's really fiction or a concealed biography! Whichever; he has crafted a story that's brim-full with humour to make you laugh and feel good about yourself ... just the tonic for this unhappy period!

I can't help but think; is there just the faint delicate blush of Harper Lee's characters lurking within this story?

Elizabeth Haran.

International bestselling Author of twenty books published in ten different languages that have even made the prestigious German "Der Spiegel" best seller list selling well over two million copies.

www.facebook.com/aussieoutbackauthor

FLYING FOX ACROSS THE MOON

BEN LAFFRA

PART ONE
The Loots clan!

BEN LAFFRA

1
The Loots shady past!

THE EPIC BATTLE AND SIEGE OF ARCOT way back in 1751 established Sir Robert Clive in the English History Books as a hero and forevermore marked a sea change in the fortunes of the East India Company in the sub-continent of India.

Some seventy years later Arcot was the scene of another change of lesser significance, but just as permanent.

Since 1709 the surname of Loots had withstood the test of time and the scourge of corrupted spelling (which was a common occurrence at that time) until it took a dramatic turn in the 1820s. The offender who started it was none other than my great, great Grandfather George Francis Loots. He was a soldier in the East India Company and was serving in the very same garrison fort at Arcot of Robert Clive fame.

George Loots married Martina Nancy Nicholas at Arcot on the 20th of February 1821 and very likely collected his East India Company claim of one "Gold Mohur" in doing so.

He also appears to have "married" a second time to a Mary "something or other", though this piece of information is under a serious cloud of suspicion! Did shifty George surreptitiously acquire himself a concubine so he could pocket another "Gold Mohur"?

This, of course, throws up another mystery; to wit, from which side of the blanket were we Loots descended? Was it Martina Nancy or concubine Mary? This was a scandal of epic proportions and an awful skeleton in the cupboard never to be revealed, discussed, hinted at, or even dare think about by the Loots clan.

There were other reasons why old George was considered "quia undesirable" as there was a grave suspicion he was a bit of a scoundrel to boot. He sometimes used the name of "Frank Letts" and there was the sneaking belief that he was into the business of illicit brewing and bootlegging of "arrack"; which was a very popular and potent liquor brew.

However, no matter what his nefarious activity might have been it did not affect his career or it might indeed have even advanced it. George Francis Loots became the Farrier Major in the Governor's Bodyguard, 7th Native Cavalry, Fort St George, in Madras India.

His "august" position advanced his libido, as well, as the blighter produced thirteen children between Martina Nancy and Concubine Mary. In the process, it was presumed the arrack he brewed also muddled his brain. At the christening of his substantial brood he managed to corrupt the spelling of our surname "Loots"; not once but in five of his thirteen brood who ended up being christened with various misspelled variations of the Loots surname!

George Francis died of dysentery in 1865. He must have accidentally guzzled the local water instead of his illicit arrack!

Having consigned "Philandering George" to the vault of secrecy it was far safer for the Loots Clan to throw up shaggy dog stories of earlier forebears of the Loots. And while I took care never to air my contrary views, I must confess, with the sliver of the old scoundrel lurking within me I rather liked old George Francis!

2
The Loots and the British Raj of India!

IF THERE WAS EVER A WRITER that eloquently captured the "nuance" of the period of the British Raj it was Rudyard Kipling. I loved Kipling's story of Kim. It was stirring stuff and reading. I wanted to be Kim one day and work in the British Secret Service and I swore a secret oath I would. But alas, like many of my ambitions the spine of conviction was missing and changed frequently on the inspiration and the moment of the day. I never did honour that oath. That aside, Kipling wrote a vast number of poems one of which was titled Gunga Din.

Kipling copped a fair bit of criticism about his writings on India. Some of his critics accused him of being patronising toward the Indian peoples in his works and some even accused him of being an "Imperial racist". But I am perhaps less unkind, for if Gunga Din is picked apart for its subliminal meaning it captures the romantic haunting memory of The British Raj. On the one hand, you have the British Soldier who admits to his constant persecution of the humble Indian water and ammunition carrier on the battlefields of the Afghan wars of the 1800s; yet, when he, the soldier is badly wounded in the battle, its Gunga Din who gives him water, carries him to safety, dresses his wounds and in the act of saving his life sacrifices his own.

The soldier laments:

"By the livin' Gawd that made you; You're a better man than I am, Gunga Din."

We Anglo Indian's mimicked the British way of life in every possible way and that has to do with how we came into being and why we lived in a "twilight" bubble of our own. It was inescapable because we were born, raised, and believed we were just "darker copies" of the British. It shaped our lives completely as well as the standards, mores, and foibles of the time.

We believed in the pristine provenance of an anglicized name; like Jones or Smith or Macfarlane and so on, while blithely ignoring their complexion. In short, those favoured by Mendel's Law were as white, freckled, blue-eyed and blond as any Englishman while others not so favoured varied in complexion from the "touch of the tar" through the full spectrum of jet black. Nevertheless, we set ourselves apart as a "superior tribe". So; some Anglo Indians affected a very pronounced British behaviour, some tried to fake themselves as really being British, others wanted to be superior to the "natives" so were downright ignorant racist's; and a few simply accepted they were different and could do without the prejudiced phobias.

Will Loots raised us to accept others as fellow human beings and that we were simply different. I think living in the bush, surrounded, and living with the local indigenous folk embedded his philosophy within our subliminal. I never once heard him speak a derogatory word about the local folk, but I did hear him gently chastise (as was his way) his sisters for doing so. His older siblings were racist.

I was to learn a lesson one day as well. Will had a new Assistant posted to him by the name of Nathan. Will told Carrie that Mr Nathan had told him he enjoyed "English" food and would eat anything so one night he was invited to dinner. Mr Nathan went through a helping of soup followed by two big helpings of Jemima's beef stew that would have challenged even Hansie's appetite! Anyway, Carrie asked him courteously if he would like some more: "No thank you Madam" he replied tapping his pretty full midriff, "I am fully fed up!" There was a split second of silence in which my childish guffaw was embarrassingly clear. Will looked at me, as only Will could when angry and quietly said: "Now that you've finished your dinner Thomas you can wish Mr Nathan good night and go to your room okay?"

I did as told and toddled off to my room and bed feeling pretty miserable on two counts. I felt I had let Will down and secondly I went without my favourite burnt custard dessert. I didn't get any left-over dessert either because Carrie gave the bowl to Mr Nathan to take home. Sometime the next day I sort of mumbled a sort of apology to Will. He gave my thick spikey mop a forgiving rub before adding: "It's all right Tom so long as you remember that English is not his language and yet can speak it. Anyone who can speak another language should be respected okay?"

Well, it was a lesson learned; at least for a while!

There is an interesting process on how the British Raj of India came into being, how ingeniously it was crafted and how it led to the engineering of the Eurasian or Anglo Indian tribe. I was just about the age of intelligent curiosity (for a change) and started to wonder about what was what! I had figured out that we Loots were different from the local country folk but stumped as to why and how? Will, who knew everything from bridges to bugouts and everything in-between and while I never saw him read the Bible; read National Geographic with the same religious intent, was bound to know. He did.

It started with the Greeks under Alexander the Great way back in 325 BC who were the first Europeans in India. They came overland on a meandering torturous route through Teheran and Afghanistan to finally arrive at the Indus. Now while there is a great deal of myth, fact and fiction surrounding his exploits in north-west India he did encourage his troops to intermarry with the local peoples. Their progeny were perhaps the first Eurasians of India, who were to disappear in the mists of time and the milieu of the indigenous population. The Loots was not from this era.

The next Europeans to arrive and stay for a long time were the Portuguese much later in 1498 AD. They came by sailing ship via the Cape. They finally established Goa as their main trading centre and just like Alexander; Afonso de Albuquerque encouraged intermarriage with the Indians. He was a wise fellow as he was known to even personally solemnise these inter-racial weddings. This Portuguese European and indigenous mixed progeny came to be known as "Lueso's and Goan's". The Loots were not of this early era either, but I was beginning to get the drift.

Meanwhile, an important event happened in 1526. The Mughals from the region of Persia invaded and occupied the North and most of the central region of India and brought the Muslim religion with them. Their rule lasted around 330 years and had a profound influence in India. Strangely it was the powerful Mughal's who were linked to the rise of the British Raj over time and in turn the Eurasian tribe and we Loots.

Attracted to the honeypot of India the Dutch followed the Portuguese almost 100 years later; the English shortly after (a sea voyage of about 22,000 km), then the Danes and finally the French. They all came as traders and with the blessings of the Mughal rulers they established trading enclaves on the East and West coasts, but it's the Brits that finally stayed to conquer.

The Brits under the East India Company liked what they saw in India and set about getting a piece of the action. You know; "useless stuff" like diamonds, gold, silver, timber, silks, jute, indigo, spices and a lot more including snuff and opium!

After a while, the Brits started to think about expanding throughout India. Why not exploit the opportunity? They took stock of the situation and identified the two hurdles to be overcome. The first being the North Central region controlled by the powerful Muslim Mughal's and the second being the warring Hindu kingdoms in the rest of the country.

Now, while the Mughals were the dominant rulers much of the rest of the country was ruled by a bunch of small rather despotic Maharajas. Astonishingly, there were about five hundred of these little eccentrics sort of ruling the roost in their little realms and living it up at the expense of their poor taxpaying citizens.

Almost a hundred and fifty years ago some of these egocentrics, aside from several palaces and a bevy of beautiful concubines (lucky them!) had their private gold reserves, had their own currency, had their own postal service and stamps and their own army to safeguard their power as well as to fight amongst themselves! To top it off, over time some even had their own private state steam-powered railways. One of them had a golden throne in his carriage and another had his carriage covered with ivory striping and all the hardware made from gold; all obligingly built for them by the Brits for a handsome sum! As per Will the Maharajas took a great deal of pride in their Railways and described their steam engines as "polished gold-bees".

Again as per Will, the significant step the clever Brits took toward the goal of British Raj was the policy of "divide et impera" or divide and rule.

First, they ingratiated themselves with the Mughals convincing them that they were no threat to their rule. The second step was to form alliances with the plethora of fabulously rich Maharajas through bullying and coercion, quite confident that the Hindu Maharajas did not trust the Muslim Mughals to come to their aid. However, not all the Maharajas were push-overs and that was a problem that had to be dealt with.

Another problem that confronted them was competition from the Dutch and the French who were equally keen on expanding their power and the Brits didn't like that! So they set about getting rid of the Dutch and the French with a few major punch-ups on the battlefield. The Dutch had better things to do in Batavia in Indonesia and nicked off, while the French sulked and then withdrew into a few isolated enclaves to lick their wounds. The Dutch and the French were not celibates and their liaisons with the local native girls had a very natural result.

However, the wily Brits knew that they could not control India without an army they could rely on. England was a long way around the Cape and recruiting and retaining a standing British army in India was very expensive. India was about fifteen times larger than England with a population of around 300 million with some of the areas still very hostile to their presence. So what did they do? They did two smart things. The first was to recruit and train the Sikhs who had been persecuted for ages by the Muslim Mughals and hated them anyway, as well as their cousins the Jats who also loathed the Mughals and finally the excellent mercenary Gurkhas from Nepal. So the Brits now had a standing "native" army.

Next, European women could not suffer the long sea voyage or survive the rigours of the harsh Indian conditions so there were none of them to marry. Just like the French and the Dutch, it's hardly believable that something like fifty-thousand East India Company employees and its Soldiers were "sworn celibates" is it? So miscegenation with the very comely native Indian women was probably already rife. Why not give it official sanction and reap the progeny as a reward? So, the clever Brits now officially encouraged and recognized intermarriage with local Indian women and in some cases actually paid them the handsome sum of one "Gold Mohur". Their men took to it with enthusiasm including my Great, Great Grandfather George Loots.

George Loots was, however, no comparison to one David Ochterlony who was appointed Resident to the Mughal court of Delhi. While George had thirteen children David had thirteen Indian wives, or concubines and a string of children! Perhaps to show his macho libido he paraded them and his children on elephants each evening through the streets of Delhi. Lucky him!

Over centuries, the progeny of these "engineered marriages" were termed variously as Indo-Briton, Country Born, Native-Born, Indian Colonials and Eurasians; and no doubt a few other rather choice and colourful colloquial terms as well! The term Eurasian stuck as the most common description for a long time. The English speaking and loyal Eurasians, who aspired to be British in every way were to become the backbone of the East India Company Army and in time the mainstay of the vast infrastructure that was crafted during the British Raj.

For around two hundred and fifty years, the Brits with the help of their native army as well as the expanding numbers of Eurasians gradually ate away at the power of the Mughals to finally establish themselves as rulers of India.

Okay, now what? They had a vast country to govern and a vast population to control with some areas still rather hostile toward them. So, just like the clever little beavers, they set about creating an infrastructure of canals, roads, telegraph lines of communication and railways while taxing the Indians for the privilege as well!

Will reckoned that the Brits didn't go about building this huge infrastructure because they loved the Indians or planned to make India a future tourist attraction, it was done to feather their own nests. That's what Imperialism is about anyway. Firstly, the roads and the rail were to move garrisoned troops quickly to any trouble spot around the country and second; they were strategically built to connect the productive hinterland to the shipping ports so they could carry off the produce to good old Blighty in their ships!

Nevertheless, Will said the Brits did a very good job over the years of stabilizing the country with a proper structure of civil law and order, an impartial judiciary, an honest and proper tax system, postal, excise and customs systems and a single national currency. They also encouraged the establishment of very good hospitals and universities and instituted English as the general Franca lingua. They also established well designed and comfortable Cantonments across the Country to house the Army. Bangalore Cant was one of the best. So, to be fair, the Brits created wealth to appropriate; something the French and Dutch never learned to do. Again as per Will who knew his history better than most, the Brits were the master colonisers.

It's also fair to point out that while the overall British policy was self-serving many Brits amongst the Civil Service genuinely loved India and its peoples; albeit in a paternalistic fashion and many were second and even third-generation sons of Civil Servants who worked in India because of this attachment. Many even retired to stay on in India for the rest of their lives. Living was cheap in the pleasant and salubrious hill stations of Kashmir, Shimla, Darjeeling, Coonoor, Bangalore Cant and other regions. As Will said, "why would you go back to England to live in a comparative hovel and freeze in the process?"

The issue of manning this vast infrastructure with loyal English speaking subjects, at least the middle management was resolved by the presence of the loyal Eurasian's. Bingo, the future prosperity of the British Raj was safeguarded! To show their gratitude to the Eurasians, the Brits formally recognised and gazetted the community as "Anglo Indian". Very kind of the Brits indeed! They must have had a reason, though even Will had no idea what it was.

The strange paradox, however, is that the vast majority of the peoples of India, especially in the rural areas never saw us as Anglo Indian or Indian but as some sort of strange foreigner! However, despite we Anglo Indian's subliminal desire to be in all things very British, they said we were Indians with some European blood while the Indians said we were Europeans with some Indian blood. Gosh, what a jolly mess, but as the wise Will said; "What we are, we are and there's no point pretending to be something different."However, Will was sure many Anglo Indians struggled with the fragility of this twilight status and unfortunately many were bloody-minded racists to boot, and he might just have had the Loots clan in mind when he said that.

The railways were the most important and certainly the largest of the infrastructure projects undertaken by the Brit's in India. It peaked during the British Raj to 41,200 miles of railway track. Pretty good going, considering the total rail track in "Mother England" was only 19,500 miles. To serve their purposes the Brits made India into the third largest rail system in the world after the USA and Russia.

It made sense to run the telegraph and telephone lines alongside the track to control the safe movement of the trains as well as for communication from one station to the next. In short, the telegraph connected every small wayside railway station to various towns and thence to cities and every post office in-between simply by following the railway line. These telegraph lines comprised the arteries and veins of a vast communication system. And the railways, post and telegraphs, Police, Customs, Forestry, Mining and many other services around the country were operated by us Anglo Indians!

To further show their appreciation of this loyal tribe the Brits made a couple of concessions. First, every Mail and Express train had a section of 1st Class compartments signed: "Reserved for Europeans and Anglo Indians only," which meant no ethnic Indian person could enter these specially reserved compartments. The second was that in every major railway colony there were two Railway Institutes; again one for the Europeans and Anglo Indians and another for the indigenous Indian folk. The European

Railway Institute was fully furnished and well equipped with a large wooden dance floor, bar, and billiard room while the Indian Railway Institute was a small building with a few chairs and card tables. Now if this wasn't a version of racist segregation one wonder's what is! Will was quick to point out that we smug Anglo Indian's now elevated socially (in some instances at least) to the lofty station of the Brits were very gratified with our superior position and showed no guilt about it either!

I got my education from Will. The Loots Clan were part of this Anglo Indian tribe of "bitsers" or fruitcakes or whatever sobriquet one might conjure up including some rather colourful and derogatory ones like "half-tickets", "eight-annas" and "half-castes"; but as Will would often say: "If you're stupid enough to call the local people "wogs" and "pariahs", don't complain if they return the compliment!"

3
The Cantonment Loots!

THE CANTONMENT OR BANGALORE CANT was the spiritual home of the Loots even before Sarah loots time. It even had its own Cantonment Railway station. If you "belonged" so to speak and had established your credentials as a true Cantonment inhabitant you never said just "Bangalore". It sounded too common from the elitist convention. Snobbery required it to be referred to as "The Cantonment" or "Bangalore Cant" and only true residents may refer to it as "Bangy" between themselves and not any outsiders. They would be dubbed "pretenders" and to be shunned. In short, Bangy residents were social climbers, name-droppers and obstinate snobs and had airs about them.

Such was the conceit that Cantonment inhabitants even had to differentiate and firmly stamp their superior status on the unfortunate occupants of adjoining Bangalore City who they looked down upon. If truth be known Bangalore City was much higher in elevation to the Cantonment and even needed a banking engine attached to the rear of the trains at the Cant to push them up the steep gradient to the City station. But the Cantonment snobs considered this a mere accident of inconsiderate topography and consigned the issue to the "bin of inconvenient truths".

There was some rationale to this snobbery though and that was thanks to the foresight of the Brits of yore. Searching for a place with a fine salubrious climate and fewer mosquitoes; a British military engineer in the East India Company, John Blakiston discovered "Bangalore". He soon drew up the plans for the "largest and finest" Military Cantonment of the peninsular of India to house the Infantry and Cavalry in 1809. The Cantonment developed with wide roads and shady avenues and was strategically dotted with public parks and not one but two vast botanic gardens. Garrison Churches, Cathedrals, Schools, hospitals a central Market and fashionable residential suburbs with fashionable names were included in his layout. All this made the Cantonment a very desirable place to live in and the snobs a sliver of credibility.

Meanwhile to the West and outside the Cantonment; the unfortunate Bangalore City was left to its own devices to develop into a teeming mass of narrow streets and overcrowded dwellings. So even though Bangalore City was at a distinctly higher altitude the Cantonment snobs could look "down" on them from the rampart of conceited society!

As far back as anyone could remember three stories constantly swirled around in the Loots Clan as to the "foundation" of the Loots in India and folklore was the standard currency. The dominant Clan folklore was there was a Dutch forbear who was of such immense girth and height that he had to have a special horse to carry him around. The second yarn was that being such a huge man the ring on his middle finger was so big it could fit around a baby's wrist! I was giddy with this knowledge.

But by the time Will and his siblings came along, none could boast this Dutchman's immense build and on the contrary, all were rather short. The story of the ring however lingered on. As folklore had it the huge ring was broken down, some gold added to it and rings made for only the males of his offspring. Consequently, Will and his male siblings now had rings with still a smidgen of gold from the original. This was accepted as gospel especially when Aunty Bunny, the renowned family snob confirmed it with a touch of envy and a curve of her thin lips.

The third tall tale was that this mighty big Dutch ancestor married a Muslim Princess no less, who also happened to be a divorcee! Unfortunately, this romantic yarn didn't quite suit the facts as was found out a long, long time later but the folklore did get one thing right; Nicolas Benjamin Loots was Dutch.

Bernice, known within the clan as Bunny was Will's eldest sister by a fair few years and she was the proverbial snob of the clan. She was not happy with this lacklustre Dutch forbear and floated her own shaggy-dog story that the Loots, as well as the ring were actually descended from a very prominent Swiss banker who was the one that really married the Muslim Princess and not this "banal" Dutchman! She was privately and decisively outvoted on that story.

Now we were not the only Loots of Bangalore Cant as there was one more Loots family who lived on "the other side of town". The inference of the "other side" being the suburb they lived in did not carry the pristine provenance of a fashionable label like Fraser, Langford, Cooke, Richmond, Benson or even St Johns Hill but the rather common name of Shoolay. It had the ring of poverty about it and it was looked down upon by the snobbish fraternity of the Cantonment. We Loots of "up-market leafy" Fraser Town were not completely devoid of snobbery, at least some of us anyway.

Bunny was the doyen of the Loots for snobbery. She had the right to occupy that position. She was the eldest sister, had buried two husbands at a fairly early age, was wealthy, lived in a fine home, a respected member of the RSPCA, a collector of fine paintings and period furniture, bred Australian "Sydney Silkies"; one of which was a snarling vicious little beast was a pillar of three churches (depending on which Padre was the flavour of the month with whom she didn't have a lingering disagreement), attended public auctions with the same regularity of Church and grew a magnificent red poinsettia in her front garden.

By the time I was growing up Aunty Bunny was a lot older. She had a broad forehead, a narrow mind, hard lines around her thin lips that were permanently pursed, a hairdo every week, bandy legs that must always be covered in cotton stockings that looked loose on her skinny legs and an acid tongue that could remove the rust from a long-discarded plow in the paddock.

"The Shoolay Loots are no relation of ours," she would announce with total conviction. It wasn't the first time she had said it in the presence of others. She seemed obsessed with the Shoolay Loots family. What constituted a relationship in her view was based not on blood but on where they lived! Shoolay being the poor suburb of the Cantonment the Loots family living there couldn't possibly be related, could they? The snub didn't stop there either. Blondie Loots of Shoolay was so named because she was blond, fair and very good looking too. No one seemed to know or care if she had a real first name. But that was poor compensation for Bunny as she expanded: "That daughter of theirs, Blondie, has airs about her doesn't she?"

Aunty Ivy who was a dear compared to Aunty Bunny was not to be outdone by her much older sibling and chimed in with a guillotine-like slur of character assassination without the slightest shred of evidence: "And she's not shy to trade on it either my dear. Have you seen the ridiculous high heeled shoes she wears?"

Since neither Ivy nor Bunny could wear high heeled shoes, and if they tried they would topple over, it was the sealer on Blondie's fate. The ensuing snigger from Aunty Bunny meant she thought the very worst of the poor innocent Blondie and all because she lived in Shoolay and wore high heeled shoes.

Granny Sarah Loots, who was the only one who probably knew the facts wasn't about to tell: "They do share rooms on the main road though and not in the patch Bernice." The patch was the colloquial term for any section of any town where the poorest of the poor working class lived.

Bunny scoffed at this minor distinction: "It's still Shoolay Mother."

Sarah still tried to assert some semblance of long vanquished authority over her now rich daughter: "It's still within the Cantonment Bunny."

Bunny pursed her lips in annoyed exasperation at this minor geographical error: "Well it should be moved out then."

Granny Loots twiddled her thumbs, a long-held habit, and left Bunny to shift centuries-old municipal boundaries at will because of the Shoolay Loots!

Puzzled by this logic I asked Will what all this talk meant and why we couldn't be related since we had the same name?

"People who talk that way have bile on the liver Thomas." His opinion was delivered with the incisive brevity the envy of any Supreme Court Judge.

Having bile on the liver sounded pretty serious so I figured from his answer that Aunty Bunny and Aunty Ivy badly needed an enema or at least a good helping of Will's powerful homebrew of omum water which according to him fixed everything.

Now there was nothing I disagreed with on what Will said, he sort of knew everything, after all, he read every issue of the National Graphic that was ever printed, but young as I was I drew the line on his magical omum water. It was vile stuff I reckoned.

I never discovered if the attractive Blondie was, in fact, a cousin!

4
The delicate art of name-dropping!

OVER THE YEARS THE LOOTS OF THE CANTONMENT had developed the fine art of name-dropping. Rubbing shoulders, so to claim, with the rich and famous was quite useless unless it could be swanked about. The Clan spared no opportunity to do so. Just the quiet hint, the shrug of the shoulders, as if it was of no real significance yet nevertheless required "public airing" without too much elaboration at a Church tea, wedding, a party or the most reliable of all gossip exposure; the quiet tété-á-tété.

"Oh quite; we Loots's know Sir Yoonus Sait and the family rather well" would do. The Anglo Indian community was small enough and garrulous enough for the gospel to spread and to be duly embellished. If truth is known, it was only Sarah Loots who could make such a claim and later Kate Loots but that small matter was judiciously overlooked.

Once that seed had been duly sown on the verdant ground to bloom, the next casual name-drop would be: "Oh by the bye, have you heard that Sunoo is back from another successful tour in London and Paris?" Sunoo being the Clan's "proprietary" name for none other than Ram Gopal the world-renowned classical Indian dancer. There was a tad more veracity in the declared connection to this famous man, but the nuance and the mystery of the relationship had to be seen as "delicate".

Again, it was Sarah Loots who was the real conduit as she brought Bissano Ram Gopal into this world. He was the son of a Rajput Barrister and a very attractive Anglo-Burmese mother. Sunoo was delivered by Sarah Loots in their palatial home "Torquay Castle" on Millers Road, complete with a swimming pool and a tennis court.

While there was the Clan story that Sunoo's father was dead against his only son's proclivity for and obvious skill for classical Indian dancing. He wanted him to be a Barrister as well, while his mother encouraged his love of dancing. Sunoo continued to practice and train diligently. While still a child, Sunoo was invited to dance for the Yuvaraja of Mysore at the Lalita Mahal palace in the presence of the Viceroy. Bejewelled like the Boy Krishna and fortified with a gulp of champagne, he danced his heart out. He was rapturously applauded. It changed his father's mind. Sunoo went on to become a world figure on the artistic stage of Indian classical dance and now danced his way firmly into Loots folklore.

Early in his career, he received a break that was to catapult him into international fame. La Meri, the internationally famous American folkloric danseuse, and her troupe were in India and she was enchanted by Sunoo's grace and performance. She invited him to join her tour of the Far East and it was in Tokyo that he received rave notices of his performance: "The soul of a genius and beautiful to behold in every movement … The perfect dancer."

Sunoo went on to America and with the patronage of Sol Hurok, a celebrated impresario gave his recitals in New York and at Hollywood, there to fraternize with the likes of Cecil B. de Mille and Arthur Rubinstein. He loved Hollywood and perhaps as a consequence went on to act in two successful films of the 1950s; "The Planters Wife" with Jack Hawkins and Claudette Colbert, followed by "The Purple Plain" with Gregory Peck and Win Min Than.

All of this, of course, was superb grist for the Loots Clan mill to be judiciously "broadcast" and sort of wallow in some sort of united recognition. Bernice Loots-Joslyn could convert a very slight relationship, with the right choice of words into an association of considerable substance!

Sunoo danced at some of the most famous and reputed theatres in the world. The Grand Theatre, Opera House in

Poland, the Palais Du Louvre and Musée Guimet in Paris, the Aldwych in London, and the Town Hall in Stockholm. He danced for Mahatma Ghandi, Prime Minister Nehru, and Queen Elizabeth who bestowed an OBE on him in 1999.

All this glory was of course duly "shared" by the Loots Clan and to cement the relationship it was duly conveyed to anybody who would listen; that when Sunoo gave one of his rare performances in Bangalore the Loots's received "special invitations". The special invitations being an oblique reference to free tickets; "free tickets" sounded too cheap.

However, while it was not for "public consumption" there was no doubt that Sunoo's father was very gracious and kind to Sarah Loots. Since she had suggested when Sunoo was a child he needed Horlicks to develop, he, in turn, ensured Sarah was always supplied with Horlicks and financial support even after she stopped working for the family. Kate Loots-Clarke worked as his Secretary in his Law Firm for a time and was very friendly with his sister Jessie.

Cousin Christine Loots spent time at Torquay with Granny Loots and watched Sunoo practising on the marble floor of the great hall. It's something I couldn't boast about but she could in our eternal fights of one-upmanship!

Led by Bunny, the Loots's were not averse to name-dropping. Now armed with the pristine provenance of such lofty connections with the Sait's and the Ram Gopal's what chance had the unfortunate Shoolay Loots?

I'm not sure if Will ever engaged with the Ram Gopal family, he never mentioned it but Carrie assuredly did and a visit to Torquay Castle, whenever she was in Bangalore Cant was a must.

Carrie, who had the looks, panache, and the style to go with it tried to give the Loots family their own "star". She was in Bombay holidaying with Uncle Don and Enid

Plunkett (while dad sang "Stormy Weather" at home with only me for companionship). Uncle Don was the Chief Boiler Inspector of the State and visited us quite often when on tour. He seemed to cry a lot after a few sherbets so I wondered if Will had given him a clip behind the ears, but it turned out not to be the case. Will explained Uncle Don had been an Engineer on a merchant ship very early in the war which had been sunk and he had somehow survived the ordeal and this had affected him. He could have been my hero after being torpedoed and all that but his crying cancelled that out!

Anyway while in Bombay Carrie heard or read that a famous Movie Producer, Shorab Modi, was recruiting women for his epic movie Jhansi Ki Rani. Carrie had visions of a starring role when in fact he was only recruiting "extras" for a particular scene in the film.

Carrie was none the wiser as she rocked up on the set at the appointed time hoping for that star role. She was selected, told to remove her fancy high heeled shoes, and go bare feet. She was duly dressed in a colourful sari by some helpful attendants (since she had on a frock) and then herded into an area that was made to look like a village street, with a hundred or so other "hopefuls". They were told that when the bloke on a megaphone told them to go they had to rush down the narrow street toward the village square while waving their hands and screaming their lungs out. They were given a couple of practice runs in what they had to do, and Carrie, despite hopping on the bare ground without shoes (which she was not used to) gradually worked her way into the front line to make sure the movie camera "focused" on her. All went well up to that point until the "call to action" came and that's when Carrie discovered that sprinting on bare feet and in a sari, which she had never worn in her life was impossible, and secondly the other hundred or so extras all had the same idea to get into the camera field. Poor Carrie was lost in the melee and horde of yelling wannabe's!

She returned home with a bad cold, sore of foot and a bruised and trodden on ankle; yet gushing about her movie role and surfaced only to flaunt the fact for ages. Will would listen politely each time but I reckon I could read his mind better than Carrie could since I constantly lived on the edge with my tomfoolery. I could gauge his moods. In my case, when Will's furrows sort of flattened out and he didn't blink I knew he didn't believe a word of the pipe-dottle I was giving for some misdemeanour of mine. I reckon he had that look now listening each time to Carrie's caper and was thinking about a caper she had once carried out: "Carrie that was a harebrained caper just like sitting on the toilet in the Residency"; but he wasn't about to dash her thrill.

Undaunted, Carrie wrote letters by the dozen to the entire Clan, to friends in India and even overseas telling them of her caper and to look for her "star" role! Poor Carrie was to be disappointed as the camera didn't pick her out at all not even for the briefest of seconds.

Carrie being a favourite of the Loots Clan, especially Bunny (except for Granny, of course), was not criticised for her failure at being a movie "star" so the generous verdict was: "Carrie tried her best, but what else can you expect from those Indians?"

Selective racial prejudice can be added to the Loots Clan's trait, at least for some of them anyway! And once again it took the common sense of Will to expose the deceit: "You can't curry favour with the Sait's and the Ram Gopal's and at the same time sling mud at the other can you?"

5
Sarah Loots!

THERE WAS NEVER REALLY A "GATHERING" of the Clan so to speak because they were all scattered around the country, but ad hoc meetings would take place between "Clan Members" in Bangalore Cant the substance of which was duly circulated by Sarah Loots to the other Loots's as she was the "Clan conduit".

The taciturn widow Sarah Loots was the doyen of the Loots clan until she was replaced by her rich daughter Bernice.

As far back as I can remember Granny Sarah Loots was old and "little" and never seemed to grow any older. She always wore small checked pattern button-up dresses, had silver blond hair which she did up in a bun behind her head, wore glasses that were permanently tied above her forehead with a shoelace, and never used them when reading the tiny print of the newspaper. When Granny wasn't reading the newspapers she couldn't find her glasses! She could also expertly pinch with her toes. If you asked her "what's the time Gran?" she always responded: "half past kissing time, time to kiss again" yet I never saw Granny Loots kiss anybody!

Sarah Loots never spoke about her past life, her husband, or about her married life and she never celebrated a birthday. She couldn't really because she didn't know when she was born! All that the Clan knew was she had been a Cantonment Smith before she married William Edwin Loots in Bangalore Cant. He was a railwayman and worked in Podanur. Family folklore has it that she was married at the age of thirteen or fifteen and the age was always debated in the Loots Clan. Since she didn't know when she was born Granny remained tight-lipped. Come to think about it Granny Loots wasn't very communicative at all.

Sarah Loots had six children and Will was the youngest with a fair gap of seven years between him and his next sister Ivy. Grandpop Loots suddenly died when he was just thirty-nine and when Will was only four years old. Sarah Loots, who was perhaps around thirty, was tough and used to hardship. Like many others, she was the daughter of a soldier who deserted his family and skedaddled back to Chelsea in England. She packed-up her brood of six and headed for the Loots' spiritual home of Bangalore Cant. She did her nurse and midwifery training at Lady Curzon's and battled along. Will's older sister Ivy had to forego her schooling and look after him while Sarah went to work.

Sarah Loots must have been pretty good at her job because she was engaged to work in the grand mansion of a famous and wealthy business entrepreneur Haji Yoonus Sait. In fact, he was considered the richest man in the south of India with interests in property, department stores, gold and manganese mines, cotton mills, sugar mills, and distilleries; you name it.

Golly, he must have been rich and important because the King of England made him a Knight.

Will had told me that to be Knighted you had to kneel in front of the King and he'd place his sword on your neck. He probably said shoulder, but somehow the "neck" word stuck in my brain and I promptly decided I didn't want to become a Knight. I'd seen my friend and minder Mahmood at home cut the neck of a chook a heap of times; what if the King's blinking sword slipped? Nope, I decided privately it was a risk I was not going to take when I grew up! However, since Granny Loots knew Haji Yoonus Sait very well I confided in her that I didn't want to be a Knight. I didn't tell her why but she sort of looked at me and smiled and I figured she knew the terrible risk with the sword as well!

Anyway, Yoonus took the risk with the King and his sword and was made a Knight, becoming Haji Sir Yoonus Sait.

Adam, his youngest son had met and married a very attractive English lady while all this was going on and Sarah Loots ended up working in their mansion too; delivering their babies and being their nanny as well.

While the Maharaja of Mysore owned a stable-full of grand cars, Sir Yoonus Sait was the first person to own a car in the Cantonment. So Sarah Loots who started out without a brass razoo to her name rode in a car long before a lot of Cantonment snobs did!

6
Bertie Loots!

BERTIE WAS THE ELDEST OF SARAH'S BROOD and Will's eldest brother by about fifteen years. He did his apprenticeship in the Telegraphs in Delhi and would you believe his luck? He was appointed to the Viceroy of India's entourage. Now, India was the "Jewel in the Crown" and the only colony of the entire British Empire, which comprised about sixty countries, that boasted the presence of the Queen's own representative in the grandeur and presence of a Viceroy. All the others were governed by lesser lights and titles far removed from the British Crown.

During summer the entire Viceroy's panoply of state moved from Delhi to Shimla in the Himalayan foothills and Bertie went with them. Will said Bertie was dashing; he wore a suit and waistcoat and spats when he wasn't in boots and putties and khakis. He was friendly and very helpful in supporting Granny and his younger siblings during his bachelor days. Being the eldest son he became the first to earn a decent wage working in the Viceroy's staff.

Unfortunately, his generosity came to an abrupt end when he got married and therein rests a weird tale to be told, but suffice it to say in Will's words: "Bertie lost his backbone after he married Nora".

Tales of Bertie are aplenty and worth the telling. As per both Will and Maurice Loots, Bertie never worked a single day in his life; that is at his real job of being a telegraphist in the Viceroy's communications centre. Instead, he was the unofficial shikari or professional hunter to the Viceroy's vast entourage and his job was to keep the Viceregal Lodge supplied with fresh venison, blue bull, and wild pork meat.

His second unofficial occupation was to take the Brits wild-game hunting. Bertie always claimed he didn't approve of trophy hunting animals like the black bear, leopard and tiger; though this was disputed and scoffed at (in his absence) and helped by the presence of strong arrack during a Loots clan meeting, with the question: "If Bert didn't shoot big game what was he doing owning a big game gun?" That was a question that was never answered.

Hiking and hunting were Bertie's passions. He used a Mauser 7.92 Sporting Rifle for smaller game and, whether he used it or not, he owned a Rigby 470 Nitro Express DB for the bigger dangerous game! Now a 7.92 mm has the kick of a mule but a 470 Express had the kick of ten mules! How in heaven's name Bertie could use it without landing on his backside every time he fired the weapon I will never understand.

Bert was not averse to indulging in a bit of moonlighting to earn money on the side about which the Clan approved, even though it bordered on the "illegal"; since he did send money to Granny Loots. He hunted crocs on the side and sold the skins. Of the three species of crocodiles in India, he mainly hunted the Mugger and the Gharial for their soft belly-skin which was highly prized and fetched a very good price. The Gharial, unlike the Mugger and its estuarine cousins, has a bulbous nose and vicious razor-sharp teeth. It grows to around twenty feet and could weigh over three-hundred pounds.

Now, croc hunting is an art because the only time you could get one is when it's sun-bathing on the river sand-bank or in very shallow marsh waters. Bert would use a long native dug-out fishing boat with low gunwales and camouflage it with tree branches and then float downriver to get within close range. This was open iron-sight hunting and no such thing as telescopes were used. The croc's upper skin is like armour plating and so it's only real vulnerable spot is its brain, which is about the size of a golf ball and located just below the "eye-brow horns" behind its eye's. The second alternative and less reliable shot for a clean kill is the spinal section behind its head and body joint. If it's not a perfect shot the wounded animal will thrash and slither into the deep river water and die a slow painful death.

Bert claimed he never took even senior British Officers trophy or on any hunting expeditions because they were not experienced "shikaris". This again was hotly disputed by the Clan (again in his absence) because he blotted his copy-book claim by sending Sarah Loots a couple of photographs: "So how come Bertie is showing off posing in a photograph with some "big-wig" with a dead tiger?" Again, a question that was never answered! There were a couple of things the males in the Loots Clan did agree on though, and that was Bertie was a crack shot and always hunted by tracking his game on foot.

However, there was a shaggy-dog story circulated by Bertie that became Clan folklore. He was ordered to take a well-connected visiting senior ranking officer on a croc hunt. Now, where Bert would normally shoot and have it skinned on the sandbank or in the camp by the local peoples the officer wanted to bring back the entire croc to show off at the regimental mess. So they had to take extra men to get a heavy croc into the boat.

Considering the unusual demands Bert considered it prudent to hunt the shallow marsh Gharial crock rather than the river estuarine Mugger. The boat could be poled much closer to the target as the reeds provided better cover and the shot could be taken by cautiously wading closer to the target in the shallow marsh rather than from a semi-stationary boat in the flowing river. The brave white hunter of a Brit at first refused to wade in a marsh full of crocs until Bertie explained that the Gharial was the "Brahmin" of croc's, fed mainly on fish and rarely attacked humans or small game so he was quite safe.

The Brit was using a Service 303 which he was familiar with and claimed he had been on many hunts with

Maharaja's, while also declaring himself to be a crack shot to boot. That boast would hardly have impressed Bertie. Maharaja hunting was usually from the back of an elephant or perched comfortably in a tree machan while hundreds of "beaters" herded the poor quarry into a killing field, which was a far cry from patiently tracking the game stealthily through dense forest for hours on foot with the help of a local tracker.

However, Bert carefully explained the precise procedure and the importance of the first shot. He added that for safety's sake he would put a couple of solid rounds from his rifle behind the shoulder of the croc soon after he fired to make sure. The Brit was annoyed at this impertinent suggestion but had little option when Bertie told him it was very unlikely he would get his trophy if he didn't.

The tracker spotted a reasonably sized Gharial and the two of them stalked closer and closer in waist-deep water, crouching in the reeds until well within killing-range. The Brit aimed carefully, fired and Bert followed up with his rounds into its neck. The croc looked stone brain dead. The dugout pulled up and after a lot of effort from the five or six of them, they got it into the boat.

They were poling back to the land area and the Brit, now fascinated with his trophy and probably confident that the Gharial was not a man-eater, started poking at the large bulbous nose of the croc with the toe of his boot when suddenly all hell broke loose. The brain dead Gharial suddenly opened its jaws and went "snap"; almost tearing off the Brit's foot. Fortunately, he had on a pair of very stout boots but apparently, the sole was almost torn off.Everyone bailed out of the boat into the shallow marsh waters before you could say Jack Robinson. Fortunately, the Gharial could not move as Bert retrieved his rifle and blew its brain out from point-blank range.

As Bertie was not an Army Officer he was not invited to the Regimental Mess night and the presentation of the croc carcass. Nevertheless, gossip has it that the croc, now possibly ponging a bit, was duly placed on show on the Mess veranda with the Officers damaged boot strategically placed in its jaws. The visiting high ranking Brit gave his own highly coloured version of the croc hunt and was quite the hero. The boot in the croc's razor-sharp jaws might give some inkling to the Brit's account of events!

Nevertheless, after that caper, Bert claimed never to have taken a Brit croc hunting again, no matter how senior, experienced, or well-connected he was!

Hunting aside, whenever the Viceroy's entourage moved from Delhi to Shimla during the summer Bertie's pastime was to trek the mountains for days on end. All he carried was his rifle, some food in the haversack, and dressed only in his shorts, boots and putties. There was plenty of good eating game in the forests around Shimla, including the Leopard that lived on the game.

Another shaggy-dog story of Bert's was that the favourite prank of the Brits in the Viceroy's vast entourage was that when a new (and usually naïve) Subaltern was attached to the staff, he was promptly told by his crafty superiors to go on a trekking expedition with Bertie Loots to gain experience in his responsibilities. The poor bugger would be exhausted at the pace, altitude, and steep hill track climb. Within a few hours, he'd be begging to turn back or stop. The young Subaltern would be told: "Either keep-up Sir or find your own way back." The stories went that the young fellow would almost pass out from sheer exhaustion and be carried back on a litter by local hills tribesmen!

What was undeniable in the Clan's view was that Bertie was a fitness freak and the fittest bloke in the Clan!

If you have conjured up a mental picture that Bertie was built like one of those big white hunters in Hollywood movies like King Solomon's Mines, Mogambo or Bawana Devil; but sadly not so as he took after his mother Sarah Loots. He was white all right, but stood about five foot eight in his boots and weighed less than a hundred and seventy pounds wringing wet!

Perhaps because of his pint-sized stature, he had to be super fit, shoot with the biggest bore rifles going around and even ride a 7.5 HP Harley Davidson with a sidecar at break-neck speed.

It was never proven but as per Clan folklore, Bertie was roaring home on the Harley one night on a lonely country road from a hunting trip when he hit a man head-on. Anyway, he pulled up at the next small-town police station, woke-up the sleeping policeman, and reported the accident. His statement (or story) was the man he had run over was a Dacoit who had stepped into the road and pointed a muzzle-loader at him as he was approaching. and to save himself he ran the bloke down. The police found the man the next morning. By then he was dead and no musket was found.

This was the time of the British Raj so I guess it was hushed up, as the saying goes and leaves a skeleton in the cupboard of Clan folklore!

7
Bernice Loots!

BERNICE, BETTER KNOWN AS BUNNY within the Clan was second in line. As per Will, his eldest sister had a very bright and happy personality when she was young. She married a Brit with the fancy name of Frederick Dalton Hansen-Martyn in a place called Calicut, just on the border of Mysore State. Its claim to fame was that it was the centre of the historic Indian spice trade, was first colonised by the Portuguese, then the Dutch and finally the Brits. How Bunny got to be there I have no idea but everybody deemed Frederick a good "catch". He was not only a very nice bloke, sort of friendly and charming but he also had a good position as an engineer. Shortly after they were married he was posted to the Silk Parachute Manufacturing factory located in the bush about fifty miles from Bangalore Cant.

During the British Raj any industry based in the bush of India, be it sugar, coffee, tea, tobacco, jute, mining, forestry or whatever, was comfortably fitted out. The Brits usually established enclaves of beautiful large furnished bungalows, shade trees, manicured lawns, gardens, and even a small club with a tennis court. It was the only way or compensation if you like to attract and keep the Brits working in the bush.

The new bride moved to a place called Goribidanur into elite company and comfortable surroundings. She would have fitted in well for Bunny was a born toff. Even her expressions of surprise were different. "Go away!" she would exclaim when we common folk might say, "Is that so or really?" But unfortunately for her, the perfect catch had a concealed problem. He was the perfect gentleman and loving husband when sober, but he would go on the binge every so often. Will said he turned out to be "an alcoholic in disguise". When drunk he would become violent and assault her. Bunny would sometimes have to run to the neighbours and sleep there overnight. Despite being brutalised every so often by a drunken husband, as per Clan folklore Bunny remained very loyal to him and paradoxically never lost her happy genial personality. The alcohol finally caught up with Frederick Dalton Hansen-Martyn and he died an untimely death.

Will reckoned they could have put a match to him and he would have gone up in flames because he had so much alcohol in his bloodstream. He must have been serious because Will was not known to drop unkindly remarks. He just didn't approve of men assaulting defenceless women.

For some reason Bunny, now still a youngish widow moved to Madras rather than to the Loots "spiritual" hometown. Not long after she met a bright IPS Police Officer with a fine career ahead of him, having been awarded an MBE apparently for his sterling work in tracking down and arresting the anti-British "fifth columnists" known as the INA. But, as per Clan gossip her new suitor, despite his decoration, had two distinct disadvantages in Bunny's view. First, he was rather dark in complexion, and secondly, he had the rather plebeian surname of Joseph! She couldn't change her suitor's complexion but made him change his name to a more fanciful "Joslyn"!

That pesky snobbish matter settled she married Christopher Joslyn in Madras. Once more the story goes that while she was brutally treated by her first husband she now ironically browbeat her second husband; despite his amiable personality and who neither smoked nor drank!

It was 1943 and WWII was in full swing and it was serious stuff. Singapore had fallen, Burma captured and "Tokyo Rose" was broadcasting from Rangoon that India was next. Japanese aircraft bombed two seaports along the east coast; Cocanada and Vizag causing some damage but the threat across the Bay of Bengal was looming. These ports were long way north of Madras but everyone believed that Madras City was going to be their real target because it was a major Military and Air Force base that even housed American squadrons. The British authorities took the threat seriously enough and encouraged non-essential civilians to leave the city (which they did in chaotic droves), black-out of the City was enforced and trenches and sandbag emplacements against air raids were present in the streets. They even evacuated prisoners to inland jails and shot all the unfortunate wild animals in the Madras Zoo. Fear and panic amongst the population were clear, especially when escapees from Burma told stories of massacre and cruelty meted out by the Japanese forces on innocent civilians.

However the threat never did materialize and the closest Madras got to being bombed was when a lone Jap plane, which might have lost its way, tried to bomb Fort St George that housed the British Garrison. The Jap Pilot's aim was way off target and it landed some distance away killing a few civilians and animals. Nevertheless, this "near escape" compelled Bunny to make an "executive decision" that she and Christopher should seek safer climes; and what could be a safer place than the bush?So Christopher managed to wangle some leave and they drove a couple of hundred miles to stay with us in the blinking bush!

While Carrie always got on very well with Bunny; Will now didn't. He reckoned that her personality had changed from being carefree and happy to one of arrogance and autocracy. Conversely, he was very fond of her husband Christopher and considered him a gentleman. Anyway, as they had no children Bunny approached Carrie one day and quietly asked if she and Christopher could adopt me. I was a precocious five years old at the time. Will promptly said no. If it wasn't for Will I suspect Carrie would have gladly traded me in because of my constant rebellion!

Bunny buried her second husband, John Christopher Joslyn when he was barely fifty-five. He died of a heart attack and Aunty Bunny was once again a widow and a wealthy one at that! This time she repaired to the Loots spiritual home town and bought a beautiful home on leafy Mosque Road, Fraser Town.

Bunny went everywhere by rickshaw and had her regular rickshaw-wallah. The poor blighter must have had a large family to feed to put up with her! Cantonment streets went up-hill and down-dale and pulling a rickshaw was no mean feat especially since the poor fellow was half-starved to boot! She would sit in the rick and if she was in a hurry she would poke the poor bloke in the back with the pointed end of her umbrella and yell at him to hurry up. But, the mind-boggling thing was that while she never felt sorry for the poor human pulling her rick she had an obsession to treat animals with considerable warmth.

Bunny would sit on her front veranda and when she saw a bloke whipping the old nag, or bull pulling a laden cart up the slope of Mosque Road, she would rush out of her house and front gate with her walking stick, berate and threaten the bloke on the cart for beating the animal. She was an ardent animal lover and was a life member of the Bangalore RSPCA. The Clan gossip goes that on more than one occasion, the bullock-cart driver seeing this crazy Memsahib rushing at him waving the walking stick menacingly hopped off the cart and bolted with Bunny in hot pursuit. Meanwhile, the overladen cart gradually started to roll backward down the hill with the poor bull now back-peddling!

Golly, the Loots were indeed a bit of a funny lot as Will said!

8
Maurice Loots!

NEXT IN LINE OF THE CLAN was Maurice Loots and he worked in the Railways way up north of Calcutta in East Bengal in a place with the exotic name of "Lal-moni-rat". He was Will's favourite elder brother and he always went up there as a young fellow to spend his holidays with him.

Maurice had fine features, short light brown hair parted high on the left and always well-groomed. He had eyes that always seemed to laugh, a square jaw, firm chin and an aquiline nose. He was shortish, though certainly taller than his elder brother Bertie. His build was square and solid as was his forearms just like Will. Though several years separated them he and Will were built alike but didn't quite look-alike as Will had a flattish nose and the furrows on his forehead deeper, and while Maurice was as fair as Granny Loots, Will was not.

Maurice took over where Bertie left off in supporting Granny Loots. He married a lovely looking girl by the name of Gwen King who had exquisite eyes and a friendly smiling face. Sadly, she died when giving birth to their only child Christine.

Gwen was utterly fastidious about hygiene. The floors had to be swabbed twice each day with phenol and even the doorknobs of the home wiped down with Dettol to kill-off any germs that might have been left by the cleaning servant, and yet in one of those inexplicable ironies of life she tragically passed away from septicaemia infection at the hospital when giving birth to their daughter. And that's how Christine was raised by Granny Sarah Loots.

Maurice Loots definitely harboured a generous splice of adventure and daring within.

In 1947 the Brits (in their wisdom) had planned the separation of India and Pakistan on communal lines; that is, an arbitrary line was surveyed and drawn from East to West in the north of India that divided Hindu from Muslim predominantly occupied areas. In the process, the province of Bengal was divided into West Bengal which was majority Hindu and East Bengal which was a majority Muslim population. It now became East Pakistan on the partition but had no common border with the rest of Pakistan in the west. In short, it was an "island of disaster" as East Pakistan was completely separated from the rest of the newly created nation of Pakistan by several India states.

The newly formed eastern island of East Pakistan where Maurice worked was "born in bloodshed" when the partition was put in place and degenerated into a total administrative mess to boot.

It triggered horrific communal conflict between Muslims and Hindus and the largest mass migration in the modern history of about ten million people between the two fledgling Nations. The communal rioting and killing between Muslim and Hindu were cruel and ghastly. The Brits in the meanwhile had withdrawn their troops and took the stance of "non-intervention" while the army of fledgling India and Pakistan was in the process of being reformed. What troops were available were busy trying to keep law and order in the Western border region of the Punjab where most of the migration was taking place, and as a consequence, the Eastern region of Pakistan was neglected.

Maurice went through some sickening experiences. Only the remaining skeleton crews of Brits, Anglo Indians and Indian Christians could run the railways and would not be molested or attacked by either Muslims or Hindus. Their orders were to keep the trains running at all costs to desperately try to evacuate the Hindus out of East Pakistan to the safety of India; and in-turn ferry Muslims out of India to the safety of East Pakistan. Civil law and order had completely broken down in East Pakistan and the poorly armed and undermanned Police Force just could not cope with the pillage and murder that ensued, while the small Pakistan army personnel posted there had been hastily formed and showed little interest in protecting the Hindu population.

Sitting under the stars in a mini Clan gathering I would listen in awe at the exploits of Uncle Maurice during that turbulent period.

Though he held a senior position in the Railway, because of the desperate situation he was required to now return to the job of an engine driver on the one available passenger line still operating between East Pakistan and India.

Along the way, a mob of murderous thugs armed with knives, swords and spears would place rocks, boulders or tree trunks on the track that would force the train to a standstill. Maurice would then make himself very visible on top of the engine coal tender with his rifle held at port. Seeing the "white sahib" and armed to boot, the murderers never came near his engine. But he still had to helplessly stand-by as the mob of Muslims would enter the carriages behind and butcher every Hindu; man, woman and child they could identify.

What was happening was bizarre as after finishing their grisly work the thugs would then clear the track of the barrier and yelling their slogans wave the "ghost train" on to continue its macabre journey. He reckoned that the only explanation he could give for this weird action was that the Muslims wanted the Hindus "on the other side" to see what they had done. The extreme irony of this was a tit-for-tat response, for he was forced to witness the slaughter of Muslims in exactly the same way on the other side of the border when doing the return trip. He described this mindless butchery as a nightmare that went on for some time until heavily armed seasoned troops from the Army could be spared to guard the trains. Over a million civilians were killed in this orgy of communal killing in both East and West Pakistan as well as in India.

Due to the administrative breakdown Banking transfers between East Pakistan and India were frozen though the currency remained the same. Maurice decided he'd had enough and planned to resign but found himself in a tight spot when he decided he had to extricate himself out of the country with his money and get to India. He was a brave and resourceful Loots. He resigned his job and gradually withdrew his savings from the local bank over some time and stashed the cash literally under the mattress. Now, with his life's savings in money belts around his torso, a haversack with some tinned food and a canteen of water he moved to a railway friend's place as close as possible to the Indian border.

One dark night, he started his trek to India hiding and avoiding the Pakistan Army and Police patrols. Due to the chaotic situation, there were a lot of thugs and dacoits around and he had to avoid the villagers. He could not carry a heavy rifle as well for protection so he only had a revolver for safety. He made it safely into India after two nights of trekking and holing-up in the countryside and forest during the day. When safely across, he caught a train to Calcutta exhausted but relieved.

Again, because of the administrative breakdown, the postal service barely operated so none of the Clan, though constantly worried were any the wiser of his adventures until he wrote a letter to Sarah Loots from Calcutta. He now planned to migrate to the UK, so he stayed there for some time so he could arrange to get British passports for himself and Christine.

Though the Brits were renowned for their upstanding honesty, apparently this was not the case with issuing British Passports. Money changed hands and he had his and Christine's passport within a week!

British passports in hand the next hazardous business was to exchange his Rupee currency to British Sterling on the black market; a thriving but dangerous caper because it was always conducted at night and in dark sleazy neighbourhoods of Calcutta. Many an Anglo Indian found himself fleeced of his money by unscrupulous black-marketeers and with no recourse to the law. Maurice was smart. He armed himself with his revolver, which he made visible before the transaction and then exchanged only certain amounts at a time, never going back to the same place twice.

Stirring stuff isn't it, but more drama was to follow. Having now settled the money affair Maurice now wrote a second letter that he planned to bike (bicycle mind you not on a motorbike) from Calcutta to Bangalore which is over 1,200 miles away. His reason to undertake this caper was he just wanted the experience of the bike trip! As you can imagine all hell broke loose at this announcement. Sarah Loots was beside herself; her son Maurice would be waylaid, robbed, even murdered! The entire Clan thought the same. Even Will, who knew his brother well was worried enough to seriously say to Carrie: "Utter madness. What's gotten into Maurice?"

Of course, at that time none of the Clan knew of his horrific experiences on the trains, his collecting his money, his hazardous border crossing escapade or his dealing with the greedy and dangerous illegal money changers; so cycling along a Grand Trunk route from Cal to Bangy was a picnic to him by comparison. Well, Maurice did just that in bicycling from Calcutta to Bangy that took around three weeks. It was all just another Loots caper and no need to make a fuss over it!

Historical folklore has it that in 1756 the same Lord Clive of Arcot fame marched his troops of nine hundred Brits and 1,000 Sepoys from Madras to Calcutta to rescue the beleaguered Brits imprisoned in the "Black Hole of

Calcutta". It was an epic performance. I just wonder if Maurice Loots, who travelled the same route some two hundred years later from Calcutta via Madras to Bangalore Cant, was the first to ever do so on a bicycle?

Surely Will didn't include Uncle Maurice amongst the Clan's daft lot? He was a legend in my young mind. The spirit of Nicolas Benjamin Loots, who left his native Holland on 28.02.1789 on a sailing ship to make his fortune in India, was alive and well!

The religious riots and killings were pretty serious stuff that prompted a Brit, Patrick Hugh Stevenage, to write about his dreadful experience with the communal atrocity.

"As Independence Day, 15 August approached, the troubles that some of us had expected began. Hindus massacred Muslims, and in turn were massacred by their Muslim neighbours, who had lived peacefully beside them for so many years.

In Bezwada, I witnessed a small part of the madness that had taken over a hitherto peaceful country. The Grand Trunk Express was perhaps the most important train in India. It ran from Delhi to Madras, taking about 52 hours to travel some 1300 miles. Rumours began to spread that on many occasions en-route it was being attacked, and the passengers slaughtered.

At Bezwada, where the train moved from Muslim Hyderabad State into India, I found proof of this. On several occasions when it arrived the only people left alive on the train were European or Indian Christians. As the train passed through Hindu areas the Muslims were killed, and as it progressed into Muslim areas the Hindus passengers suffered the same fate. The terrified remnants of what had been fully loaded trains were taken off at Bezwada and treated to hot meals and drinks of tea or coffee in the refreshment rooms.

The train itself was pushed into the traffic yard, and the sweepers were put in to wash away the blood which caked the floors of the compartments, inches deep. This happened on several occasions while I was on duty at Bezwada."

9
Kate Loots!

KATE OR KITTY as she was affectionately referred to, was next in line and essentially flew under the family radar so to speak, but not the microscope. Sarah Loots had worked in Sir Haji's mansion and one of his sons had married Renée an English lady. Kitty was very attractive and in time became a friend and constant companion to Renée. I guess Renée was lonely in a huge mansion full of Muslim women most of whom couldn't speak English.

In time Renée's husband as is the Muslim custom decided to take another young bride. She jacked-up at this idea, packed her bags and two young children, Miriam and Kenny and ostensibly went back to England on a holiday and took Kitty with her for companionship. In fact, she had no intention of coming back.

After a year or two, a bit of fishy innuendo started to float about in the Clan conversations. This was led of course by Bunny, not overtly mind you, but enough to create the suspicion. Comments such as: "Why is Kitty so attached to Renée?" … "Why is Kitty staying with Renée?" … "Why hasn't Kitty come back?" … "What's going on between Renée and Kitty?" … "Why hasn't Kitty found a young man to marry?" … etc., etc. No one was game to say what the Clan suspected and that was that Kate and Renée might be having an "affair"!

What hope could there be for the unfortunate Shoolay Loots when they were ready to point the bone at a fellow Clan relative despite there being no proof? The Clan could be malicious of a fellow member as well!

Finally, Kitty did return to Bangalore Cant and met Fred a widowed Officer in the British Army. He had a terrific personality and had two daughters by a previous marriage, one of whom was Dolly who was very sweet to me. Anyway, Kitty and Fred married and he whisked her off way-up north to the Military Cantonment of Quetta, 5,500 feet above sea level and on the border of Afghanistan.

To drive a nail into the family gossip coffin, Kitty soon after gave birth to a bonny wee baby girl. Kate was so overjoyed with her baby girl she named her Joy!

The Clan's gossip cupboard was bare once more!

In time, Uncle Fred received his discharge papers and returned to the roost to settle in the Cantonment. Dolly went to Bombay to start a career and the young Joy remained in Bangy. Joy was as pretty as the morning star and an accomplished pianist to boot, but she was so far up herself that even the sunlight couldn't follow her! When the very good-looking Joy passed by her cousins on her bike, she would cock her pert nose into the air and turn her face the other away. Ouch!

In time Fred and Kitty decided to emigrate. England was too cold and out of the question. Australia was considered seriously but finally rejected because there would not be any servants, so Rhodesia was chosen on the advice of friends. It was so much like the India of the British Raj; to wit comfortable large bungalows, gardens and servants at one's beck and call, so off they sailed to Salisbury Rhodesia.

10
Ivy Loots!

IVY LOOTS WAS THE LAST OF Will's siblings and looked after him as a tacker so they were very close. In fact, of the three sisters, she was a sweetie and had the crazy habit of whistling old tunes all the time while pottering around in her home. She did not believe in the old Irish saying of: "A whistling woman & a crowing hen are neither good for God nor men". She just kept on whistling! She was rotund in every way, both face and body, full of the joys of spring and as happy as a dog with two tails. That took some doing considering the bloke she married.

Anyhow she met Arthur Healy who also worked on the railways and like the rest of Will's siblings headed way up north to Kanpur. In time, they had a son named Tony. Now, this story is more about Uncle Arthur than Aunty Ivy, since unlike her two elder sisters who sort of governed their husbands she was subservient to hers!

Arthur was a belligerent character and the total opposite to Ivy; once again a true benchmark of the saying that opposites attract. He had a craggy long face, a slightly crooked bulbous nose, eyes that could bore through a steel vault door (except that his glasses were permanently smudged), short stiff, salt and pepper coloured hair that could stand straight up in a force ten gale! He didn't speak much and sort of grunted a lot; but when he did speak with anyone it was never a conversation it was a challenge!

He was built like the proverbial brick dunny and had a temper to match it. He loved a stoush and would take on anybody just for looking at him! He ultimately lost his job because of his temper for clocking his boss with one punch. His boss was a Brit (if you don't mind) and Arthur's actions were not the done thing at any time, let alone during the Raj!

So, like the rest of the Loots they finally returned to the spiritual roost to settle down; figuratively speaking that is, as literally speaking Arthur hardly settled himself down. Consequently, his evening's entertainment was to deliberately ride his bicycle after dark on the road without the compulsory oil lamp. When stopped by a poor, half-starved skinny bow-legged local cop and asked where his bicycle lamp was, he would point toward the streetlight. When the unsuspecting cop looked up toward the light Arthur would clock him one right on the chin then ride off to another street and repeat the caper on another unsuspecting cop that might stop him. And when he couldn't find an "obliging" cop to stop him, he went looking for British Tommies who might be prowling around looking for a local girl. If there was just a pair of them, Arthur would pull-up, start an argument and a fight and blinking clock the both of them. This was his evening's entertainment and he didn't drink either!

If that didn't make him a daft bugger, he had another addiction. He was determined to make his only son Tony into a rough and tough boxer like himself. So he would stand by his front gate and when he spotted a big made Anglo Indian lad passing by, he would call him into the front yard and tell him he could earn himself a few annas if he could beat Tony in a fight. Tony was a bit on the skinny side and when the strapping lad saw him, he would be into it. So out would come the boxing gloves and Tony was forced to fight the bigger boy.

"At first the poor blighter used to get a hammering" Will said disapprovingly, "but Tony gradually became a dashed good boxer himself. Big strapping Anglo Indian boys now gave their house a wide berth after that."

Despite his father's daft ways Tony went on to be an Aeronautical Engineer in Pan Am in Idlewild Airport New York International in the States.

And that was Uncle Arthur!

Will was right; with a few exceptions, the Loots's were indeed a bit of a daft lot!

11
Will Loots & Carrie Morris!

ALL WE KNOW OF CARRIE'S side is her family folklore. She was certainly born in Rangoon Burma and always reminisced of holidays in a lovely hill station place called Mandalay.

Her father was of English and Burmese heritage though Mendel's law seemed to have effectively suppressed the "English" while highlighting the "Burmese" in his case. Her mother was apparently of French and Indian heritage. I saw very little of either of them but remember Carrie's dad to be very quiet. He had a bald shiny head that I was forever tempted to give a rub before leaving. He was always reading the newspaper on the veranda and would look over the top of it briefly at me and greet me with a nod and a half-smile on the rare occasions when we did meet.

He did have one special skill though which I admired greatly and would watch closely in constant expectation. He always smoked those powerful Burmese cheroots that you could smell down the street and into the next suburb if the wind was in the right direction. Every so often the newspaper would move a fraction as he turned his head, and with a perfectly aimed "phessht" he would send a stream of tobacco juice into a spittoon three feet away. Gosh, he was good at it, he never missed!

It must have been sad for Carrie as he just sort of died one day and all I can remember of it is what Will said: "The poor old man was too tired to live."

Carrie's mum, who we called "Nanna" scared the lot of us including Hansie and Hansie didn't scare easily. She was tall and raw-boned so to speak, had a long freckled face, sunken cheeks and scary faded blue eyes that pinned you to the floor! Jeanne my cousin who lived with them said she was very strict and religious and if she suspected anyone was telling a fib she would bring out the large family Bible, locate it in the centre of the dining table, place a pair of blinking scissors on it and then spin it. If the spinning scissor stopped pointing accusingly at the poor victim the "guilty" verdict was confirmed; followed by a religious tirade of going to hell for telling lies. Jeanne swore that the scissor's always stopped while pointing at her quarry. That yarn was sufficient reason for me to keep a healthy distance from Nanna and to never open my gob. I would just nod or shake my head to her questions if we ever visited to save myself from the scary scissor pointing ritual. On one occasion frustrated by my just shaking or nodding my head, she demanded: "Haven't you got a tongue Thomas?" To which I nodded vigorously and stuck my blinking tongue out. Though Carrie was not impressed fortunately Nanna thought it funny and laughed.

On the way back in the gharry Carrie demanded; "Thomas why did you behave so badly."

"I'm not taking any chances with the scissors and the Bible Mum."

"What fib is that now?"

"Promise Mum. Ask Jeanne." And I told her about the scissor and Bible caper. Carrie went all silent and methinks she just might have suddenly recalled similar incidents of her long-forgotten youth.

So, I guess you could say that with Indian, Dutch, English, Burmese and French blood in our veins we were a true "bitser" family; that means, with "a bit of this and a bit of that" in our lineage or if you wish to be more romantic you could describe us Loots as "exotic". This potpourri of race may account for the fact that Carrie was very good looking. Everyone said she was a dead ringer for the Hollywood actress Ava Gardner.

Carrie's father held a pretty high position in the police force in Rangoon and when he retired just before the

Japanese invasion, he moved his family to Bangalore Cant and settled down.

In those days, bachelors, especially those working in the bush as Will was, depended on Church Hall or Institute dances in the cities to meet and court a girl when they came on their annual leave. Carrie was full of life and loved dances while Will was just the opposite. Quiet and reserved, he could barely dance and in fact, Carrie always said he had two left feet! Nevertheless, as the saying goes, opposites attract and that's how they met and fell in love.

Now, this is when things get rather bizarre in how the respective parents of the young couple viewed things and the whole matter deserves some explanation because it sort of ordained our lives and relationship with our grandparents.

Let's return to Sarah Loots. Will was her youngest and her absolute favourite son to boot because he was just four years old when he lost his father. So, she probably considered Carrie an interloper when she married her favourite son. Added to this was the strange mind-set of Granny Sarah Loots in having no time for the female gender anyway. In short in Granny Sarah Loots's world, men and boys came first and women and girls came a distant second. This meant she had no time for Carrie either. Again, in short, they did not like each other. Carrie loved everybody in the world except Sarah Loots. It was never open warfare mind you but there were the usual snipes and jibes to keep the flame going when they were alone. Will's presence meant that they were at least civil toward each other.

On the flip side of the coin, there was Carrie's mother. While Carrie's father was quiet and rather dignified, her mother was a snob if not a bit of an autocrat. Because Carrie's father had held a high position in the Police Force her mother had an even higher opinion of herself! She was always reminding anyone who would listen that her maiden name was del Ganin!Consequently, she viewed this insignificant railway employee with the banal name of William Loots to be below her beautiful daughter's station. In short, she didn't approve of Will.

It was the perfect parental example of quid pro quo.

Despite this handicap, the courtship developed and William Loots and Caroline Morris got married at St. John's Church in the Cantonment.

Will, being the serious reserved type just ignored his mother-in-law for the rest of his life and there was very little if any contact with Carrie's parents and her entire family including her four younger siblings. I cannot remember Will discussing his in-laws except once when he heard that his mother-in-law had joined the Seventh Day Adventist Church denomination. He promptly dubbed them, "Seventh Day Adventurers" and the subject was closed.

We children were forever raised as Loots and that was that!

Grownup folks can act awfully strange and still lecture little larrikins on how to behave!

BEN LAFFRA

PART TWO
The Loots of the bush!

BEN LAFFRA

12
The bush Loots!

THE NUCLEUS OF OUR BRANCH OF THE LOOTS family was Will and Carrie, Hansie and Nanette my two older siblings followed by me. There was also Mahmood my minder and our cook who we all called Jemima. How she got that name I have no idea, perhaps from Will who on the rare occasion when he couldn't remember the name of some lady would say: "Jemima Jones". Anyway, Mahmood and Jemima had been with us since Adam was a boy and were treated like family. I have to reluctantly include Cousin Christine Loots within our family core because she spent so much of her life with us, though I use the word "reluctantly" with very good reason. Chrissy always had the wood over me in any argument or scrap, and they were countless, and I could never get my way with her. Yep, Chrissy was tough rivalry and a tom-boy to boot and was a pain in the bum; but she did on one occasion saved my life. She never ever let me forget it!

Will Loots had "sayings"; I called them sayings because he would simply say it and never preach it, but there was always a "lesson" attached to it. Some that stick with me is: "Pride is not the problem; its vanity", and another: "Justice is more rational than love", and yet another: "Never judge yourself on the welcome you get on arrival but by the genuine regret shown on leaving."

As Will was an engineering Permanent Way Inspector on the railways he was for the most part posted in the "bush" and was moved around in his job quite frequently, so maybe he was referring to the "welcomes" and "farewells" at each country posting.

On arriving at a fresh country posting there would always be a small group of Railway employees on the Railway platform to welcome the new head honcho and they would place welcoming garlands on Will and Carrie. I was always left out. After his stint of three or so years, Will would have to move on. Now, in addition to his fellow Railway workers there was a crowd of the local people including the Village Munsiff on the Railway platform to farewell Will Sahib and Memsahib. The garlands were bigger, more plentiful and the Namaste's sincere. Sometimes I scored a small garland too! So perhaps they were sad to see Will go. Other passengers on the train must have thought a person of considerable importance was being fare-welled; they wouldn't know it was just the modest Will.

The places Will was posted to in the bush contrasted a lot. Some places were so hot, the mercury in the thermometer had to go around a second time, others so cold that the crows cawed in soprano, or so wet that the chooks grew webbed feet, or so dry that your spit evaporated before hitting the dirt, or so humid that you walked around in a personal sauna; while yet others so arid that the trees followed the dogs around for a squirt of moisture!

But when the blessed first monsoon arrived the agony of prickly-heat was over. The once parched earth would release its pent-up aroma of special remembrance to all who have experienced the first rains on sun-baked soil in the sub-continent of India. Its earthy bouquet is unforgettable and no Parisian perfume can rival it. And with the life-giving rains, the trees would flourish once more with new growth of leaf, flower, seed and fruit.

Between monsoons the sky was clear, the moon bright and the ghostly flying fox in their hundreds would wing their silent way across the moon to feed on nature's bounty. The cicadas would burst into song and the frogs would follow in various tones from deep bass to soprano at night. That's when the snakes would hunt and every so often, when curled up snugly in bed at night you would hear that aching long drawn out shriek from a frog and know it has fallen prey to a snake. It was also time for the rat snakes to prowl the villages hunting for rats and their nemesis the King cobra would, in turn, hunt the rat snakes. All of that was natural to us living in the country.

The term "bush" does not mean an isolated sheep or cattle station or a house on the vast prairies, as there was always a railway station, a hole in the wall post office and a village nearby that had grown-up by the station. What the bush meant to us in India was most of the people around us spoke their native language, which was usually foreign to us, yet we always managed to connect with a sort of Patois tongue. The bush also meant there was no electricity, running water, pubs, shops, grocery stores, hospitals, doctors, dentists, police or Swiss restaurants; but there were always the local roadside hawkers, slipper-maker and dhobi; that is a bloke who washed, starched and ironed clothes for a living. The starch made the clothes stiff as cardboard but the pant crease was always perfect!

There was always a village tailor as well whose skill in stitching a pair of pants or a shirt was built on guile and knack. One could have a shirt or pant, measured and expertly stitched by a tailor in the big smoke which was then given to the bush tailor with the material. He would carefully take the samples apart, stitch by stitch, then copy the blinking thing to perfection. Every Christmas Will would get the appropriate material and we would be measured-up for our outfits, except Jemima who got ready-made saris. Hansie and Nanette were kitted out in their usual school uniforms, Will his Military tunics, and khaki shirts and shorts for my minder Mahmood. I wanted khakis like Will's and Mahmood's but for some weird reason, Carrie said no they should be white. I argued and pleaded and howled until I think Will convinced her with the logic that since I was a grot and always soiling my clothes, white material would show up worse. Carrie finally agreed and I got my way!

Carrie was the only one who was privileged to choose her own material and dress fashions by a "ladies tailor" in Bangalore Cant. She loved dressing up no matter where we were and she loved wearing costume jewellery too; usually made with base metals and simulated stones but it looked good on her. It was not Will's way to show overt affection but there was no doubt he loved his Carrie and it was his way of recognising she had given up the city life she loved to devote herself to him and the family in the bush.

We lived with the occasional outbreak of life-threatening cholera or plague in the district and the constant threat of malaria. The floor was regularly swabbed with Phenol that had such a strong smell it probably sent plague and cholera packing! We slept under mosquito nets and Carrie always had more gallons of Flit than there were mosquitoes in the entire district. Fresh vegetables were always washed in Condi's crystals and the drinking water always boiled.

There was the Gregorian calendar and an old Railway Station Clock that Mahmood would religiously wind-up each morning. They hung on the dining room wall, and despite the loud tick, tick, tick of the clock to attract attention to it; we paid little or no attention to it or the calendar. The centuries-old "Bush Calendar" linked to sunrise and sunset, seasons of the year, the monsoons, the harvests, the village market days and the arrival from somewhere and departure to somewhere of certain tradesman services served the purpose.

The bush calendar dictated our lives with a gentle tranquillity ordained by the harvest season.

The first to appear each year would be the village Shaman. He would start at Will's office to break his coconut and chanting his mantras would dispense his blessings of sandalwood incense in all the rooms, the stores and the workshops. He would receive his "prasadam" from the staff and a "baksheesh" from Will and then according to tradition he would politely ask if the Sahib's home also needed his blessings and the removal of evil spirits. Will always said yes and he would hold his palm out for the second baksheesh.

Carrie was never keen on the Shaman's blessings but Will had told her it was a harmless tradition of the ages to be respected and not to fuss over it. Nevertheless, she stayed well out of his way when he arrived at our bungalow. He was a little birdlike figure that seemed to flit his way from room to room chanting his mantras of blessings in a sing-song voice. He was wizened, bent over almost in two and had eyes that never seemed to focus. I would follow him from room to room all over the house but he never seemed to ever notice my presence. His last stop would always be at Jemima's kitchen where she would give him a big prasadam of Indian sweets; ludoo's, jelabies and dood peda. Jemima fancied herself as a Shaman as well! Because Jemima and I were sworn enemies I figured she was an evil spirit and the Shaman should have cast a spell over her and made her disappear. The Shaman let me down and my fervent wish each year was never granted.

Once a year, at his appointed time of the bush calendar the travelling "knife sharpener" would arrive with his ancient wooden "A" frame contraption of a sandstone wheel driven by a pedal and pulley. All the scissors and knives including Jemima's would be honed. Jemima would watch her prized possessions like a hawk for a time lest I stole one to do some digging for worms or tree carving. I had to bide my time until she relaxed her vigilance. When I could steal them her pots and pans made super loud drums, cymbals and containers for mixing mud and cow dung for my dinky toy battlefields. Jemima did not agree and it was one more reason why we were sworn enemies.

The knife-sharpener would be followed by the "tic-man" or cotton-beater to fix up the flat and hardened mattresses we slept on. He would open up the mattresses and beat up the cotton with an implement that looked like a longbow. He would heap the flattened cotton and gradually work his way through the heap whacking the string of the bow with a wooden mallet and the string separated and fluffed up the cotton fibres. I would sit for ages watching him work, fascinated with the cotton fibres flying up in the air like little clouds. He would then add some more cotton if needed, re-stuff and "re-button" the mattress, so for a time you felt as if you were lying on a brand new mattress. He was a kindly old man as ancient as the hills and forests, skilled in his trade and a pearl of wisdom that was a companion to his patience with me for I would try to beat his "harp" with the mallet and send the cotton flying all over the room. He would just smile and never complain.

Following the tic-man and arriving at his appointed time of the bush calendar was the "bottle-wallah". He was a shrewd man with a long face, a pointed white beard and sharp eyes whetted from the practice of bargaining. I never went near him, for once when I was being particularly naughty Carrie threatened me with: "I'll tell Jemima to trade you to the bottle-wallah if you don't behave yourself." I was already a legend in the family for getting up to some mischief or other.

So it was always Jemima, who was equally shrewd as the bottle-wallah, with a sharp tongue and shrill voice to match who was appointed to deal with him. Mahmood would collect all the old newspapers, magazines, bottles, clothes, cans and any old junk that could be recycled and set it out on the back veranda floor. Then an epic battle on price would take place between Jemima and the bottle-wallah that could go on for an eternity. I always watched from a respectable distance and ready to bolt just in case Jemima included me in the bargain! I think Jemima and Mahmood shared the hard-fought-for proceeds.

That's how simple life was and that roughly describes our bush in India in which I grew up as a tacker during the twilight of the British Raj.

13
The Metaphor of Will!

HANSIE, NANETTE AND CHRISTINE were boarders at school in Bangy while I was still a tacker at home so Carrie was in charge of my "pre-school education" like teaching me my ABC's and learning my numbers. This was conducted at the dining table each morning for an hour. That was the only mistake I reckon Will ever made because I would play-up with her. On one rare occasion, I did have a useful brainwave as I decided I would like to write postcards to Hansie in school. Carrie suggested I should also write to Nanette and Christine but I said: "no Mum they're in a girl's school." That fine piece of logic of mine escaped her but after some argument she finally conceded. She thought it was a good idea anyway because it would at least get me to write something. There was a lot of palaver about the rules of this brainwave of mine that had to be resolved.

"Can I have my own postcard Mum?"

"Yes you can, but you must only write one short sentence."

"What's that Mum?"

"Well, a postcard is small to start with Thomas so you can't write like you prattle on." She gave me a few examples. I was not impressed but after a while, the drill was worked out. I had to say something short and Carrie would write it out in capitals on my slate. I would then laboriously copy the words in pencil on the postcard. Carrie would fill in the date and address and I would finish it off with signing "Tom." Good beginning except for another problem; I wanted to write whoppers and another huge argument took place.

"I shot a leopard with my Winchester". The Winchester happened to be a toy gun.

Carrie said no. "I told you no fibs, Thomas." She would never use Will's word of "pipe-dottle" for fibs.

"I had custard pudding". Carrie said no to that as well, even though it was not pipe-dottle. The reason she gave was it would make poor Hansie hungry and feel left out.

"Skip said to say hello". Carrie said that was okay even though I knew he couldn't talk! I cheekily asked her how-come that was okay?

She was smart. "Because Skipper wags his tail smarty-pants and that's like saying hello."

I conceded and the first of many missives and arguments with my rigid "censor" was finalised and I went with Mahmood riding on his shoulders to make sure it was posted.

"Dear Hansie, Skip said to say hello. Your loving brother, Tom".

Carrie was not very complimentary. She said the one line which I had so laboriously and carefully copied on the postcard looked like Egyptian hieroglyphics; whatever that was! I accused her of getting that piece of information from Will's National Geographic. But in time my writing improved as per Carrie's verdict because it now looked like Chinese characters. I didn't mind that because we played Chinese checkers and so it must be an improvement. And so again, according to Carrie, my writing progressed to look like Japanese, Russian, Greek, and every language in-between to finally resemble Roman English.

I was miffed because Hansie never replied to my postcard until Carrie explained that he was allowed only one postcard a week and he did always say hello to me.

"You know Mister"; Will would call me Mister when he was cranky with me, "you have been nothing but trouble from the day you were born."

That was my dad Will giving me a dressing down for some particular tomfoolery I had been up-to. Everybody called him Will except Carrie who called him William and not because it was his real name; it was actually Wilhelm but she didn't like it. Will wasn't upset with that, so long as you didn't call him "Bill" as he never fussed over a thing which was inconsequential in his opinion. He was just as happy with being called William or Will and I had this bottled-up urge to call him Will as well. I did once. Just once and that was when he was going to give me the dreaded enema because I hadn't been to the bog for three, or maybe four days. Or was it five?

I'm sure Will had somebody spying on my "thunderbox" who reported to him that I hadn't had a bog. Maybe it was the "Matharani" who emptied and cleaned the thunder boxes with phenol each morning, or maybe she told Jemima, then Jemima told Carrie and she told Will. Whatever the process Will would come to know and out would come the enema can for a serious clean-out of my "innards" which was a favourite term of his for my stomach.

I hated the sight of the enema can as well. It was a white enamel container with a long pink rubber tube with a straight black plastic spigot and a sort of tap contraption on it that hung menacingly on Will's bathroom wall. I had to lie on my side on the bed while Will would mix up some soapy water; that's right just Lifebuoy soapy water, then insert the spigot with a smear of Vaseline on it right up my Khyber pass, open the tap and hold the can high as the dashed stuff slowly dribbled into my innards while I protested loudly in vain. I was so aggrieved after one such episode I announced, between heaving sobs: "I don't love you any more Will".

No shock, no anger, Will just looked at me in his quiet way and said: "well Tom, in that case, I wouldn't want to give you another one so just you lie there and hold it in as long as you can before heading for the bathroom."

And that was Will; and though it's hardly a pleasant impression to insert an enema episode into a story it sort of epitomises the quiet yet steely resolve of Will and the fact that I never called him Will ever again.

The name of "Will" sort of suited him. He was not very tall but he was solid, square and dependable, never spoke a lot or laughed loudly, seldom cross at home except with me for good reason, patient when he had to be and had just a quiet smile when required. He had permanent furrows on his forehead that just got deeper and deeper as he grew older and I think I might have been the cause of it. I reckon that "Will" was the metaphor for my dad.

And the following is what Will was probably thinking of when he said: "You know Mister; you have been nothing but trouble from the day you were born."

Brother Hansie was older than me by four years and sister Nanette by two. As with the earlier confinements when the time was approaching Will and Carrie would head off about three or five hundred miles by train to Bangalore Cant. They would stay with Will's mum Sarah Loots who had "taken rooms" with Granny Long. Granny Long was no relation but that's what we called her. Taking rooms was a polite way of saying renting a portion of the house. The house was located on Mosque Road in Fraser Town.

Being the third to be born Carrie figured she had sufficient experience and confidence about when I was due to pop-out before having to go to the hospital. She should have consulted me because I decided to push toward the big wide world ahead of time apparently at the ungodly hour of one or two o'clock in the morning and she went into intense contractions, or so I was told years later by Will.

Will hurriedly put on a shirt, pulled on a pair of trousers, tightened his belt (he always wore one) and rushed off to the stables behind the house where the "gharry-wallah" was sleeping to hook up his nag quick smart for the trip to the hospital which was about two and a bit "alpine" miles distance.

Now Will's mum, Sarah Loots, was a qualified midwife and a nurse to boot who had safely delivered heaps of babies in her time, so you might well ask: "Why all this blinking drama when Granny Loots could have saved the day?" But no, Carrie did not get on with her mother-in-law Sarah Loots and there was no way in the world she would trust her to deliver her babies.

Grown-ups could be awfully strange!

Bangalore Cant is known as a "hill station" which meant it was built on undulating long climbs up the roads and the reverse going down. That made the going slow uphill and a bit of a hand-break operation going down to stop the horse from slipping on the tarmac. The gharry-wallah could understand the urgency from the cussing and swearing of the stressed-out Will, but I wonder if the poor old horse being whipped to go faster did!

To add to Will's stress Carrie's "water burst" (a quaint expression I never got to learn the meaning of) while still in the gharry. Gosh did the gharry seats get an unwelcome bath? Another minute or so and I'd have had the remarkable distinction of being born in a four-wheeled ancient horse-drawn gharry, drawn by a flea-bitten old horse with a top speed of five miles an hour! But, it was not to be. Later there was some debate I was actually born on the wheeled stretcher as per Carrie, but apparently, the nurse in charge pooh-poohed that story and that she had made it to the hospital delivery table with not a second to spare.

Will's patience had been sorely tested earlier but he didn't have to pace the hospital corridor for long when the chief delivery nurse, who was well known to Granny Loots came out and said to him: "Will, you have a healthy baby boy with a thick mop of hair and a pair of lungs that could be heard in the last row of a concert hall. Carrie is doing fine and resting so you can go home now, have a rest and come back anytime later this morning. And oh, tell Sarah

I'll drop in to see her when you fellows stop producing babies at ungodly hours." She then pointed down to the bottom of his trousers, adding tartly: "and you can now roll your pyjama bottoms up so they can't be seen before you go." About three inches of brightly striped pyjamas were protruding. Will tended to stutter a bit when embarrassed. He was.

Will later declared that this narrow escape, or, in his words "a close shave" of almost being born in a gharry, accounted for my habit of getting into trouble!

I was born in The Lady Curzon Hospital that was built on the same design of the Laraboisierl Hospital of Paris in 1868. I arrived at the start of the final decade of the British Raj in India, as well as the start of the "Phoney War" period that was the precursor to World War II. Being the youngest he named me Thomas. Will was not a religious man in conventional terms but methinks he did have some serious misgivings about me for ages in keeping with "doubting" Thomas of biblical fame!

When Carrie was ready to travel home, Will with his two small children and his newborn son in tow, who already showed alarming signs of having the lungs of an opera singer, headed back to the bush station where he worked.

Barely three months old and I was to disturb Will's composure once again. For some reason, Carrie couldn't breast-feed me after a time. No sweat, Will had a cow.But fate decreed otherwise as a month or so on the blinking cow suddenly dried-up! Again, no sweat as while there were no cows in the nearby village, the friendly village Munsiff promptly provided a milking buffalo. But that created another problem. I had a bad reaction to buffalo milk and suffered a severe dose of the runs despite it being diluted. And apparently, to show my distaste for buffalo milk I would bite on the nipple of the feeding bottle, rip it off and spill the contents all over myself and my baby cot. I don't remember doing this. Since there were no doctors within cooee the furrows on Will's forehead deepened.

Once more the village Munsiff suggested to Will he could have a choice of several "wet nurses" from his village, but this time Carrie firmly knocked that idea on the head. I was never told why. Maybe she thought I would never be able to speak English or suffer some other diabolical side-effect from sucking on the teats of a "native" village woman! For the second time, I was not consulted!

The usually resourceful Will was running out of ideas but fortunately not the friendly village Munsiff. He called the elders of his village together to find a solution for Will Sahib. They quickly concluded donkey's milk was good for everything including babies and so a milking donkey with its foal was promptly procured. The wise village elders were right. Will's Thomas took to donkey's milk with unrestrained enthusiasm much to the relief of all concerned. Donkey's don't produce a lot of milk so family folklore has it that Will had to keep a yard full of milking donkeys and their foal's to cope with his son's appetite!

Since I was raised on donkey's milk Will declared this accounted for my possessing a rather pronounced stubborn manner!Being a man of considerable prescience, he was proved right on both counts. I had the happy knack of constantly getting into trouble and also of being rather obstinate!

Carrie used to always tell me: "They broke the mould after you were born Thomas." She was probably right, too!

And that's the eventful start of the larrikins life!

14
The trials of Tom!

THOUGH I WAS THE YOUNGEST of three siblings "trouble" was my middle name. Hansie was the quietest of us three and you could barely get a word out of him. He showed signs of a tradesman's skills very early and loved to make things with his hands like bows and arrows, shanghai's, tops and woodwork stuff. Though gentle by nature Hansie was as wiry and tough as a starving bushranger on the run from the troopers. He also had the appetite of the bushranger's horse!

Come to think of it, it was the quiet Hansie who got me into strife and my first brush with Will's wrath according to my version. Hansie always disputed that and believed that Will had "skelped" me umpteen times before that incident. He's probably right. Will used the term of "a clip behind the ears" but Hansie stuck to the term of skelp! Whatever, we were hanging around in Will's workshop making different spikes for the tops he had brought back from boarding school. He also told me all about a new play-toy called a yoyo which he wanted to get for me but they were too expensive. "They're easy to make though Scoot," he said, "I've figured it out."

Now Hansie was the only one who called me "Scoot". I reckon he gave me that nickname after noticing I would scoot at the first sign of trouble, but he didn't want anybody else to know. It was just between him and me. And that was Hansie's way.

"How ya goin to make it Hansie?" I was deadly keen to possess this new invention called a yoyo.

He explained that if you took an empty thread reel, cut it at the spindle joints, turned them inwards and put a piece of a lead pencil through the hole of the reel as an axel, then get some thick string and fixed it to the axel and wound it around; bingo you had a homemade yoyo. My mind was racing like a cheap two bob watch with a broken spring. Where can I get my hands on some empty thread reels? With my "fertile" brain the answer didn't take long.

"Hang on Hansie, I know where I can get us some empty reels and we'll make us some yoyo's" and before he could ask me where and how I was off. I bolted home and as the coast was clear with Carrie reading in the front veranda I stole into her sewing room and checked out her sewing stool. It had a hinged seat and a deep compartment beneath; and there, amongst sundry sewing stuff were six reels of different coloured thread. I knew Hansie would balk at pinching the reels and removing the thread so I nicked three reels and repaired to my hiding spot behind the banyan tree and set about removing all the thread. Gosh, I couldn't believe how much thread was on a blinking reel. Anyway, I finished the job leaving a massive mess of coloured thread strewn in the dirt and headed back to the workshop.

"Where'd you get 'em Scoot?"

"Mum's got heaps of empty ones stored in her sewing stool," which of course was bare-faced pipe-dottle which was a unique expression of Will's for fibbing and lies. I never heard anyone else use it and maybe because he smoked a pipe. "I'll go get us some pencils and string from the Head Babu now." I was brave because I knew Will was not in the station and had left early to go on track inspection. The Head Babu gave me one partly used pencil and sent me to the Store Babu for some bricklayers twine. It was perfect. I returned with my loot. Hansie was impressed and made us three champion yoyos and like everything I liked to do, I became a little champion at yoyo-ing.

All was well for a few days while I was busy developing my yoyo skills. Carrie didn't miss any thread reels as she hadn't been sewing and then to my bad luck a strong wind blew up; and what did it do? It took the thread lying in the dirt and made an intricate design of knotted coloured thread on the fence wires of our compound. It hung there like incriminating gossamer. I'm sure it was Jemima who took a closer look at this strange phenomenon and waddled off to Carrie to also have a look as well.

When the whole yoyo story was finally unravelled Will didn't even interrogate Hansie. He just knew who the culprit was and I got a severe dressing down and a clip behind the ears. Poor Hansie was mortified that he had got me into strife and quietly said to me; "sorry Scoot."

And that was Hansie.

When all had been forgiven I showed Carrie how useful her thread reels were with a demonstration of my new-found yoyo skills. "Perhaps you can be just as good with your ABC's and numbers Tom," she said. I guess she was not impressed!

In-between the two of us was my sister Nanette. She had our mother's sweet nature. Because she was sandwiched between two boys she had to cope and put up with my constant teasing, pinching kicks under the dining table and even a pull of her hair. But the best prank, oft-repeated, was when Nanette was sitting on the floor completely engrossed in playing with her miniature tea set and dolls. She would even talk to the silly things, or at least I thought so because dolls couldn't talk back! Anyway, I would belly crawl silently up behind her with my new Christmas present cap pistol and go BANG, right next to her ear. She would jump a mile high and scream with fright while I laughed my little head off with malicious glee.

You see, I had tucked away in my mischievous little brain that Nanette was scared stiff of thunder. One day we were hanging around Will while he was working outside making some alterations to the chook-house. Nanette was hanging around with the claw hammer in her hand while he sat on his haunches working away when suddenly there was a huge flash of lightning followed by an almighty thunderclap. In her fright, Nanette walloped poor Will right on the head with the blinking hammer. Fortunately, she was only a tacker like me at the time. Will ended up with a bit of a lump on the head and probably a headache to boot.

Cousin Christine who was more a sister than a cousin and just a year and a bit older than me had lost her mum at childbirth and while she was brought up by Granny Loots in Bangalore Cant, she spent most of her holidays with us. I never thought of Christine as anything else but my sister albeit a heck of a lot more boisterous than Nanette. In fact she was a regular tomboy. She hated being called Chrissy and made the mistake of telling me. So to get back at her I would deliberately yell out: "Hey ya Chrissy wat'cha 'doin you blinking sissy". Her face would turn scarlet with anger, her eyes would narrow into invisible slits, her lips would purse as if she had just sucked on a lemon, then bunch her fists and let fly if I was within range. Yep, she was always ready for a scrap and she would never, ever give-in. Nor would she cry. I never heard or saw Chrissy cry except a couple of times and in both cases, I was involved.

One other first cousin, Jeanne, was also part of our holiday lives on a few occasions. She was the first cousin to us on Carrie's side. Jeanne was the only one from Carrie's family that we had any regular contact with. She had a slight squint, which made her self-conscious, a pert nose and large black eyes. She needn't have worried about her squint. She had a generous nature and where I couldn't get Christine to fetch and carry for me Jeanne would happily do so.

I guess what bound Christine and Jeanne into our family was Carrie. She was the total opposite to Will (that is when it came to punishing me) with a sweet and caring nature and with rarely a harsh word. I think that when she did get cross with any of us it embarrassed her. Will was the reliable rock in the family and the disciplinarian. Most often a stern look from him was enough to keep me on the straight and narrow, at least for a time.

Now, Will wasn't always strict and grumpy. When he was in a good mood by my reckoning he would keep singing a few bars of his version of the words of the song "Lambeth Walk" and whistle the tune in between. Maybe I hadn't been up-to any tomfoolery to make him cranky. I liked the jolly sound of Lambeth Walk. While it wasn't funny for him, I thought it funny as when he sent Carrie away for a short holiday anywhere, or to fetch Hansie and Nanette from school, Will would completely forget Lambeth Walk and start whistling and singing that doleful blinking song "Stormy Weather". Never mind, since he and I were alone together without Carrie I was always on my best behaviour to avoid getting into "stormy weather" myself.

I'm afraid that out of all of us Loots "siblings" I was the chronic larrikin who gave everybody a hard time. None were inclined to share my belief but I like to think I just had an adventurous spirit that stretched the envelope of Carrie's and Will's patience to the limit!

Living in the bush meant I grew-up in big rambling old homes built by the Brits with no electricity, no running water, thunder-boxes in the dunny, mossies, midges, snakes, frogs, lizards, goannas in the roof, big black hairy scorpions that hissed and little boy's tall tales!

Scorpions were pretty common in the bush, and the little Red Scorpion was the worst poisonous critter around. It was nasty fellow because it wasn't very big, around a couple of inches "stretched out", could scurry at a hundred miles an hour and loved to come into the house and find a spot to hide in. Its sting was pretty painful and would last for hours as it went up your arm or leg to settle in the glands of the armpit or groin. Aside from watching where you walked, shaking out the shoes and dusting out the clothes and hat before putting them on was just second nature.

There was another one, the Giant Black Scorpion which had a deadly poisonous sting but it was nocturnal and rarely came into the house. Because of its size, "stretched out" it was eight or nine inches long, it was slower moving and so easier to spot.

One morning I was mucking around minding my own business playing "top's" with myself when the top landed on its side and whizzed away to disturb some wood pieces nearby. I was gobsmacked to see a champion big black scorpion raise its sting, pause ready to strike, then "seeing" no danger it crawled back under the piece of wood again. This was an opportunity too good to pass up. I got myself a stick, made a knot-loop of my "jathi" or string that was used to wind around the top, and with the stick turned the timber piece over. Sure as there are no fleas on a dead cat the scorpion was up in arms, it raised its curved tail ready to sting, so I carefully hooked the loop around its tail and tightened it. Bingo, I raised my wriggling prize up into the air. All I needed was a pair of Carrie's scissors to snip its sting, nick one of her shoe boxes for its house and I would have myself a giant black scorpion as a pet! Now taking it into the house was risky as I would have to pass the hawk-eyed Jemima so I tied my prize to the stick and sped in. To my bad luck, Carrie was at her sewing machine where the scissors were kept.

"Mum, can I borrow your scissors please?"

Carrie didn't turn around, busy with her sewing. "What for Tom?"

I went into a long explanation of playing top's etc. ending with: "I got myself a big black scorpion for a pet Mum. It's a beauty at least a foot long and it's tied to my jathi and I need the scissors to snip its sting off."

Carrie pivoted on her sewing stool quicker than you could say Jack Robinson: "Oh my God don't tell me you've been playing around with a poisonous black one? And you haven't even got your shoes on; what on earth are we going to do with you?"

"But Mum it's attached …" She didn't let me finish.

"Go and fetch Mahmood immediately Mister and tell him to kill it immediately. No, go to your room and just stay there."

"But Mummmm …"

"No, if's and but's Thomas; do as you are told immediately and I'll tell your father when he gets home." Crikey, Carrie looked angrier than a cut snake that scared me more than a giant black scorpion could. As I turned to go she fair yelled at me; "and where is this wretched thing?"

"I can show you …"

"No go to your room and tell me where it is."

"In the white ant woodpile Mum and it's got my top jathi on its tail. Can I have it back?"

She glared at me and strode off. As per Mahmood, he found my jathi but no scorpion. He got the shovel and turned the woodpile over, found it, flattened it, sliced off its poisonous tail and fed the rest to the chooks. So instead of ending up as my pet, the scorpion had a nasty ending!

The white ant woodpile was Will's idea for good chook feed which he must have got from reading National Geographic. The woodpile was very old railway sleepers that were piled in our back yard which Mahmood would keep wet so that the white ants would hone in to nest and multiply. Every so often he would extract a piece and throw it in the chook pen and they would go crazy feasting on white ants like it was Christmas.

Will did not give me a clip behind the ear but he was really angry and gave me a right royal dressing down about the danger posed by poisonous snakes and scorpions! Perhaps in the back of his mind was the only thing he could remember of his father was that he was a keen naturalist. Will was only four years old when his father died.

So, with all these nasty dangerous critters slithering or crawling around you would expect that I would always put my shoes on. But no, I had the shocking habit of persistently running around barefoot. I loved the freedom of bare feet and that of course frequently got me into strife and flirting with the dreaded "clip behind the ears" from Will.

Aside from the dangerous critters, it was not quite pukka during the British Raj to be seen running around barefoot! That was the preserve of the "natives", not the British, and we Anglo Indians had to ape the Brits in every possible way and that included always wearing hats and shoes and the shirt tucked into the pant. I'm afraid I consistently failed the British dress code in all three departments!

When the first monsoon rains broke it could rain for days. Lovely warm rain that made our large backyard into a slushy, muddy, tempting ankle-deep pond, except for the stepping stones that led to the out-houses which were the servants quarters. I could watch the deluge happily from the back veranda as the big droplets made myriads of little fountains as it hit the surface of the muddy water. When the coast was clear, and I was on my own, and Carrie was having her afternoon nap I would slip outside and gleefully squelch and stomp around in the pouring rain and mud, under and over foot and up-to my shins.

This is one time my trusty four-legged friend Skipper would hang back. He didn't like to get his paws wet if he could help it and come to think of it, he didn't like getting wet at all. Skip hated baths and would stand there in the bathroom looking very unhappy and forlorn while Mahmood gave him his monthly! That's one dislike we both shared with a passion; having a blinking bath. But he had far less reason to complain than me about the evil business of having a bath. Mine had to be once a day at least, and more often even twice while Skip had one only once a month! So Skip would sit on the back veranda and after a bit, start to bark like heck because he couldn't, or more correctly wouldn't join in the fun of playing in the mud and rain. Then sure as there are no fleas on a dead cat Carrie would appear at the back veranda door and start yelling at me to come in from the rain. I knew what had happened; Skip's barking would have attracted Jemima's attention, she would have seen me playing in the mud and rain and waddled off to wake Carrie up and sneak on me. Jemima was always sneaking on me, she was!

Jemima and I were sworn enemies and our fights legendry over her pots and pans and cooking implements, that were temptingly laid out on the long table in the rear veranda after cleaning and polishing with wood ash. I was skilled as a Sioux Warrior at pinching her "valuables" when she wasn't looking; her frying pan or pot to mix mud in, or to use as some sort of drum while I played at marching soldiers, or nick her sharpened clever to do some practice chopping on the wooden sleepers.

I had a thick spikey head of hair which prompted Carrie to sometimes refer to me as her "wired haired terrier." I also had three "cowlicks" or whorls on the back of my head; and Jemima, who also posed as the shaman in our family, confirmed that it meant I would in time have three wives! Maybe that's why she didn't like me. Anyway, it was definitely mutual and war declared with no end in sight!

I never won the fights with Jemima as Carrie always took her side.

Life was very unfair to little larrikins!

When Will was not around, Jemima would insist on treating my cuts and bruises with the application of spit and cobwebs. Since Carrie couldn't stand the sight of blood she usually got her way. I balked violently once at this "medical miracle" that was to be applied up my bloodied nose! Mahmood came to my rescue that time and instead pushed some cottonwool up my nose instead of spit and cobwebs.

Anyway, once more Jemima had got her back at me by summoning Carrie to see me doing my rain dance in the mud and slush.

"Tom, Tom, Tom." I would pretend not to hear until Carrie raised her voice several octaves in anger. "Thomas, I'm warning you to get out of the rain immediately before you catch pneumonia."

Now I'd heard Carrie yell that I'd catch the dreadful pneumonia last monsoon, not that I knew its meaning, but I'd figured that it had something to do with getting wet. And since I got wet almost every day when forced to have a bath why didn't I get pneumonia then? I thought it better not to ask her that as I would surely get a clip behind the ears from Will for being too insolent.

I would finally squelch my way slowly and reluctantly toward her. "No, you don't dare come inside. God, just look at you, your shorts, legs and feet, they're filthy with mud just like a little "chokra". Now go the back way to your bathroom immediately and have a bath. And change those clothes while you are about it."

"But Mummm, I've already had one in the rain."

"Don't try to be smart Mister, or I'll tell your father when he gets home. Now do as you're told immediately." She told Jemima to take the parasol and to fetch Mahmood from the quarters.

Before leaving I gave Jemima my best "death-stare" and stuck my tongue out at her. Jemima never died from my death stares though I tried really hard.

While Jemima and I were avowed enemies, Mahmood the gentle giant and faithful family manservant, who was also charged to look after me was my friend and confidant. He had been there with Will and Carrie even before Hansie and Nanette and now finally me. He was over six foot tall with an oval face and dark black eyes that couldn't hide the kindness. He always shaved his head and wore a turban but rarely shaved his chin. His turban's always had a blue stripe in it and since he knew I liked it he would wrap his turban around my head and swing me up onto his broad shoulders and race around the yard, or place me on the branch of a tree, or hold me while I swung "like Tarzan" on the long trailing air roots of the banyan tree, or sit on his haunches and watch me play with my Dinky Toys, or show me how to milk the cow or churn the milk to make white butter. He played tops and marbles with me and always let me win. He would make a great fuss when he missed an easy shot, shake his head and click his tongue at the failure; but he knew that I knew he was pretending. It was a game within a game. Perched on his wide shoulders, or piggyback he would take me to the village, the train station to watch the train wheeze in and out belching steam and smoke and to the shunting yard to watch the little engine do its work like a busy ant toing and froing.

But there was one thing Mahmood denied me and that was to play with his clasp knife. It was a "Pathan" knife, curved like a new moon that folded into its wooden handle like a penknife, but bigger with a four or five-inch blade that he kept honed like a razor blade to expertly slit the neck of a chook. He would shake his head resolutely and with finality say: "Ney chota baba." No amount of coaxing, cajoling or tantrum by me changed his mind and I gradually resigned myself to never playing with his Pathan knife. And most importantly Mahmood never snuck on me to Jemima or Carrie when I was up to mischief. He simply clicked his tongue, cleared up the evidence of my crime and swung me onto his shoulders and took me somewhere interesting.

Mahmood was family, cared for and looked after by Will with the same attention he gave to his children and he, in turn, devoted his life to us.

Anyway, I knew the drill well. Mahmood would come to the bathroom, clicking his tongue in distress (never with disapproval) at my muddy grotty appearance, undress me, scrub me clean with Lifebuoy soap, towel me and put out a change of shorts and a shirt. Come to think of it, I can never remember Carrie bathing me; it was always Mahmood.

And so my harmless frolic in the rain and mud would end with a hated bath!

I'm not sure if Carrie did ever report me to Will, but if she did I have a feeling he might have had a quiet smile. Will sort of understood little boys liked larking about in the mud and rain and forgave me these minor skirmishes with her.

There was another reason why she didn't approve of my behaving like a little chokra, not that I understood it at the time, but Carrie was an ardent Royalist and adored the British Monarchy and Will didn't. How much she idolized them lies in a yarn that happened a long, long time later when they had retired to a place called Whitefield which was an enclave of Anglo Indians situated about fifteen miles out of Bangalore Cant. But the story epitomizes Carrie's keen British spirit and a slight dose of racialism!

Queen Elizabeth and Prince Philip did a royal tour of Madras and then came to Bangalore Cant. Cheering crowds in their hundreds of thousands thronged the streets just to get a glimpse of their motorcade and the handsome young couple. Carrie was deadly keen to see them as well when they arrived but Will flatly refused. So she missed out but didn't give up!

Not far from Bangalore Cant is the picturesque Nandi Hills on which stands an ancient summer palace of the anti-British warrior of old; Tippu Sultan. Not to be outdone the

Brits also built a grand Governor's Residence during the Raj that was rarely used except for Presidential visits and such like. Anyway, the Queen and Duke at the end of their visit and probably well-worn out by cavalcades, grand entertainment and sumptuous dinners repaired to the Nandi Residency for a bit of R & R before they departed from the South of India.

The day after the Royals left, a bus trip to visit Nandi for sightseeing and a picnic was organised by the Whitefield club. Carrie who was a legend for running late for any occasion surprised Will by being up and dressed in all her finery bright and early, so they were the first at the Club to catch the bus. She was again the first to hop in and grab the front seat as well. After a few sightseeing stops, when the bus pulled up at the Residency, Will was in for another surprise as Carrie bolted out of the door like greased lightning while mumbling something about needing to go to the toilet in a hurry. Will duly followed her as she streaked ahead, raced up the stairs and went ahead of him into the building.

The wing where dignitaries stayed on their rare visits is always off-limits to the general public and is protected by a sort of ornate red silk tasselled rope placed across the entrance door on polished brass bollards. The cleaners were still working in the wing as a uniformed bloke was standing by the open door. By the time Will got through the large ornate entrance hallway he had lost sight of Carrie but after fossicking about he spotted her haranguing the uniformed guard and making a big show of needing to get to the toilet in a damn hurry, while the poor bloke was trying to convince her she couldn't go into this particular area. But somehow she got her way as the guard gave up and in she went. The poor fellow was still shaking his head in alarm when Will went up to him and told him not to worry his wife wouldn't cause any damage and gave him a couple of rupees to ease his conscience. When Carrie reappeared with a big smile on her dial he asked her what the devil was all that about. "Oh, I just wanted the thrill of being the first to sit on the toilet which Her Majesty had used!"

"Just how did you convince that guard to enter the restricted area Carrie?"

"Well, after a bit of palaver William, I told him it was so urgent if I didn't get to the bathroom immediately I would have to do my business on his highly polished marble floor!"

She boasted about her caper to every one of the tour party on the bus while Will cowered in embarrassment. The Loots family joke ever after was that Carrie sat on the same "toilet throne" as Her Majesty Queen Elizabeth.

That might explain why Carrie was so alarmed that her little grot was developing into a barefoot native "chokra"; a derisive term I'm afraid for a homeless, poor, barefoot grotty urchin with a runny nose and shirttails hanging out of his pants!

15
Tom's awkward questions!

IN WILL'S JOB, we lived in rambling old homes that were built for the Brits during the Raj, with trellised verandas in the front and rear to allow the breeze through and keep the wild animals out, or so I believed.

Will told me that leopards often came down out of the surrounding hills and jungles and crept around the villages nearby at night to grab a country ring-tail pie-dog or goat that had not been secured. There were always heaps of dogs around in the day in the villages. Anyway, Skipper our German shepherd and my constant companion was kept indoors at night on the instructions of Will. For me, that was proof enough that leopards roamed around at night in their hundreds, even thousands! Little boys have a wild imagination. We had tall louvered windows with bars (to keep the leopards out of course), thick twelve-foot high laterite stone walls and high pitched roofs without a false ceiling, bare rafters and roof frames with tiled roofs so you could see the chinks of light through the gaps in the tiles when you woke up of an early morning.

There was the "gazunder" a piss-pot in fact beneath the bed at night, "thunderboxes" in the bathrooms and concrete water storage troughs that often had a friendly frog or two bobbing around in them. But the concrete did keep the water cool. And there was a dipper or large tin mug with a handle to pour the water over you for a bath.

The monsoons also produced myriads of tiny frogs that didn't get into the water trough. They never seemed to grow bigger than about an inch and a bit in size and would invade the house according to nature's special calendar. Carrie was terrified of them and kept her distance but Will stipulated they be left alone as they just minded their own business and did no harm. These tiny beautiful creatures would merrily hop across the floor, crawl-up in single file only in the corners of the front veranda wall (they never went beyond that) and all just sit there for ages looking at each-others bum's. I never once saw one of them fall. They were friendly little fellows too. I would pick one from its corner perch and hold it in the palm of my hand and it would just sit there quite happily. The funny part was when the little frog behind saw the gap, it would promptly move up to fill the gap and all the others below would follow suit. So I would put the little fellow at the end of the queue. It was a game I would play with them all day. They never complained! Then one day they would all decide it was time to go "home" and crawl down in reverse and hop away merrily across the floor and through the gaps in the trellis, never to be seen to the next season.

I asked Will if they were the same ones that came back each year. He said he didn't know and that was a severe disappointment. Will knew everything! Anyway, I suggested I tie a piece of string to a few of them to check it out but he gave me a firm no! That was a second disappointment.

There were times like this that I felt life was very unfair to curious little boys!

Things can happen in the bush that can be a tad scary. Late one evening, Nanette and Carrie were sitting in the veranda having a mother and daughter yarn when Nanette noticed something moving on the trellis just behind Carrie's head. They both bolted for safety screaming blue murder! It turned out to be a snake, a common krait that grows to about three feet. Mahmoud got rid of it by "bagging" it and then put its lights out.

Will always said that the cobra was the "gentleman" of snakes because it rarely if ever would strike first to bite and would always "flare its hood" and hiss a warning; while kraits he reckoned were bad news because they were small and slender size and had a bad habit of coming into homes looking for really small rodents and insects. The actual bite of a krait he reckoned couldn't be felt and so was dangerous as its venom was deadly. We all learned to check what we touched and where we moved at night. It just became second nature and except for Carrie and Nanette, we were not scared.

I had a friendly goanna that made its home in the rafters as well. I've no idea what it did for its tucker, but when it was over a hundred degrees in the waterbag and I was forbidden to go out in the scorching sun to play barefoot in the dirt, which was a crime according to Carrie's standards, and without a hat which was one more of many offences as per my her; I was confined to bed until the cool of the evening. And if I stretched to look around the overhead mosquito net there he was high in the rafters. I always called him Mr Goanna. I don't know why, because whenever he peered down at me he would stick his tongue out. I would return the favour but he didn't seem to care.

"Hello, Mr Goanna! One day you're going to slip and fall and I'm going to catch you by the tail and put the frights up Mum who hates creepy crawlies!"

Mr Goanna never did fall and Will told me a story as to why they wouldn't.

"They have strong leg muscles Tom, and claws that can grip to the rough surface of the stonework of the wall. In the olden days, the enemy would creep up to the fort walls in the dead of night with their goanna's." A tingle went up and down my spine with excitement as the story unfolded as a true story or not just didn't matter. "They would put the goanna on the wall and hang onto its tail while it slowly and silently climbed to the top and that's how they took their enemy soldiers on the fort ramparts by surprise, stabbing them with spears. Mind you, their goannas were much bigger than that fellow in our roof."

So Will knew about my secret Mr Goanna. Why did I think he wouldn't? Will knew everything!

At sunset, each evening, the Petromax lights and hurricane lanterns would be lit and Mahmood went around the house with the Flit pump to keep away the flying bugs and mossies. We played games like caroms, drafts, cards or Chinese chequers by lamplight. It was fun because I would always like to cheat a bit to win and would get caught.

On the stone paving outside our bungalow, Mahmood would put out Will's long easy chair that had funny leg supports that swivelled out from the stout armrests so he could put his legs up and lounge back on it. Reclining comfy cane chairs were for the rest of us. This is where we gathered after dinner in the comfortable world of our family time. No phones, TV, or visitors. The only "proper" English speaking folk lived probably over a hundred miles away or whatever. It was a simple yet beautiful life governed by the seasons, sunlight and darkness and not the calendar or watch.

Carrie smoked cigarettes like a train and Will smoked a pipe; sort of off and on. Will was never a regular smoker as he would suddenly start smoking his pipe and then after a month or so he would put it away only for it to appear again a few months later. But when he lit his after-dinner pipe the aroma that wafted lazily through the still air was oh so nice. I loved the rich ripe smell of pipe tobacco.

"Make smoke rings Dad" I would urge.

Will would take a gurgling suck on his pipe and blow smoke rings that hung like silvery circular ghosts in the still night air. Carrie could blow smoke rings as well when I badgered her to do so. Actually, Carrie blew better smoke rings than Will but I never told him so. Will was best at everything!

"Belly gone tuff Dad?" This strange and somewhat muddled expression of mine meant I wanted to climb onto Will's lap, stretch out and look at the heavens. The air was always pure, and except for the monsoon seasons, the sky would be brilliantly lit by stars. The big yellow moon looked awfully close and the flying foxes gliding like silent black ghosts across the moon were a wondrous sight. There were often hundreds of them lazily winging their way to the huge silk cotton, giant gold mohur poinciana or mango tree that would be in flower or fruit in our compound. When they settled there and started feeding however, the ghosts became as noisy as a bunch of silent Monks thrown out of the Order of Carthusians!

"Why is the moon so bright, Mum?" I once asked.

"Because it's a big yellow balloon with a big candle in it!"

This is when Will would clear his throat, a sort of tight-lipped silent signal that he didn't approve of little boys being told fantasy stories about the moon. He believed that if a child asked a sensible question it should be answered correctly even if they didn't understand it completely. But this very admirable belief of Will could, on occasion, have its drawbacks.

I was with him by the chook pen one day while he was throwing some green feed to the chooks when I saw the big rooster chase a plump hen, catch her and jump on her back while pecking the coxcomb of the poor hen.

"Dad, Dad, look at the rooster bullying that poor hen!"

There was silence from Will but little boys have an insatiable curiosity. The rooster finished with that hen, flapped his wings in triumph, let out a "Cockle-doodle-doo" and promptly repeated the process on another hen. This time I had a direct question.

"Dad, what's the rooster doing?"

"I think we better go inside young fellow."

And that was the answer I got. So much for responding honestly to a child's question! But worse was to come.

Now, Skipper who was my constant tail, friend and faithful companion of many an escapade, witnessing many a piece of mischief I was up-to and never dobbing me into Carrie or Will, was after all just a dog. Not that I appreciated that as we used to have "conversations" though I never noticed they were always one-sided.

Stray dogs were rare around our wire fenced compound. The servants had strict instructions to shoo them away and throw a few stones at them for good measure lest Skipper catch, rabies, fleas and ticks from them. But one quiet afternoon when no one seemed to be around, except me and Skipper, a stray dog managed to breach the wired sanctum. Skipper made a ferocious charge at the stray and I thought he would finish it off; instead, he pulled up short, gave a bit of a sniff at the rear of the cringing stray and then did what the rooster did to the hen! This was something I had never seen for sure.

"Hey Skip, what' cha up to? You can't ride piggy-back on that one. You're too blinking big."

He ignored me and looked pretty pleased with trying to ride piggy-back since his long tongue was hanging out as proof!

Then, unexpectedly all hell broke loose and I was thrown into fits of laughter. All of a sudden Skipper was back to back with the stray, stuck together so to speak and the stray was yelping. Skipper didn't look too happy either. His ears were stretched back and not standing straight up as usual. Skip was hopping this way and that, pulling and tugging like heck and the both of them were going around in blinking circles and looked as they would go all giddy. I figured somehow he'd gotten himself into deep strife. I thought in alarm my friend Skip was fair dinkum anchored permanently to the other dog!

"Hang on, Skip!" I yelled. Hang on? Hang on? This was possibly not quite the right choice of words. "I'll tell mum. She'll know what to do."

Into the house, I rushed to Carrie who was having her afternoon siesta.

"Mum, Mum, wake up! Skipper is stuck!"

"What do you mean stuck Tom? Stuck to what? And where's Mahmood?"

"Dunno Mum, but Skip's stuck for good to another dog and it's yelping like blazes! What's happened Mum?"

Carrie was now sitting bolt upright and wide awake.

"Go to your room at once and stay there Tom."

"But Mum, Skip is hooked up to the other dog like a shunting engine! How're you 'goin to get him unstuck?"

Now I figured Carrie would at least understand that rather fitting description since we had often seen such engines hooked up to each other, busy as bees shunting wagons around in the railyard! But obviously, she didn't.

"I said GO to your room, Thomas." Her otherwise normal sweet tone had somehow become menacing!

"But Mummm...!" I was not allowed to complete my plea and I was now hopping around from one leg to the other in agitation.

"Do as you're told, AND RIGHT NOW!"

There was not only a certain finality to Carrie's "NOW" but a higher than normal pitch to her voice as well. I figured I was nearing a category three reportable offence to Will, never mind a category two; so I skulked off reluctantly to my room and lay on my bed, thoroughly pissed-off. After all, I'd been the one who raised the alarm that my friend Skip was in desperate strife!

It was times like this when I felt life was unfair to little boys!

I could over-hear a fair bit of commotion going on outside now and soon after Skipper came tearing into my room and settled down beside my bed, licking vigorously away at his "wee-wee!"

"Hey Skip; you'll be in trouble as well? It might be your turn to get a clip behind the ears from Will eh!" I savoured the unkindly thought.

Skipper always looked at me when we talked to each other, he did now and I somehow thought he had a funny glint in his eyes.

I was primed and dying to pop the question to Will about Skip being stuck to the other dog like a shunting engine; with which I was sure he was very familiar with but I didn't get a chance. I think a secret pact had been made between Will and Carrie to take my mind off asking the shocking question. I came to this conclusion because they talked about everything under the sun, and the moon, and the stars and the blinking universe so I couldn't get a word in edgeways! Very early in the piece Will popped a timely question that he knew would distract me.

"Like to come on line with me tomorrow Tom?"

"Yep Dad." My immediate and excited response was forthcoming of course. He knew I loved going on the rail trolley with him.

"You better get ready early then. I'll give you a call."

I didn't need telling as I usually slept like a log at night and was up at dawn each day. Every minute was precious for play.

"Can Skip come too Dad?"

"Yes Son, he can come with you. Put his harness on first thing in the morning. Okay?"

"Can we take the gun Dad?"

"Yes, and now it's time to get to bed young man." I think I detected a touch of relief in his voice as I headed off.

I was not yet out of earshot when I heard Carrie say; "well thank goodness for that. By tomorrow he'll forget all about that and come up with something new I imagine."

My ears pricked up as I stopped dead in my tracks. I was a skilled eavesdropper!

"He's an inquisitive little cuss, no doubt about that. Not that's a bad thing mind. It's good to have a curious mind Carrie though it does get a bit trying at times. The scoundrel has a "why" for everything. Maybe he'll be a lawyer when he grows up."

"Well, he tells enough fibs to qualify for one now." Carrie and Will laughed quietly together.

What's a blinking Lawyer and a fib telling Lawyer at that? I couldn't dare ask Carrie or Will or I would give the game away. My mind was ticking over like a run-a-way two bob watch when the solution arrived. I would ask my friend Ghokale the Store Babu. He was sure to know and I was sure he wouldn't tell Will.

I heard Will say; "come on mother, let's go to bed." I bolted to my room as I heard Will call out to Mahmood. I went to sleep none the wiser I'm afraid but with a vague sort of unrequited suspicion.

Later my friend Ghokale, the Store Babu told me a Lawyer went to court (whatever that was) and argued the case before a Judge (whoever that was) so that the guilty person was punished and not the innocent. It sounded pretty good to me.

"Why does he tell fibs Ghokale?" He took his cap off as usual and scratched his head, a sign that usually meant he didn't understand me, so I explained: "You know, he tells lies."

"Ah Tom Baba, he is speaking untruths you say?"

"Yep, the Lawyer tells untruths."

"That I am not sure Tom Baba. I am not a Lawyer. Who knows? I am thinking maybe he tells the untruths to save the innocent person? Yes?"

That logic sounded good and suited me as well. I was innocent because I always told fibs; or as Will would say, pipe-dottle.

16
Romancing the steam train!

STEAM LOCOMOTIVES AND TRAINS ran on ribbons of steel and nothing can equal the thrill of watching a large shiny behemoth, belching smoke and steam thundering through the countryside. The golden romance of the steam era was to last a hundred and twenty-five years and to this day still has its adoring fans around the globe.

These drivers had a love affair with their living mechanical monsters. Just listen to the romantic lyrics of Charlton Ogburn Jr., author of Railroad & the Great American Adventure:

"In the cab on a moonlit night, seeing the light flashing on the rods, the flames dancing in the firebox, looking back at the smoke trailing over the train, the steam gauge steady at 200 pounds and hearing the old girl talking in a language that only you and she understood. There is nothing like it in the world!"

These big puffing black behemoths had captured the imagination of people, especially little boy's ever since they appeared. Even songs were written about them and the most popular toy trains were steam trains.

If you have ever stood beside the twin ribbons of steel watching the roaring approach of a black behemoth and felt the very earth tremble beneath your feet as its six-foot two-inch driving wheels pounded past, and if you have heard the raging thunder and seen the eruption of smoke from its chimney and the hot steam squirting from the piston rods as it bore down on you; you have lived. And especially in the silence of the night if you heard the haunting engine whistle that created its Doppler effect as it tore away from you on its run through plains, jungles, hills, and mountains you have lived twice; because there's nothing like it in the world!

Now, these engine drivers were to me the chocolate topping on the churned ice-cream. I think they loved their locomotives because the engines were always groomed like a bride at her wedding. The copper pipes were burnished and shining on the black greased background of the massive engine boiler and the brass valves, gauges and instruments inside the cab, polished like gold.

Will said some of them looked like "gold bees", which is a golden stag beetle. They had a very shiny greenish-gold colour and a very collectable pet for young boys, especially in the bed to fly around inside the mosquito net. Carrie was never impressed with my insect pets.

Riding the foot-plate meant the cab of the engine and looking forward the black boiler seemed to stretch a very long way to the front of the engine that was connected to the coal and water tender on some sort of pivot beneath the chequered steel floor of the cab. The engine would buck and sway at high speed differently to the movement of the tender. So, balancing on the centre steel dividing plate produced an exhilarating ride of its own.

I think I liked firemen better than engine drivers. Engine drivers always wore white, sometimes even dressed in a neat white cotton suit and tie, while firemen were always in thick blue cotton drill pants and a short-sleeved shirt with the collar stylishly turned up. Their blue drill clothes were grease-stained and sweaty and that appealed to me. Their fingernails looked filthy black with black coal oil and that appealed to me as well! But it was their sweat-stained blackened faces that broke into a creased smile, their white teeth even whiter against the black of sweaty oily coal dust which made them heroes in my mind.

I surreptitiously wiped some oily black on my face and pants to wear as badges of honour hoping Will wouldn't notice. If he did, he never said anything.

Firemen were always friendly and would give me a handful of "waste", which was a sort of grey, blue and red cotton strings all balled together that served to wipe your greased and sweaty hands. When Will wasn't looking, I made sure I did a bit of wiping, just like the firemen did to make the waste dirty like theirs. I always got a knowing wink and a smile from them. They treated me as if I was one of them. Again, when Will wasn't looking I hid my dirty grubby waste quietly in my pocket to show off to Carrie. She would order me to get rid of it; I would, by hiding it under my mattress. Carrie almost fainted when one day she was supervising Mahmood turning all our mattresses and found a whole swag of dirty waste under my mattress.

"I'll tell your father when he gets home."

It was a category three reportable offence but I got away without a clip behind the ears. Ever after Carrie made me turn my pockets inside-out after a trip on the engine to make sure I wasn't smuggling any more dirty waste into the house.

There were special moments as well when "riding the footplate". The ubiquitous Thermos would be opened from time to time and bruised and battered enamel mugs hanging from some part or other of the engine would be produced. The coffee would usually be sweetened with condensed milk and if it wasn't hot enough the mug would be placed on the shovel and held in the firebox for a bit to come out piping hot. I would be given a mug and then I'd do my best to slurp the coffee as loud as the firemen did. Will didn't seem to mind, but I bet Carrie would have been horrified at me noisily slurping from a dirty chipped mug. It felt good though. I felt grown-up. I asked Carrie to buy me a chipped and dirty fireman's mug. She glared at me and I guess that meant a definite no!

In-between shovelling coal into the deep insatiable burning red maw of the beast, the Senior First Fireman (there were always two) would hoist me up so I could tug on the wire of the steam whistle. What fun! I could never have enough of pulling on the steam whistle. Aside from larrikin boys having fun "blowing" the steam whistle it had a special function. There were quite a lot of various codes, communicated by short and long whistle blasts that were used by the crew to interact with the guard at the end of the train, the station staff that the train was passing through, to warn railway crossings ahead and of course engineering staff working on the track. And there were special times when the friendly whistle would sound in the dead of night as the mail or express train thundered past the station and a friendly driver would give us his individual signal on the whistle to say: "Hello there Loots family this is George or Harry or David!"

Steam engine firemen were my heroes and not for nothing. They performed heroic acts every day and night. Picking up the line clear on the run at forty or fifty miles an hour when passing through a station rather than stopping; was quite an art if not a risky caper as the timing had to be right or an arm could be broken or worse still the line clear dropped that would cause a huge delay and drama.

Clearing the line meant a heavy metal ball was extracted by the station master from his line block control instrument. Once extracted it meant no train could enter the section in the opposing direction from the station ahead because it was a single line. The ball was placed in a leather pouch attached to a bamboo leather-covered oval hoop, about two to three feet in diameter resembling a very large tennis racquet without strings.

I watched the heroic act from the safety of the cab. From a distance, the First Fireman showed me where the "line-clear" man was standing by a marker holding the hoop high at arm's length and told me what he would do to pick it up. My heart raced as the distance to the man closed rapidly. The driver gave a coded blast on the steam whistle that they had seen the line-clear man and was ready to pick-up on the run. I think I missed a few heartbeats as the

Fireman climbed down lower on-to the lowest steel footsteps of the cab. He was hanging on by one hand to the stanchion and had the hoop from the section we were clearing in the other. At a predetermined point, he tossed the "clearing line-clear hoop", then leaned far out and hooked his arm through the new hoop exactly at the moment of passing. The momentum of the engine caused the hoop to smack loudly against the cab side metal panel and I jumped in fright. The First Fireman calmly climbed back into the cab, checked the ball number, hung it onto a hook and gave me a wink. The driver gave a coded blast on the whistle to the Station Master and the train Guard to confirm all was okay. Gosh, it was a thrill because it all happened quicker than it took me to tell the story later to Carrie.

But if that got the adrenalin going, picking up the line-clear hoop at night sent my adrenalin through the engine cab roof! The headlight of the engine (which was never very bright) would pick up the lone figure standing at his marker in the otherwise pitch black of the night. In one hand the man would extend the hoop at arm's-length and in the other he'd hold a modest oil-soaked blazing flare behind the centre of the hoop. The flaming torch was barely a pinprick of light in the distance. The steam whistle sounds above the thundering engine to acknowledge sighting of the line-clear man as the pinprick of the sputtering flare would keep growing bigger, alarmingly quick for my pulse rate. The pitch-black dark made it seem as if the engine was speeding forward at a hundred miles an hour, its powerful six-foot driving wheels inexorably propelling it faster and faster toward that sputtering torch while my head and eyes kept swivelling giddily between the sputtering torch and the Fireman. Despite the dim light in the cab, he must have noticed for he gave me a wink then calmly stepped down and hung perilously onto the stanchion. It was a matter of seconds and the timing had to be perfect, for, as the headlight on the front of the engine passed the line-clear man only the flare was visible in the darkness. My breath had long since stopped by the time he unerringly hooked his arm through the hoop while the man dropped the burning flare out of harm's way at the precise moment. I jumped out of my skin with the loud thwack of the hoop against the cab and that started me breathing again; just like a doctor I was told, smacks a new-born baby on its back to get it breathing. The drama of the moment had my adrenalin pumping. The fireman gave me another wink and a wide grin.

Yes, I decided I was going to be a fireman and took to turning up my collar and rolling up my sleeves. Carrie was never too impressed with Will taking me on the engine but he knew that I just loved the experience.

I curled my little arm up and tried hard to show my biceps that would qualify me for a fireman job. I had none of course. "Dad, Dad, look at my muscles."

"The muscles on your brawny arms stick out like spider's knees, Son!"

I was not sure how big spiders knees were but it didn't sound too encouraging. The knees of the "daddy-long-leg" spiders that abounded around the house were definitely disheartening. I'd have to check Will's National Geographic magazines where maybe I'd find big spiders with big knees!

With my head dizzy with trains and riding the footplate and trains whizzing here there and everywhere I guess calamities are bound to happen and sure as there are no fleas on a dead cat Carrie would be involved! She was going on a trip to Bangalore Cant to see her parents, do a bit of shopping and spend time with Hansie and Nanette while Will sang "Stormy Weather" and I was on my best behaviour.

Carrie had to change to an overnight train at Madras and told the luggage porter in very proper English;

Bangalore Mail! Perhaps the way she said it sounded like another similar-sounding place. So he takes her to the wrong Mail train leaving about the same time and Carrie blithely makes herself comfortable in the 1st Class Ladies coupe; "Reserved for Europeans and Anglo Indians" and all on her own. The next morning the train is still travelling and finally pulls into "her destination" at well past midday and Carrie duly alights and the railway station looks very strange. The waiting porter duly confirms her worst fears; its Mangalore Central and not Bangalore Cantonment. However, the Station Superintendent, an Anglo Indian, as usual, looked after everything. He informed Will over the railway telephone network, made her comfortable in the Ladies waiting room, arranged for lunch and dinner took her home to visit his family and finally put her on the night train to Bangalore City, all at no additional cost.

When she returned I heard Will say to her: "How on earth did you manage to catch the wrong train to Mangalore? Didn't you look at the signs on the carriage hoarding and the reservation card on the compartment door?" Of course, poor trusting Carrie hadn't done either!

I was dying to tell Hansie of Carrie's misadventure so when we got around the dining table for the weekly "postcard session" I came up with:

"Mum caught the wrong train".

"Don't you dare." Carrie was still smarting with embarrassment.

"But its true Mum and you said I can't write fibs?"

"Never mind and don't be a smarty-pants or I'll tell your father."

I didn't get my sneaky way and couldn't tell Hansie about Carrie's trip so I returned to try my luck with some of my own fibs.

"I shovelled the coal" … "I picked up the line clear even at night" …"I'm going to be a fireman".

Carrie disallowed all of them forcefully and I ended up with the dull truth:

"Dear Hansie, I went for a ride on the engine. Your loving brother. Tom".

17
Pentecostal bedlam!

GRANNY LOOTS WAS TINY and had silver sort of blond hair for as far back as I can remember. She always kept her hair drawn back into a bun, wore her glasses perched above her forehead tied with an old shoestring and could read the daily newspaper The Deccan Herald without using her glasses. I could never work that one out. She roomed with Granny Long and got the newspaper second-hand from her.

Granny Long's house was a large lovely old colonial bungalow on a corner block and so it had a big compound with plenty of trees to climb and have fun on. Most of the old homes were pretty big because Bangalore had been a Military Cantonment from way back because of its cool climate, never too hot or too cold and these residences had been built by the Brits. For yonks, the Cantonment was known as the "Pensioners Paradise" for the retiring Brits and now the Anglo Indians. There was a stable behind Granny Long's house in which were housed the gharries; one of which took me on that exciting journey to the hospital. These carriages were available for hire and regarded as the genteel form of transport for the snobs who could afford it. Those who couldn't had to travel in hand-drawn rickshaws or on bicycles.

Situated right opposite Granny Long's home was a small general store and I think the owners of the store actually owned the gharry business and just rented the stables from Granny Long.

Whenever Will took a holiday we would pack-up and go and stay with Granny Loots despite Carrie and Sarah not being on "good terms". Over time, all of Will's siblings had left the roost and struck out to all parts of the country to find their way in the world then return to our spiritual home of the Cantonment to settle and buy homes of their own.

One of my favourite pastimes was to stand at the closed wooden slatted gate of Granny Long's house and watch the people pass on the road through the gaps of the wooden slats. I was fascinated with the numbers of Anglo Indians around who looked just like me! They were as thick as thieves. Gosh, I saw more in one minute than I would see in a lifetime in the bush where we lived. My inquisitiveness with these Anglo Indians kept growing and I wanted to see them and they see me, or so I thought. I nipped inside to Granny Long's big open veranda, offloaded the heavy brass jardinière plant pot with great difficulty from its carved wooden stand, dropped the pot halfway onto the stone floor that put a big dent in it and then half dragged the stand back to the front garden wall. I could now climb onto the jardinière stand and look and lean over the wall where I could see the road and the folk better. From this vantage point, I happily tried to engage them in conversation.

"Hello, what's ya name?" … "Where you goin?" … "What'cha got in the bag?" … "What'cha buy?" … "Did'ja buy Bulls-Eyes?" … "Where do you live?" … "Have you got Dinky Toys?" … "Do you have a dog?" And any other rubbish that came to mind.

Some of them smiled or waved to me, others just glared but most ignored the irritating brat over the wall! However, this pleasant pastime was very short-lived. I couldn't keep still while standing on the wooden stand; the blinking thing toppled over and I with it and did myself an injury. I was confined to bed for a time after my scrapes and bruises had been treated by Gran and escaped a clip behind the ears (scrapes or no scrapes) from Will, only because of the presence of Granny.

Will must have been furious and I don't know what apology and restitution he made to Granny Long for her prized banged up brass jardinière. But Granny Long was a sweetie and never held that piece of mischief against me because I would wander in unannounced and have a chat with her telling her lots of fibs of living in the bush; including leopard's prowling outside my bedroom window snarling at me! I think she enjoyed my fibs because I never went away without a small packet of sweets. However, she was a bit cranky with me once when I denuded her guava tree of almost every piece of fruit so I could try to pelt the chooks with them. I never hit a single chook but I reckon they enjoyed the game and had a peck at the ripened guavas. I got a stern lecture and a clip behind the ears from Will for that caper though!

Granny later told me that Granny Long sold the fruit to "pickers" to make an extra quid and warned me off of the Sapota, Pomegranate, Custard Apple and Mango fruit. I had to spend the rest of the holiday and watch them hanging temptingly in frustration, especially the Bull's Heart that had turned big and red and ripe.

On the many occasions when I came a cropper and did myself an injury while swinging like Tarzan from the banyan tree air roots or trying to jump over our wire fence or do cartwheels; Carrie would say to Will: "William that son of yours will get himself killed one day."

"He'll learn the hard way, Carrie. Don't worry."

Nevertheless, I scored a small paper bag of "rat's dirt" for my scrapes and bruise from Gran after falling off the jardinière stand and not long after almost made Carrie's words prophetic!

Now, Granny had a strange attitude that I did not quite understand at the time and I never figured out the reason for it either but she had no time for the girls in the family and that included little Christine. The boys and men came first. Full stop! Will was her favourite son and, you guessed it I was Granny's favourite grandson!

I could do no wrong. I would chase her chooks around the yard, hide her glasses, shoes, walking stick and even her "wee-wee" tin and all I would get was an affectionate pinch on my cheek. Now, Granny's wee-wee tin was so named because she had trouble making wee's. So when she sat on the thunder-box she would put that tin under the tap and open it to a trickle. The tinkling sound made by the trickle into the tin helped her do the job. She was a nurse after all, so who was I to argue about its effectiveness? But I could hide the tin, couldn't I?

Gran had a favourite chook and whenever it wanted to lay its egg it would climb the three stairs into her front room clucking away merrily. Gran would reach down beside her chair and put a hessian bag on her lap. The chook would then hop up onto her lap and settle itself to do her job while Granny kept on knitting or reading the paper. This was a routine almost every morning.

Cousin Christine lived with and was literally brought up by Granny Loots, as her dad, who was Will's elder brother lived and worked way up in the Northeast of India. She, of course, played second fiddle to me when I happened to be "in residence" with Granny. She was a girl remember? So if you get my drift, Granny was fond of me, I was very fond of Granny and Christine who was left out in the cold wasn't fond of either of us! She took her anger out on me in vicious pillow fights which she indulged in with the distinct glint of murder in her eyes. I was just fortunate the pillow was not a blinking club!

There was a very famous place in Bangalore Cant called the Egyptian Bakery that made everything from big Wedding Cakes to tiny coloured "rat's dirt" and everything in-between. Actually "rat's dirt" consisted of caraway seed covered with hard icing sugar and had a peppery sweet taste. The trick was to put a hand-full of "rat's dirt" in your gob and crunch away. At least that's what I would do when Carrie wasn't looking.

One day, Will, Carrie, Hansie and Nanette went off to Commercial Street, the Cantonment's famous shopping precinct and left me and Christine to our own devices and Granny's care.

Thanks to my flourishing relationship and amusing tall tales with Granny Long I scored a bag of big fat egg-shaped Egyptian Bakery almond sweets she bought from the Store across the road. Christine and I were sitting together on the floor and I was playing the ass, as usual, transferring the almond sweet from one side to the other in my mouth, pretending I had two of them in my gob. Suddenly the lark backfired and the large egg-shaped sweet ended up in the back of my throat blocking the air passage. I finished up lying on the floor trashing around like a hooked cod unable to either breathe or howl.

For a time Chrissy thought I was playing the ass until she saw my eyes go all cockeyed (that was her very unkind description mind you) and my face going rather blue. She now started yelping in a panic for Granny Loots. She took one look at me and the almond egg sweets on the floor and figured out the problem. Lifting me by the legs, she started whacking me on the back while I was suspended upside-down. It worked a treat and out flew the lovely Egyptian Bakery almond egg sweet and I started to breathe again.

Granny was a tiny person so what she did was a feat of Charles Atlas proportions, especially when one considers that Chrissy had been so terrified she hung onto little Granny's legs like a blinking octopus all the while screaming blue murder in the process! She denies this, but Gran told me she did and I would take her word any day over Chrissy's!

Well, apparently after a few deep breaths I came good and Granny said she had never heard anybody howl as loudly in her life! She reckoned the whole of Fraser town would have heard me. After that close shave, lovely big fat pink and blue egg sweets were banned by Will.

I guess I very reluctantly have to admit I owe my life to Chrissy because if she hadn't been around I would have been cactus as sure as the sun rises. There must have been times when Chrissy regretted saving my hide; times when she had to suffer some devilment at my hands but she hotly denies this.

Sometimes little scoundrels can get a bit lucky!

Now it wasn't from some deep sense of gratitude, or some sort of religious re-awakening that I had escaped an ignominious and untimely death by a whisker from an almond egg sweet; but not long after the incident we all went to church, except Chrissy and Granny. I don't think Granny Loots ever went to Church anyway and poor Chrissy was crook with a temperature, maybe because of a reaction to my flopping around like a dying fish! I asked Gran why she didn't go to church. "Those who go need it Thomas" was her response. Try working that one out! I wondered if she had her daughter Bernice in mind. She probably did.

Aunty Ivy, Will's elder sister who had looked after him when he was a tacker and her husband Arthur had come back to Bangalore Cant and settled down. They opened up a small store in the area known as St John's Hill and so named it "Hill's General Store". It was in the neighbouring suburb not too far from Granny Loots.

Aunty Ivy was rotund, friendly and a sweetie while Uncle Arthur was tall, big-made and a grump. She would slip you a bar of chocolate or lolly from the shop when you went in but you wouldn't get a hello or the blinking time of day out of Uncle Arthur.

They also had a pair of German Shepherds and Uncle Arthur used to breed and sell the pups. That's where my Skipper came from and I remember that Will was cross with Arthur because he charged his own brother-in-law full tote odds! Never mind, Skipper was worth every cent.

Arthur had a bad temper and was damn good with his bare knuckles and he used to beat-up the British Tommie's and local cops for entertainment. In short, I was convinced he was daft and always kept my distance from him.

Anyway, daft as he was he and Aunt Ivy went regularly to church and they must have persuaded Will and Carrie to go with them one Sunday. We were to meet them there before the service but as usual, Carrie was late getting all dressed up and by the time we got to the church most of the folk had filed in to take their places. The usher, upon seeing a family of new shiny faces and the opportunity to swell their congregation plus add a bob or two to their coffers, walked us all the way up the aisle to sit us in the third row behind the toffs. A few of the toffs turned around and gave us a gracious smile.

As we were going up the aisle I waved out to Aunty Ivy with a big shiny grin. She waved back with a smile but Uncle Arthur scowled at me. Maybe he was miffed because we were getting seats up front near the swells!

Will made sure I was sitting right next to him, and then in turn came Hansie, Nanette and Carrie in the pew. It all proved a great experience for me. The ladies in the front rows all wore big funny hats and even white gloves but right down the back in the last rows sat some Indian folk in their best shirt and pants or saris. I made a note to ask Will about this later because he had already given me strict instructions to be on my best behaviour and not to chatter in church.

His instructions always carried a bit of a threat when he was serious. "No talking and playing the fool in church Tom or you'll get a clip behind the ears." Will was a bit cranky too because we had been late to enter the church. He was a stickler for keeping time but never succeeded when Carrie was involved. He was not known for his humorous sayings but he did manage one; he often referred to Carrie as: "The late Mrs Loots" for never keeping time.

"Yes Dad, I promise!" I assured him after his warning not to chatter. Making a promise was, of course, my pet expression though keeping one was, of course, a different matter. Will knew this so I had to sit right beside him.

There was a small organ in the corner and the organist was a lady with a hat as big as a blinking umbrella perched on her head. All went well in the singing of the opening hymn. I thought it loud and cheerful and even the long prayer led by the tall skinny preacher on the dais in front was entertaining for despite his skinny frame he had a deep bass voice and a funny drawl of an accent I'd never heard before. He didn't look like a preacher to me. He had on a cream cotton suit that sort of hung on him like he was a clothes peg. Even his face didn't look anything like a preacher. It was sort of long and bony, with a beak of a nose and his dark eyes were sunk into his head like inkwells. Worst of all he had long white hair and badly needed a haircut.

From this you can gather I was paying little attention to the church service and all brought about by my musing about the limited experience I had with Anglican Padres. They all appeared well-fed because they were fat and wore flowing white robes with fancy coloured "scarves" hanging around their necks! This Preacher looked like a blinking grave digger, not that I had ever seen one. He was a gravedigger with a deep voice!

My happy mental wanderings were disturbed when suddenly all went quiet as the preacher stepped up to the Bible lectern and again sent up a long fervent prayer to the Almighty, blessing those present and reeling off a list of names of those who were sick and all sorts of other things. I reckoned the blighter would never stop! To pass the time, I thought of my new Bata shoes, my new socks, my new white short pants and white shirt, my Dinky toys and battle-plans, Skipper, bugouts and everything else I could think about except what the preacher was saying. I even wondered if Mahmood ever went to church! I couldn't understand a word the Preacher said anyway so I kept sneaking looks at him because I could now see him clearly and hoping he would stop. Fortunately, Will's eyes were closed. I thought of the shiny new copper coin Will had given me for church collection. Fishing it out of my pants pocket I slipped it into my new Bata shoe. Much safer there I figured and maybe I could keep it too!

Stop he finally did after an eternity and a booming deep "Amen" came from inside an empty forty-eight-gallon drum just behind me. I quickly snuck a look behind to see this huge fellow, sporting equally big white whiskers sitting just behind me in a black suit and looking mesmerized at the preacher. He looked as if he was hypnotized or worse a stunned mullet because his eyes were glazed. He ignored me, but his equally big wife but sort of sideways with hips like battleships glared at me. I got a jab in the ribs from Will for good measure.

The Preacher man now started his sermon in earnest; his tongue rolling off words such as the evil Devil that kept you from coming to church (I thought of Granny Loots), temptation, hellfire, hell and damnation, wicked thoughts were as bad as fornication, gambling, drinking, gossiping, the day of reckoning was surely coming for the unrepentant sinners and something like being punished by frying in some eternal fire! Now if ever there was a scary thought; I mean like sitting in a frying pan on the fire forever and ever? Every so often, the big geezer behind me would suddenly let out a bellow of "Amen" or "Hallelujah". I sort of jumped out of my skin every time he let fly!

But the bloke behind me was not alone mind you as there were heaps of others in the congregation carrying on with Amen's and Hallelujah's like they were going out of fashion. Their hollering got louder and louder and the preacher got more and more worked-up, holding up the Bible in one hand and walloping it with the fist of his other hand for emphasis, and all the while I got more and more scared!

"What the heck is going on here?" This question had hardly entered my head when the big geezer behind jumped-up and started waving his hands in the air like he had a fit or something worse, yelling gibberish at the top of his booming voice. At least I thought it was gibberish because I couldn't understand a blinking word he said. I took one look at him carrying on like a daft bloke and started to duck under the bench in front of me when Will's hand grabbed me by the scruff of the neck and hauled me back onto my seat. He leaned over and whispered fiercely in my ear: "Where do you think you're going Mister?"

"Under the bench Dad, that big bloke behind is scaring the heck out of me and I reckon he might grab me anytime."

"He's not going to so sit right where you are." I wasn't so sure about Will's reassurance. I snuck a sideways look at Nanette and I reckon she was scared too because Carrie had her arm around her shoulders while Hansie was typically unruffled by all this yelling and carrying on.

So I sat where I was but nothing could stop me from darting glances back at the big fellow despite more fierce whispers and several digs in the ribs from Will. I wasn't taking any chances as the big geezer looked as if he was ready to grab me at any moment. I sat on the very edge of the bench, as far forward as possible ready to duck under the bench in front if he tried to grab me; never mind about Will's instructions. Honest, if I had been on the other side of Will next to the aisle I would have bolted for the door before you could say Jack Robinson! I had never heard or seen such bedlam even in the Russel fish market let alone a Church.

The Preacher-man, who looked like a grave-digger and with a deep voice of a grave-digger finally quit stirring up the congregation and gradually the bedlam died down. I was just recovering from the bedlam when the Preacher man produced a bottle from beneath the Pulpit and went down to the front row on the other side of us and started to pour some drops on the people's heads. I couldn't resist a whispered question to Will: "What's he up-to Dad?"

"Sssh he's putting oil on their heads."

"How come, Dad, don't they have any Brylcreem at home?"

"Quiet Tom; I told you no prattle in Church." But somehow his fierce whisper lacked the usual threat and I had the feeling he wanted to laugh. Will would always use a dash of Brylcreem himself.

It was time for a jolly song again and the usher came around with the collection plate. I watched this in some consternation as he got closer and closer. My copper coin sat in my brand new Bata shoes. He stopped by Will who put his collection in the plate while I looked fondly at all the money in the plate and did nothing. I got a dig in the ribs from Will and I shook my head. I got a second dig and still shook my head. The furrows deepened on Will's forehead as the plate went all the way down our pew. He leaned down to whisper fiercely once more in my ear: "Thomas, what have you done with the coin I gave you for collection?"

I was about to bend over and take my shoe off but suddenly couldn't remember which shoe I put it in! Was it the left or right shoe? So I did the next best thing. I put my hands in my empty pockets and pulled both white cotton pocket lining's right out. The big geezer behind grunted something and his wife sniggered. Will must have heard them and looked toward the heavens for guidance. From the corner of my eye, I caught Nanette grinning like heck and Carrie with her handkerchief clasped firmly to her mouth. I had a feeling she was near to hysterics.

The usher must have been a nice bloke who wasn't into yelling loud "Amen's" and "Hallelujah's" because he smiled when he saw me pull my pants pockets inside out. Will took the returning plate and held it well over my head before returning it to the usher. Maybe he had a hunch I would have a go at helping myself from the collection plate instead! I would have if I could mind you because those shiny silver coins looked much better than my copper one, but everyone was looking.

Aunt Ivy invited us back to their place for tea, cake and biscuits and Hansie and I had a good guff. Carrie was chattering away with Aunty Ivy and the rest of us were quiet like. I tried to keep my distance from Uncle Arthur when we sat down but ended up right opposite him in their narrow veranda. I didn't see him carrying on with his hands in the air and yelling gibberish but I figured he looked just the type who would. I wasn't taking any chances. I just couldn't take my eyes of him chewing on his cake. In fact, I was staring at him.

Despite his smudgy glasses, he must have noticed and he suddenly growled: "What are you staring at boy?"

I was fascinated with his jaw's that seemed to pop out of the sides of his face while chewing. I piped up, pointing to my jaws: "You got funny muscles there and there when you chew."

A tense silence followed this exchange and I just heard Will say: "Now Thomas, watch yourself will you!"

But Aunty Ivy broke the ice by saying: "Uncle has muscles everywhere Tom."

The tension relieved Arthur suddenly guffawed, his big frame heaving with mirth. Everybody sort of laughed in thankful unison. When he sort of settled down he said to me: "Got a copper on you sonny? I'll show you something." I shook my head violently. There was no way I was going to part with the coin in my shoe. "Never mind" and he fidgeted in his pocket and took out some coins and selected one just like mine. "Watch this now young fellow." He started to first rotate and press the coin with both his left and right thumbs and fingers for quite some time. When he was satisfied he held it between his right thumb and second joint of his forefinger and bent the blinking thing almost in half. He had gone beetroot red with the effort. "How's that sonny? I got muscles in my fingers too" he crowed. I was not the only one gobsmacked, as Hansie who was into doing push-ups, pull-ups and exercises had got up and watched him closely in case he was pulling a trick. He grinned and tossed the coin to Hansie who looked at it in admiration and instead of putting it into his pocket (as I would certainly have); he just nodded in admiration and gave it back.

On the way home in the gharry Will suddenly asked me what I'd done with the collection coin. Eyes downcast I fidgeted a bit wondering what my punishment might be since Will was already cranky at being late for church and my cheeky brush with Uncle Arthurs jaw muscles. Anyway, I bent down undid the laces of my new Bata shoes and took the both of them off because I still wasn't sure in which odd I put it. And there it was, bright and shiny in my left shoe. I thought I might just get a clip around the ears instead when I glanced up at Will he had a smile on his face. "Next time put it in the plate Thomas."

"Yes, Dad I promise. Can I keep this one?" He nodded and by this time Carrie was hysterical with laughter, Nanette was laughing too and even Hansie had a grin on his dial. I looked at my acquisition fondly, the first money I ever had. I asked Will what it said on the coin.

"It's a one quarter-anna coin, Son."

"Can you bend coins Dad?"

"No, I can't. I'll leave that to your Uncle Arthur." I was disappointed but tried not to show it. Will could do everything!

"Was it a trick Dad?"

Hansie piped up "No. He did it fairly." I wasn't about to take Hansie's word and looked to Will for confirmation.

"You heard your brother, didn't you? He was watching carefully."

"Whose picture is that Dad?"

He checked the coin. "King George the VI."

I wondered if he was the same King that put the sword on Sir Haji's neck. I also toyed with the idea of sneaking across the road and buying myself some almond egg sweets with my copper coin when we got back, but that was risky and I gave up on the idea. Anyway, encouraged by Will's good mood and getting-off with my caper I then asked him: "What's that funny church Dad?"

"Don't say funny Tom. It's a Pentecostal Church."

I tried to get my tongue around it but ended up calling it "Pentecosting", and that's what it remained as in my brain.

"Why were all those people carrying on like they were daft Dad?"

This time Carrie got the giggles again for sure and didn't have to put the handkerchief to her mouth. Will didn't answer. He seemed deep in thought.

"And why were all the village people sitting at the end Dad?"

"We'll discuss that another time Tom when you are a little bit older, okay?" Then added after a pause: "Now just keep quiet for a time will you?

But, we never went "Pentecosting" again. We stuck to being plain old sober Anglican's.

Some years later I had gone home for the school holidays and Will and I were going for a walk with Skip in tow when he suddenly asked me if I remembered my question to him while going home in the gharry after the Pentecostal experience. I had to admit I didn't remember. "Well," he said, "you were very little but had a curious mind and you asked me a question about religion and about the local people, I told you I would explain when you were a bit older."

With that, he explained to me his philosophy on religion. It was for me a revelation for Will had rationalised his views of religion when certainly in India, if not the world, the Christian religion was still buried in arcane beliefs. Church dogma was so strong for example that even when an Anglican boy wanted to marry a Roman Catholic girl, the girl would be excommunicated unless the Anglican agreed to marry in the Roman Catholic church and all their children had to be baptised Roman Catholics as well.

In a nutshell, Will explained religion was the dogma and rules of the Church that often did not meet his ideal. "Spirituality," he said, "is far more important and it was how you led your life. To do good and practice justice was far more important than just going to church and praying selfishly for yourself or for anything else." Anyhow, in his view God didn't make Heaven only for us Christians. He pointed to the folk working in a field: "You see those people Thomas? They are Hindu's and go to a temple to worship. Now if God made us, and made them as well why can't they go to Heaven like you and me? Everyone who does good no matter their religious belief or the colour of their skin had an equal right to Heaven." It was profound stuff but typical of him, he never openly spoke about such things yet was always willing to share his thoughts with his wayward son.

Will had worked out the conundrum of religion long before the anointed Ecclesiastics of the Church did!

18
Tom's experiment backfires!

NOW, WILL WAS A VERY WISE PERSON at least I thought so because he knew everything! After all his favourite reading was the National Geographic magazine and he even tried to get me interested in them as well, or at least to look at the pictures as part of my education. I think I might have disappointed him.

Will had some sort of arrangement with a second-hand book shop somewhere far away in the city up or down the line that would send him a whole big bundle of second hand National Geographic's as well as magazines for Carrie. She liked romance and detective story magazines with grisly murders yet was scared stiff of creepy crawlies. In return, Will would bundle off what had been read back to the book shop with the payment.

The logistics of this two-way free delivery service must have been phenomenal because it would have to be passed on from one Railway Guard of the train to another until it reached its destination. But I guess that this had been a well-developed kindly railway practice of years aimed at looking after the folk posted to isolated stations.

Will had a peculiar belief, the only one perhaps which I didn't share and that was a "clean" stomach of a morning was essential to good health.

"Have you done your business this morning Tom?" This was his way of checking whether I had been to the bog and such questions usually happened on his Sundays off from work.

"No Dad, I didn't feel like it."

"Now go and do your business immediately!" he'd say, pointing a finger imperiously in the direction of my bathroom. Off I would go and sit on the thunder-box for ages swinging my legs, humming to myself and planning the day's activity. Skipper would, as usual, be curled up by my side for company. The ploy was that hopefully Will would get fed-up and forget. But no such luck. When I came out after ages he would ask me again.

"Well, have you done your business?"

There was no use lying as I knew the drill by now and if I tried to bluff I had "done my business" he would go and inspect the thunder-box for the evidence.

"No Dad, but I went twice yesterday, promise; once for today and once for yesterday!" This, of course, was a complete lie! I hadn't "done my business" for the past two days (maybe three or four!) but the sheer logic of my fib sounded pretty good to me!

"Don't give me that pipe-dottle Thomas; you must have cast-iron guts."

Actually, I'd long held the suspicion that Will conducted secret thunder-box inspections. But there was no escape and Will now seemed to favour Epsom salts over the enema so out came the dreaded packet of Epsom salts that I hated. The stuff would fizz menacingly in a full tumbler of water and he would stand there to make sure I drank the lot. Still, it was better than a blinking enema administered through my Khyber Pass!

"Up to the nose and down she goes, Son!" That was Will's favourite expression of encouragement when administering a dose of salts to fix my cast iron guts!

It's in times like these when I felt life was unfair to constipated little boys!

Later I found out where Will had got this merciless idea from that regular bowels meant healthy little boys. As far as I was concerned constipation had nothing to do with health. The idea had come from none other than Granny Loots. Mind you, Hansie and Nanette suffered the same fate of the dose of Epsom salts whenever they came home on holidays.

"Dear Hansie, I had Epsom salts today. Your loving brother, Tom".

Carrie, my vigilant sensor approved immediately so riding my luck I asked her if I could add something else. "Yes you can add a short postscript."

"No Mum I don't want to add such a big word."

Carrie looked at me wondering if I was being insolent or innocent. She decided on the latter and explained what a "PS" was; upon which I asked her to add:

"PS: I can count to 100."

"No you can't" the censor promptly ruled, so we settled on 20.

Now there were three things I hated with justifiable little grot's passion; cutting my nails, having a hair-cut and having a bath and as sure as the sun rises all three pet hates had an inexorable cycle that I could not appreciate, fathom or escape. Having a bath was when I could no longer dodge one by telling a fib that Mahmood had given me one early in the morning. Carrie would inspect my nails, behind the ears, behind the knees and between my toes and check with Mahmood.

"Get in the bathroom now Mister or I'll tell your father when he gets home!" This was followed by further instructions at a furious pace. "Now scrub properly with soap or you will get ring-worm, and keep the door open so you don't pretend you're having a bath either and change your filthy clothes as well when you've finished."

I was a little grot and a larrikin!

The use of the word "Mister" and not Tom, or Teddy Bear meant she meant business. I had long worked out that Carrie had three scales of threats for me.

The first and lowest scale was: "You don't want me to tell your father, do you?"

The second scale was that she might or might not dob me into Will: "Just wait till I tell your father what you got up to when he comes home!"

The third and really serious scale was what I called a "reportable offence": "I'm going to tell your father when he gets home."

More often than not I was on the "reportable offence" roster!

On the other hand, Will had some favourite threats he would frequently deliver that sounded far more threatening and sort of followed the same scale as Carrie's.

"If you don't watch out Mister you'll get a clip behind the ear."

"I'll give you a hiding if you don't behave yourself, Mister."

"You do that again Mister and I'll string you up from the rafters."

Both Will and Carrie used the word "Mister" when angry with me. Gosh, I had gone pretty used to the first one of "a clip behind the ears"; but the threat of the hiding and being strung-up from the rafters scared the heck out of me.

Returning to Carrie, a reportable offence usually resulted in a clip behind the ears from Will. So into the bathroom, I would go. Splash, splash, splash, most of it around the walls and not on me, loud yelps and a lot of sounds to pretend I was bathing, plus more yelps from the cold water and whistling; a quick superficial rub of the large pink brick of Lifebuoy soap, followed by lots more splashing of water.

"Stop wasting water Tom." Oops, she wasn't bluffing she was waiting there and listening.

"Yes, Mum; I mean no, Mum," and I'd finish my cat's lick.

The clean, rough-textured towel felt good and it took off any of the grime I had neglected to soap away. I would duly change into the clothes that she had laid out on my bed for me and be off once more to play outside and get dirty again.

I was a happy little larrikin!

Now you'd think that Carrie's mention of getting the dreaded "ring-worm" would scare me. It didn't! As far as I was concerned, worms, including ring-worms though I'd never seen one were all the same and to be found a-plenty in the garden especially in Will's vegetable patch. He had a passion for growing only two vegetables. A strange thick leafed climbing spinach and an equally strange hairy thick leafed plant called "oumum"; from which the leaf was brewed into a tea and supposed to cure everything from earaches to farting, headaches, burping, indigestion and every blinking ailment in-between!

Will took daily doses of oumum brew but I figured it never worked on his flatulence and burping. Yet, since he never complained about headaches and earaches it must have worked a treat on them.

Oumum, if you have ever had the misfortune to take it tasted terrible and smelt worse. Believe you me I hated it so much I made very sure I never complained of anything just in case I got a dose of oumum water. I reckoned Epsom salts was poison enough!

But spinach I loved, not because I liked the taste but Will said I would grow big muscles if I ate it. Hansie ate spinach too but Nanette and Christine would turn their noses up at the mere mention of it. But girls didn't need muscles, did they?

Will's vegetable patch was a great source of big fat worm's since it was regularly watered and fertilised with cow-manure by Mahmood. So, armed with a rusty old "dog-spike" I had long ago pilfered from Will's railway yard of discarded railway equipment I would dig out worms and take them to the chook pen, not so much to feed the chooks but for entertainment! A chook would grab one and run off with the long wriggler while the others chased it around and around the yard and tried to grab a piece of it out of its beak.

I was not just a larrikin but a sadistic little larrikin as well!

Digging in Will's vegetable patch was not without risk.

"Now, just who has been digging up the spinach patch?" This was an alarming clip-behind-the-ear statement rather than a question delivered by Will with his eyes riveted on me over the lunch table. Gosh, maybe I'd forgotten to put the soil back after digging for worms. I looked away pretending innocence. "Well, who was it?"

Will wasn't about to let up.

"Not me Dad, promise, it must have been Skip."Hearing his name Skip looked at me anxiously.

"Don't give me that pipe-dottle Mister. I suppose you thought him to use a dog-spike as well? Next time you'll get a clip behind the ears."

Gosh, not only did I forget to put the soil back but also left the incriminating evidence of the dog-spike as well!

I was not only a sadistic little larrikin but a disloyal larrikin as well even ready to blame my faithful four-legged friend Skip!

Now I'm not sure how I got to hear that if you bury a chook egg in the hot sand for about a week or two it would hatch. Maybe it had something to do with Will's National Geographic and how sea turtle's buried their eggs in the sand to hatch. He would tell me things from the Geographic that would stick in my head. Well, I was going to find out. So one fine morning I nicked an egg from the chook-house, retrieved my rusty dog-spike, dug a hole and buried the egg in a secret spot, duly warning Skip not to dare dig it up because a little chick would be born.

I lost track of time and don't know how long after I remembered the buried egg, but sure as the good Lord made little green apples no baby chook had surfaced either! So, I carefully searched around and finally found the spot and carefully dug the egg out. Was there a little chook inside? Maybe it suffocated. I had to find that out as well.

So, with the help of the chisel end of the rusty dog-spike, I carefully tried to make a hole. The smell put even Skipper off and Skip had a strong nose; after all, he used to bury his bones and dig them up to chew on.

"Here, Skip, have a blinking sniff of this!" He turned his head away. No, it was too much even for him.

If I had thrown away the offending egg nothing would have happened but instead, I had an idea; though all I wanted to prove was that I was on a par with Will in certain manly practices.

In addition to his wisdom I reckoned, Will did have a very macho habit and that was farting or in polite parlance a touch of the flatulence, which Carrie thought was disgusting. Sometimes his farts sounded like the slow rumbling thunder that accompanied the monsoons. I was so taken with his ability that I tried hard to emulate his farting skills without success. All I could manage after a lot of straining was a pathetic short soprano squeak!

Since Carrie would constantly admonish him for "making a bad smell" I came to the sound conclusion I could at least create a very bad smell that would lift me to his lofty level. So, I hid the stinking egg under my shirt right side up mind you and stole quietly via Carrie and Will's bathroom and into their dressing room. She was as usual on the front veranda busy reading her magazines.

I carefully looked around the room for a suitable hiding place. I cautiously considered Carrie's wardrobe and Will's chest of drawers and discarded those spots because I figured the smell would be masked by the closed doors and drawers. The shoe rack looked very, very good and Carrie's high heeled black and white dancing pumps (at least that's what she called them), looked ideal. So I carefully tried to insert the egg right-way-up into the dancing shoe and failed. The blinking thing toppled over quite simply because it couldn't stand-up and the smell was bad. In fact the room stank! Hells bells it was time to bolt. Smelling the problem Skipper bolted outside before me! That was strange. He usually followed. Never mind. The job was done and now all I had to do was wait patiently for the fun to begin.

The fun began after our lunch together as Will was on line and Carrie went to the bathroom before her afternoon siesta. The fun turned out to surpass whatever I could have imagined or planned. She came fair flying out, yelling to Mahmood that there was a dead rat somewhere in their bedroom or dressing room. Skip and I decided it would be better to stay out of harm's way.

After some time Mahmood came out with the "dead rat" in the shape of Carrie's dancing shoe and headed for the water trough outside to clean it.

"I think Mum will have to learn to dance with one shoe Skip!"

My cockiness was short-lived. Mahmood, the gentle giant came out and told me Memsahib wanted to see me now. Mahmood my minder, companion and friend looked very serious and clicked his tongue in disapproval. I took his big rough hand for comfort and headed for the house.

"I think I'm in trouble, Skip. Coming?" He didn't look too keen but in we went and I put on my best, most innocent look. Mahmood disappeared.

Carrie looked awfully mad to me. In fact, she was angry. "Do you know what you have done?" I shook my head innocently. "You've ruined an expensive pair of dancing pumps your father bought me for Christmas. That's what you've done!"

"But Mummm...!"

"No ifs and but's, Mister. Go to your room at once and stay there. I'm going to tell your father when he gets home."

Now that was a category three reportable offence and meant the dreaded clip behind the ears from Will. Aside from that, she sounded near to killing me so I had to try once more. I looked at Skip for help and inspiration but he seemed to avoid my eyes. He had an innate knowledge of when I was in strife. I made one last desperate plea which I thought had considerable merit.

"But the chook could have climbed up and laid the egg in your shoe, Mum!"

"AT ONCE, Tom Loots and stay there till your father gets home!" The finger was pointing authoritatively in the direction of my bedroom and her eyes were blazing like firebox in the steam engine.

Carrie just didn't appreciate my logic, which of course was an absolute lie and how a chook could balance on a shoe rack to lay its egg in a shoe defies imagination, except that of mischievous scoundrels. Still, it was a plausible story or so I thought anyway. I lay on my bed, one leg cocked; the other crossed over at the knee and played with my toes. A habit I had when I was thinking or planning mayhem or in this case awaiting execution in the shape of a clip behind the ears from Will.

I declared war on National Geographic for it was to blame for the idea of burying eggs in the first place. What's the difference between turtle and chook eggs after all? A chook should have been born and if it had been born like little turtles I wouldn't be in strife, would I? Yes, I decided I would destroy National Geographic with the full force of my Dinky toys. It wouldn't stand a chance against my Spitfire, tanks, artillery gun and heaps of trucks. I felt a lot better after that decision as I waited for my execution.

My desperate defence that National Geographic said that the buried egg would hatch a little chook was in vain and in the end, I did get the dreaded clip behind the ears from Will. National Geographic was very lucky to survive the blitzkrieg I had planned but did not execute!

I thought I should caution Hansie in my next PC just in case he tried to bury chook eggs.

"Dear Hansie, Don't bury chook a egg. It won't hatch."

She almost killed me with a dirty look and that honourable attempt did not pass the censorship test! I had to change it, after several tries to:

"Dear Hansie, Say hello to Granny. Your loving brother, Tom".

It's times like these that I felt life was unfair to little larrikins; especially when it's true that buried chook eggs don't hatch, as I proved and even got a clip behind the ear for my well-intentioned experiment!

Will, being the thinker he was despite his anger at my "experiment" quietly set to work designing a "kerosene lamp incubator" and had it made in his railway workshop. It was an oblong wooden cabinet which had a drawer on one side that was metal lined in which there was a big "railroad lantern" on a metal ring base fitted with a big fuel tank. There were holes only on one side at the top of the drawer to allow the heat from the perforated top of the lantern to circulate into the main cabinet and a chimney at one end of the cabinet with a damper. There was a metal grill in the main cabinet that could hold a dozen eggs. The egg cabinet had a thick glass window on the front door and a thermometer hanging inside to check the "constant" temperature which Will said had to be at 100° F which was not a problem because the weather was pretty hot anyway. The whole incubator was then covered in some padded insulation material.

The first I saw of this wondrous invention was when it was placed in my bedroom on its own table and Will gave me a lecture on how "we" were going to hatch eggs in an incubator. Will said he had been testing it out in the workshop for a time on how high the flame should be and when the tank needed filling. Gosh, was I excited and one of my tasks was to turn the eggs four times a day; under supervision. Will had marked the shell of each egg with a pencil with the numbers 1 to 4. For three weeks I was on my best behaviour, glued to the incubator and completely involved in this mind-blowing experiment of hatching a chook. Even Skip couldn't get me away from the incubator. I think about two weeks after setting Will produced his flashlight and said we had to check if a little chook was being formed.

Will had a fascination with flashlights. While most folks had just a two or four-cell torch Will had an eight-cell monster more than a foot long that could be adjusted from a wide arc to a super-narrow beam. I used to love "spotlighting" the flying fox hanging upside down, thick as thieves in our trees. Their eyes would glisten red and some would let go and flop all over the others to find another perch. It was great fun but never stand beneath the blighters because they seemed to keep crapping all the time.

Will put each egg against the torch and sadly three of the twelve hadn't formed into a "big black blob" which he showed me. He removed them and threw it into the chook pen; something I should have done when my "experiment" failed! On around the 18th day, Will said to me: "all right Thomas you can stop turning them now and set the egg to stand on its pointed end." I looked at Will aghast. Didn't he know the dashed thing would topple over like it did in Carrie's dancing shoe? I shook my head determinedly.

"What's wrong?"

"They'll fall over Dad."

"No they won't Son, see the grill? Well, just you carefully put the pointy end into the open part of the square." I was weeing my pants but I took the risk and found that they didn't topple over after all, and one morning a couple of days later I hopped out of bed to find nine fluffy yellow chooks squatting together. It was a sight to remember. They were carefully transferred to their private shaded pen separated from the other chooks with their own "lock-up" chook house. All the chooks retreated to their lock-up each evening to protect them from the roving mongoose and other predators.

Will could have as usual allowed Mahmood to set aside a "brooding" hen to hatch little chooks but it was Will's way of teaching his wayward son a valuable lesson.

19
Tom escapes!

THERE WERE NEVER ENOUGH HOURS OF PLAY in the day. A small boy's imagination to occupy himself with playing is boundless. Cowboys and Indians; bang, bang, bang! I shot Jemima a thousand times in the back without feeling any qualms of being unchivalrous. She ignored me. She was used to being shot. Or playing soldiers while creeping around bushes and trees, or, diving to the ground; bang, bang, bang! Climbing up a tree and sniping at anybody who came into the yard; bang, bang, bang!

Nothing and nobody got killed as a result of my heroic efforts. Will had a toy wooden gun, just like a Winchester lever-action painted black and silver and shiny that he'd made for me in his railway workshop. It was a beauty.

My Dinky Toys were all dark green Military coloured ones and absolute magic they were. There were different kinds of trucks, an ambulance, several jeeps, a petrol tanker, all with wheels that spun and tanks with real guns that went "ka-boom, ka-boom, ka-boom!" ... Well, I was the one who made the boom. I even had one Spitfire, which I highly prized. It roared through the house with me firing its machine guns ... "rat-tat-tat, yeeeoww, vroom, rat-tat-tat, rat-tat-tat, rat-tat-tat, rat-tat-tat", which drove Carrie mad until she yelled at me to go outside and play. Dinky Toys were beautifully made of lead, at least I thought so because they were heavy!

I had some toy soldiers as well but they were funny blue, red, and white painted soldiers with long hats. Most of them were a bit shabby and broken and must have been second-hand cast-offs. I didn't like them and set them aside or regularly killed them as the enemy.

Little larrikin boys could be hard to please, as well!

But, having a collection of military Dinky Toys and not putting them into action at the enemy just wasn't fun.

One had to create the battlefield and the imaginary enemy and what better real battlefield option than the clay-like dirt outside? The challenge, however, was to first dig up the sun-baked dirt and what better tool to use than Jemima's heavy meat cleaver? I stole it, while she wasn't looking for the job at hand. Now, I had somehow learned that cow dung made the soil nice and gooey. The village huts and floors, as well as their courtyards, were plastered with it so it must be good I figured. No problem. We always had either a cow or buffalo or two and plenty of dung and so with some cow dung, a saucepan for water, also stolen from Jemima's hoard plus her meat clever, I set-to industriously. I soon had a nice old pile of clay mixed with cow dung in the saucepan. I created my battlefield with trenches, hillocks, tank traps from sticks and a fort with stones and even a moat around it. I decided I needed to build a secret camouflaged tunnel to hide the Spitfire; but how?

I suddenly remembered there was a nice really big Horlicks jar of Will's pickled onions in the meat-safe. Will loved his pickled onions in vinegar. I, on the other hand, didn't like pickled onions and so I supposed the Horlicks bottle would be the perfect thing to shape and build a tunnel with.

Now why it was called a "meat-safe" I've no idea. It was large, had four short legs that stood on cement water bowls and panels of mesh all around. Maybe it was to keep the meat "safe" from the leopards that prowled around? Perish the thought; a leopard prowling around the house was not a nice prospect. But still, I had my faithful Skipper who always slept at the side of my bed. But gosh, Will said leopards ate dogs! The thought of Skipper being eaten by a wild animal right in my bedroom frightened the heck out of me. Henceforth, I slept with my trusty Winchester beside me in bed. I would deal with Mr Leopard and shoot it with one bang right between its eyes. I told Skip not to worry!

I felt better and so my clothes now smeared with mud, cow dung and dirt and a face probably the same from trying to wipe my snotty nose or swat the pesky flies I stole back into the house and retrieved the bottle of pickled onions from the meat-safe. You beauty! I emptied the pickled onions onto the ground nearby and used the now empty jar for my tunnel. It made the perfect mould for a secret tunnel complete with a powerful tank and Spitfire that were hidden inside. I was busy fashioning a cow-dung smooth runway for the Spitfire when my magnificent battlefield world fell completely apart.

A flustered Jemima went searching for her blinking meat cleaver and I was sprung. There on the ground lay the mud and cow-dung covered incriminating object in question, a shiny large saucepan smeared with muddy cow-dung, along with an unappetising pile of pickled onions in the dirt and the bottle coated with mud and dung! Jemima shook her finger angrily at me and hurled a torrent of invective to boot. Picking up her beloved meat cleaver and saucepan she waddled off at high speed to report the incident to Carrie. As she did so, I shot her in the back with my trusty Winchester … 'Bang! … Bang!' But she didn't drop dead as she should have!

"I reckon I'm in big trouble Skip!" Skipper cocked his head sideways in sympathy.

Unlike Jemima, Mahmood was my friend but also the usual bearer of bad news. He arrived to tell me I had been summoned to Memsahib's presence. He was clicking his tongue and shaking his head too, which meant real trouble. Carrie must have been furious and all for nothing, in my view. I took his big rough hand for courage. On the way in we passed Jemima in her kitchen washing her precious clever and saucepan and she gave me another broadside of invective. I gave her my best "death stare"; it didn't work, she didn't die so I stuck my tongue out at her.

Carrie glared at me over her glasses. "Just look at you. I can't believe anybody could get so filthy."

Gosh, she had gone stark raving mad at me. I looked at my arms and clothes. They didn't look filthy to me?

"And what's that terrible smell?"

"Dunno Mum."

"And oh my God look at all that filth on your feet!" Fortunately, we had no such luxury as carpets. The floors were always made from black Napa slabs. I looked at my feet. They weren't too bad, just heaps of brown gooey smudge and lumps of sticky mud between the toes which had clung on when I was trampling the soil and cow-dung to make it soft. "Get into the bathroom at once and I'll send Mahmood to give you a proper scrub. You stink. How you don't get sick I don't know. I'm going to tell your father when he gets home."

Carrie's angry pronouncement meant it was yet another category three reportable offence; or even worse, a category four which was the threat of a "damn good hiding"! Whatever that was it sounded bad!

Mahmood gave me a thorough scrub all right, clicking his tongue all the while. The blighter used up half a cake of Lifebuoy soap in the process!

I knew I was in deep strife. Will would be ramping wild when he got home, especially since he had lost his precious stock of pickled onions; so maybe I would get a "hiding" instead of just the clip behind my ears.

Now a clip behind the ear from Will never really hurt mind you, but the fear of getting one hurt a lot more. His threats in the past of giving me a "damn good hiding" sounded even worse. I had to use some cunning or self-preservation this time to avoid a dreadful hiding. As soon as I heard him coming from the office, I threw Skip's tennis ball out from my bathroom door and as he tore after it I locked the door to keep the blighter outside. I then scurried to the small room where there was the gun cupboard and the dirty clothes or soiled linen box and climbed into it.

Now I must tell you our dirty clothes box was one of a kind and made in Will's workshop, of course, like all our fine teak furniture was. This was a perk of the Brits that continued. It was about 36 inches square and about five and a half feet high. It had close fine slat panels all round to allow the air through. It had a hinged lid at the top through which Mahmood or Carrie would pop the dirty clothes in and a hinged door down the bottom from which the dhobi extracted the clothes for washing.

Having scrambled in through the bottom door I piled the dirty clothes over me to hide.

After a bit, while Carrie probably told Will what I had done with his prized stock of pickled onions I heard him bellow my name. After repeated calls, Will came searching, even into the small room but never thought of searching inside the dirty clothes box. I was desperately holding my breath. He didn't have to check the gun cupboard because that was always locked.

Again, after a time the servants were called in to do a pukka search. The hunt for Thomas was on in earnest. They searched high and low; in the bathroom, under the beds and every nook and cranny of the rambling old home. Then, they scoured the chook house, the cowshed, the rooftop of the chook and cow shed and every tree in sight. They even searched for me in Will's workshop yard and stores and made enquiries at the railway station and the local village. Still, no sign of Tom!

Soon, the hunt for Thomas took on a touch of panic as I could hear it in Carrie's voice and had a silent chuckle.

But it was Will, always Will who knew his larrikin son all too well. "Where's Skipper?" I heard him ask.

I pushed some clothes aside and peeped through the slats. Someone had let Skip back in and there he was curled up by the side of the dirty-linen box. "Skip, Skip, skedaddle quickly Skip before dad sees you here!" My urgent whispered pleas to Skipper were useless. All he did was sit-up and sniff at me through the open slats of the soiled linen box. "Go away Skip. Go fetch your tennis ball!"

Skipper was a dead give-away because there he was, waiting for me to climb out. You see, when I played hide and seek with Skip, one of my favourite hiding places happened to be the tall soiled linen box!

Will opened the lid of the box as I burrowed down deeper amongst the clothes. He just looked down at me sternly.

"All right young fellow your number is up. You can come out now."

That sounded ominous and the dreaded hiding instead of a clip behind the ear was definitely coming. I crawled out of the bottom door, let out a sob or two for insurance, wiped my nose in my shirttails and when I dared look up, Will was smiling. He tousled my thick mop of untidy hair then said quietly: "You won't do that again, will you?"

"No, Dad I promise." My promise was duly accompanied by a further loud sniffle or two for good measure.He knew, as did I that I never kept my promises.

But I was forgiven this time and Carrie was relieved her Prodigal son had been found. So, I got an extra share of burnt custard dessert that night after dinner. Not bad, eh!

Sometimes, but only sometimes mind you, a naughty little larrikin can get lucky!

The tall soiled linen box that saved me from punishment was to have an opposite consequence for poor Carrie. One day, as she was putting in some dirty clothes she suddenly let out a yelp of pain. Something had stung her on the upper arm and she was in severe pain. At first, it was thought to be a scorpion but after a careful search by Mahmood, it was discovered that a big hornet had built its nest in the back corner of the lid. Will, later identified it as the Asian Giant Hornet that was known to have a very powerful venom in its sting and can sting repeatedly.

Carrie fell very ill for a week and I was concerned enough to behave myself during her illness while poor Mahmood felt the pain as much as Carrie and felt it was his fault the hornet had gone undetected. He didn't just Flit the blinking hornet, he drowned it in Flit and then removed its nest and grubs.

"Dear Hansie, Mum was sick from a sting. I have been a good boy. Your loving brother. Tom. PS: I learnt my 3 times tables".

That one passed the censors test. At first, I wanted to ask him if he got pickled onions in school but that was not approved and I got a fierce look from her for my suggestion.

I announced to Will I was going to take the Flit gun and "shoot" all the hornets flying around our shrubs and trees. He patiently explained to me the difference between wasps and bees and that bees were actually very good insects that even made honey.

A month or two later and lo and behold two wooden "beehives" was installed in our compound complete with bees. Will fashioned some mosquito netting to go over the hat and face and his khaki stockings lopped off at the "ankles" to go over the arms and he showed me the wonders of the wax combs forming on the frames inside. We made our own honey to pour over our morning porridge.

Just like the incubator; that was Will's way of teaching his problem child something sensible.

20
Hansie's Dick Whittington caper!

"**HAVE YOU EVER BEEN CHASED** by somebody with a table fork and murder in mind? I was by brother Hansie!"

Hansie had a long fuse and it would take a long time for him to bust his boiler, but one day when he was home from school and Will wasn't there I was giving Hansie a lot of stick despite Carrie telling me to stop it. But she was a softie and of course, I wouldn't listen. Suddenly Hansie got up, fork in hand, murder in his eye and that's when I bolted. He chased me out of the house brandishing the fork, but the one thing I had over him was the ability to sprint faster. Self-preservation developed this skill over time. Nevertheless, he chased me until I scurried up a tree yelling my lungs out for help as if the picture house was on fire! Help arrived in the shape of Mahmood who took the fork from Hansie and coaxed him away.

I gave him time to cool off before climbing down.

"Why didn't you help me when I was in trouble, Skip?" He sort of grinned at me. He liked Hansie too!

Anyway, it was fights and incidents like this duly reported by Carrie to Will that convinced him to write off to somebody in Bangalore Cant to buy a pair of second-hand boxing gloves from the Goodge. That, he figured, was the answer before I was deservedly murdered by my own brother. Will showed us how to lace up the gloves, patiently explained the Queensberry rules (whatever those were) and supervised a few bouts to make sure we followed the gentlemen's rules before leaving us to our own devices.

So boxing or sparring was a favourite pastime. Hansie was bigger and stronger, but so typical of his gentle nature he would never hurt me, while I did my best to whack him a few mostly under the belt or throw in a kick or two despite Mr Queensberry's rules! Will incidentally, had written to the School Principal not to allow Hansie to box because he had a deformity of his chest commonly known as "chicken chest". That aside he was fit and strong as a Mallee bull!

While Hansie was my main sparring partner, that is when he was in the mood, I tried to convince Carrie to give me a fight. She just glared at me, but Nanette had a tad of spirit and would oblige until I plonked her one on the nose and then all hell broke loose!

"You damn bully!" she would yell at me and run off to Carrie to undo the laces on the gloves. But she was game and would come back for more after a few days.

While Nanette wasn't keen on the boxing caper, she loved to play backyard cricket. I don't know why but Hansie flatly refused to play cricket. Tops and marbles he would, but not cricket. Will made us wicket stumps in the workshop; we had an old cricket bat from somewhere and used a white hockey ball because we didn't have a regular red cricket ball.

If one lived in a railway colony you could always get a few Anglo Indians together to have a game of back-yard cricket but it was a different kettle of fish in the bush. When we set up the wickets I always had to bat first, according to "my cricket rules". Nanette was permitted to bowl underarm and do all the skinning, which was jargon for fielding until she threatened to pack it in and then I would allow her to bat.

Now Skipper was the fastest and best fielder in the team and would willingly skin all day except for one problem, the blighter would never give the ball back in a hurry and Nanette would turn her nose up at all the saliva he left on the ball when he did give it up. No worries, I would happily wipe the ball clean in my shirttails and toss it back to Nan.

I was a legend for making up rules so I could bat again, one of which was, if Nanette missed hitting three balls in a row she was "out". I sure as heck introduced the baseball "three strikeouts" rule to cricket! If Nanette complained about any rules I had made up I would swear blind it was a regular cricket rule and she didn't know anything about cricket because she was a girl! As if I did!

Most often a few village boys would hang around watching us and that's when I really came into my own. As the poor blighters didn't have a clue about playing cricket I could cheat like hell. In short, they did most of the skinning while I had a great time batting! Sometimes I had to give them a hit to keep their interest going, but if they happened to hold the bat the wrong way around I would promptly call the batter "out" before even bowling the ball! But, they enjoyed playing with us and always rocked-up for a game.

Trust the larrikin to manipulate the rules to suit himself!

Anyway, one afternoon Carrie confined all of us to our bed-rooms because it was too hot to play outside. I couldn't argue because Will was not on line and was in his office nearby.

I was playing as usual with my toes. Hansie who was always quiet this day seemed particularly preoccupied with his own thoughts and not interested in talking at all. Not that he did much talking anyway and if Hansie didn't want to talk there was no way I could get him to. I once complained to Carrie that he wouldn't talk with me.

"That's because you could talk the hind-legs off a donkey Tom and nobody can get a word in edgeways." I wasn't sure how to take that, seeing I was brought up on donkey's milk!

I craned my neck around my mosquito net and spotted my friend Mr Goanna snoozing on the roof truss.

"Hey there Mr Goanna I'm going to catch you one day."

"You better watch out Scoot, goanna's have teeth." Crikey, Hansie had spoken?

But I had to continue to bait him to talk, even though baiting Hansie was a mug's game. He just couldn't be baited. "Nah, Bugouts don't have teeth."

"Goannas are not bugouts."

"Of course they are, 'cept bigger."

Hansie went quiet, which meant he had closed the conversation and refused to be baited into an argument. He was lying on his back with his eyes open and digging his nose. This habit meant he was thinking very seriously about something.

"What'cha thinkin 'bout, Hansie?" I got no reply. I started humming tunelessly to myself and playing with my toes to pass the time.

"I'm going to run away Scoot."

I stopped humming and playing with my toes and sat bolt up-right in speechless shock, and that's saying something in my case! This was a hugely exciting decision. Did I hear right?

"What? Why? Where? When? How?" Five rapid-fire questions from me with a mix of bewilderment, shock and a little bit of uneasiness.

"Dad doesn't love me Scoot. He yelled at me and skelped me."

"What fer Hansie? What'cha do to make dad angry?"

He didn't reply and I knew he wouldn't tell but I had a feeling why. Hansie hadn't done his school holiday's homework despite repeated reminders from Will which I had overheard. But I didn't tell. So there was no point in pestering him to get the reason; nevertheless, I got to thinking seriously. If Hansie reckoned that after just one clip behind the ear Will had stopped loving him, then logically Will must hate me heaps! I was a legend for being yelled at, threatened and getting clips behind the ear. It was such a common event nobody even took notice about it anymore. Not even Carrie; except me of course!

But the very rarity of it for Hansie had hurt him deeply as it was his first time. I figured that if I got closer to him he would tell me more. We had single beds. I hopped out of mine made him shove over and sat by his legs crossed legged and facing him.

"What'cha going to do?" My move to sit on his bed worked a treat. After all the long silences Hansie opened up and started to tell me of his plans. I'd never heard him speak that long ever before.

"I'm going to Uncle Bob's forest in Dandily. I'll catch a train there."

Now Hansie had no money for a train ticket, but that wasn't a problem. Being the son of Will Loots was enough to travel anywhere on that line without a ticket and in 1st Class as well! Uncle Bob was the District Forest Officer, so that part was okay too. But what about the wild forest animals?

"There are tigers and leopards in the forest. They'll eat you up Hansie."

"No, they won't. I'll stay with the elephants and tigers are scared of them Scoot. You know that."

"You mean you're going to be like Sabu and stay with the efelants?" As a tacker, I could never get my tongue around the elephant word and always said efelant.

"Yeah, I'll be just like Sabu, 'suppose."

Gosh. Hansie had been planning and thinking things out very carefully. This was hugely exciting because we had seen Sabu in "The Elephant Boy" in the travelling Tent Cinema that came around from time to time. And what lent total credence to Hansie's plan was that Will told us that parts of the movie had been made in the Mysore forests and I now concluded it had to be in Uncle Bob's forest. My heart was racing with excitement like a two-bob watch gone totally mad!

"Maybe you can stay with Sabu Hansie. He's in Uncle Bob's Dandily forest for sure." I could see he hadn't thought of that because he looked at me and gave me his crooked smile.

"That's an even better idea Scoot. I can stay with Sabu."

"Can I come with you?"

"No."

"I'll be really good, I promise. I won't get you into trouble." Why anybody would want to believe my promises, I don't know. I was a legend for making and breaking promises. Hansie knew this.

"No." He shook his head with finality.

When Hansie said no, he meant it and I'd learnt long ago there was no point in cajoling or arguing with him. He would just go silent. I would have to find another way.

"What about carrying your things? I can help with that can't I?"

"No. I've got a stick already and I'll carry my things in a bundle tied to the end of the stick."

Gosh, Hansie's plans were well advanced. "You mean just like Dick Whittington did?" He sort of half nodded. Long ago Carrie had read us the story of Dick Whittington and his cat and showed us the pictures of him carrying his things on a stick over his shoulder. I suddenly had a brilliant idea that would convince him to take me with him.

"You'll need a red cloth to tie your things in Hansie. Dick Whittington's bundle was tied in one. I'll go get one for you in a jiff. Get the stick ready in the meantime."

I was off before he could change his mind. My offer to get the red cloth, generous as it was had its drawbacks and fraught with danger. I would have to be careful and crafty. I snuck out of the house easily enough as Carrie and Nanette would be snoozing at this time. I carefully made my way to Will's office and his railway stores close-by. The problem was I had to get by Will's office to get to the stores. I dared not go via the front as the punkah-wallah or somebody inside the office was sure to spot me. I crept around and behind the office and bumped straight into the trolley-man spraying water on the cuscus blinds right behind Will's office window to keep the office cool.

"Sssh!" I said and put my finger to my lips. He nodded and grinned good-naturedly at me.

Having negotiated that obstacle the rest was easy. I fair flew into the stores to confront Ghokhale the store Babu. I knew him well. I was always in and out for nails, screws, off-cuts of timber and anything else I could think of to build battle-fields for my Dinky Toys.

"Hello, Tom Baba. What is it I can do for you today?"

He gave me a huge smile as Ghokhale was my friend with good reason. He was in charge of the railway material stores and a source of all sorts of odds and ends I needed for my imaginary battles. I had trouble following his English at first because he confused me by mixing up his words in a sentence. I once made fun of Ghokhale's way of speaking English with Carrie but Will stopped me in my tracks, admonishing me that if I learned to speak the Marathi language as well as he spoke English, I would be doing well. I never made fun of Ghokhale again.

"Hello Ghokhale, my dad said to give me a big red gangman's flag." It was, of course, a load of pipe-dottle.

"Aaah, Tom Baba, so what game are you going to play today? Will you be fighting the Germans again?"

Ghokhale knew all about my previous battle plans to fight the "Germs". I had no idea who Germans were but knew all about germs from Carrie and so I figured Germans were sort of enemy human soldier germs. In short, germs were Germans in my mind. Anyway, I had to find a story quickly to satisfy my friend. I couldn't tell him it was for Hansie who was going to run away.

"No, Ghokhale. Today I'm going to be a real engine driver and Hansie is going to be the guard."

"Ah, very good idea, Tom Baba; so you will also be needing one green flag as well?"

Gosh, this was getting complicated. I hadn't thought of that. Plus, every minute spent in the stores I reckoned increased the danger of Will showing up; and if he did he would skin me alive when he heard what I was up-to. Mind you, I was sorely tempted to take up the offer of a green flag as well but fortunately decided against it.

"No, Dad said only a red flag Ghokhale" which was another shocking lie, "but I can come back for the green one later okay?"

"Certainly, certainly Tom Baba and you will be wanting a new red flag?"

What luck? Fancy a brand new red flag for Hansie? I nodded my head in vigorous agreement

"Tom Baba will sign for it so I can show it to Bada Sahib?"

Hell's bells this was getting dangerous. First off I didn't know how to sign. I could, of course, agree to put my left-hand thumb impression as I had seen the gangmen do when I went with Will on the Pay Special; but worst of all I could visualise myself swinging from the rafters if Will heard about this caper; never mind a clip behind my ears. I was in deep trouble and had to get out of it.

"Can't you just give me one Ghokhale? I mean, just give it to me because I don't know how to write my name. I'll bring it back. Promise!" This, of course, was another big fat lie because there was no way I could bring it back. It would be with Hansi in the jungles of Dandily!

He scratched his head for a very long time in deep thought while I sweated.

"I can give you an old one without signature Tom Baba."

My cheekiness knew no bounds. Here was a solution but I still wanted to make sure it was a good red flag. "Okay. Can I see it first, Ghokhale?"

He disappeared into the back of the store and came back with a big flag which he opened up on his desk.

"I have for you selected the best one Tom Baba."

It was a bit faded and oil-stained but still red. I nodded happily. "You won't tell my dad now will you Ghokhale?"

"No, no Tom Baba, it is not necessary for such things."

I heaved a huge sigh of relief. "Thanks, Ghokhale. You are my real friend."

We shook hands solemnly once more to seal our friendship and I was off back home via the same route with the flag tucked under my shirt for good measure. Meanwhile, Hansie had collected his pith hat, a couple of pairs of khaki shorts, shirts, and socks and had neatly laid them on his bed. I presented him with the red flag with flair. He smiled. A bit sadly, I thought but my good deed was not without a cunning motive.

"Thanks, Scoot. You're a real brother."

"Can I come with you now? I risked my life to get you that red flag."

"No, Scoot. I don't know what I'll do for grub and I'll have to sleep out in the open till I can meet up with Sabu and the elephants."

That declaration promptly cooled all my desires to go with him. Sleeping out in the open with leopards and tigers roaming around was not a good idea, trusty Winchester or not.

"You better take some grub from the meat-safe with you then."

We stole into the back veranda and kitchen area where the meat-safe was. Jemima was snoring her head off in the kitchen. He collected a spoon, a bone-handled knife, a few left-over chapattis and curry mince-patties, homemade biscuits, a carrot, and two bananas and then started cutting into the dish of pumpkin halva. Now, pumpkin halva was a treat Will made for us and it was scrumptious. Risk my life I would to get him the red flag but my brotherly love balked at sharing the pumpkin halva. The blighter was cutting out a big piece as well!

"You can't take halva Hansie it'll blinking melt" I whispered fiercely. Once more, so much for brotherly love when it came to pumpkin halva!

"I'm just taking my share.'"

"Yeah, but don'tcha take too much. It will turn to goo and you won't be able to eat it."

Which was probably rubbish of course but any story to save the halva was required. Hansie ignored me. He tied it all into the red flag and onto the stick he had. We shook hands solemnly.

"Be seeing you sometime Scoot." Hansie gave Skip a cuddle and then slung his stick over his shoulder with a certain flourish.

"Say hello to Sabu for me and write me a postcard okay?"

"I will. Say cheerio to Mum and Nanette Scoot, and don't tell anybody where I'm going okay?"

"I won't. Promise!"

Skip and I watched Hansie in his pith helmet, stick and red bundle over his shoulder striding off with confidence toward the railway station nearby. He turned once to wave cheerio before I lost sight of him. "Hansie won't be coming back" I confided in Skip and he looked at me sadly.

I went back to bed and played with my toes while thinking of Hansie's thrilling odyssey. It was bigger than when Hansie and Nanette went to boarding school for the first time. After some time I figured I had better tell Carrie. After all, Hansie had made me promise I wouldn't tell anybody where he was going but didn't say anything about his running away. I went to her room.

"Mum, Mum, wake up! Hansie has run away." She opened her eyes and looked at me with a puzzled expression. "Hansie has run away Mum. Promise!"

"Don't talk rubbish Tom."

"Truly, Mum. I saw him go just like Dick Whittington did with a stick and all."

She now sat bolt upright. "Go where?"

Now, this is the part I had promised I wouldn't tell. "I dunno Mum. He didn't tell."

Carrie got out of bed, put on her shoes, tidied herself, brushed her hair and put on her lipstick and some jewellery. Hansie could have reached Dandily and been eaten by a tiger by now but she never went out unless she looked her best. Hearing the going's on, Nanette came out of her room looking scared as heck. The idea of Hansie "running away" from home frightened her. Carrie set off toward Will's office with determined strides. I tagged along and I reckon she didn't even know I was following. The moment she entered the office all the staff stood-up and salaamed out of courtesy to Memsahib. She gave them all her dazzling smile.

Everybody liked her. She was the friendliest person on God's earth and the only one, Will said who could conduct an hour's friendly conversation with the village Munsiff or headman without either of them understanding a word they said to each other. The Munsiff might be seriously telling her that he had already seen Will Sahib, and had now come to see Memsahib to warn about a leopard that was very active at night in the surrounding villages and to be careful to lockup the animals. At the same time, Carrie would be blithely telling him of her last trip to the Cantonment or how the children were faring at school! Anyway, with her dazzling smile and a heck of a lot of hand signals they always parted in full agreement; or sort of!

As we entered his office Will looked up at us over his glasses with some surprise.

"Yes Carrie, what's the problem."

"William, Tom has just told me Hansie has run away."

Instead of responding to her anguished and earnest statement, Will looked at me up and down seriously. I was fidgeting. "Why haven't you got your shoes on Thomas?"

Gosh, of all the things Will should be concerned about in the middle of this hugely important family crisis, did he have to pick on my bare feet?

"William...!" She couldn't finish her agitated outburst.

"It's all right, Carrie. I know where he is. The Station Master phoned me some time ago and I've already sent Mahmood there to keep an eye on him. He won't be going anywhere. He's in the Station Master's office amusing himself. Don't worry. He'll be back soon enough."

"I'd better go and fetch him then."

"No Carrie, just leave Hansie alone. He'll get over it and come home. Don't worry."

That was Will. Always in control and cool as a cucumber!

"He'll be hungry." Why she would think of Hansie's stomach I don't know.

"I doubt it, my dear. He's eaten something he already had with him plus half a dozen bananas and a cup of coffee the Station Master gave him. So go home please and just leave him alone." Then he looked at me, stern as ever, "and you better put your shoes on whenever you go outside Mister or you'll get a clip behind the ears."

Its times like this when I felt life was unfair to little larrikins!

Carrie took my hand for comfort and we walked home together.

Will was right. Hansie came home well before dinner time. He'd eaten all the grub he'd taken from our meat-safe including the halva much to my chagrin. And to add insult to injury, Carrie gave him an extra big slice of pumpkin halva for dessert. I glared at him and tried to give him a kick under the table but he ignored me.

Nothing further was said about Hansie's caper that night at the dinner table or any time thereafter, but I tried to get my revenge after Carrie had kissed us both goodnight and put the hurricane lantern wick on low. I leaned out from beneath my mosquito net and hissed at him loudly. "Hansie, you scoffed more than your blinking share of pumpkin halva you did."

My venomous hiss didn't work. All I got for an answer from Hansie was a loud grinding of teeth. The blighter was already asleep, probably dreaming of pumpkin halva!

Hansie ground his teeth at night like heck. I once asked him if he did that in his sleep because he was getting at me for the day's teasing. He gave me that lovely half crooked smile he had and shrugged his shoulders leaving me to guess.

And that was Hansie.

Anyway, nobody remembered me risking my life to get him the red flag. Nobody remembered how I kept my promise not to tell how and where he was going. His running away episode just entered the Loots Clan folklore as: "Hansie of Dick Whittington fame."

It's times like this when I felt life was unfair to little heroes!

21
Will in a storm!

ASIDE FROM HEAPS OF HELPERS in the shape of trolley-men around the house (whenever needed), another privilege left by the British Raj was the tradition of the Engineering meetings. This was held about every two years and Will was on the Committee. More by design than happenstance, the meetings were always held in Goa and with very good reason that had nothing to do with the important Engineering Railway problems at hand. Goa was a thriving cosmopolitan duty-free Portuguese colony. Duty-free European imported luxuries, not available in India were cheap as chips and plentiful in Goa.

So when the meeting date duly arrived, six "conscientious" senior Permanent Way Inspectors of the M&SM Railway would make their way to Marmagoa via Londa Junction and the border Railway Station of Castle Rock. At their destination of Marmagoa and the rail terminus, six independent 1st class compartments would be drawn up at the end of the station platform in addition to one carriage for their serious deliberations.

Now it was too much of a risk for Will to leave me alone with Carrie for one whole week as Hansie and Nanette were back in school. I would cause uncontrolled mayhem for her. So it seemed to him far more prudent to take me with him and keep an eye on me instead. Of course, I was pleased as punch to make the trip with him but would have to be on my best behaviour since he was always within arm's length in a fairly confined carriage, reminding me of the ever-present possibility of my getting a clip behind the ear.

The rail track from Londa junction through to Castle Rock travelled over the Western Ghats and a real treat with long, slow, steep climbing curves when you could see the steam engine straining its every "sinew"; tunnels galore and thick jungle scenery. It was tiger country and none other than Uncle Bob's Dandily Tiger Reserve. I reckoned Hansie was lucky not to try and find Sabu and the efelants as the tigers would have got him for sure! The rail line crosses a bridge and I craned my neck to look all the way up to the top of the one thousand foot drop of the cascading white Dudhsagar Falls. Wow, how good was that and I tucked it away to boast about to Hansie.

I had a great time seeing new and strange places and learning about the odd habits of the local people. Goa was full of luxury goods, the best of liquor, Scotch, champagne, wine, material, fashion clothes, cigarettes, watches, radios, chocolates, jewellery, and even comic books all from Portugal and duty-free. But there were two oddities. Footwear was outrageously expensive and so was beer. I figured out the reason; shoes couldn't "walk" the distance from Portugal and beer suffered a "tummy-ache" over the long journey. As a result, shoes and beer were imported from next-door India and expensive. The locals could do without the beer but shoes were a different prospect.

The local Goan folk were very cosmopolitan, "Westernised" loved Western-style music and were also talented musicians, so entertainment and dancing was a frequent event. The curious thing though was to see the local people, stylishly dressed in the finest European material; men in tuxedo or suit or ladies in fashionable dress walking barefoot down the suburban street to a local dance, or celebration of some kind, while carrying their shoes in their hands. They also drank a local brew similar to liquid gun-powder, called Fini.

Will bought me comics to read to keep me occupied and also a stack of Mars bars, as well as a big block of lovely dried dates to snack on. Instead, I made the main meal of it all by polishing off the lot and spent the next two days on the toilet! I learned my lesson too late. The matherani who came to clean and replace the toilet pan below the carriage had to work overtime.

Old habits die hard. I was a gluttonous little larrikin!

Since the carriages were literally at the end of the Railway Platform I could wander down to the Station Masters office and have a yarn. He was always smartly dressed, much better than our Station Master back home, and very friendly. Each day I would have a snack and a coffee with him and spin my yarns. He had plenty of time on his hands as there didn't seem to be too many trains.

It looks like the six important Committee members were exhausted by the morning's serious deliberations and so almost every afternoon they would split up and go off into town or make their way to someplace or other, sightseeing or shopping or knocking back the grog in a bar. Marmagoa was located near Vasco da Gama, the capital at the tip of a peremptory overlooking a large bay and harbour. We could cross to the other side by a motorised ferry launch to visit the exotic-sounding place called Panjim.

One afternoon Will and I went to Panjim on the ferry and while on the return trip, a freak storm suddenly blew-up just as it cleared the river mouth. The launch was old and rickety and as usual, it was overcrowded plus top-heavy as the people were allowed to load all their stuff on its roof. Fortunately, the roof had only a low railing surrounding it so it all went overboard as we were being tossed around like the proverbial cork in the ocean. Will was relieved to see various items floating off on the huge waves as this stabilised the launch a bit. He even had a half-smile on his face despite the blinking storm.

The storm was so serious the crew started to dish out the old kapok and canvas-covered lifebuoys with ropes looped around. There were not enough of them to go around. They gave preference to the families with children and explained to them how to hang onto the looped ropes.

While this was happening the boat was being tossed about like the five o'clock wave!

Goa is a religious place and the Catholic priest sitting next to us started to recite his rosary at a hundred miles an hour. I could hear him even over the storm he was so fervent in his prayer. He got a lifebuoy and didn't miss a beat as he grabbed it and hung onto it while praying. We being "foreign" looking were also given preference and a crew member offered a lifebuoy to Will. To my disbelief he politely refused it. I looked at him in some shock and I must confess, with some fear. He leaned close to my ear and I shall never forget the gist of his words.

"There are about two dozen lifebuoys Tom and about a hundred people on this damn tub. If she starts to go over you can bet everyone will panic and desperately fight to grab and hold onto the first lifebuoy nearest them and probably drown in the process."

"What will we do Dad?" My teeth were chattering out of control as I popped the question. He must have noticed but said nothing about my trembling teeth.

He pointed to the long sturdy planks that served as seats. "Plenty of these seat planks to go around Soldier. They're only sitting in rebated sections and will come off, so I'll grab one and we hang onto that and I'll swim you to the shore. Now first take your shoes and socks off and leave them here and next tighten your belt as much as you can. Now when I say get ready you hang onto my belt behind and don't let go. Once we are in the water I'll use your belt to keep you afloat and we hang onto the middle of the plank and strikeout for the shore. We go overboard together with the plank, okay?" He repeated all of this while yelling into my ear because of the strong sound of the wind.

"Right Dad."

When Will called me Soldier I knew he was asking me to be one. It was our special bond of understanding despite the legion of clips behind the ears. My teeth stopped chattering. Only then did I look around at the other passengers. Men, women, and children their faces covered in fear, their eyes windows of terror. I don't remember anybody spewing. Perhaps we were all too scared. Some women and children were crying while the priest kept praying. Was he praying for himself or for the people I wondered? Perhaps unkindly!

The launch skipper seemed to know what he was doing because he somehow got it to ride the waves and did not try to drive into the storm. It would have been like trying to drive through a brick wall and it would have simply pushed us backwards and probably swamped the boat. Running with the storm, however, did cause waves of water to sometimes wash over both the sides. It had one good effect though, panicky people rushed to the centre of the launch and stayed there, clinging onto anything they could. It would have been cactus if the people panicked and all rushed to one side of the tub. She would have gone over as sure as there are no fleas on a dead cat!

Fortunately, the storm subsided just as suddenly as it had blown up. There was heaps of timber and flotsam blown-up on the foreshore as we approached the jetty after a lengthy detour, mute signs of the havoc the storm had played. Somehow the old tub survived the battering or the Captain was an old hand at the caper, but we were safe.

Despite being wet and sorry we were not cold. Goa is a warm place.

Anyway, despite the recent scare I couldn't help but chuckle as I noticed the priest go ashore and immediately kneel and start saying a loud prayer of thanks. The only problem was he was still hanging onto the lifebuoy! But like I said, Goa is a religious place and he soon had others kneeling around him as his prayer of thanks got louder and louder. I couldn't understand what he was saying. I guess it was Latin or something.

"Wonder if that priest will take a collection next Dad?" Will just grinned at my attempt at a joke and we sat on the steps of some building or other to put on our equally soggy socks and shoes.

"Maybe he thought he'd float to Heaven on the lifebuoy Tom!"

Will was hardly given to an obvious sense of humour so that was a real gem. We both laughed like little boys as we sat there on the steps. It was a special moment between father and son that's impossible to forget.

Even naughty little larrikins can remember special moments with their father!

"Well Soldier that was a close shave. Now let's go and have something to eat."

We happily squelched our way toward the roadside stalls. Will knocked back a couple of pegs of Fini and he certainly deserved it. Goan's are mighty good cooks so we had a good feed of fresh Prawn Curry and rice.

Golly! Did I have a story to tell Carrie when I got home; and when Hansie, Nanette and Chrissy came on their Christmas holidays I'll boast about it as well.

The next day was our last in Goa. The meeting was duly adjourned early and all went shopping for duty-free stuff. I didn't know what Christmas presents Will bought for the family, he told me I couldn't see. But, I had a pretty good idea what Hansie and I would get when he went into a music shop with a window full of harmonicas and a toy shop displaying Meccano sets and Dinky Toys. He also bought a bottle of brandy, I think, and several tins of fifty 555 State Express cigarettes for Carrie, as well as Mars bars. Besides, we picked up a dozen of the newfangled stretch nylon socks as well.

Our special VIP carriages were hooked onto the end of the train and we said goodbye to Goa as we headed off to the border check-point of Castle Rock. On the way out the train would be halted for about two hours at Castle Rock to undergo the Customs check.

There was no such thing as a duty-free quota. Everything imported into India was subject to duty. So the moment the train steamed to a halt at Castle Rock checkpoint, India's customs inspectors would lock all the carriage doors on both sides and nobody was allowed to get out of their compartments; except of course the august Railway engineers in their VIP carriages. Just one more perk left by the British.

The Inspector of Customs, Mr Gorham, a Brit rocked up for a chat. He knew every one of the PWI's by name and it was a rare opportunity for him to catch up with a few of his old cronies. Castle Rock, like our place, was a lonely out-post though of course, he had Goa a hop skip and a jump away.

Now, unlike overzealous stupid customs inspectors one might encounter, Mr Gorham had a simple set of common-sense rules. No lethal firearms of any type were allowed but if a traveller had a small portion of duty-free stuff that was obviously for personal consumption his staff would close a blind eye. They were after the professional smugglers trying to smuggle gold, jewellery, expensive watches in steel trunks with false bottoms packed with cigarettes. As well as those who overstepped the bounds of reason. These people would get the book thrown at them. Except ours, of course, everyone's luggage was searched and the compartment stripped for hidden goods. Suspects were taken away for a body search as well.

Being a sticky beak I got Will's okay to go for a wander along the platform. And boy, did I get an eyeful of the Custom's activity. There were long tables laid out with tin trunks being emptied of their contents and pleading owners trying to make every excuse possible for being caught with contraband.

Later, Will told me that the customs had a hard time catching professional smugglers who used the road and jungle tracks at night to cross the border. They had to use informants and set-up armed ambush patrols to catch them. "Unfortunately Tom, the smugglers they catch and imprison are only the carriers who take all the risks. The real rogues are the merchants in Bombay who hire them for a pittance to do their dirty work. The merchants can never be caught."

The thought of armed jungle patrols at night sounded exciting. I secretly decided I was going to be a Customs Officer!

All of this took time so our pre-ordered lunch would arrive with trays carried by bearers dressed in fancy white regalia and fancy turbans. Wow. This was the life!

What with the Christmas presents to come and the excitement of smugglers, I was a contented little larrikin at the moment!

"Dear Hansie, I went to Goa with Dad and saw Sabu's Jungles. Your loving brother. Tom. PS: I learnt my 6 times tables".

The strict "censor" said "No fibs Tom" when I tried my best to add that I had seen tigers, leopards and even Sabu's efelants!

22
Chrissy's religious bug!

ON MOST CHRISTMAS HOLIDAYS Cousin Christine would come back with Hansie and Nanette to spend it with us. She adored Carrie especially because she'd lost her mother at childbirth. She knew this and always gave Chrissy a caring hug and made a great deal of fuss over her. It was great to have them home for the company, even Skip would bark and race around the house with joy when they arrived and I now had three victims to torture!

Hansie was not into devilment but he loved hiking. We had heaps of army water canteens with long straps and he would happily go off on his own with just a canteen of water, but sometimes I would go on hikes with him and Skipper armed with my catapult. I would happily fire away at any wildlife within range. I don't think I hit anything anyway but it was the fun of it. Hansie, who was good with his hands would make terrific catapults but would never use them. There was only one problem on these expeditions, Hansie was a lot fitter, taller and stronger and had a long loping stride so I had a dashed hard time keeping up with him. He walked with the long easy strides of a desert camel against my smaller steps. After a mile or two I would say to him: "Slow up will ya Hansie! I can't blinking well keep up with you."

"Try running Scoot."

Now that piece of advice wasn't very helpful either because after an hour or so I was plumb tuckered out, but the cunning mind of the archdevil had its advantages.

"Okay, you go. I'm not blinking going any further."

I would stubbornly plonk myself down under a tree or on a rock. It was unfair on poor Skip as he didn't know whether to stay with me or keep going with Hansie. After running between Hansie's retreating figure and me, barking like heck most often he would reluctantly stay with me.

I'd cup my hands and yell as loud as I could at the receding figure: "What'll ya tell Mum if the blinking leopard gets me eh?" Hansie would ignore my threatening yelps and keep going but I knew he wouldn't leave me alone for long and after a bit, he would return and sit with me under the tree. He wouldn't say a word or even cuss me.

And that was Hansie.

There was another thing about Hansie that I couldn't compete with or brag about and that was his uncanny ability to relate to animals. Whether it was a chook or a great big ploughing bull tethered in a village shed; Hansie would handle it, rub its forehead or neck, make funny noises between his lips and teeth and they would behave nicely. These dashed bulls weighed in at around a thousand pounds and stood over six feet tall with big horns. You can bet I gave them a wide berth because they would snort at me and swing their big blinking heads with horns menacingly, but never at Hansie!

Over time he had a big red squirrel pet that came and went as it liked and would climb onto his shoulder, a parrot that did the same and even a lovely whistling bulbul. One morning he found a bat on our bedroom door curtain that had wandered in by accident. Blow me down, Hansie started squeaking at it softly between his teeth and the dashed thing crawled its way down the curtain and into his hand. Every night it would fly away and sure as the sun rises it would be perched on our bedroom door curtain the next morning and go to Hansie when he called it.

Carrie gave the bat a wide berth but tolerated it because it was Hansie's friend; that is until one day he rocked up with a three-toed sloth that he had bought from somebody in the village.

"Hansie" she said with a firmness not normal to her when dealing with him; "that animal stays in your room. Don't you dare bring it anywhere near me you understand?" Carrie, a "city girl" was scared stiff of the harmless sloth and all such creepy crawlies and yet lived in the bush cheerfully because she was Will's wife.

Hansie smiled his quiet crooked smile and kept it in our room feeding it tender leaves bananas and fruit. The sloth was a friendly fellow and spent most of its time sleeping up-side-down until one day Hansie decided to take it out to the forest area and let it go.

"What'cha do that daft thing for Hansie?"

He shrugged. "I think it missed its friends and felt a bit lonely living here in our room Scoot."

And that was Hansie!

But there was one blinking animal that didn't take to Hansie. One day he was feeding a baby monkey he'd coaxed down from the tree with banana skins when suddenly its mother charged down and bit him severely on his arm.

Will cauterised the severe bite with raw iodine, packed it with sulphur powder and that night took him off by train to the Poona Military Hospital which was an overnight journey. He stayed with him for a few days then left him in the care of friends for weeks during his treatment. Will went every so often to check on him. Hansie had to have fourteen painful anti-rabies injections in his stomach which was the only method of treatment at the time. When he came back he showed me the angry red welts on his stomach.

"Gosh Hansie did it hurt?"

"Yeah, a little bit Scoot, but it's okay now."

And that was Hansie and no wonder he wasn't scared of leopards!

Anyway, on this particular holiday, Nanette was content to play quietly by herself or read books or spend time with Chrissy playing stuff like hop, skip and jump. The pair of them were constantly yakking their heads off and I felt completely left out.

One of the first things Chrissy would do when she came on holidays was to go to my chest of draws and help herself to several pairs of my shorts and shirts because she hated the blue "bloomers" Granny Loots made for her which she had to wear under her dress. I didn't mind. I had heaps on standby because Carrie reckoned I was a grot, which I was and needed more than one pair a day. Shorts were far cooler than a blinking dress I reckon beside it was far more practicable if she wanted to muck around with me.

Infrequent though it was, there were times when I was seriously well behaved and even useful. This could happen only once a year around Christmas time and though it was the bush, Christmas was a huge family event. There was no tinsel decorated Christmas tree and not a lot of presents either, it was just lovely family time.

About a month or so before Christmas Will would order the dried and preserved fruit ingredients which included the "secret" proportion of palm jaggery from the Cantonment market for the famous Loots pudding. He would then start the mix in a huge saucepan and I was allowed to help. He never seemed to mind me licking my fingers and hands of the sticky gooey stuff while mixing, but Carrie would throw a fit when she saw me. He would slip a shiny silver four anna coin into the mix. There would be one lucky person who would get it in their slice one day. Once it was mixed to his satisfaction it would be "dolloped" into a large tin. I think it was a Margarine tin. Anyway, it was awfully big. He would then seal the top cover with wheat dough and with a large cloth firmly tie the tin up.

The sigri was just a stone and clay structure with three sides about twelve to eighteen inches high and was usually built outside in the lee of the bungalow and out of the wind. Mahmood would chop up an old wooden sleeper or two to size and stack it nearby. The pudding tin was so large it required a kerosene tin with the top cut out to be boiled in.

Once the water in the kero tin was bubbling away to Will's satisfaction the pud would be lowered into it and a big stone or brick placed on the top for good measure. My job was to keep the sigri fire going, not without a stern warning from Will plus the threat of a clip behind the ear to never let the fire die down and the bubbling water never drop below a certain pre-marked level. I figured it was a very important job. Hansie, who was noted for scoffing more than his share of the famous Loots pudding, was never interested in its making or boiling. The blighter would be off hiking the hills with Skip and risking his life with the leopards!

Carrie, Nanette and Christine had nothing to do with the grand process of preparing the pudding mix. That was left to Will and me but once the pud was loaded into the kero tin Chrissy would happily sit in the dirt with me to keep me company at the fire. I could sit on my haunches for hours I reckon, a practice I learned in the villages. The village folk, whether it was an important village meeting or just having a yarn beneath a big old shady Banyan or People tree always sat on their haunches.

Chrissy would want to stoke the fire and add the wood but I would protect my important job with determined tenacity.

"You can fetch me some more wood Christine."

Piqued by being denied the chance to keep the fire going the eternal arguments and one-upmanship would rise to the surface. "You can get it yourself."

"Okay, you can buzz off I don't need you then." I knew she wouldn't buzz off and in the end, would fetch me the wood.

"Right ho it's time to tell Jemima to bring out a kettle full of boiling water. It needs a top-up."

"You can go yourself."

"No, I can't. The fire may die out."

"Balderdash, it's a bonfire you ass and not about to die out."

"Nah it's too risky. If it did, dad would skin me alive."

"Then you go tell Jemima and I'll tend the fire."

"You can't. It's too dangerous."

"Rubbish."

"Yes, it is."

"No, it isn't."

But in the end, Chrissy would give in and head for the kitchen and Jemima. I yelled just to heckle her "put a blinking juldi on it will you Chrissy?"

She stopped in her tracks, glared at me between her eye slits and with bunched fists and started back toward me to scrap. I grabbed a piece of the burning firewood and waved it menacingly, "hey Chrissy; sure you 'wanna 'ave a scrap?"

'Swine, I'll get you for this,' and off she went.

To be fair I had very few wins over Chrissy. I usually came off second-best in these skirmishes but this time I had the burning timber for help.

Meanwhile, the second activity would be started by Carrie, and Christine would vamoose to join the 'girls' around the dining table for the rolling of kul-kuls, the rosa-cookies and the dhole dhol mix. These three would be later fried in a big pan of oil on the same sigri fire by Will. Since I disliked all three of these Christmas treats I was ruled out of it anyway. The still trekking Hansie loved them and could have my share when they were ready; meanwhile, I would stay at my post like a vigilant sentry on duty until Will arrived at the due time of some hours to check the pud. It would be hauled out of the kero tin, opened up carefully and Will would insert a long wooden skewer to check that it was boiled to perfection all the way through. This was always a magic moment for me as I held my breath as he rubbed his fingers along the skewer to test it. "Whoosh" the air would escape from my lungs when he nodded toward me as if to say; "well-done Soldier"! The pud had been done and we would all look at its golden brown crinkly surface. The tin would be re-sealed and allowed to mature for Christmas day.

The cutting of the Loots pudding was a tradition as we all gathered around the table. Will would cut large slices and you can bet it was a ripper of a pud.

As for that lovely shiny four anna coin that was hidden in the pud? I never seemed to get it. The blighter Hansie who never helped in its making most often found it.

It's times like these when I felt life was unfair to little larrikins!

Around Christmas time we gathered around each evening by lamplight under the stars and sang Christmas Carols and funny old songs. Carrie had a good voice, Nannette was equally good, and Will, who was good at almost everything wasn't a very good singer. I squeaked on, Hansie played his harmonica and I could swear that Chrissy couldn't sing a blinking note. At least that was my jaundiced view of her singing because blow me down she could sing better than me and I was not about to concede that publically.

One of our favourites was "Old McDonald had a Farm"; that could go on forever because of all the birds and animals each one of us, in turn, could name. Hansie would imitate the animal honk, grunt, squeak, moo and neigh or quack, you name it, to perfection. Will would contribute his favourite ditty of: "I paid my one rupee to see the tattooed she" and we would all join in the chorus: "And I went back, and I went back and paid another rupee!" Carrie's rendition of: "Somewhere over the rainbow" was an all-time favourite and her rendition of Silent Night in which we all softly joined is a haunting memory of the wonderful family time in the bush.

Now I knew Christine was no push-over. She was a tom-boy without a doubt and whether it was pinching, pushing, shoving, punching, wrestling or pillow fights, she would never give in. She only had one discernible weakness and that was running. Chrissy, bless her heart would trip over her own two feet but always get up laughing like a gurgling drain. Nevertheless, I had to get even with her because she would never "give-up" when I demanded it. She would just keep fighting until I was exhausted. She had the energy of an Opel fossicker who didn't know the time!

But one particular Christmas holiday Chrissy arrived with some sort of stupid girlie composure. She helped herself as usual to my shorts and shirts but that's where it stopped and there was none of the banter, one-upmanship arguments or scraps and fights. She was behaving like a proper young lady to even preferring Nanette's company to mine and this didn't sit well with me. I was perplexed and disappointed as this strange attitude of hers lasted the whole of her first day. It usually took only half an hour after she arrived for the two of us to start a scrap!

Now, to be honest, religion was not high on our family agenda. Will believed that doing good and the practice of justice was far more important; not that I understood his philosophy back then. Anyway, saying grace at mealtimes was a personal and private thing and closing one's eyes were indicative of saying grace. I, of course only had my eyes half-closed ready to tuck in. I had a healthy appetite though I could never compete with Hansie.

The first inkling that Chrissy had caught some terrible blinking religious bug struck me at dinner the very first night. She closed her eyes, folded her hands, bowed her head and started rambling on in a loud voice; blessing the food, Will, Carrie, Hansie, Nanette and everybody else in the world including me! I was so gobsmacked you could have knocked me over with a feather duster.

Will looked serious, Carrie had a gentle smile for Chrissy, Nanette and Hansie didn't seem to care and I fairly scowled at her in disbelief. She wouldn't look at me.

Now, like I said before Will never held to saying grace aloud, but it was at one Christmas lunch sometime before when Jemima and Carrie cooked up a storm and we all tucked in, after which Will suddenly said: "God be praised, my belly's raised, six inches above the table." We all burst out laughing and even Will had a bit of an embarrassed smile on his face.

I remembered this impromptu outburst of his and figured I would use it to get back at Chrissy. I bided my time as Chrissy continued her sermons and one day when she finished and said aloud "Amen" I promptly piped up: "God be praised, my belly's raised, six inches above the table!" This time though no one laughed. It went down like a lead balloon. Carrie looked a tad puzzled, Nanette and Hansie didn't seem to notice at all, Chrissy was glaring at me, her face as pink as a sliced watermelon and Will was caught between a rock and a hard place, because, while he wanted to give me a dressing down he knew that he had uttered those very words himself! Anyway, he cleared his throat and mildly said: "Thomas, I don't think you should be joking about that just now so I'm sure we won't hear that again okay? Now let's eat shall we?"

And that was Will.

Encouraged by me being put in my place by Will, Chrissy's caper continued with even greater zeal each mealtime, now including breakfast, lunch and of course dinner. She dragged each prayer out longer and longer. Even Skip, Mahmood and Jemima got included in her praying and I was gobsmacked again! What the heck is going on? I quietly checked with Nanette if she said her prayers at night as well, and strike me pink she confirmed that she not only did but had her in on the act as well! I concluded privately that she had caught a serious life-threatening religious bug!

For once I was so stunned I didn't know what to do with her. I was scared to confront her as meddling with religion and God was dangerous as I still remembered I could end up permanently in that "Pentecosting" frying pan. I repaired to my bed one afternoon and played with my toes for guidance but nothing came out of it except the sudden thought that she must have gone to the "Pentecosting" church with Aunty Ivy and Uncle Arthur. That's where she must have caught the blinking bug.

Hansie was no help when I asked him. He just shrugged, gave me that quiet crooked smile of his and mumbled something like; "leave her alone Scoot. She'll get over it."

Skip was as nonplussed as I was when I asked him what to do.

I was too scared to go to Will or Carrie in case I got another lecture or maybe even a clip behind the ear. And like I said, I was too scared to bale Chrissy up lest I ended up in hell on that deadly everlasting frying pan! I was caught between a rock and a hard place and it never occurred to me that I was the only one worried about her religious bug. But maybe, just maybe I had the premonition that these sorts of things had the nasty and inevitable habit of getting me into strife, and sure as there are no fleas on a dead cat that's exactly what happened one afternoon.

"Pssst! Pssst! Tom, come with me."

It was Chrissy peeping around our bedroom door curtain and crooking her finger to motion me to come quickly. Hansie was snoring and all was quiet. I hopped out and followed her outside with Skip in tow.

"What's up?" I was now suspicious of Chrissy ever since she had the religious bug.

"We've got to save Aunty Carrie."

"Gosh; from what?"

"From smoking you ass."

Now Chrissy had called me an ass, swine, bully or an idiot a zillion times before so it never bothered me, it had long since become almost terms of endearment coming from her. I looked at her gobsmacked.

"Why?"

"It'll kill her that's why."

"How the heck do you blinking know? It hasn't killed her so far."

"Because God told me you ass."

"What? When?"

She nodded seriously; "Just last night."

Hell's bells, this was serious stuff. If God was involved I'd better help. Besides, I shrewdly figured He wouldn't send me to the frying pan if I did. But this was also a God-sent opportunity to ask her about the "Pentecosting" bug at last!

"You haven't been going to that church where daft people go, have you?"

"What on earth are you talking about you idiot?"

"You know, it's the one that Aunty Ivy and Uncle Arthur go to? It's called the Pentecosting church where they wave their blinking arms in the air and yell and carry on like they're daft?"

"You mustn't say wicked things like that."

"Well, have you?" I had her over a barrel and she looked as guilty as a nun squatting in a cucumber patch!

"I went with Aunty Bunny a few times. Why?"

"What? Why did Aunty Bunny go there of all places?"

"Because she said she had a difference of opinion with her Baptist minister."

"Then why didn't she go to St. Johns?"

"Because she had a tiff with the padre over there as well; that's why. But it's all been patched up now with the Baptist preacher."

Strange as it might appear all this made perfect sense to me. Aunty Bunny, I figured would fight with her own shadow. Anyway, the burning question had been cleared up at last so back to the dreadful business at hand. Just how would we save Carrie?

"Did God really tell ya to save mum from smoking?"

She nodded wisely. "Uh-huh."

"Did ya actually hear 'im? What did 'e sound like then?"

"It's sacrilegious to speak about God like that."

"What's that supposed to mean?" Chrissy looked puzzled; "that big word you just said."

"I don't know what it means, I heard Aunty Bun say it often about somebody."

"Then it's a bad word to be sure Chrissy. I wouldn't be saying it."

"You're trying to dodge Thomas."

"No, I'm not. So what did God sound like? You know, gruff or squeaky."

"Don't be an ass. God speaks to you in a different way."

I was still fishing to get out of the stew. "Now, what's that suppose' 'ta mean?"

"Never mind He did and we have to destroy her cigarettes."

"What?" I was completely gobsmacked. "You don't mean the ones in tins do ya?"

Will and I had made another trip to Goa and as usual, he had brought back cigarettes for Carrie, Charles Atlas springs for Hansie to exercise with, a talking doll for Nanette and I got my Dinky Toy.

Chrissy nodded sagely and was off before I could stop her, then came back with three tins of the prized imported State Express 555 Will had smuggled back from Goa. I knew she would have had to get them from Carrie's dresser drawer but she was sleeping and had a habit of doing so with a pillow over her face. This was a serious caper, God's dictates or no God's decrees and I now anxiously figured I had better get some insurance cover!

"Let's wake Hansie up and tell him as well."

"No, only the two of us have to do it."

"Now, who blinking well said that?"

"God, you ass. Who else?"

Gosh, why did God pick me? He could have chosen Hansie, or even Nanette?

"Wait a tick I 'gotta think Chrissy." She didn't blink an eye at my calling her Chrissy any more.

"Think about what?"

"I'm thinking about why God chose me? He never chose me before and I'm always in strife with dad."

"That's because you listen to the Devil. That's why."

"How do you blinking know who I listen to?" In my reckoning, I only listened to Will and he certainly wasn't the Devil. Jemima maybe was a She-Devil.

"Well if you listened more to God you wouldn't get into trouble now would you?"

Chrissy's logic sort of floored me. Maybe it was true. So after considerable deliberation, I figured that if He Okayed it He would protect me as well.

"Umm okay, what do we do?"

"Drown them."

"What?"

"You heard me, you idiot."

"Did God say that as well?" She glared at me with daggers in her eyes. So I tried another weak tack to distract her. "How come your shirttails don't hang out of your pants like mine always does?"

"What rubbish is that now?"

"Well you heard me; how come?" My tack seemed to be working, but alas!

"Because you are a liar and a cheat and you don't listen to God. That's why. Now, what are we going to do."

I was getting nowhere but I was still wracking my brain for some insurance cover. "I know what Chrissy. Why not bury them instead? God buries heaps of dead people in the ground every day. That graveyard in the Cantonment is full of them. I know I've seen it." This inspired idea of mine threw her. I could even hear her mind ticking as loud as a run-away two bob watch with a weak spring! I decided to put in the KO punch like the great Jack Johnson.

"I even know how to bury them. I buried an egg."

"What egg?"

I wasn't about to confess about the egg caper and the thought of what had happened to me was still fresh in my mind. "Don't worry. If we bury them they won't be found. I know plenty of good hiding places." She was still thinking because she was biting her lower lip. I figured I was winning; until…

"Yes, but you are sure to let the cat out of the bag. I know you too well Tom Loots."

"I won't. I promise."But Chrissy shook her head determinedly. She was on a blinking mission for sure.

"No, they're not eggs and besides I told you God said we had to drown them."

The mighty Jack Johnson couldn't fight both Chrissy and God together. He threw the towel into the ring! "Okay then, let's drown them in our bathroom tub." The idea was easier said than done though. How do you drown sealed tins? They just bobbed around on the water. I thought I better check once more just in case she had changed her mind.

"You sure God told you to drown 'em?"

"Of course you idiot."

"Then why aren't they drow'nin'?" Once more I thought it was an inspirational question that would stump her. But alas no! She had a blinking answer to everything I could come up with.

"Because the Devil is stopping them from drowning; that's why!"

I threw in the towel once again despite Jack Johnson! Getting into strife with Carrie and Will was one thing but getting into strife with God might sit me on the blinking Devil's everlasting frying pan!

"Then we've got to make a hole in the top."

"What?"

"You heard me. Come with me, I know how to beat the Devil."

"See, I knew God would find a way."

This time I glared at Chrissy. If God would find a way why didn't He make the holes in the tins in the first place? I retrieved my rusty dog spike and quickly made a big hole in each tin. I was about to put them in our water tub when she stopped me.

"Wait" she whispered fiercely.

"Now what?"

"We got to say a prayer first for Aunty Carrie. Hold my hand and close your eyes."

Chrissy said a fervent prayer to save her aunty Carrie, who she loved very much because she was like her mummy as well as a prayer to save Will, who she loved like her own dad. Then she added one to save Hansie, Nanette, and even threw me in for good measure. Anyway, we all had to be saved from dying from smoking cigarettes. "Amen."

I wasn't paying too much attention as I was looking at the tins perched on the ledge of the trough.

"I didn't hear you say Amen. Say Amen."

"All right, Amen."

With a bit of encouragement, we sank the bobbing cigarette tins and the terrible deed was done.

All went well until Will came home and was having a cuppa and a chat with Carrie on the veranda. After some time I heard a mighty bellow from Will.

"Thomas; come here this minute!"

I bolted outside for cover with Skip. But as usual, Mahmood arrived to escort me into his presence. Mahmood was clicking his tongue and shaking his head as usual which meant I was in big strife and this time with Bada Sahib. I took his big rough hand for comfort. Will's face seemed like a big dark black angry monsoon thundercloud as I stood in front of him and fidgeted and he was so mad he didn't even notice I had no shoes on. I was so scared I felt like weeing in my pants!

"Did you take your mother's cigarette tins?" Since he suspected me he'd already figured out that the cigarettes would have come to a sticky end.

"No Dad. I promise." I figured that much was true. Chrissy and not me had actually taken the cigarettes.

"Don't you give me that pipe-dottle Mister. Then who took them?"

I was about to dob Chrissy in and tell him it had been God's idea when I heard this scared little voice behind me.

"I did Uncle Will."

"What?" Will's 'WHAT' tore through me like a thunder-clap from the thundercloud. "You're not trying to be silly and take the blame for Tom, are you?"

That's when all hell broke loose. Christine started howling and ran to Carrie, who gathered her up in her arms and started soothing her. That's the second and only time I heard her howl, the first one being the almond egg sweet incident years ago.

"All right, where have you hidden them?" He said this rather ominously while glaring at me and not at Chrissy.

Hidden them? I sure needed God's help in a hurry. "In my water tub Dad." With this, I heard Carrie bawling as well. Maybe for her cigarettes or to keep Chrissy company I don't know which. I was too worried about my own skin!

"WHAT?" Again the thunderclap went straight through me and I might have just weed a tiny bit in my pants. "Come with me Mister."

He looked at the mess down the bottom of the tub and then at me. The long seconds ticked by very, very slowly as I fidgeted and hopped from one foot to the other. The bathroom was huge so I kept a safe distance from Will as he was fuming and I reckon he was ready to skin me alive and then string me up from the rafters.

"You put the holes in them I suppose?"

Gosh. God better come to my help and quickly. I think He did because I blurted out; "yes Dad, but Chrissy said God told her we had to save Mum from dying from smoking."

"What did you say?" It sounded like another blinking thunderclap but this time of astonishment from Will.

"Promise Dad, we even said prayers!"

I heard a grunt of total exasperation from Will, but his sense of justice and fair play had put him once more between a rock and a hard place. I might have been a willing accomplice in his thinking but it hadn't been my idea in the first place.

"All right Mister. Go and tell Mahmood to fish them out and throw them away and change the water. And you had better keep out of my sight!"

Phew; that was a close shave! Before he could change his mind I bolted like greased lightning to find Mahmood!

The only good thing that came out of drowning Carrie's cigarettes was that I behaved myself for a time and more importantly, Chrissy stopped saying grace aloud. She returned to normal and was completely cured of the dangerous Pentecosting bug!

Mahmood was sent to the local bazaar to buy Carrie her usual "Number Ten" brand of cigarettes made in India.

Do you see? Sometimes little larrikins cop it even when they are innocent!

And would you believe my luck? Ever after that, whenever Carrie told the yarn of the cigarette drowning caper she would say it was I that did it and not Chrissy that drowned her State Express 555 cigarettes.

It was an unjustified blot on the little larrikins character.

Anyway, holidays have to come to an end and I was sad to see Hansie, Nanette and Christine depart.

I did give Chrissy some good advice. "Don't go to that dashed Pentecosting thing again okay?"

She gave me a big hug and a kiss, forgave me for all the pranks I'd played on her and promised faithfully not to go Pentecosting ever again.

23
Tom's hard landing in chook poo!

ABOUT TWO HUNDRED YARDS FROM OUR HOUSE sat the dirt road that went from the Railway station to the Grand Trunk Road and just beyond that a large open field that was a sort of common area or maidān as it was called. It was used for grazing village animals, weekly shandys or market and the yearly visiting Tent Cinema and Circus.

Early one morning I was out with Skipper and could see a heck of a lot of activity on the maidān. I could see a lot of people milling around and smoke from cooking fires curling lazily up into the clear sky. The peaty aroma of the dried cow dung and hay mix was a pleasant reminder of the village cooking fires and the harbinger of a hot tumbler of jaggery sweetened chai. All of this was different from the usual activity on the maidān so I had to investigate.

What I saw intrigued me because I had never seen such people before. The women had attractive flashing black eyes; they all wore tight bandanas with tails on their heads, brightly coloured tops and big bright heavy skirts that swirled like curling smoke around their ankles to their voluptuous walk. The young ones were beautiful. They wore lots of metal necklaces and big metal rings on their arms and ankles that made music with each step. There were wizened-up old women too with deeply lined faces that had the same metal rings hanging on like silver flying fox to their ear lobes and noses, as well. Gosh, they all looked so strange but were fairer and better looking than the local people; even the men who wore funny coloured turbans! There were lots of little children too. They gawked at me and I gawked at them. All around the encampment were lots of carts, small ponies and donkeys hanging around. They had come suddenly from nowhere and set up their coloured patchwork tents.

They also had dogs. Heaps of them and a pack of them came out at Skip. He was bigger than any two of them but not a whole blinking pack. He stood his ground in front of me while they circled and snarled and barked and carried on until a bloke came out with a stick and belaboured them like blazes. The poor devils skulked off in pain and retreated to safety. He said something to me I didn't understand.

I bolted home to convey this exciting news to Carrie. I was hopping around like a grasshopper as I breathlessly gave her a full account of these strange people who I was sure she had never ever seen in her life either. There might have been sixty or eighty people in the camp but I added a few hundred to their numbers. Carrie being what she was, listened patiently and then gave me some pretty scary news.

"They are Gypsies Tom. They steal chickens and eggs and naughty little boys, too. They'll catch you and hide you under their long skirts and whisk you away forever if you don't listen to me."

Carrie must have seen a rare chance to scare her naughty son into some semblance of obedience. It had the desired effect, at least for a while.

I wore my shoes and hat, stayed indoors in the hot afternoons and played with my toes, thinking about these dangerous Gypsies who stole naughty children. After all, I did see lots of "stolen children"! I warned Mr Goanna of these dangerous people and not to get caught or they would surely eat him up. I kept a close eye on our chooks and for good measure, I kept my Winchester with me whenever I was outside. I never went near that blinking Gypsy camp.

Then one fine morning after a couple of weeks they were gone as suddenly as they had come. I was relieved.

Perhaps it was my enforced good behaviour for about ten days that needed release and led to my next piece of misfortune.

It was Hansie who once came back with the weird names of "blood-suckers" and "bugouts" for the large scaly lizards that abounded around all over, sunning themselves on the ground or scurrying in the trees. Anyway, it turned out that they were not lizards either but native chameleons and it was Will who explained the difference to me. He probably learnt it from the National Geographic! They were called "the common Indian Chameleon" and were about eighteen inches long, scaly and brown in colour. Big enough in my book for a sure shot with my catapult though I could never hit one. They were fun to watch as well, for aside from wanting to knock over a few (little larrikins can be cruel) when two of them faced up to each other almost nose to nose, their heads and half their bodies would turn a bright red. They would then puff themselves up to twice their size so the spikes on their backs would stand up and they would stare at each other. And then, both of them would start doing push-ups with their gobs wide open. They could do a lot more push-ups than I could. Then, all of a sudden they would start wrestling as if doing the waltz on their hind-legs. After a bit of dancing one would give-up and bolt with the other in hot pursuit.

Anyway, despite Will's explanation I always call them blood-suckers or bugouts, much to his annoyance and despite constantly correcting me. It was Hansie who added a version as to why they were called bugouts it was because they had eyes that bugged out. That sounded pretty convincing to me.

Now Skip would always chase the bugouts whenever they were on the ground but never managed to catch one as they scurried safely up a tree. But one day, a big fellow was a little bit slow and Skip managed to knock him sideways with his front paw and bailed him up before he could get to the tree. Instead of trying to bolt in another direction the bugout stood his ground, raised himself on his front and rear legs, changed his colour to red, hoisted the hackles on his neck and back and opened his gob wide. He certainly looked pretty fierce. Skip, I reckon was nonplussed by this show of pluck as he skidded to a halt. They were supposed to run from him. He made a grab for it, missed as the blood-sucker dodged sideways and then it latched onto his lip with determined tenacity. I collapsed laughing as Skip spun around and around trying to dislodge the blighter, twisting his head this way and that and pawed at him like heck in frustration, but the bugout had a good grip on his side lip and hung on grimly.

"Hey ya, Skip I reckon he's got a good hold on you and you need help."

It was hard to get Skip to keep his head still but after a time I was able to get my fingers around the back of the bugout's head and jaws. Maybe it was giddy from all the swinging around or it reckoned I was another enemy it had to fight, but it let go of Skipper's lip. I held him up in triumph. Strangely, he didn't wriggle or squirm in my fingers or I might have just dropped him. He just stayed quiet. Skip now wanted to get his revenge and jumped up to try and grab the fellow again. I had to hold him high above my head while yelling at Skip to cut it out.

Now, any other young scoundrel would have let it go on a tree but not me. I got the urge to show Carrie my prize, tell her the funny story of Skip with the bugout and maybe scare her as well. I knew she hated lizards and geckos and things like that so into the house I headed at a run with Skip still jumping around like a circus clown to get at it.

"Hi Mum, look what I caught." I was at the doorway of her sewing room. She was sitting on her sewing chair head lowered busy turning the handle of her Singer sewing machine.

She sighed. "What is it now."

"It was hanging onto Skip's lip Mum and he was hopping around like mad trying to get it off until I did. I saved his life Mum!" Which I thought was quite clever.

Carrie decided I was going to pester her anyway so she stopped sewing, turned around on her sewing stool, looked briefly at me holding the bugout high in the air then her face drained of blood like she'd seen a ghost or something! She fair screeched at me.

"Tom, get that thing away from me immediately!"

"But it's got no teeth Mum. You remember Dad telling me they're harm ....!" I didn't get to finish.

"I don't care what your father told you; get that wretched creature out of the house immediately." Her voice was now a very high soprano.

Now, I don't know if it was Skip still jumping around or maybe he got a nip on the bugout's tail, or Carrie's screech, or my carelessness but the dashed thing wriggled like heck and I accidentally let go. Splat; it landed on the floor. Skipper bowled me over to get at it and the blinking bugout now headed straight in Carrie's direction. Quicker than you could say Jack Robinson she climbed on top of the stool and was yelling blue murder for Mahmood while the bugout scurried under the wardrobe for safety. I picked myself up and bolted for the outdoors and for the first time Skip didn't follow me. I reckon he was still trying to get the critter out from under the wardrobe.

I shot past Mahmood at a hundred miles an hour. He was on the run in the opposite direction in answer to Carrie's shrieking, followed by Jemima waddling fast with a blinking wooden chapatti roller in her hand ready to wallop some intruder on the head. After a bit, Mahmood came out holding the poor bugout by its tail and with Skip still hopping up in frustration. He put it on a tree and it scurried up quick smart.

As usual, Mahmood shook his head and clicked his tongue and told me Memsahib wanted to see me immediately. He didn't give me his hand as usual for comfort as we marched back in. It was the first and only time my friend and minder did not extend his hand in comfort. I think he'd drawn the line at frightening Memsahib. As we went via the kitchen Jemima gave me a mouthful for good measure. I returned it with my death stare and stuck my tongue out for emphasis; yet strangely, I had a terrible feeling of guilt for once. Maybe it was the panic in Carrie's shrieking that got to me.

She was on the veranda having a cup of tea and a fag to steady her nerves. She took her time before putting the cup down and glared at me. This was a side of my her I had not experienced before and my nerves were jangling.

"You did that deliberately, didn't you?"

"No Mum promise, I was only trying to …. !" I didn't get to finish.

"Don't you give me any of your stories Tom, you've been very naughty and I'm going to give you to the Gypsies."

This was a death knell, a new one and therefore worse than a category three reportable offence to Will. I broke down and started blubbering. Honestly, I was feeling sorry and the thought of the Gypsies hiding me under their blinking skirts scared me.

"I'm sorry, Mum. I promise I won't do it again. Please don't give me to the Gypsies?"

Carrie was a softie. She hugged me, wiped my tears away and blew my nose in her handkerchief because she knew I would use my shirttails that always seemed to be hanging out of my shorts. She assured me she wouldn't give me to the Gypsies and didn't even report me to Will.

Phew! The little larrikin just saved himself from the Gypsies!

Dear Hansie, The blinking Gypsies camped on the maidān. They scared me. Your loving brother. Tom.

She censored the word 'blinking' and the rest was approved.

The Gypsies were now but a faded memory thank goodness. The monsoon had come and gone, refreshing the maidān across the road to a very pleasant grassy green. The jawar crops stood tall in the fields and their heads of ripened golden rust stalks waved gracefully in the wind. The pesky starlings descended in their thousands to get a feed of the jawar and I barely made a dent in their numbers with my catapult but I did scare the heck out of them as they lifted off in a black cloud and settled again in another cloud in another area of the field. I would follow them tenaciously.

I would wander into the local village and always received a warm welcome wherever and whenever I went.

I always went to see the Munsiff who was the village headman first, or before I left because I liked him. A cool glass of thick salty buttermilk with a squeeze of lime in it would be offered to me in any home I visited. There were times when I would sit down cross-legged on the cow-dung smooth floor and share a meal of bhakri or jawar roti, a sort of unleavened bread cooked on dried cow dung patties, a big raw red onion, dahl and a chilli hot vegetable dish all finished off with a small clay pot of rich buffalo yogurt that was so thick you could walk on it!

Now the Hindu custom is to eat only with your right hand as there were certainly no spoons and forks. There is a cultural if not a hygienic reason for this strict practice of theirs and yet they never once in all the years did they point out to me that I was using both my left and right hands.

The Mahratta fare was simple but I loved it. Chota Sahib was always made to feel welcome and they asked for nothing in return.

They would graciously ask after Bada Sahib, Memsahib and Chota Sahib's brother and sister. In my Patois Hindi I would reassure them all was well and ask for another pot of yogurt, this time with some jaggery to sweeten it. I was shameless. They were just pleased Chota Sahib enjoyed their yogurt!

The village Munsiff had a lovely piebald pony, its leather bridle and stirrup legs richly decorated with burnished copper or brass emblems. He would put me on the horse and parade me down the village street. Gosh, I felt six foot tall and grinned so much if I didn't have ears the grin would have gone around my head!

They were lovely, decent and simple people and would take great pride in showing me their latest acquisition; a new ploughing bull or bicycle or pony. Many of them rode horses in Maharashtra and their hero was Sivaji, who had not only pushed the Muslim Mughals back but gave the Brits an equally hard time. Even the poorest of homes in the village had a portrait of their hero hanging on the wall.

The Marathas were great wrestlers and even the children of the village engaged in the sport. I wisely stayed out of it. I knew my limits after a few attempts when even a smaller tacker than me would have me on my back before you could say Jack Robinson. But I did play the game of Kabaddi with them.

There was one strange practice I acquired while a tacker and that was to shake hands solemnly when I was nicking off. They seemed to appreciate that instead of the traditional Namaste. I have no idea how I acquired these quaint habits of courtesy when I was in the villages. Sometimes the Munsiff would seat me on the front of him and ride me home. I would urge him to get the pony to gallop like in the Western movies but he would never go beyond a trot. Gosh, how good was that! How much excitement can a young scoundrel have in one day!

Carrie was not sure about my village visits and my returning with a full belly but Will assured her it could only do me good to learn about the local people and their lives.

"Dear Hansie, I came home riding on a pony. Your loving brother, Tom."

Despite my pleas and promises to be a good boy she refused to budge on: "I rode a pony firing my Winchester like Gary Cooper."

It was times like this when I felt she was unfair to little boys fibs! I told her Will would have Okayed it. "Well, Mister" she countered, "why not ask your father?"

I didn't.

October would see the start of the harvest season. This was a time when the centuries-old bush calendar came to life and with it the village fairs to celebrate the harvest period. One morning as I looked out over toward the maidān I once again noticed a flurry of activity. For a brief moment, my thoughts went back to the Gypsies but when I saw the tall tent poles start to go up I knew it was the mobile touring tent cinema that had come to town. You absolute ripper!

According to the bush calendar, the travelling tent cinema was a regular feature after the monsoon was over and brought the magic of the "flickering" silver screen to the remote bush. Movies had a starring role in the harvest celebrations that took place in the various villages along the line. They showed all the old English Western movies; Billy the Kid, Jesse James, Red River, The Outlaw, Arizona and heaps, heaps more plus movies like Tarzan, Sabu the Elephant Boy, Walt Disney movies, Dr Jekyll and Mr Hyde, Charlie Chaplin and even my favourite Spy Smasher.

It was a theatre within a theatre. The audience all sat in rows on the grass and it did not matter a jot that the village folk did not understand English. They would intently follow the action and clap loudly when the hero overcame his enemy. The more fighting action the better they enjoyed it; as of course did I. The flickering quality of the images on the screen was of no consequence, nor was the occasional snapping of the film roll. Everybody waited patiently for the technician in his cubby hole to splice it and start again. Without a doubt, they enjoyed English movies just as much as we did.

It was a wonderful sight as the people came from all the surrounding villages; the women and children in bullock carts and the men riding beside them on their decorated and groomed piebald ponies. They would camp on the huge maidān for the festivities. Stalls with sweetmeats, clothing, pots and pans, trinkets, brightly painted papier-mâché figurines, wooden and clay dolls and dolls whose heads wobbled so you had to guess whether they meant "yes" or "no" to a question! They sprung up like mushrooms in a flurry of organised chaos. It was an exciting hive of activity and the evening smoke from their cooking fires once more carried such a pleasant smell.

Skip and I went off to investigate and after snooping around, I found the bloke in charge of the cinema projector.

"Hello, Mr. What's your name?" He gave me a huge smile because he must have recognised me from snooping around the previous year.

"Ah, Chota Baba, it is good to see you again. My name is Kavi."

"I'm Tom. What'cha going to show Kavi?"

"Very good picture we are showing Tom Baba; very latest Sabu movie. It is called Cobra Woman."

Gosh, Cobra Woman sounded exciting. I'd never seen a woman cobra!

"Did Sabu bring his efelants to fight with the cobra woman?" He looked at me puzzled and I knew why. "You know the big animals with big ears and long trunks Sabu rides on?"

"Ah! Sabu the Elephant boy? No, no, Tom Baba; that I am showing last year for you. No elephants this time but very much sword fighting action."

There were no efelants but sword fighting sounded great. Yet, I was desperate to see Spy Smasher again. "You're not going to show Spy Smasher Kavi?"

"For you, Tom Baba, I will show one Spy Smasher serial next week."

"Oh, thanks Kavi. I'll tell my Mum and Dad but don't forget to show Spy Smasher next week okay?"

"No, no, don't worry. Tomorrow night I am keeping chairs for you in back row?"

"Thanks, Kavi." I shook hands with Kavi to seal the deal and pelted home to give Carrie the news of what movies would be showing and that Kavi my friend was going to even arrange chairs for us. I should have known better. Carrie didn't trust tent cinema chairs. She believed they were full of bugs and so on the evening of the movie Mahmood was despatched ahead with chairs from Will's office. And would you believe it? She would instruct Mahmood to make sure he even doused the office chairs with Flit as well! I think she had bug mania as any furniture not from our house had to be doused in Flit.

We were greeted by the manager I guess and shown to our "bug-free" chairs. He didn't want to take the money for our tickets but Will insisted otherwise we would go home with our chairs. He was genuinely mortified. He didn't charge for Skip though who settled down at my feet on his leash.

We were big fish in a very small bush pond but I always felt it was the calm dignity and courtesy of Will towards the local folk that endeared us to them and them to us. Will was the model of a good decent person.

The tent was packed with men, women and children from the surrounding villages near and far. Somewhere in the throng would be Mahmood and Jemima keeping an eye out for anything we needed. Throughout the movie, they gave Sabu a heck of a clap in every scene because they all knew he was from India. There was plenty of sword fighting as Kavi had promised but I was disappointed the "woman" didn't look anything like a cobra at all! During the interval, three glasses of cool sugarcane juice were served to us. I could see Carrie turning her nose up at the grime on the outside of the glass but she took a delicate sip of it after a quiet word from Will. Since I had no hang-ups about grime I finished it for her.

Since Kavi was now my friend, I went back into his box-like projecting room to see the projector and the big rewinding reels. It was hot there but he was pleased Tom Baba had come to see him.

I rode home on Mahmood's shoulders as usual. He would go back later to fetch the "bug-free" chairs. Carrie made me a cup of cocoa before going to bed to blend with the sugarcane juice in my tummy. It was a lovely family time growing up in the bush.

I was a happy little larrikin ... if a bit of a scamp!

As promised, Kavi showed a Spy Smasher serial the following week and it drew quite a crowd even though it was a repeat from last season as tickets were half price. It was only one show on the last day because the "Cobra Woman" proved very popular. Will and Carrie didn't come and sent me with Mahmood so he got to see a movie squatting down beside me and cheering wildly with me at Spy Smasher's amazing exploits. He carried me home on his broad shoulders.

"Dear Hansi, I saw Spy Smasher jump on the crook's van. Your loving brother Tom. PS: Mum got me pencils and a rule book. PPS: I gave my slate and colour pencils to Mahmood."

The censor ruled out: "I flew through the air like Spy Smasher." I certainly did a little later with vastly different consequences.

So, as you can imagine I was taken by a scene from Spy Smasher where the hero chased two villains on his Harley Davidson, taking a dangerous short cut across the rough countryside to cut their speeding van off. He climbed a rock overlooking the road and as the speeding van approached he leapt from the high rock, his cape flying through the air like a vengeful eagle and landed on top of the careening van in a crouch, his revolver drawn and ready to fight the Nazi spies! Golly, it was so exciting that scene stuck in my head.

On another warm lazy afternoon when consigned to my bedroom I played with my toes as usual while reliving every moment of my hero's adventures.

It didn't take me long to work out how Spy Smasher flew through the air. It was his cape. That's all I needed; a cape! And so I stripped the sheet from my cot, stuck my cap pistol in my belt and slipped out via my bathroom door so Carrie or Jemima wouldn't spot me if awake. With practised stealth, I made my way to the cowshed and chook house and checked the heights out. The cowshed was taller but the inability to climb onto its roof without a ladder ruled it out. I had to settle on the lower chook house roof which I could climb onto. I clambered up, tied the ends of the sheet around my neck and shoulders, settled the pistol in my belt ready to be drawn for action, visualised the speeding van about to pass: ... "varoom", "varoom", "varoom", "varooooom" and with perfect timing, I launched myself through the air. I landed with a horrible splat on my two feet at a half-crouch and pitched forward flat on my face as the chooks scattered.

"Aaawwww!" I yelped loudly in pain. Needless to say, aside from pain in my left knee and back, I was also covered in chook poo. I couldn't smell it myself though.

Mahmood, as usual, was first on the scene. My agonised yelping had carried to Carrie and Jemima. As Mahmood carried me into the house she copped a nose-full of chook manure smell and pointed in the general direction of my bathroom. So instead of putting me on my bed Mahmood stripped me and bathed me. I sobbed all the way through it and he clicked his tongue, this time in sympathy! I reckon he went through one more brick of Lifebuoy soap to clean me up.

I'd never seen Will so worried as he checked my swollen knee and the pain in my back. He prescribed Aspros and Carrie rubbed my back and knee with her "miracle" Amrutanjan balm and confined me to bed. Mum loved her Amrutanjan and would rub it on her forehead and temples every night. My cuts and bruises were painted with raw iodine which made me yelp but Will was concerned about tetanus and he took my temperature and inspected it three times a day.

Once more I heard Carrie say: "That son of yours will kill himself one day."

Whenever she was really worried about me she would use the term "that son of yours" but I didn't hear Will reassure her this time. I reckon he was really worried too. As Hansie and Nanette were away at school the worried Carrie slept in Hansie's bed in my room for a whole week.

The little larrikin certainly caused his parents a lot of grief!

The travelling tent cinema was not the only major event on the yearly "harvest bush calendar", for about a month or so later once again there would be a flurry of activity on the maidān. This time the tent poles would be much taller and the tents more elaborate. It was a travelling circus. I would spend all day with Skip wandering around, barefoot, of course, much to Carrie's chagrin if she caught me; watching the construction which took a couple of days. Each day I would give her a full account of the progress. She always listened patiently to my elaborate and most often fanciful description, or more accurately lies, of how I went right up to the efelants and fed them a stick of sugar cane, or that I had seen Sabu knocking around with the efelants, or that I had gone right up to the tiger's cage and I never flinched when it roared at me! She had heard it all the year before. In truth, I kept my distance from the efelants chained by the rear foot to a big stake in the ground and the tigers and black bears that were in big cages.

Much to my disappointment, there was no friendly Kavi around. They were polite enough to this pesky kid wandering around asking heaps of stupid questions but I could never strike up a conversation. It never occurred to me that setting up a circus tent with all its trappings was a pretty serious logistical exercise.

There were horses and dogs as well, but my fascination was not with the trapeze and the tightrope being erected high up in the tent, but with the iron or steel "Cage of Death". The Cage of Death was a spherical metal cage and a daring motorbike rider would roar around just like Spy Smasher did on his bike chasing crooks, except this was thunderously real. He would build up speed gradually going round and round, higher and higher until he did "vertical" loops at top speed. Wow, I used to get dizzy just watching him risking his life, or so I figured. I was so taken with his daring I promptly discarded becoming Spy Smasher and would be a Cage of Death rider instead. I announced this as usual to Carrie. She just shook her head and looked at the rafters! "Thomas" she intoned "you can't be everything but you can be something if you learn to read, write and do your numbers."

The well-intended advice was lost on the larrikin.

The tent cinema was a great attraction to the surrounding village folk from far and wide, but the circus was without a doubt the super event of the year. Once more the village folk would troop in, happily sit on the ground and enjoy the show. Every act was given a huge round of applause. The applause would get louder for the daring trapeze artists and tight rope walker but you can bet your boots the biggest applause was reserved for the Cage of Death. It was always the final act.

And as usual, the bug-free office chairs would be set up in a prime position one night for the Sahib's family with Mahmood and Jemima close handy. Poor Skip, he was not allowed to go to the circus despite my pleading with Will.

Will would always allow me to see two extra shows accompanied by Mahmood and I would make the journey home perched on his shoulders, going; "verroomm, verroomm, verroomm" with each step trying to imitate the loud exhaust of the motorbike. These were moments of real magic for the larrikin to treasure.

The little larrikin was very happy indeed!

"Dear Hansie, I went to the circus and saw the Cage of Death and Sabu's elephants. Your loving brother. Tom."

There was some argument about it being Sabu's efelants, but the censor finally gave in when I asked her how she knew it wasn't Sabu's efelants?

The sensor had earlier ruled out: "I rode in the Cage of Death", and even ruled out: "I'm going to be a Cage Death rider."

"No you're not," she said firmly.

My knee healed perfectly if a bit crook but I never blamed Spy Smasher; if only I'd had his blinking cape!

24
Tom's sweet revenge!

CARRIE WENT TO BANGALORE CANT to do a bit of shopping and to once again bring Hansie, Nanette and Christine home for the school holidays.

Christine was no push-over and if you haven't guessed it there was also an intense attempt at one-upmanship on my part at least. Lazy afternoons could be spent playing the game. I never told her about jumping off the chook shed, because I think she would have promptly called me a stupid idiot. So I set about firing a series of questions at Chrissy which I figured I could win: "Have you had a ride on a pony?" ... "Can you catch a bugout?" (She had called me a swine for frightening poor Aunty Carrie when I boasted to her about what I did) ... "Have you been to a shandy"?... "Can you shoot the gun?" (She called me a liar, though I swore I shot heaps of fat wild pigeons and doves) ... "Have you been on the trolley?'" Unfortunately, she had and I'd forgotten the picnic we'd been on, so I backed off ... "Have you seen a king cobra 20 feet long?" (Again she called me a liar though I swore blind I had seen heaps); ... but I finally had Chrissy over a barrel when she admitted she didn't know what a tent cinema was. I quickly went in for the kill or what I thought would be a real winner to sink her and make her say: "I give up!"

"Bet you haven't been on an engine."

"So?"

"I've even blown the steam whistle and shovelled the coal as well. Bet you haven't." The latter part, of course, was a total fib. I couldn't lift a big shovel let alone a shovel full of coal.

"So what? That's nothing compared to what my Granddad did."

"Ha, ha, what did he do?"

"He drove the King and Queen of England's train."

"Rubbish. I don't believe you. He lives in England and that's why he's called the King of England."

"He came to India you idiot and my Granddad not only drove the train he even shook hands with King."

"It's a big fat lie."

"No, it isn't."

"Yes 'tis. Did he have a sword?"

"What's that got to do with it you idiot?"

"Well, if he didn't have a sword he wasn't a King."

"Don't be an idiot. He was a King."

"Ha, I knew it was a big fat lie."

"Then you ask Uncle Will. He knows it's true."

"You bet I will one day. I'm going to the bog now. See you later."

This line of Chrissy's was too much for me to bear. Gosh, imagine shaking hands with the same King who put his sharp sword on Younns Sait's neck and made him a Knight? I had to check this out, so I didn't go to the bog but bolted around the back way so Chrissy wouldn't see me and rushed to Will's office to find out if her story was true.

The punkah-wallah on the front veranda didn't even see me. He was, as usual, sitting on the floor with his back to the wall half asleep while operating the punkah rope around his big toe; up and down, up and down, up and down like a church bell puller. I reckon he would do that at night in his sleep!

The Head Babu in the outer office peered over his glasses and half nodded a smile. When Will was not around he was a wonderful source of pens with nibs, red, blue and green ink, copying pencils that you licked and drew with in purple, the odd rule made in the workshop and sheets and sheets of coarse brown paper from which to make aeroplanes. It was the war years and there was no such thing as white paper, steel pins, or paper clips or I would have been collecting that as well. Some bright spark discovered that acacia thorn could work as well as steel pins and a whole new cottage industry developed supplying every office in the country with acacia thorns. They were sharp and spiny and hurt like heck if you pricked a finger or hand and so even though they could be a vicious weapon against the "germs" I never used them again in my battle plans. Once poked; twice shy!

Will sat as usual at his big desk poring over official stuff and signing papers from time to time. He spotted me tearing in.

"Why haven't you got your shoes on, Mister?"

The use of the word Mister meant he was not overly pleased with me. All the staff had nodded or smiled a greeting at me but not Will and I could never figure out why he always first looked at my blinking feet!

"Sorry, Dad. I promise I'll put them on next time but I got to ask you something."

"Important, I suppose?"

"Yes Dad, promise."

"Well, what is it."

"Christine told me a big fat lie. She says her Grandfather drove the King of England's train and even shook his hand."

"She's not in the habit of spouting pipe-dottle like you young feller. Now go and put your shoes on."

"But Dad ...!"

"No ifs and buts Thomas. I'll talk to you later."

I was summarily dismissed. Unfortunately for me, he did confirm Chrissy's tale later in full. I was mortified. She was now miles ahead of me in the boasting stakes!

As it happens way back when Adam was a boy King George V and Queen Mary came to India for their Durbar. After the Durbar, he went by a Special Royal Train on a ten-day tour of the North, visiting the various Princely States and being entertained by these rich little despots. Occasions such as this always included hunting big game; like tiger, rhino and black bears. Anyway, the royal train had a specially selected crew that took them to the various stopovers along the way between Delhi and their final destination which was Calcutta. The eight hundred mile journey was hardly arduous because the train would have a constant right of way, as well as the several stop-overs. The pleasant trip took about two weeks and one assumes the special crew would not have been without their comforts at the stopovers, courtesy of the Maharaja.

On finally reaching Calcutta, His Royal Highness graciously sent for the driver of his royal train to thank him. He thanked him for his service and then asked his name.

"David King, your Highness."

"Fancy that, Mr King; I believe this is the first time a King has been driven by a King!" He then shook his hand in parting.

Chrissy's Grandpop's name on her mum's side was David King.

Shucks, I was not only gobsmacked by this revelation but also extremely peeved at the thought of Chrissy having one over me. I tried to avoid her, but she was after me like an angry honey badger on heat because she knew she had me over a blinking barrel.

"Well? Did you ask?"

"Ask what?" I was not about to capitulate without a fight.

"Ask Uncle Will about my Grandad meeting the King, idiot."

"Oh, that one; was he the same King who put the sword on Yoonus Sait's neck?"

"What rot are you talking about?"

"It's not rot."

"He doesn't put a sword on the neck anyway; it's on the shoulder."

This was good. I had her distracted from the issue. "Close enough to the neck. What if his blinking sword slips? It'll cut your head off just like Mahmood does to the chooks. I've seen that plenty of times."

"Don't be an ass."

"I'm not going to take any risks if that King wants to make me a Knight or something. I don't want to be a Knight."

"Bully for you. Now did you ask or not or do I have to ask for you!"

I was caught like a rabbit in the spotlight and forced to capitulate. I did so ungraciously as possible like a beggar who had been ignored. I would have to get even.

Little larrikins are bad losers!

Playing outside without shoes got me constantly into strife with both Carrie and Will but it was a rule I regularly disobeyed and had no trouble convincing Chrissy to do the same. She was a tom-boy without a doubt but she had one weakness, she would trip over her own two feet. I was now on a mission to get even with her; both for over the cigarette drowning caper which I hadn't forgotten, and now over the King shaking hands with her grandfather. Now I knew of a thorny patch in the grass down by the back fence and had made the painful discovery myself one day earlier before Chrissy had come on holiday.

"Bet you can't race me to the back fence."

"Yes I can."

"Okay, here's the starting line. The last one to touch the fence is a red-faced monkey."

"Right, but no cheating mind."

"I don't cheat?"

"Oh yes you do. You try to cheat every night at cards and Chinese chequers."

Crikey, I was caught again. "Never mind that, are you ready to race me or not!"

"I'm ready idiot."

"On your marks, ready, steady, go!"

I was pelting ahead of Chrissy but as I was nearing the thorn patch I craftily slowed down and she shot past me like a bolt of lightning straight into the trap. She pulled up howling with pain like a staked banshee as I collapsed on the safe grass area while laughing my head off. I had her at last.

In-between yelping she swore at me over and over again. With some absolute miracle of balance, Chrissy managed to get out of the patch on the back heels of her feet without falling over and made it to safe ground. Now that would have been even greater fun. Prickles in her bum would have been the icing on the cake!

"You damn swine, you knew the thorns were there. Just you wait Tom Loots I'll get even with you!"

I just kept laughing.

Hearing her howls of pain, she couldn't walk obviously, Mahmood came rushing from somewhere followed by Carrie. I wisely stopped laughing and pretended to look for thorns in my foot as well. Neither of them bothered about me. I wondered why!

Mahmood ignored me and headed for the yelping Christine, clicking his tongue in sympathy; "Missy Baba, Missy Baba." He picked her up gently and carried her into the house. He and Carrie knew the emergency drill since I had been the first patient only a month or so earlier, but only just a few prickles in one-foot mind before I hopped out on one leg and started howling.

Chrissy's case, I knew was fair dinkum severe because if the head of the thorn had broken off, the pointed shaft had to be literally dug out with one of Carrie's sewing needles and extracted with her eyebrow tweezers. I was already full-bottle on this painful procedure. Mahmood would do this with gentle, steady hands. It was beyond poor Carrie. She was terrified when any one of us was hurt because as you know there was no doctor within cooee.

I didn't feel too sorry for Chrissy though because I figured Mahmood had already practised on me and she would have an easier time.

"I think we better skedaddle and lay low Skip! Mum might be cross with me."

Lay low I did but within ear-shot of the bedroom window that Christine and Nanette shared. The delicate operation went on for a long time and much to my mirth there were yelps of pain from time to time from Chrissy. There's one thing I was sure about Chrissy, she would never sneak on me to Carrie or Will or I would have definitely got a clip behind the ears or worse still a hiding.

Serves her right though for not giving up!

I was an unsympathetic little larrikin as well!

When things had quietened down I snuck back into the house hoping to stay invisible. Oops! I bumped straight into Carrie coming out of Chrissy's room. "Why didn't the two of you have your shoes on Tom?"

"We were going to have a race Mum."

"Well, next time race with your shoes on Mister."

"I got thorns in my foot too Mum." This, of course, was pipe-dottle.

"Well, serves you right if you didn't learn from the last time. Now go and wash your feet immediately. They're filthy."

"Yes Mum."

I was aggrieved not to get any sympathy at all and it's in times like these that life seemed unfair to larrikins who told lies!

"Can I go and see Christine Mum?"

"Yes, after you've washed first and don't get up to any mischief."

I had my cat's lick in my bathroom then stuck my head around her door. Christine was lying down looking quite chirpy and beside her bed sat the ubiquitous thunder-box. She was sipping something from a mug and looked as if she was enjoying it. Her feet were all bandaged up but I could see the gentian violet of the antiseptic on her exposed toes.

"What do you want you swine?"

"Yer toes are purple. Ha-ha!"

"Get out you damn swine."

"Okay. Come on, Skip. Let's go." I stepped out of the door and waited. I knew her curiosity would get the better of her.

"You still there?" Back in I went. "What do you want."

"Your toes are purple and look 'jes like carrots."

"Shut up you ass, besides carrots are not purple. Go and get one from the kitchen and we'll see."

"Never mind the colour your toes look just like carrots."

"No, they don't."

"Want a pillow fight?"

"Are you mad? My feet are killing me."

"I'll only whack you on your head."

"I don't trust you."

"Are they hurting real bad?"

"Of course you idiot. What do you expect!"

"M'ebbe if I gave them a squeeze it'll get better."

"Don't you dare I'll scream."

"Watch ya drinking?"

"Hot chocolate, it's nice. Want a sip?"

"Yep." I drank the whole lot smacked my lips and wiped my mouth in my shirttail. Her face had gone red with anger by now. "It was nice" I added.

"You … You … bastard" Chrissy exploded. "You drank the whole lot!" She spluttered with righteous anger just as Carrie came back at that precise moment into the room. She covered her mouth, not in shock but in unrestrained laughter and then turned around and left.

"What's a bastard Chrissy? I bet you don't know."

"And I suppose you do?"

"Yep. Dad showed me heaps when I went on line with him. It's a big bird. I think it looks something like a vulture." Will, of course, had shown me the Great Indian Bustard that stands a little over three feet tall. However, "bustard" or "bastard" was one and the same for now.

"See; I knew I was right to call you one. You're a bastard vulture. You drank up all my chocolate."

Now, this was not going to plan. My recent lofty display of natural science in enlightening her on the meaning of bastard had backfired. I was being called a vulture. Better to change the subject. I pointed to the thunder-box. "How are you goin' to go 'fer a bog if your feet are killing you?"

"None of your damn business."

"Show me."

"No."

"I know what will happen. You'll wet your bed and make a stink."

"Get out."

"Okay. Come on, Skip. Send for me when you get another mug of chocolate."

"Get out you swine. You knew the thorns were there all along."

I was a spiteful little larrikin!

Their holidays came to an end all too soon and I was back on my own with Skipper but I gave Chrissy my "gold bee" as a parting present to ease the painful memory of "three-cornered-jacks" in her feet!

Will said it made the papers of the era that in ten days, HRH and his coterie of "fearless shikaris" managed to kill off thirty-nine tigers, eighteen rhino and four bears. They were shot from the safety of an elephant's back and the animals had no chance considering they were herded and trapped in a circle of elephants; literally like sitting ducks. Carrie, ever the "royalist" had been impressed with the historic occasion years earlier but Will was not! Trophy hunting in his book was a senseless act.

25
Will's close shave!

THOUGH I COULDN'T READ Will's favourite National Geographic I always blamed it for giving him some bad ideas at least as far as I was concerned and one of them was that I was forbidden to handle the rifle. Will had it locked away in a wooden case and placed in a locked wardrobe along with his twelve bore. I longed to handle the rifle and even shoot it. Will knew this because of my constant pestering. So I was warned not just with the usual threat of "a clip behind the ear" but with the far more dire threat of "getting a hiding!" That sounded awfully bad. I was sure National Geographic was to blame for this utterly unfair ruling of Will! The rifle was totally out of bounds to me!

It's in times like these that I felt life was unfair!

I was dying to have a shot at the bugouts, not to mention squirrels and the noisy black crows as there were heaps of them in the trees.

The gun in question was Will's .22 bolt action rifle and one day I struck gold, or at least I thought so at first because he invited me to help him clean and oil the gun. This was a major breakthrough and so while I sort of helped him clean the gun, he went about patiently explaining everything about the parts and working of the weapon.

Will knew how to get my attention and that was to call me "Soldier." Not Tom or Son, but Soldier. It was a sort of self-image builder because of all the things I wanted to be when I grew up, and that ambition could change daily, to be a soldier stayed on top of my list. Of course, when he was cross with me he would say "Mister" and that's when alarm bells would sound in my mischievous mind.

When he opened the gun case there it was folded snugly in a recessed section, the three crossed rifle BSA trademark engraved on the beautiful wooden stock.

"This model rifle is folded Soldier and do you know why?" I duly shook my head "because it can be easily carried around in a bag or case, unlike the old blunderbuss." Will always called his single barrel twelve bore a blunderbuss. I stopped fidgeting and hopping around with excitement. I had to be a soldier and give him my total attention.

First off, Will showed me that to fold the weapon the spring-loaded catch behind the bolt had to be slid back and went on to explain that for safety reasons if the gun was cocked the release button could not be even accidentally depressed because the cocking piece covered it. Now, none of this made the slightest sense to me but I still listened intently as the lesson continued. After locking the hinged barrel section to the stock with a "snap" he went on to patiently explain the function of every bit of the weapon. From the foresight, the wind-up adjustable "V" notched rear sight, the two cleverly recessed leaf aperture sights located behind the rear sights, that snapped up for fifty and one hundred yard sighting, the breech-block mechanism of the bolt action, the safety latch and the trigger. Again; nothing of this made any sense to me at the time but somehow I knew that it was an important lesson.

Finally, Will extracted two cartridges from different boxes and once more explained they were rim-fire rounds; not that I understood that either; and the difference between a "short" and a "long" round. "They don't look too big do they Soldier when compared to the blunderbuss cartridge but don't be fooled by its size. These are high-velocity rounds and aside from being very accurate are also very, very dangerous, even up-to a mile distance if you don't take good care when shooting. If the bullet hits a fellow in a vital part as the head, you will kill or seriously injure him. So when shooting this rifle, never think it's like the BB. This is a deadly weapon and must be used with care. Understand?"

I did understand the need for respecting a weapon; after all, it could kill somebody. Will had once told me the story of an Anglican priest who was thoroughly annoyed by the crows cawing in a tree just outside the window of his rectory. He took his .22 rifle and fired a few rounds at the pesky crows. One bullet ricocheted off a branch and seriously injured a man walking along the street.

After showing me how to clean the barrel with the "pull-through" and oiling it with the special gun oil, Will finally allowed me to heft and shoulder the rifle and this is when I discovered even the meagre five lbs was really too heavy and big for me. Of course, being a larrikin, I was only half convinced!

Wow, was I awe-struck with all this knowledge and later on made sure I gave my garbled version of the rifle lesson to impress Carrie! I don't think she was impressed but she listened patiently. She didn't particularly like guns I concluded because she told me she had never used one.

Despite all this enlightenment, the gun was still strictly off-limits for me but I did stop blaming National Geographic! I would have to settle to continue using my catapult. But that night I had wondrous dreams of knocking over heaps of bugouts, crows and squirrels with the rifle!

And that was the wisdom of Will. Young as I was he knew that I would be using a gun one day and had given me a lesson on how to respect and use a dangerous weapon. His knowledge ranged from guns to bugouts and everything else in-between!

Now, Will had what was called a railway section under his control. The section could vary in distance but it was around seventy-five miles of rail track on average and there would be small way-side railway stations along the way and as always there would be a village nearby the station. To inspect his section Will had a trolley that ran on the rails and each day he would inspect a pre-determined portion of his section.

A rail push trolley was a slatted wooden platform with a front bench with a back to it that sat in metal sockets on the trolley platform. Just beside the bench was the hand break and in the middle, behind the bench was a flag pole with a red flag. At the back of the platform there were two metal supports at an angle with a wooden handle threaded to the top. These handles served to push the trolley and each was positioned to be directly over the rail track. The frame had four U-shaped bush bearings bolted to the undercarriage of the platform and these went over the slotted axels of the trolley wheels and secured by a "cotter pins". Four trolley-men took turns in pairs to push the trolley.

The amazing thing was that these remarkably dexterous trolley-men were barefoot and would push and run along the top of barely two inches of the steel rail line. They would build up the momentum of speed and expertly hop on to sit on the pushing handle. As it slowed down, they would expertly drop one foot onto the track, slide on for a foot or two to gauge the forward momentum and then the second foot would drop onto the track in a running motion. Pushing up an incline was a slog and done at a walking pace until the top of the incline, then they'd do a quick run to build up the exhilarating speed down the slope after which came a welcome rest for the trolley-men. That's when I felt the trolley travelled lightning fast! Or so I described it to Carrie.

Will would pull-up and let Skipper down so he could run beside the trolley. That was his time of fun. He would bark with unrestrained joy and even tear ahead of the trolley alongside the track and bound along the sleepers between the rails. But when Will stopped to do an inspection Skip had to be back on the trolley and the head trolley man would hang onto his collar. Skip was always obedient, except for one failing. He could not resist chasing cow's or donkeys and grabbing onto their tail and hanging on. The animal would be kicking out angrily with its hind legs to dislodge Skip but he would somehow dodge the dangerous hoof.

Will would have his railway issue diary on his lap making notes of what needed fixing on the track; that is, jobs such as packing joints, hammering in loose dog-spikes, replacing wooden sleepers, realigning, lifting or even replacing rail-lengths and so on. When it came to deep cuttings, bridges and tunnels Will would alight and do a thorough inspection with a torch and long-handled hammer. The location of all these jobs was identified by the marking on the telegraph poles. Every "gang-beat" had its sub-section of gang-men under the control of a supervisor or Maestri.

When we came to where a gang was working on a job, Will would pull-up and first check the Maestri's muster book and this is when all hell would break loose on occasion, and I discovered why Will went wild. These men had a habit of cheating. In short, they would have fifteen names marked as present and working while only fourteen blokes would be present. This meant that the Maestri on pay-day would pocket or share the wage of the absentee. Will would fly into a rage while the Maestri would try to come up with a lame excuse that the missing man had gone to the toilet or gone home sick; all to no avail as Will knew all the stories. Will would sometimes jump off his seat and belabour the fast retreating Maestri or grab the flag-pole and chase the fellow down the track. When things settled down and the poor fellow came grovelling back with a "thousand apologies", Will would issue him with a stern warning then note in his workbook the jobs to be done on the "beat".

One day this went completely awry. Will was chasing the Maestri in a rage when Skip got loose. He bounded off the trolley, overtook Will in a flash and grabbed onto the Maestri's long shirttail trailing behind. It looked too much like a cow's tail and he couldn't resist it. Will, for once was flummoxed as he didn't know whether to belabour the Maestri or Skipper for being disobedient. In the end, Skip got a clip behind the ears and ordered back to the trolley while the miscreant was lucky to escape with a dressing down and a stern warning.

Despite this show of uncontrollable rage and sometimes walloping the Maestri he gave me a lesson I never forgot. "You know Tom, wallop or demote the scoundrel but never sack him. If you sack him his wife and children might starve."

The little larrikin never forgot this lesson!

Now while there were plenty of trees beside the railway line, for some reason that even National Geographic never explained was that lots of big plump doves would perch in long rows on the telegraph wires that ran alongside the rail track. It seemed to me to be their favourite pastime. This was the highlight of my going on line. Will would pull-up, load the small-bore rifle, carefully aim and whack. With a brief puff of feather-down, a dove would drop, all this without getting off his trolley seat. Will was a crack shot and I swore when I got hold of the rifle one day I would be one too!

What fascinated me was that when there was a clean hit the other doves would just look down at their dead mate with curiosity and might just find they would suffer the same fate with the next shot! Sometimes the dove would only be wounded, in which case the head trolley-man whose duty it was to collect the doves would screw its neck to put it out of its misery. It never made me feel squeamish as Will had long ago told me that an animal must never suffer from a bad shot, even if you have to track it down and put it out of its misery.

"Even a wounded tiger or leopard Dad?"

"Yes Thomas, even a wounded tiger or leopard; though you shouldn't shoot one in the first place. Always shoot for the pot, not for a trophy."

Lesson number two. I shivered at the prospect of following up a wounded leopard.

There were certain locations where the railway crossed a main "grand trunk" road. Here there would be a gateman who swung the gates closed or open. The train always got preference. On the roadway, there would be long lines of huge ancient native banyan or wild fig-trees on either side that shaded the road for the weary traveller. But the fig-trees were also popular when in fruit season with the big plump wild green pigeons. So off would come the trolley and with the head trolley-man in tow, we would set-off for a green pigeon hunt. While there were heaps of them in the huge banyan trees, they blended in well with the thick foliage. "Look out carefully for their bright yellow feet Tom, that's the only way you can spot 'em."

We would return with a bag-full and for sure that night we'd have dove and pigeon pepper grill. Absolutely delicious!

A "shandy" in India was not a blend of lemonade and beer but a street market at a particular village located usually near a railway station. Shandy day's had a native calendar of centuries as to where and when they would be held for just one day and the head trolley-man always knew this information. People from all over the local countryside would come to the shandy to sell, or barter, or buy fresh fruit, veggies, meat that was usually goat's meat, chooks, pots and pans, clothes and all sorts of necessary items for daily living. Most of the stuff would be laid out on the ground but some sat in carts on wheels like the sweet-meats stall, which of course was my favourite. It was always a colourful affair, busy and cheerfully noisy.

Will would pull up at the railway Station Master's office to clear the line of his presence and off we would go to the shandy with the head trolley man in tow. With practised eyes, he would examine the fare at every stall.

Now, whenever Will picked up a chook at home he would always hold it under its tummy between its legs but not so at the shandy, the poor things were usually transported hanging head down on both ends of a bamboo by their legs. Gosh, if I did a head-stand for that long the blood would stay permanently in my head!

The presence of a Sahib, complete with pith hat dressed in Military outfit (it was the war years and Will was an Officer in the army) khaki shorts and shirt, khaki long socks and polished brown boots, was always an attraction for the local vendors who mistakenly had the belief they could diddle him on the price of something or other. Not so; Will knew everything about everything from rifles to bugouts to a fair price of a chicken, pound of meat or tomatoes! It was fun to watch him ask the price of something and of course get an inflated quote. He would make a counteroffer and that was usually refused by the vendor. So Will would pretend to walk off and that's when all the yelling, pleading and cajoling would start. After a fair bit of palaver the price would be settled. The funny part of this was that this palaver would take place at every purchase he made.

"Never pay what they ask, Tom" he warned, "if you do they would think you a fool and not respect you. Bargaining is part of their culture and a way of life."

That was lesson number three or four or whatever for the day which was wasted on me since I never had any money!

The routine of going on line would continue until at some predetermined railway station, right on time a freight or passenger train would arrive with our lunch cooked and sent by a man all the way from home in a long green "tiffin-carrier" which was insulated with cork to keep the contents hot. Once more, the logistics of this operation I never really understood but it was routine. After lunch, off we would go again until Will had completed the inspection of the predetermined sub-section, usually around late in the afternoon. The trolley would be dismantled to be loaded into the "brake-van" of freight, local or passenger train that would arrive to take us back home and I would get to ride on the engine.

The engine ride was the finale to a perfect day.

And what a day and what yarns to tell Carrie? I tried to convince her when Will was not around that I'd shot a few doves and pigeons.

"You're telling fibs again Tom. Now go and have a bath before dinner. You are full of grease and coal dust and put your filthy clothes in the soiled linen box as well while you are at it!"

A bath, really? What a total let-down to the excitement of the day.

I still hated baths. It's in times like these that I felt life was unfair!

Going on line on a trolley had its hazards as well. Trains would enter or leave a section between stations only after a safety process of a "line-block or line-clear", but not so an inspection trolley. Will's only safety was to issue a "caution order" to the station master before entering the section. It was his responsibility to insert it into the pouch of the "line-clear hoop" for trains entering the section behind him and also to signal the caution-order to the station master ahead in case a train was cleared for an entry that was coming from the opposite direction.

The engine crew would keep a sharp look-out for the trolley when there was clear visibility ahead and sound the warning code on the steam whistle if there were blind curves and steep cuttings. The drill was to stop the trolley at a safe distance as soon as a train was approaching and the trolley-men would manually haul the trolley off the track and out of harm's way.

Trains were a lot faster than the poor old push trolley; however when the head honcho or District Engineer inspected Will's section a motorised rail trolley was used. It was powered by a small two-speed air-cooled motor and connected by a belt to the rear axle. The throttle and brake controls were handled by Will like the captain of a ship does. It could go at a good clip up and down dale but certainly not as fast as a steam engine. So the drill of taking it off the track was the same, by four hefty trolley-men on the whistle warning approach of a train.

One fine day his District Engineer, a Mr Iyengar, better known as MOS was doing his inspection of Will's section. Will said he was a very clever engineer who he liked and respected for being a straight shooter. Anyway, toward the end of the day, they were running behind time as they headed toward the end of Will's section. MOS was keen to make the next station ahead to catch the train now coming behind, his reason being he was scheduled to play a tennis match at his HQ.

Now, Will was fully aware of the express train that was coming up their backsides because he had been briefed by the last station master when he was issuing the caution-order.

The section they were travelling through had a lot of curves and deep "cuttings" this means the rail track was cut into the hills with almost vertical walls on either side. Sounds are deceptive in such conditions but Will could gauge from experience that the engine's warning whistle meant the express train wasn't too far behind. He told MOS they had to stop and take the motorised trolley off for safety. However, they didn't have far to go and he pressed Will to keep going because he was desperate to catch that blinking train.

Will told his head trolley-man to stand up facing backward, keep a sharp ear and eye out for the express coming behind to give him a warning and to keep his crew ready to take the trolley off the track in a hurry.

The little two-stroke engine was going flat chat but trying to out-run a steam train, let alone an express was akin to dicing with the devil. Will could hear the warning steam whistle getting closer and closer. The dreaded tap on his shoulder and a shouted warning came from his head trolley-man that the express was right up their Khyber Pass.

Will cut the trolley engine, threw out the anchors and they all bailed off as the trolley-men worked desperately to get the trolley off the track to safety. They almost did except for a corner portion that still infringed near to the track as they dived for cover. Will had bailed off to the right while MOS jumped off on the left where the trolley had been offloaded. The big black behemoth started screeching to a halt with sparks flying off the rails as the driving wheels were arrested when the engine driver threw out the anchors. But a speeding train cannot stop on a dime and the steel "cow-catcher" section of the engine just clipped the infringing trolley and flicked it like a toy against the cutting sides smashing it almost to smithereens.

All hell broke loose of course and would you believe it? Except for minor cuts and bruises, the only one to sustain an injury was MOS. A shard of wood from the trolley smashed into his thigh and blood poured out of the wound as he lay beside the track. It wasn't a serious injury and the Guard of the train, which was always equipped with a basic first aid box, fished out some cotton wool iodine and bandages and Will patched up the leg of MOS.

Well, he caught his train all right and had to be helped into his special District Engineer's carriage that was pre-attached to the end of the express in the expectation of picking him up at the station ahead. MOS asked Will to travel with him in his carriage the short trip to the station. The train was restarted after a long delay of course. Will knew he was in serious trouble and the least punishment he could expect after the rigmarole of an enquiry was to be demoted and a pay-cut to boot.

MOS shook his hand on parting and apologised. "Don't worry Mr Loots I will attend to this matter."

He did.

Will went through the enquiry conducted by the AEC but never tried to blame MOS. It was pointless anyway because according to the rules, it was his responsibility to pull up when he considered it necessary and could not be over-ruled by a superior. He was the Ship's Captain so to speak. He simply stated that it was an error of judgement because of the difficult terrain.

Will never heard anything after the enquiry. The incident had been quashed!

Carrie ruled I couldn't write to Hansie about Will's "narrow shave with death."

Sometime later Granny Loots, unbeknown to Will, wrote a handwritten one-paragraph letter addressed rather vaguely to "The Senior Engineer, M&SM Railways, Madras." In it, she explained she was getting very old and would he please post her youngest son William Loots somewhere close to Bangalore Cant on compassionate grounds.

Now, on the vast railway network, there were "choice" postings and "dog" postings and Will never expected to get a desirable one. So he was duly amazed and surprised when he received a series of plum postings for the rest of his career. Somehow, Granny Loots's letter appears to have travelled the labyrinth of railway bureaucracy to reach the right person.

By that time the Chief Engineer of M&SM Railways was none other than MOS!

Perhaps Granny Loots's letter had an unintended effect on Will's career opportunities as well since he had now come back to the attention of MOS. Will received three opportunities for a promotion to Assistant Engineer and he turned all three down. That would be a surprise to most: "Why would you turn down a promotion?" Will's justification was simple. In his opinion, an Assistant Engineer was a "sham" position created by the Brits during the Raj as a reward for long service for someone who wasn't good enough to make the responsible grade of a District Engineer. As a consequence, in his opinion, an Assistant Engineer did nothing but shuffle papers and report on his subordinates. Will reckoned reporting on your colleagues was not his cup of tea.

Carrie was sorely disappointed for she fancied the title of "Assistant Engineer" but try as she might Will was firm. "I'm not going to sit at a desk all day twiddling my thumbs and shuffling papers Carrie."

And that was Will's way.

26
Tom's Cobra panic!

LIKE THE ENGINEERS MEETINGS IN GOA the "perks" the Brits left behind continued to flourish in Will's time. A large portion of his rail section ran through dense forest on either side of the rail track. Even though it was tiger country Will said he had never actually seen one while going on line inspection but one morning he did come across a signalman perched high up on the signal and frantically waving them down.

The fellow had gone to the signal early one morning as usual to extinguish and trim the wicks of the "outer signal" kerosene lamp and as he got there a tiger appeared. Fortunately, he was close enough to scramble up the ladder to safety. Now, the Station Master noted his long absence and figured out what had happened but no one was game enough to go and rescue the poor fellow so he had been sitting there for the last three hours. The tiger, of course, had long gone. He climbed down with relief and got a ride on Will's trolley back to the station.

The thick forest also made for an ideal camping spot to set out for shikar and much earlier some enterprising Brit chose an idyllic way-side railway station and had an entire 1st class carriage (with its wheels removed) hoisted onto a high plinth made up of railway sleeper's right alongside the forest and near the local "way-side" railway station. The carriage was fitted out with running water from the overhead railway tank, a kitchen and pantry area and of course each compartment already had its "long-drop" toilet and the comfy sleeping berths.

Especially during the holidays when Hansie, Nanette and Chrissy were down the Loots family plus Jemima and Mahmood would climb onto Will's trolley and off we would go the fifteen or so miles to the camp-site and spend a week there and in-between their holidays we would spend a few nights there as well.

We would go for long leisurely walks more alongside the track than deep into the forest. Will would carry a twelve-bore for safety but never ever had to use it as we didn't go to shoot any game. My absolute and total confidence in Will was shaken when he casually said that he couldn't hit the side of a barn with a twelve-bore, but could shoot the head off a matchstick at fifteen paces with the rifle! So I'm glad we didn't come across a tiger.

Ever since the ferry episode in Goa I had been pestering Will to teach me to swim. The added pressure was that Hansie had learned to swim at school and Will said the had become a very good swimmer. There are no swimming pools in the bush but there was a huge big open well near the campsite that was lined with granite stonework and had stone steps jutting out from the sides about every eighteen inches that spiralled around the wall of the well. One fine day he seated me on his shoulders and down we went on the steps.

He sat me on a step waist high in the water and told me what we would do. By now my bravado and desire to learn to swim had completely vanished. I was in a blue funk and the cold water around my waist made me want to wee. I looked down into the beautiful clear water and the blinking steps seemed to go on forever and ever, which meant it was deep as heck. Yep, it looked awfully deep and by now I was in a purple funk! And bobbing around in the water away from us were heaps of huge, big, fat green and yellow frogs. They didn't scare me but the deepwater did.

"Lie flat on your belly and hold onto my hand's Soldier and start kicking out. When you get the hang of that, I'll let go of your hands and I want you to do a dog's paddle. Now I'll show you what you have to do." Will swam out a bit and showed me what he meant by kicking as well as the dog's paddle. By now my teeth were chattering and I couldn't help but do a piddle in the well. I never said a word though and hoped the frogs didn't mind.

"All right Soldier. Ready?"

He'd used the magic word again. I had to act like a soldier. After a bit of trashing around and a rest and giving it another go and a bit of a rest, I started to get the hang of how to use my legs for kicking and enjoy myself. I fancied I was swimming by now despite Will holding my fingertips.

Carrie was watching from the top looking a bit concerned but she did have the trusty Kodak Brownie ready to photograph the epic event!

After a bit more practice while Will still held my hands, he suddenly let go of my fingers and I now had to trash away with my arms trying to keep my head above water, but every so often I would go under ... and there was his hand pushing me back up each time as I came up spluttering. This sinking and trashing went on forever in my fear-ridden mind though it was probably less than fifteen seconds; when suddenly my head stayed above water and I was paddling like a little frog and not sinking.

"Dear Hansie, I learned to swim in the same deep well with frogs. Your loving brother. Tom".

The censor firmly ruled out earlier attempts of: "I dived into the well"... "I can swim better than you"

There were lots of fireflies flying around at home and they were easy to catch. I reckoned they were friendly insects and even Carrie seemed not to be scared of them. Hansie, Nanette, Chrissy and I often caught them and put them in a jam bottle or under our mosquito nets to watch their tiny winking glow as we fell asleep.

Carrie once called them little fairies with lanterns and Will cleared his throat. As I said, he believed little children must be told the correct thing; that is, except when he was unsettled by my embarrassing questions!

But here in the forest fire-flies were thick as thieves. One night from our carriage window I saw a tree covered with fire-flies and the whole area surrounding the tree glowed in the dark of the night. We watched this incredible phenomenon for ages before we retired for the night; something that's hard to forget. I had never seen that before or since.

Yes, the pristine forest held its secrets and surprises and saved them for those who ventured within.

There was a marshy wetlands area not too far from the carriage that Will said was a good hunting spot for wild ducks at certain times of the year. One evening as we stopped by the marsh we saw another amazing sight. There was a smallish tree that overhung the marsh and hanging from its branches was a heap of green snakes. Will reckoned there were about fifty of them just hanging there doing nothing, like a conclave of green pointed-nose cardinals! I was dead keen to get closer and have a shot with my catapult, pretty sure I wouldn't miss but Will stopped me and Carrie was ready to bolt back to the carriage.

We went back the next evening and they had disappeared into the marsh. I had never seen that before or since either.

As you can imagine I was sure that I heard tigers roaring and leopards coughing during the night.

"Did you hear them last night, Dad? They were right outside the carriage I promise!"

Will would smile knowingly each morning as if he'd heard them as well. I imagine he didn't want to ruin my imaginings.

"Did they scare you Thomas?"

"Nah, Dad. I'm not a funk!" Very prophetic words indeed!

Now I certainly knew Will was no funk. The Loots family were travelling somewhere by train and we were all fast asleep with only the dim compartment night light on and the train going at a hundred miles an hour when Will heard a suspicious sound from the compartment door. The window shutter on the door had been latched partially open to allow the breeze in. From his bottom bunk, he quietly watched the hand of a man come through and unlatch the window and push it up. The bloke was standing on the steps of the carriage door outside while hanging onto the handle with the other arm. He then undid the bottom latch of the door but couldn't reach the top latch; so he started to haul himself through the window. That was the moment Will was waiting for and all hell broke loose.

He pounced on the bloke, grabbed him under his armpit's, dragged him through the window and body-slammed him face down onto the hard wooden floor. For good measure, Will hammered his foot into his back that drove the wind out of his lungs with a whoosh, and for insurance, he slammed his foot into the back of his head.

Will was swearing at him like a trooper in the process, but his swearing didn't drown the yelps of pain coming from the bloke on the floor. He was curled up in a ball by now, the front of his face and nose a bleeding mess and he was crying for mercy. By now all of us had come wide awake.

The bloke turned out to be a uniformed soldier who had gone AWOL. Will further scared him out of his wits when he showed him the Officers "pips" on the epaulettes of his own uniform. He made the bloke fish out his Army Pay Book from his pocket and took possession of it. After a time Will put him in the bathroom and calmly told him if he wanted to jump out the window he was free to do so. Jump he would have to because there were certainly no steps to stand on. The three steps were only at the doorway and jumping out of a train at night while it was clickety clacking along at full pelt would have been suicide for sure.

Carrie wanted Will to pull the emergency chain and hand the bloke over to the train Guard but he wouldn't have a bar of it. He knew that stopping the train meant long delays to restart it and a hell of a lot of inconvenience to the other passengers. The bloke was handed over to the Railway Police at the next major stop and we all went back to sleep or at least tried to. Hansie was the first to do so because I heard his teeth grinding. Nanette climbed into Carrie's berth for mutual comfort and I played with my toes for ages with excitement before I dropped off.

Now if it was me that had been the hero the whole world would have been told about it, but not Will.

"Poor devil" he would say "I wonder what drove him to such desperation!"

And that was Will's way!

Our camping carriage compartment near the jungle had six berths; three lower berths that served as comfortable lounges during the day and sleeping berths at night and three upper bunk berths as well. Despite my howling protests, Carrie would not let me sleep on the top berth. She was sure I would fall out of it at night and do myself a severe injury. Sleeping on the upper berth seemed more fun but I was confined to the lower berth at night and had to cope with the imaginary tigers and leopards that prowled around just outside my window every night.

One night I was startled by the reality of what I was sure were tigers and leopards growling around just below and right outside my window. I shot bolt upright and whispered or yelled loudly; "Dad, Dad, the tigers and leopards are here!"With that warning, I shot out of my lower berth and was off like a bride's nightie into the upper bunk! Will got out of his bed and picking me up plonked me right back down on the lower berth.

"It's all right Thomas. There's nothing to be scared about. They're only wild boar rooting around outside." And of course wild pigs they were probably rooting around for the kitchen scraps that Jemima had turfed out that night.

Obviously, this little larrikin was a funk!

Will's work complex not only had the store with my friend Ghokhale in charge, there was also a blacksmith's and carpentry shop as well. There was also a large yard for storing old sleepers, metal fish plates, dog spikes, lengths of the old rail line and all sorts of old permanent way stuff including a broken-down old push trolley.

Will had placed the yard out of bounds to me because the grass would grow up high during the monsoon and dry up in the summer leaving a thick dry thatch. It was also a source of zillions of bugouts and small lizards and probably field rats.

Of course, being placed definitely out of bounds and the threat of a clip behind the ears as a minimum punishment only increased my craving to explore this wonderful playground full of odds and sods and see what I could come up with. After a few furtive sorties, I got the brilliant idea to build a railway line and put the trolley on it; but figured that I had to wait for Will to go on the monthly pay special so he would be away for at least a couple of days. The opportunity came as I knew it would and so I was into the forbidden playground early one morning.

My friend Ghokhale must have spotted me because he turned up. "Hello Tom Baba, you are being out very early? Are you planning to fight the Germans here today?"

I was relieved. Obviously, Will had not passed the word that it was out of bounds. "Hello, Ghokhale. No, I'm not going to bomb the Germs Ghokhale, I'm going to build a railway line."

"Oh? That is very good."

"I'm going to build the line all the way to Bangalore Cant to my granny's house." Bangalore Cant was a mere five hundred or so miles away!

"But there is already a rail line to Bangalore Tom Baba?"

"But not to my granny's house Ghokhale."

"Ah. Yes, yes I see. You are making a very good point." My friend would always find a way to humour me.

"I'm going to build the line and put that trolley on it so I can go on my own to see her."

"How you will build the line?"

I was stumped and fidgeted, but only for a minute. "There are stacks of old sleepers and plenty of old rail lines. I'll use them. I'll start over there Ghokhale and keep going." I went over to a piece of ground to show him my starting point. My good friend scratched his grey head for a time on this major enterprise of mine.

"I am thinking Tom Baba you will be needing some help?"

"Why?" I wasn't keen on anybody else snooping around lest they told Will!

"I am thinking sleepers and rail lengths are very heavy Tom Baba."

Gosh. I'd never thought about that. I conceded gracefully that I needed help. So for the rest of the morning my friend Ghokhale somehow wangled a few men from time to time to place some old sleepers in a neat row at the required distances and place two old rail lengths complete with securing fish plates at either end. All of this activity was duly supervised closely by me.

As a precaution, two short rail lengths were placed across the track at either end so the trolley would not run off the rails. Actually, that was Ghokale's idea; after consulting with me! My dream had come true in less than a day and to see the old trolley sitting on the track gave me a thrill. Under the watchful eye of my friend, I did a few practice runs up and down the thirty-foot or so rail length.

I was quickly cured of trying to walk on the top of the railway line while pushing the trolley as Ghokhale was shaking his head vigorously and clicking his tongue with disapproval. "No, no, Tom Baba, you must not be trying to do that. You will cause yourself an injury and what will the Bada Sahib say to me?"

I didn't want my friend Ghokhale to get a clip behind the ear so I pushed while stepping on the sleepers.

I had a quick lunch with Carrie and as soon as she had retired for her afternoon siesta I bolted back to my railway line. I don't know how many times I enjoyed myself pushing it up and down, perching on the handles like the trolley-men did and sitting on the rickety seat to issue instructions to imaginary gang Maestri's.

I could have spent endless hours pushing from one end, which was our home railway station to the other end which was Granny's railway station and back again; until at one station change-over I suddenly felt a horrible pain in my foot.

I'm sure the howl I let out carried all the way to Granny Loots in Bangalore Cant! It definitely carried to my friend Ghokhale, to the Head Babu and all of Will's office staff, the carpenter, the blacksmith and many Will's workers nearby. All hell broke loose as my howling increased and everyone dropped what they were doing to investigate what had happened to Chota Baba; who they found sitting in the dirt and hanging onto his right foot while howling his head off.

I can but imagine what happened and can only relate what I was told much later.

I was immediately carried home screaming blue murder with pain and put to bed. Carrie must have been terrified. My red and swollen foot was washed and plastered with sulpha powder and bandaged by Mahmood who could not find any puncture marks. But that was no guarantee I hadn't been bitten by a krait. Meanwhile, just in case a snake catcher was sent for and a whole workforce of men started to carefully restack the sleepers nearby. A snake catcher was a low caste Hindu who was expert at catching snakes and an invaluable presence in Indian country life. And sure as there are no fleas on a dead cat, a cobra was found amongst the sleeper stack that was duly caught and bagged by the snake catcher and with that, there was the immediate conclusion that Chota Baba had been bitten by the venomous cobra. The Village Munsiff who had despatched the snake-catcher now wisely made the decision not to inform Carrie about this or I'm sure she would have passed out!

A cobra's venom can cause death in about thirty to sixty minutes depending on the severity of the strike and condition of its victim. Once again, without Carrie's knowledge, a whole new series of measures started to be put into motion that was well known and practiced on the railway at that time.

While there is never going to be a rational, or scientific, or Will's National Geographic explanation for it; there was a humble station master at a lonely wayside station who had the extraordinary "powers" to cure cobra and venomous snake bites from afar. His name was "Pambu Narsaiah". He was so well known during the British Raj era that an unwritten rule stated that when a snake bite victim was hurriedly brought to any railway station, day or night, the priority on the control telephone line was immediately given from that point to Pambu Narsaiah's station.

Narasaih would take the call, ask a few pertinent questions about how much time had elapsed since the bite, which part of the body the victim had been bitten, instruct that the cobra be released unharmed if it had been caught and then repair to a tree nearby. There, he would tear a strip of cloth from the dhoti he'd be wearing and tie it to a branch of the tree while repeating certain mantras. Once finished, he would return to the telephone line which would be kept open and tell the Station Master at the other end that the patient would recover.

So while Chota Baba was still howling and bringing the house down this practice was carried out. Pambu Narsaiah duly went through the procedure, performed his rites, came back to the phone and told his counterpart at our railway station that I had not been bitten by the cobra but probably stung by a scorpion and unfortunately, his powers did not extend to scorpions! He did advise however that a poultice of certain herbal leaves be applied and a small pinch of "kacoramu" powder be placed on my tongue.

Everybody was relieved at this good news, except me. I was in bloody agony for hours and the whole village around could hear my howls of pain.

Surely, Pambu Narsaiah could have learned how to cure a blinking scorpion sting?

The Village Munsiff who was there all along was a tower of strength to poor Carrie. He promptly sent for the Village Shaman to carry out his "mantra" and apply the medication as per Pambu Narsaiah instruction and maybe the pain was less or my lungs tired, but I stopped howling.

Meanwhile, Will had been advised about what had happened and handed over charge of the Pay Special to his assistant then caught a train home. Will was not angry with me and never spoke about wearing shoes; the furrows on his forehead were just a little deeper. I was quarantined for ages and Mahmood wouldn't let me out of his sight.

"Dear Hansie, A cobra bit me and I nearly died. Your loving brother. Tom".

The now much-relieved censor disallowed it. The cobra was replaced with "scorpion sting" and nothing about nearly dying.

It's times like these that I thought life was terribly unfair to little scoundrels who ran around in bare feet and wouldn't put his shoes on!

Believe what you will and phew phew what you don't but you would have had to live in the bush of the subcontinent to experience the mysteries of life in the raw. The following is an account by Patrick Hugh Stevenage a Brit who was working on the M&SM Railway during the British Raj, regarding Pambu Narasiah.

"I was at this time working as assistant station master of the joint Madras and Southern Mahratta Railway and the Nizam's railway station at Bezwada, where the broad-gauge and metre-gauge services met. One morning, in the control office, I was surprised by the arrival of a bullock cart, from which a young man was carried unconscious and laid on the ground outside the office. He had been bitten by a cobra. Distraught relatives dashed in the office and demanded that a message be passed over the control telephone line to 'Pambu' Narasiah, one of our stationmasters down the line. In a few minutes, he answered the phone and asked only two questions. When had the man been bitten, and was he conscious or unconscious? There was a short pause and then he reassured the anxious people that they were not to worry and that the lad would live. About 20 minutes later the victim of the snakebite, which often proved to be fatal, got up, asked for a drink of water, climbed back into the cart and set off for home.

This experience would have been absolutely astonishing, had I not heard about Pambu Narasiah and his strange powers from a friend many years earlier. "Pambu" in Tamil means snake, and Narasiah was a railway employee who had the "power" to cure snakebite from a distance, as I had indeed witnessed. He had refused promotion many times, asking only to remain on the mainline where he could be reached by the quick railway telephone system."

Reproduced from: "Last Children of the Raj". By Patrick Hugh Stevenage

27
Tom learns about the birds & the bees!

GRANNY LOOTS LETTER to the Chief Engineer of Railways worked a treat as Will received a plum posting as Inspector of Buildings to Perambur Madras, the Headquarters of the M&SM Railway. This being the HQ there was an enormous infrastructure of large railway workshops and buildings to be maintained.

Perambur was a suburb of Madras that was a few hours journey by rail to Bangy.

For the first time, we had a very nice bungalow with terraced roofing, electricity and running water. Thunder boxes, however, remained as a reminder that Will was not quite up the totem pole but rather his position was just a segue to a different job.

While our bungalow was not within the very large railway colony, after a long time there were Anglo Indian friends to make and lots of them. While Hansie and Nanette continued as boarders I started to attend the local Railway Primary School and discovered that Robert, a classmate, lived just across a small lake at the side of us. We became fast friends and so did Carrie and Will with Robert's parents Mallee and Mable.

There was an enormous European and Anglo Indian Railway Institute just to the side of us with a large polished wood dance floor, a stage, live dance bands (that Carrie was chuffed about), billiard and snooker tables and an Anglican Church. The Railway Institute was the focal point of all celebrations especially over Christmas and Carrie made-up for all the years of Christmas in the bush by going to every blinking dance.

Christmas, whether it was in the "big smoke" or the bush was a time for family. Between Christmas and New Year there was always too much eating and in some homes, too much drinking. Nevertheless, visiting for lunch or dinner was a daily affair over the festive period which prompted one more of Will's sayings: "Thank the Lord He had only one son!" The implied reference was that if He'd had two or three sons then we would be celebrating Christmas three times a year and over-indulging!

Will was not a humourist.

And if we needed reminding about Church, the common wall in front of our bungalow belonged to a Baptist church. I figured this proximity of churches might at least keep me out of that Pentecosting eternal frying pan; but as happenstance would have it its proximity placed me awfully close to that everlasting frying pan!

I even became a choir boy at the Anglican Church along with my new friend Robert. He always disputed it but I don't believe Rob could sing a blinking note though he indignantly claimed otherwise. But in a large choir, and it was a large choir he got away with it. Rob had another contagious habit, he would doze off during the long sermons, and I, sitting alongside would soon follow suit. Uncle Mallee who also sang in the choir and did have a good voice always sat just behind us and would give us a dig every so often to keep us awake. I suspect that our antics just might have given the congregation the spiritual lift that was absent from a boring sermon!

Since my testicles were still at their zenith I sang soprano! And there was another jolly good incentive to become a choir boy; the princely sum of four annas a month pocket money to do so.

Mallee had two passions; homing pigeons and motorcycles. While he could not interest Will in the flying "poop machines" he captured Will's imagination on a two-wheeled machine and that was to own a motorcycle. Besides, that Will had special access to petrol coupons because of his job and that proved another reason as it was still the post-war years and petrol was strictly rationed.

It wasn't long before Mallee rolled-up on a beautiful BSA 3.5 HP with a polished black frame and chrome plated petrol tank with green panels. The hand gears were mounted on the petrol tank and a pillion seat had already been fitted by the previous owner; a British Army Officer returning to England. Will was sold and bought it immediately on Mallee's recommendation because he had already checked it out mechanically. It was a beauty.

Off we all went to the lush green railway maidān up the street that was used for playing hockey, cricket and soccer. Will had never ridden a motorbike and did a few practice rounds under Mallee's tutelage. After a few rounds, he reckoned he had the hang of it. He was so confident about his skills he asked Carrie to hop on. She had never been on a motorbike either and wasn't sure how to hang on sitting side-saddle on the pillion. Will let the clutch out a little too quickly and she ended up on her bottom on the grass, while Will, still unaware he had lost his prized passenger roared off and even started a conversation asking her what she thought about the motorbike! He didn't wake up to this fiasco until he did a turn to come back and could see Carrie standing where he left from.

A worried Mallee helped her up, but after dusting herself off and rubbing her sore bottom for a bit she burst out laughing and we all joined in. The look on Will's face was worth a winning lottery ticket. He was so mortified and embarrassed he never said a word. I kept a straight face for fear of copping a clip behind the ears.

Perhaps because of this debacle or his desire for his children to also enjoy the motorbike he asked Mallee to find a matching side-car and fit it up. He did. For about four years we enjoyed this grand possession, especially me because Will would sit me on the petrol tank and we would ride around the maidān while I made a great show of hanging on to the handle-bars as if I was doing the riding.

About fourteen miles away was a backwater called Ennore which was a popular picnic area. We often went there and waded in the shallow waters when Hansie, Nanette and Chrissy came on holidays. How we all managed to get there I can't remember. Maybe Will made a couple of trips because it wasn't that far and the traffic those days was non-existent though there were plenty of pot-holes in the roads to be avoided.

"Old man Bailey", up the street from us loved his fishing and had proper fishing rods. The three of us would go off to Ennore, hire a small fishing rowing boat and fish all day. Will thought it was a mug's game and I agreed because aside from tiddlers I caught nothing. Secondly, it was so much easier to buy fresh fish from the local fishermen. Most often we returned with their netted catch rather than what we'd caught with rod and line, but if old man Bailey caught a fish he would be so chuffed the size of it grew with each passing mile on our return! Crikey, the entertainment each way was old man Bailey himself who was comfortably sitting in the sprung side-car, constantly yelling out to dad: "Watch out, Will … pot-holes, pot-holes!" He never stopped this pot-hole hollering every blinking trip!

As I now actually had friends to play with I was rarely if ever involved in some mischief or other and subject to a clip behind the ears. Yet, despite this, I got the worst hiding of my life from Will around this time.

Friends of ours were visiting Carrie one afternoon, Bruce and Muriel Evans. Uncle Bruce was the morning broadcaster on the Armed Forces Radio Station still active in Madras. Anyway, I couldn't get my way with something or other that I wanted from her, threw a huge tantrum and called her a very, very local language bad word I had recently picked up and refused to apologise. Everyone present was horrified and it was a category four, rather than category three offence. She reported me to Will when he got home and I have never seen him so angry in all my years of tomfoolery.

Will had an innate appreciation of justice. Mischief and pranks in a high-spirited boy needed to be kept in check but not eradicated; conversely, disrespect and vile abuse of my mother, no matter how innocent I was of its actual meaning had to be nipped in the bud. I ended up with a well-deserved walloping on my be-hind and made to apologise to Carrie, then sent to bed still howling. As I've said before my mother was a complete softie and no matter how well deserved the punishment she couldn't bear to see any of her children cry without giving them a cuddle to ease their feelings.

She was probably ready to come to her "Teddy-bears" aid when I heard Will tell her she was not to go to my room and give me a cuddle to ease my grief! "Leave him alone, Carrie. Thomas has got to learn the meaning of respect and what's right and wrong. He must never believe he can be abusive toward you if he can't get his way."

Carrie's "Teddy-bear" sobbed himself to sleep! Nevertheless, I quickly recovered and the hiding never had any effect on my sense of liveliness.

Unbeknown to Carrie and Will, the Baptist Church opposite us was to advance my knowledge of the "birds and bees" by light-years in one short afternoon.

Robert and I were playing marbles in our front yard one quiet afternoon when we heard voices from over the wall at the back of the church. Robert listened in to the conversation because he could understand the local language and told me to go quickly and get something to stand on so we could peep over the wall. Keen to investigate I sped in and brought a wooden chair, set it next to the wall and Rob climbed up and cautiously peeked over. He'd barely had time for that when he ducked his head back down again with a funny look on his face while his eyes were as big as saucers; accentuated by the fact that he had very grey eyes!

"What's up, Robbie?" I whispered.

"Ssssh!"

A tense conversation between Rob and myself ensued in whispers. "The Sexton of the church is having a go at a girl."

"What do you mean having a go?"

"You know. He's got her blinking clothes up to her waist and he's shagging her."

"What's shagging?" I must have still had a blank look on my face while Robbie was looking at me in either astonishment or disbelief. He had the benefit of a city upbringing while I was a country bumpkin! I got to hopping around anxious to have a look. "Heck Rob, what's going on?" I was concerned that the action that so engrossed him might end before I had a chance to see.

"Here Tom climb up on the chair and have a look for yourself."

Two pairs of very astonished eyes were riveted on the Sexton and the girl for the rest of their tryst as the sexton heaved away with ecclesiastical zeal. I received a first-hand explicit demonstration of what shagging meant as I had never heard the word before. I reckon I didn't take a breath throughout their frenzied panting and heaving and came awfully close to self-inflicted asphyxiation!

At long last, I learned what the rooster and Skip had been up-to. Now I'm not sure if rigour mortis set in a certain part of my anatomy, but I suspect the Sexton's frolicking in the grass may just have dropped my left testicle a sixteenth of an inch lower which meant I could now sing "alto" in the church choir!

Alas, all good things must come to an end and even though I kept a daily vigil on Rob's advice. Much to our regret, the Baptist sexton failed to further advance our education. On the other hand for the first time, I had about three and a half years of proper schooling.

I didn't dare write about the Sexton to Hansie and neither did I boast about it when he came on his holiday. For once I kept my mouth shut.

Will's tenure in Madras was over and he was concerned that I was growing up without steady schooling. He chose a transfer back across the peninsula of India, once more to the Western line in Maharashtra to a "plum" station that had proper private schools.

Meanwhile the larrikin's questionable "knowledge" had been advanced considerably in the city!

28
Tom's startling vow of marriage!

BEING MOVED AROUND THE COUNTRY was quite normal for us and packing up and moving a lot of furniture was always taken care of by Will's workmen. Carrie just supervised the process. A complete wagon, would you believe, was allocated by the railways to send our stuff ahead. A wagon was also allocated for the cow or buffalo we had. So duly stacked with feed and water, Mahmood would accompany the animal safely to our new destination.

Will promptly enrolled me in a Catholic private school.

Belgaum was a large township, which was also the Army Regimental HQ of the Mahratta Light Infantry. There were military parades and stuff like that which we attended.

I was definitely going to be a soldier again!

It was not a railway colony as such but we did have some branches of the railway people stationed there. It had an ancient Anglican garrison church of Gothic architecture, built way back when. St. Mary's didn't have a choir or my newly acquired testicle lowered "alto" might have come in handy!

Belgaum wasn't quite the bush but we returned to large, rambling old homes without the luxuries of Perambur, so we were back to Petromax lights and Hurricane lanterns. But Will did keep the Shortwave AC/DC radio he'd bought in Madras and with his amazing ingenuity rigged-up a system from railway carriage batteries to power it. Aside from the Short Wave Armed Services radio station from Colombo Ceylon, he was able to tune into Radio Australia transmitted from Darwin. The programmes appeared to be beamed to Asia and the sub-continent, and so, with a very tall aerial mounted on our roof, we got reasonable reception. Every evening we would gather around the radio to listen to the kookaburra call sign.

Gosh, we were fascinated with the kookaburra laugh and blow me down it wasn't long before Hansie could imitate it to a tee when he came on holidays.

Christmas Dances at the military mess got in full swing over the festive period. Hansie and I were not taken to the shows not that we were interested in dancing anyway. Now, Hansie was not one for mischief but he did have one weakness and that was the flicks. When Will, Carrie and the girls were off to the dance the two of us would bunk to the late show movie. We never got caught by Will.

There might have been a respite for tomfoolery while in Perambur but I was not cured of it.

Will had made a pair of "Bowie" knives in his workshop some time ago and they were beauties. They had heavy blades made from carriage spring steel and were a good ten or twelve inches long, complete with deer horn handles with brass handle guards and butt.

We had a half dozen turkey hens and one male gobbler that roamed around freely in the back-yard. The gobbler reckoned he owned the backyard and if anyone came near the hens, he would carry-on like he was going to attack and peck one to death. He would "gobble" loudly, raise himself with all his ear and neck flaps purple-red, and scrape the tips of his wings on the ground. Even Jemima who had to make the trip across the yard to the bungalow cursed him loudly every time for she seemed to be one of his favourite targets.

Hansie and I were mucking around in our back yard shaping bamboo for a bow and arrows and minding our own business when the idiot of a gobbler decided to put on an act just behind me; for the life of me I don't know why I did it but I took a swipe at his neck with the Bowie and knocked his block clean off. The blood from the severed neck was going everywhere and Hansie stared at me in disbelief. I handed him the knife and was bolting when blinking Jemima came out of the kitchen. What she saw was Hansie holding the Bowie and the beheaded bird still flapping in the dust.

When Will got home he didn't even ask Hansie if he did it he just collared me and I got more than one clip behind the ear.

The clips behind the ear didn't stop the roasting of the turkey for dinner though. I was stubborn and refused to eat it despite the angry glares from Will. "If he's stubborn he deserves to starve," Will declared, still angry with me and if it wasn't for Carrie I would have gone hungry. Hansie had no such qualms and tucked into the turkey roast like a starving bushranger

While on one of the school holidays Hansie went down with a terrible illness called enteric. He was admitted into the Military Hospital and despite the best of treatment available, he was not responding to it. He was gravely ill and Carrie spent all day at the hospital and Will stayed with him at night. For a change, I was on my best behaviour as there was a crisis in the family. Honestly, I've never seen Will so worried as the furrows on his forehead deepened. For the first time, he was not in control and Hansie was damn near death. Finally, the Doctors told Will that a new antibiotic drug was available only on the "black market" in Bombay called Penicillin, that it was very expensive but was the only thing that could save him. Perks and comforts we had but not money as even senior PWI's were poorly paid. Will didn't hesitate; he sold the motorbike and sent Sorab, a Parsee friend to Bombay to get it. I could imagine his heartbreak to part with his BSA motorbike and sidecar but Hansie's life was at stake. Penicillin saved Hansie. He was late getting back to school and missed a whole term as he had to recover, and recover he did along with his appetite!

We had not been very long in Belgaum when I heard Will confide to Carrie that our next-door neighbour was a Mr George Phillips and that he was the Signal's Inspector.

"I think George is a bit of an eccentric Carrie. He keeps cobras as pets." My ears started flapping like an African elephant's as I eavesdropped on their conversation.

"What? For heaven's sake is he mad?"

"I wouldn't say that as he keeps snakes as a hobby with good reason. He milks them of their venom and supplies it to the government anti-venom lab which is a good thing. Now I don't know if it's a yarn or true but he once took one on inspection in his line-box and caused quite a stir in the compartment when he calmly took it out and displayed it."

"Then he is mad. What does his wife think about his stupid hobby?"

"George is a confirmed bachelor, my dear."

"Well, no wonder. Anyway, neighbour or no neighbour William we're not going to have anything to do with him."

This conversation might have scared the wits out of Carrie and placed Mr Phillips out of bounds socially but I was as excited as heck. For over three years in Perambur, I had been starved of anything resembling the bush, now I was living in a town with no bush *per se* around the house and right next door was snakes; and blinking cobras at that!

I wasted no time and when all was quiet that afternoon I snuck around to the neighbour's back door. He had a manservant who told me Sahib was reading. He must have heard me as I heard him call out to come on in. His bungalow was just like ours and I looked around carefully to see if his blinking cobras were knocking around the room because I suddenly realised I had no shoes on either.

"My name's Tom and I live next door, Mr Phil."

"Yes, I know. You must be Will's son. Well, sit down Tom. What can I do for you?"

"Can I see your cobras?" I thought he threw me a slightly puzzled look for a time.

"Aren't you scared of snake's young fellow?"

"Yep, Mr Phil, I was once almost bitten by one." This was a huge lie, but it did get his interest and I told him my hugely embellished story and about Pambu Narashia. He nodded wisely but a story or no story he pinned me to the floor with his next question.

"Have you told your mother and father you want to see the snakes?"

Gosh, Mr Phil was not daft at all. He was just like Will with his questions. The name of Mr Phil, instead of Mr Phillips just sort of stuck in my head but he didn't seem to mind. I had spied on him many a time in his backyard dressed in his pith hat and khaki clothes but this was the first time I'd seen him up close. He had long hair, combed back and it was mostly grey. I reckoned he was a lot older than Will but bigger. He was a big bloke with a quiet voice.

"No Mr Phil. If I do my Mum won't let me come here. She's really, really scared of snakes."

He was lost in thought for quite some time and I thought he was going to tell me to buzz off, but he didn't.

"Well, at least you're honest, but it's a good idea young fellow to wear shoes and long pants when you are around snakes. Got any long pants?"

I shook my head. "Never mind, but just remember that for the future okay?"

He had not one but three cobras. He showed me their specially made wooden boxes, each about the size of a large tin trunk but higher with mesh panel sides. Inside, I could see dirt, leaf litter and thick dried tree branch pieces at the bottom. He told me he fed them on eggs, tiny young chickens, rats and such like. He told me that cobras spit out the eggshells after digesting the contents. He went on to tell me they couldn't see very well, especially at night and I was surprised when he told me they had no hearing but could sense the slightest movement and vibrations from its prey through its tongue.

"Cobras are shy Thomas and will not bite unless cornered, threatened, or accidentally stamped on. The best way to avoid being bitten, even by accident, especially at night is to have a stout stick and bang it on the ground as you go along. Most snakes will quickly move off as they feel the vibrations from their bellies. Incidentally, Tom, you can eat a cooked snake but make sure you take the head off first well below the poison glands in its neck."

"Have you eaten them, Mr Phil? What do they taste like?"

"No young fellow; I've never been that hungry!"

He laughed softly. I liked Mr Phil. I was never allowed to take his snakes out of the box and he never allowed me to handle one unless he had "milked" it and then he would hold its head anyway while I let it curl around my arm. I discovered that they were awfully strong.

"Have you ever been bitten, Mr Phil?"

"If you work around snakes Tom you must expect to be bitten some time. I'm pretty careful as you can see and when a cobra has been kept in captivity, looked after and fed well; they sort of get used to being handled and are not as aggressive as a wild one. Mind you they get a bit cranky when I'm milking their venom."

One day he showed me how he milked them of their venom by gently moving his fingers on the glands in its neck, but made sure not to "drain" their venom sacs "dry" and told me that they could refill their venom sacs pretty quickly that way. He milked them about once a week or once in two weeks. The special venom milking bottles were supplied by the government hospital and stored in a big Thermos with ice; ready for immediate delivery back to them with the venom.

I was never afraid of snakes before but after my time with Mr Phil, I learnt how to handle one and had quite a few experiences with them over the years. Strangely, Hansie who got on so well with any creature or animal on

God's earth didn't like snakes. He once came across one near the chook pen. He promptly fetched his hockey stick and finished it off. Will was quite pleased with this because it was a Russel's viper and very nasty fellow's they are. Russel's Vipers were "bad-tempered" as confirmed by Mr Phil, and will strike at any animal or person that ventures near them and so was responsible for a lot of deaths in the villages.

Belgaum was Uncle Bob's HQ for the forest industry. Will and Carrie were happy because they now had the regular company of Uncle Bob and Aunty Olive. We would head off together to the forest Dak Bungalow in Dandeli for a few days every so often. Dandeli had a variety of wildlife and birds; elephants, tigers, black panthers, crocs in the Kalanadi river, snakes a-plenty and the unpredictable wild buffalo that had strange "white socks" on its four legs. This was definitely Sabu's territory. I had lost my fear of leopards and I could now pronounce the word elephant correctly rather than "efelant"! I think Carrie was relieved.

The huge four-bedroom Dak bungalows were all alike with high ceilings and timber louvered windows and doors to allow the air in. They were built by the Brits all over India at strategic locations to house the visiting officials on their periodic inspection rounds. They were fully furnished including the traditional "thunderbox" in the bathroom, though it was wise to take one's personal linen. Each was permanently manned by a "kansama" or cook and a couple of helper's.

From Circus and Tent Cinema "chair" days Carrie still held the firm belief that the beds in the Dak bungalows were all infested with bugs. She was probably right for the first time. Since Mahmood couldn't come poor Will had to turn every mattress over and give them a massive soak with the Flit Pump as she didn't trust the Dak Bungalow servants to do it. If the Flit didn't kill the bugs, to be sure the blinking smell did as thanks to Carrie's insistence our rooms reeked like the Flit factory!

However powerful Flit was in killing bugs it didn't kill my desire to shoot and Dandeli was the perfect chance but Will would only let me do some target practice under his supervision. "You're not ready for it son, maybe next year." And that was that.

I was off the censor's list by now and writing my own PC's but not as frequently as in the past. Writing without Carrie's supervision was another major alteration in my life but the habit of writing at least "partial" fibs appears not to have declined!

"Dear Hansie, I hope you are Okay. We have been making super trips to Dandeli with Uncle Bob. Saw plenty of deer and buff but no elephants or panthers. I'm now shooting the rifle so when you next come on your holidays we'll go hunting with a proper rifle. Your loving brother, Tom".

Aunty Olive had two girls and a big gap to a baby boy called John. I became attached to the elder girl Ingrid because she was a bit of a tom-boy like Chrissy and willing to run around barefoot against the rules! Inge was as pretty as a rose about to blush, though to be honest, I didn't quite notice her that way at the time. We were simply playmates with Hansie and Nanette away at boarding school and whenever the two families got together and that was quite often.

One warm Sunday, the Kerr family came to lunch and as usual, after a big meal the small talk became desultory and in a semi-comatose state they would all doze off in their chairs. I skedaddled to play outside and was soon joined by Inge. We took off our shoes and played hide and seek for a time until I got another idea. We had milking cows and a big haystack sat at the side of our house.

"Let's climb up the haystack and slide down the side, Inge."

Inge was game and I went up first and showed her how. She came sliding down on her backside and the front of her dress fluttered up to her waist in the process. She didn't have on any "chuddies" or knickers and I got an eyeful of the "second face of Eve". My eyeballs might just have challenged the extremity of my face as had Robbie's that fateful afternoon over the Baptist church wall!

Now, granted that my carnal knowledge had been substantially advanced thanks to Robert and the Baptist sexton; but the actual image, shape, or form of that specific part of the female anatomy had remained a mystery to me; and here it was in all its glory and wonder captured in the "Kodak" of my puny brain.

Unchartered territory this may well be, but I suspect my testosterone levels advanced rapidly to a higher age group and for the first time I experienced an unquestionable effect in a certain part of my anatomy normally associated with a militaristic function termed; "Attention!"

"Let's do it again, Inge." And up we went and down we came as each time I gathered additional eyefuls until she stopped and defiantly faced me with hands-on-hips.

"Gosh, how often do I have to come sliding down this haystack?"

"Once more Inge, just one more time okay?"

"No, I'm tired of the game."

I conceded reluctantly, confident the view was now imprinted on my mind. She was sweaty by now and pieces of hay were stuck all over her, her clothes and in her short curls.

"Do you think I can get a glass of water Tom?"

I could certainly have done with one myself as my mouth and throat were parched and it wasn't from the ambient temperature. "Yep, but first let's get the hay pieces off us or Mum will kill me if we bring them into the house."

I found hay pieces stick like stubborn limpets to sweaty smooth skin. I was on my knees and taking my time picking off the little pieces, starting at her feet and working upward with cunning intention; and that was to have a real close-up peek at the female anatomy. Having achieved my objective and gawking in wonder; for the life of me the words tumbled out of my blinking mouth; "Inge, you're not wearing any chuddies you know."

Inge grabbed my left ear, twisted it and hauled me up. "So that's what you were staring at Tom Loots?"

I must have looked as guilty as a Nun squatting in a cabbage patch and tried to bluff my way out of it. "Looking at what?"

"You made me slide down that haystack a dozen times to gawk at my wee-wee didn't you?"

"Uh, ah, well just a bit I guess."

"More than a little bit I think, so don't you tell fibs!"

I might have grinned sheepishly but what came next wiped the grin clean off my dial and replaced it with astonishment. Ingrid stood on tip-toe and gave me a mushy kiss right on my lips followed by a gobsmacking declaration:"I'm going to marry you when we grow up Tom Loots."

She took my hand now with some assertion of ownership as we walked to the back door. My very agreeable and slightly trancelike feeling continued and then suddenly evaporated with the sudden thought that Inge might tell her mother that I had been eyeballing her "wee-wee". It sent a shiver down my spine and had a definite adverse effect on that part of my anatomy as I hurriedly disengaged my hand.

"Aren't you coming in Tom?"

"Not just now Inge, I better tell Mahmood to tidy up the haystack before dad sees it or he'll kill me."

Now a trick I had learnt long ago in times of peril from angry parents was to delay the confrontation for as long as possible and allow their temper to sort of cool down a bit.

Well, I had to go in some time and I figured since Will and Bob hadn't come looking for me with the twelve-bore shotgun, it was safe. Rather than all of them being out for the count as we had earlier left them they were now wide awake and laughing loudly. I sauntered in as if nothing had happened but would have dived head-first into a sewer for safety if one had been handy at what Aunt Olive said: "Hello Tom, what have the two of you been up to? Ingrid has just announced she is going to marry you when you both grow up so I've told Carrie and Will that they better save you for her."

They all laughed again except Will as I looked at him in some trepidation. He wasn't laughing with the others but had that atypical thoughtful look on his face and the furrows on his brow had deepened. The word GUILT must have been flashing like neon lights on my brow with no furrows to hide it! I looked around hurriedly but couldn't spot the sewer cover.

The little larrikin knew a lot more about the "second face of Eve" than he should have at his age!

Hansie and Nanette arrived for their Christmas holidays with Christine. Gosh, I suddenly realised how much they had grown. Hansie, now a teenager was as tall as a beanpole and Nanette and Christine were nearing their teens.

About this time Hansie's school Principal a Mr Andersen came to Belgaum for a Methodist convention and stayed with us for about a week. Carrie prettied up our room for him and Hansie and I would sleep on camp cots on the back veranda. Will cautioned me to be on my best behaviour and even Hansie said: "Don't be coming up with any daft ideas Scoot. Remember Andy's my school Principal."

He was a big tall man, with twinkling blue eyes behind his glasses. "Has he skelped you Hansie?"

"No, Scoot, you get the cane if you step out of line in school. But he's fair and rarely uses it. There's another master we call Mitchy and he's a bit free with the swagger stick."

"Gosh, I better watch my step then eh?" Hansie gave me his crooked smile, more of disbelief than conviction.

But we rarely saw Mr Andy, except for breakfast and sometimes for dinner as he spent most of his time at the conference. He was up and about early one morning in the backyard though and he asked me if I knew how to milk our cow. I certainly did as Mahmood had thought me long ago how to tease the udders first with warm water and draw the milk. At milking time the next morning, Mahmood tethered its hind legs, gave it a bucket of "chunis", a mix of rice and wheat bran with molasses and with the due flair of a natural show-off I gave Mr Andersen a demonstration. If I could read the expression on Hansie's dial I'm sure he was hoping I wouldn't spray his Principle's polished shoes with a squirt of milk from the cow's teat! I didn't tell Hansie I was tempted to do just that as he was standing very close peering into the milk bucket.

A lovely Parsee family lived in a great white mansion a couple of streets behind us. In it lived "old man" Dalal who had the shape, size and looks of a walrus and a deep voice to go with it. He had two son's living with him, the eldest son Sorab who was a bachelor and had been in the Merchant Marine, and the second son Cawas and his very sweet wife, Parvin.

Cawas was an Inspector in the police and perhaps due to the troubled times of the "Quit India" movement was armed with a service revolver. Gosh, how I loved watching him clean and oil it. If truth be known I was a gun nut, but always respectfully. They had a son Cyrus who was younger than me and we became fast friends.

Sorab was the mildest mannered and kindest person you could ever meet and had long been the travelling guardian for Hansie and Nanette. His mild exterior belied his incredible strength of character, obedience to his father and affection for the youngest of the three brothers, Pacie.

Sorab was a civilian unsung hero of WWII. Pacie, his youngest brother by a fair few years was an officer in the Indian Army and was listed as "missing in action or captured" by the Japanese in Burma during the war. At that time the Japanese were "posing" as saviours of the Indian and Burmese people from the wicked British imperialists and were trying to indoctrinate British India Army personnel who they had captured to turn against their comrades. They were placed in special POW Indoctrination Camps with the traitorous INA troops to "turn" them.

Despite the contents of the formal Military letter Sorab's father believed Pacie was still alive and had been imprisoned by the Japs. He gave him two gold sovereigns to use in emergency and ordered him to find Pacie and to get him out. The resourceful Sorab disguised himself as an Indian religious Sadhu and travelled up to the Northeast of India where the bitter fighting was taking place at Imphal on the border of India and Burma. He trekked across the war zones of Assam and Burma, a terrain largely covered by rugged mountains, forests and rivers with nothing but tracks to follow. In keeping with his disguise and with little money, he quite literally "begged" his way for weeks in Burma, always in constant danger of losing his life if exposed.

It would have been a trek of epic proportions in normal times but to do it in a war zone is beyond human comprehension. He found his way from POW Camp to POW Camp, in itself a mind-boggling mission until at last he found Pacie.

I cannot recall the specifics except that he somehow rescued his brother by using the gold sovereigns, dressed him as a Sadhu as well and got him safely out of Burma. That was easy as Pacie was malnourished, bearded, long-haired and gaunt. He said he would have looked like a Sadhu without the disguise!

Sorab would never say anything about his incredible odyssey, even though I asked him many times.

Things didn't go well with me at the Catholic school and I even heard Will tell Carrie it had been a mistake to put me in there. As we had moved around so much, my early schooling (despite Carrie's tuition) was always disrupted and I just couldn't keep up with the class. Most of the teachers were priests in brown cassocks; I reckon the blighters were brown clad sadists. Even though Will had told the Principal that I would probably need special attention and tuition, the only special attention I got was constant detention and whacks on the knuckles of my hands with the twelve-inch wooden line rule they all carried around. My knuckles used to be red and raw with the whacks and my studies went backwards. Others in the class also suffered the same fate and some would even cry, but I hated these priests so much I wouldn't cry to give them any satisfaction. I reckon the blighters whacked me harder!

About six months of this and Will reckoned enough was enough and mayhap Mr Andersen had suggested I be sent to join Hansie as a boarder. Will was never one to waste too much time once he came to a decision; Nanette was promptly withdrawn from her boarding school and sent as a day's scholar to a local girl's school. She was happy to come back home.

When Hansie and I returned to school Will would get a 1st Class return Guardian's pass for Uncle Sorab to escort us. I now stood on the platform about two in the morning with Will and Uncle Sorab. It was my turn to go as a boarder!

I was certainly suffering a large dose of the blues and close to tears. Carrie started that by wishing her "Teddy-bear" a teary farewell at home, Mahmood had worn a doleful expression all day and even blinking Jemima cried! I didn't think that Jemima would feel sorry to see me out of the way. Skip's ears were laid back all day for he had seen the packing of Hansie's and my tin trunk and kit bag. He knew well what it meant from previous years when Hansie and Nanette were leaving and knew they wouldn't be around the next day.

Hansie was quiet as usual as he sat on the station bench and I was unusually muted.

Suddenly, Will said to me; "Did you remember to say cheerio to Mr Phillips, Tom?" I shook my head glumly and in some shock. "Don't worry, I'll tell him you said to say cheerio I'm sure he'll miss your company."

And honestly, that was the innate understanding of Will. He knew all along about my regular clandestine visits next door to see the snakes and Mr Phil had probably told him anyway. He simply trusted him to take care of me and teach me something about wildlife; even dangerous creatures but he didn't want Carrie getting hysterical about it. Even though he knew all along he'd never said a word to me for all those months.

A tiny bit of excitement improved my mood as when the Poona Bangalore mail slowly pulled in and despite the ungodly hour of about two am the Bombay and Poona batch were wide awake in their carriage, cheering, calling out and carrying on.

Will wished Hansie telling him to keep an eye on his younger brother and then me as we shook hands. He did not believe in hugs. "Look after yourself Soldier and study hard, okay?"

I nodded. I couldn't voice my usual chirpy; "Yes Dad, promise".

I hugged Mahomed. He had been my friend, companion and protector for so long he was my family as well. The gentle giant and my protector of many years took his turban off and wiped his eyes. I almost started bawling.

As the train slowly pulled away I could hear the boisterous rendering of ...

"Wish me luck as you wave me goodbye
Cheerio, here I go, on my way
Wish me luck as you wave me goodbye
Not a tear, but a cheer, make it gay"

The little larrikin, at last, was going to find out the hard way what discipline really meant and I never went barefoot again much to Carrie's relief!

For about the next eight years, off and on, I was to be part of a train group and after being blooded in that first term, loved every minute of boarding school.

I was barely nine years old when I went off as a boarder and Belgaum was the last time in my life I was to spend with Carrie and Will, other than on brief holidays.

29
Hansie and the road roller!

COMING HOME FOR THE SCHOOL HOLIDAYS now with Hansie and Christine was just grand. The three of us had grown and while Chrissy never gave up the habit of promptly helping herself to my shorts and shirts she was not as feisty as before, though the tongue was scathing as ever and the pillow fights more violent! I guess we had all grown and in the process, I appeared to have lost my penchant for mischief which was replaced more with a spirit of mulish adventure.

I was now allowed to freely care for and use the small-bore rifle but only with the short round. I even started reading National Geographic despite my getting into trouble over the rotten egg and was now actually glad I didn't annihilate it with my Dinky Toys. The Dinky Toys had been put away somewhere and I hadn't touched them for years. I guess I had outgrown them.

There was a mighty old fort in Belgaum that was built by some warring King over seven hundred years earlier. It had a wide moat all around it and the massive stone walls were over thirty feet high. It covered a huge area and inside there were temples, mosques, shrines and a large building that was once the British Military garrison. The fort had another claim to fame that took place before we arrived in Belgaum; Mahatma Gandhi was imprisoned there by the Brits during the Independence movement. Anyway, Hansie and I never got tired of exploring this old place, climbing all over the ramparts and going through all the dungeons and old buildings. It reeked with history. There was so much to see and explore in Belgaum including "sacred sites".

Belgaum once had a big Parsee community with a fire temple and even their "Tower of Silence". The Parsee's don't bury their dead but take the body up to the top of the tower and leave the corpse there to be consumed by the vultures. Hansie and I had surveyed it out of interest and I got the urge to take a closer look up top. Fortunately, the stout entrance door was padlocked and I couldn't get in. Hansie had already threatened me with his leaving me and nicking off back home. I guess he had better sense and more respect for the dead than I had!

The fort was also a great spot to shoot feral pigeons and we usually came back with a decent bag. They all sat in rows facing outwards along ledges in the ramparts. The soft lateritic rock and trajectory also made for a safe shot with the rifle. The short rounds didn't make too much of a bang so as I dropped one they would all take off and circle a bit and return to their perches. To be honest it was pretty easy shooting. Hansie would never shoot one but it never stopped the blighter eating the pepper grilled pigeon either!

But one day this went a tad overboard. I shot a ground cuckoo and figured it would be good eating as well. Jemima was not too pleased with plucking and cooking this strange bird. She cooked it anyway but nobody would touch it and a glare from Will indicated that the two of us would have to finish it. It was tough as old boots and didn't taste like pigeon or dove at all. And yet, the black koel is pretty good eating! Poor Hansie who didn't like shooting anything had to live with my folly and Will's edict; "you shoot it, you eat it"!

One day Hansie and I headed off on our bikes for a shoot. He only really came to keep me company and for the bike ride. On the way, we passed by acres and acres of lush sugarcane crops coming into harvest. The canes were thick, juicy and heavy and I pulled-up and eyed them.

Hansie could read my thought's by now; "don't be getting any ideas Scoot and try something stupid. There are plenty of farmers still knocking around in the fields and you'll be caught for sure."

I'm not sure what they would have done with us for nicking their sugar-cane but I was damn sure what Will would do to me.

"Hansie, we'll come back tomorrow late in the evening with the Bowie when the farmers are not around and cut us some nice fat canes."

He didn't look too happy about my idea but that evening he came with me anyway. I guess he figured he couldn't let his little brother go it alone. The workers in the cane fields took their own sweet time knocking off and by the time they cleared off, it was near dusk. Hansie was not happy because we had a long ride back and it would be in the dark. But I was not going to give up. As soon as the coast was clear, in I went while Hansie stood KV with the bikes. I selected a half dozen big fat juicy canes and made quick work of it with the Bowie. Hansie had brought a rope and tied all six canes to the crossbar of his bicycle because he still reckoned it would be too big and heavy for his little brother.

And that was Hansie.

They were so big and long the canes stuck out a mile in front and at the back of his bicycle. Anyway, we slowly wended our way back in single file and by the time we reached the outskirts of town, it was pitch black and no street lights had been installed on the outskirts. Only the military cantonment and the railway station were electrified. Hansie wore glasses and whether it was that or the cane bundle being awkward and he wasn't paying attention, he ran smack into the back of a huge black steam-powered Road Roller parked on the side of the road. Crash … bang!

"How the heck did you manage to run into that blinking big thing Hansie?"

"Because I didn't see the dammed thing, that's why!"

Hansie was not one for talking much, never mind about swearing but the calamity caused him to go over the edge. Hansie was mad as a cut snake, still swearing under his breath at me and my "daft ideas". I wanted to laugh but somehow managed not to. I reckon he would have killed me this time for sure with a thick sugarcane stick instead of a table fork!

He had lost his glasses in the process, the cane had broken loose and it was a mess. Anyway, he picked himself up and dusted himself off as I groped around and found his glasses. They had not broken thank heavens because they'd landed amongst the cane fronds. Fortunately, his bike was not damaged either thanks to the fact that the cane was sticking out a mile in front.

"Let's leave the dashed cane here Scoot and head for home."

"What for, we've come this far?"

"What will we tell dad?"

Frankly, I hadn't even given that a thought. "Don't worry Hansie I'll tell dad the village Munsiff gave us the cane. Leave it to me." We somehow got the load retied and off we went once again. With all the kerfuffle we were late for dinner and Will listened while I spun a long yarn about being held up by the nice village Munsiff who gave us chai and the sugar cane sticks. He listened without interrupting my pipe-dottle, but he had the last word.

"Well, you better clean yourselves up and have your dinner. And Tom, you better not go back for any more sugarcane. Understand?"

I knew instantly he hadn't believed a word I said.

And that was Will's way!

For the next week Hansie and I, joined by Chrissy and Nanette sat contentedly on the bathroom doorstep, chewing and spitting out the sugarcane husk. We had strong teeth and somehow stolen cane tasted sweeter; because the supreme irony of it was that if we'd asked the farmers for the cane they would have happily given it to us!

We went to Dandeli with the Kerr family and I think Hansie fell in love with the forest life and industry. He would head off to the sawmills and spend hours watching the process or would go trekking on the logging trails. I went with him a couple of times and was scared as hell as we came across fresh elephant dung on the track, but nothing scared Hansie. Meanwhile, Aunty Olive still couldn't forget Inge's promise and teased me like heck. We had both grown up a tad and I reckon I was embarrassed and so was Inge as in the back of her mind would be the memory of my eye-balling a certain part of her anatomy. School discipline and the full busy daily regime of a boarder tended to knock any thoughts of the hidden face of eve out of one's head; though a tale was to follow.

We got to do one more caper before Hansie and I left for school. I had spotted a heap of peafowl in a village out of town and was keen to bag one. If the turkey was fine to eat I reckoned a peafowl would be even better.

Hansie was busy tinkering with the Crystal Radio set he had made complete with a "pricker" and a pair of old earphones. He could get radio broadcasts on it or sort of, but it worked anyway. I put the proposition of the peafowl to him. He was half listening as he kept tuning his Crystal set. I hung around like a bad smell in a lift so he finally gave up.

"Why?" he wanted to know.

"To eat the blinking thing, of course, what else?" I had no interest in eating it I just wanted to bag myself a peafowl.

"You can't eat peafowl Scoot."

"Yes, you can. Same as turkey they are. You ate that blinking big gobbler, didn't you? Anyhow it's a dashed side easier than trying to shoot twenty-five pigeons and wasting ammo for the same amount of meat. Just one round would do the trick."

I didn't have a clue what it tasted like of course but a fib was necessary. He looked at me with that atypical half-smile of his. I wonder what he was thinking. He pulled his mouth organ out of his pocket and the blighter started playing it. Now I could sing fine but couldn't play a blinking note. Hansie couldn't sing a note but blimey he could play the mouth organ, but at the moment he was giving me a hard time.

"Hansie, what about the blinking peafowl?" I yelled, interrupting him.

He tapped the mouth organ professionally on his thigh to get the spittle out I guess. "Like the sugar cane, I don't think it's a good idea Scoot."

Now the mention of the sugarcane caper meant Hansie hadn't forgotten my wonderful plans and ideas. But I was not going to give up. "Well, I'm going after one tomorrow morning. You can come or not come but I'm blinking going."

Hansie came with me. I knew he wouldn't let me go it alone. He said nothing all the way there. The village sat well off the road and there was reasonable but interspersed bush cover. He waited by the road with the bikes while I loaded the rifle and crept ever closer to the grazing peafowl. There was a long white Muslim shrine behind where they were grazing so I figured it was a safe shot. I was going to have to break one of Will's rules though and that was to go after a peahen because they were smaller and I figured their meat would be tender. I knew I had to get a chest shot to bowl one over. Easier said than done I have to admit; because even though I was well within range none of them would keep still. I sweated on one for a long time and while it was pecking away in the grass I fired.

All hell broke loose. Obviously, I didn't get a clean kill shot. It flew up in the air awkwardly letting out an ear-splitting "keee-yok, keee-yok, keee-yok", and before you could say Jack Robinson the whole blinking lot of them were flapping around and "keee-yoking" their heads off. A couple of village people came out, then a few others followed by even more as the wounded hen flapped around in pain while the rest had flown into the trees. I stood there in full sight like an idiot with the rifle, hoping to finish it off or to try and grab it and twist its neck when a lot of finger-pointing started. The small mob advanced rather threateningly while yelling and gesticulating. A few started throwing stones at me. I figured it was time to bolt and I was off quicker than a bride's nightie on her honeymoon!

Hansie glared at me but didn't say a word. I had broken two of Will's rules in one hit. I shot at a hen, not the male as he had thought me to and I didn't finish it off! Not a word was said when we got home.

Despite the boarding school discipline the larrikin hadn't abandoned his old ways entirely!

BEN LAFFRA

PART THREE
Tom's tales of boarding school!

BEN LAFFRA

30
Tom's dubious school record!

AFTER ALMOST SIX YEARS the 2nd WW was over; India had achieved independence after some 350 years of British rule yet the lifestyle and influence of the British Raj were to continue for several more years. Everyday life remained uncomplicated and simple. Transport was by steam train, horse-drawn tongas, jutkas and gharries, two-wheeled hand-pulled rickshaws and the ubiquitous bicycle. Communication was through letters and postcards. Emergency communication was transmitted via Morse code and telegrams while telephones were only for Government departments or large companies and a domestic rarity. The circus and the cinema was the most common form of public entertainment. Music was played on wind-up gramophones, scratchy vinyl records or provided by live bands. Domestic shortwave radios were a rarity. Contemporary serious reading material was only the local newspaper. Magazines were generally from the UK and US and were usually months old and widely circulated second or tenth hand until they fell to bits.

Though frowned upon and considered "trashy" the clandestine reading of smuggled in American comics were the staple compelling reading of children. They included heroes such as Dick Tracy, Captain Marvel, Batman and Robin, Wonder Woman, Tarzan, Jesse James, The Lone Ranger and a host more that are long forgotten. Oh, there was a second "forbidden fruit" for us and that was chewing or bubble-gum. Disgusting though it may appear, sharing it after it had been chewed on was not uncommon between boarding school mates. Since money was as scarce as rocking horse poo such niceties took second place and the gum was shared around. Well, none of us ever got sick or contracted some terrible disease from it.

Our knowledge of the world was minuscule by comparison to the youth of today. There was no TV, Computers, Internet Highway, Twitter or FaceBook. We may not have been sophisticated but we were certainly imaginative and physically and mentally strong.

The boarders were divided into three dormitories on the two upper floors. Young Dorm had a partition with meshed windows separating it from the Middle and Senior Dorm. That also separated me from Hansie since I was in the Young Dorm and he was in the Senior Dorm. We all had tall "lockers" in which to stash our gear and as was the practice the "newbies" always finished down at the very end.

Now, I thought that Epsom salts was an invention of Granny Loots and that Will had inherited the bad habit from her. I found out that was not true. The first official activity each term for every boarder on arrival was the "medical parade" conducted by Major MacDonald. Long before me, some wit had nicknamed him as "The Vet" and that stuck. The first medicine administered by the school nurse was a Hobson's choice of a big glass of Epsom salts or a dose of castor oil followed by a teaspoon of sugar as a reward. The theory being to "clean us out" of the holiday rubbish we had eaten and blinking clean us out it did!

Soon after the "poison" was swallowed you next marched into the Vet's room for the rather basic medical examination. He had a brisk staccato-like Army voice so his first command made me jump with fright: "Stick your tongue out ... Open your mouth wide"; as he shone a torch down your gob and throat. Then he'd yell ... "Now spread your hand's palm down, open your fingers"; followed by checks behind the knees, neck and ears checking for signs of ringworm or scabies. The final command would be: "Drop your pants and cough" and with the help from the tip of his swagger-stick, he closely examined your crown jewels. The final command would be a rough bellow of: "Right, off you go. NEXT!!"

On my first medical examination, I wondered if the Vet detected any unusual signs in my crown jewels as a consequence of my perceived advanced education administered by the Baptist sexton and my eyeballing of Inge's second face of eve! If he did, he never said anything.

Not long afterwards we would all be hanging on to our churning pain-riddled guts while queuing for a spot in the bog. That was my introduction to boarding life.

The infirmary was not all that bad a place mind you. A bout of the measles or mumps and one ended up in "isolation"; here to thoroughly enjoy watching one's mates troop to class while one generally bludged. But more importantly, "sick bay food" was extra special along with treats of burnt custard pudding, blancmange and jelly. Now, how good was that? We all tried desperately to get measles but only the lucky some would be successful!

I had to quickly adjust to the regime of boarding life. A boarder's day, as in the army is governed by a strict regimen of both time and activity. It had to be if there was to be a disciplined orderly routine each day. It was the job of the Duty Master (or DM) and the House Duty Captain (or DC) of the week to regulate this and keep things running smoothly.

The bugle Reveille from the Military school across the road or our 6.00 AM gong started the day off.

The first activity every weekday was physical training or PT on the main playing field for half an hour, conducted by our ex-Army Games Master, Captain Holmes. The blighter never gave you a second to catch your breath or pick your nose and had us doing a regime of exercises non-stop. Once completed we had to rush back and change into school uniform and shoes and head down for breakfast; so everything was done on the jog or run.

Before breakfast, we were all lined up in our respective "Houses" under the control of that week's DC. After this the DM would go down the lines, house by house to inspect our attire, polished shoes, stockings straight, hands for dirty or uncut fingernails, etc. If one was late to line-up or the DM spotted a shirt not properly tucked in, or socks sagging, or any one of a million things the DC would promptly order the poor miscreant to fall-out and run once around the quad; or twice if he happened to be a recidivist. I found out DC's had long memories. The quad run was a good two hundred yards and you risked your breakfast being pecked at by others at your table by the time you got in so I quickly learned never to infringe.

The boy's all sat at tables of six or eight on wooden chairs in our respective "Houses" and one's "table spot" was permanent for each year. You advanced "up" the tables as you gained seniority until you sat at the House Captain's table; and then finally to the Captain's chair if you made it to that august position. An un-written time-honoured strict code of practice governed this process. Gosh, I had to absorb all this quickly.

Gosh, shades of Chrissy's Pentecostal bug struck me the very first day. As soon as we trooped in for breakfast, lunch or dinner the DC would ring a small brass bell and we all had to stand to attention behind our chairs in silence as he pronounced the grace:

"For what we are about to receive oh Lord make us truly thankful. Amen"

Fortunately, unlike Chrissy's grace, it was short and delivered with the rapidity of a machine gun!

But every so often our patience and hunger were sorely tested. A school Principal who preceded our present Principal was one C N Weston, better known as "Wessy". He was revered in the school as he was the architect of much of the funds that both saved and expanded the school and grounds including a swimming pool and sports pavilion. His drive and energy in securing the funds from donors in the USA made him a legend and he still lived on the school premises in rooms attached to the Principals bungalow.

Wessy, however, had been in the 1st WW and had been in the thick of the fighting in the trenches of France and consequently suffered the after effect which at that time was called "shell shock". He was barely seen by us around the school grounds except on occasion. Every so often he would appear at dinner and would deliver a religious sermon all the way through and would have kept going all night if not "politely" stopped by the Duty Master.

School folklore had it that Wessy in his time as School Principal was a very strict disciplinarian and very free with the cane for the slightest misdemeanour. The story goes that on one occasion when the senior class had finished their final High School examination he asked the group if any one of them had been through his school career without a caning. One idiot proudly put his hand up, upon which Wessy produced the cane and gave him "three of the best". True or not I don't know, but I'm dashed glad he wasn't the Principal during my time or I would have had a permanent appointment with the blinking cane!

There was one redeeming feature of Wessy though and that was his love of sport. It didn't matter what it was, whether, at just practice or an interschool match, sunshine or rain Wessy would always be there on the sidelines to cheer us on.

Breakfast was a plate of porridge of ragi or sago (better known as "frogs-eggs"), two very thin slices of bread with a scrape of butter, a banana and coffee (better known as "dishwater"). The dishwater was always from the ubiquitous tin jug proudly sitting in the middle of the table. Once a week we got a hard-boiled egg as well. Depending on the "stratum" or layer the egg occupied in the huge cooking pot, it could be rock-hard-boiled like a hand grenade, half-boiled which was the prize, or almost raw, meaning as runny as somebody's nose with a bad cold!

Lunch consisted of a plate of rice with a vegetable curry, dhal (a lentil) and once again the ubiquitous tin jug proudly in the middle of the table, this time full of pepper water which one liberally added to one's plate. Like the dishwater, at breakfast, the pepper water was best described as "hot and wet".

Dinner would be a meat side dish or "SOS" which translated meant "same old stew" with two slices of bread and pudding, usually a rice pudding. For a few years, the SOS was made from army surplus canned Donald Cooks. The empty cans were piled up outside alongside the kitchen and sold for valuable scrap. Once, on a visit by Carrie, I was proudly showing her around the school and she spotted the mountain of cans. "What's that?" she asked, to which I laconically responded: "SOS Mum." Poor Mum, all she could say was; "Oh". I must confess grub was very Spartan and we all felt hungry all the time or maybe we were growing up fast.

The ringing of a big brass school bell "ordered" every activity which was done on the jog.

Post breakfast we all had to present ourselves in the games shed in our houses, now joined by the day scholars before trooping into morning Chapel after this the day's classes started.

Every weekday evening was spent in compulsory sport, usually playing the game of the season. The first term would be hockey and boxing, the second term cricket and swimming and the third term soccer and athletics. This regime was followed by all the "European" schools and so enabled the interschool matches.

After a quick wash-up and a change out of games clothes we all trooped into the study hall; the Young Dorm for half an hour and the Middle and Senior Dorms for one hour. Then, we'd go to dinner followed by a bit of free time. Finally, the last bell of the day would be sounded for us to troop to our dorms. We had a final job before the DC bellowed "Lights out!" and that was to vigorously polish our shoes ready for the next morning.

There was a strange practice in the Cantonment courtesy of the Metropolitan Electricity Department; the lights would flicker over the entire city at 9:00 PM and this was the signal for lights out, by which time we had to be in bed. I can tell you after the day's hectic activity my lights were out and the hard coir stuffed mattress and pillow just didn't matter! Testosterone was now being engaged far more productively and sadly the "second face of Eve" rapidly disappeared from my Kodak roll memory into the school routine and boisterous sport!

My first teacher, a Miss Aggie was a kindly soul used to handling youngsters just starting in a senior school. Unfortunately for me, on the very third morning of my first year in boarding school, she took ill and various teachers were required to fill in for the day.

Earlier, Hansie had given me a rundown on the various teachers in the school and warned me to watch out for a strict disciplinarian he called "Mitchy", a nick-name for Mitchell. "He always carries a military swagger stick with a silver knob on it Scoot and he'll wallop you on the bum if you step out of line; so watch out okay?"

As fate would have it Mitchy, normally a senior class master was filling in on a particular subject that day for Miss Aggie. He announced that before the period ended he would ask a series of questions on the subject we had covered and those who knew the answer were to put their hands up and he would choose each in turn to answer the question. Well, the process started and you'll never guess it. The very first question he put, this clever little dick, me, jumped up and answered it. He warned me not to do that again and to put my hand up instead or I'd get the stick. On the very second question, for the life of me, I bobbed up and answered it again like an idiot! It's hard to accept as true but I was stupid enough to do it a third time.

Mitchy had had enough. He called me up to the front of the class, bent me over and gave me three whacks with his swagger stick on my behind. Believe me, they were painful as hell and though I was damn near to tears I managed not to blubber. Still, I had a dashed hard time sitting down for a few days.

Hansie, however, had heard about it and in our once a week postcard home he wrote to Carrie and Will about the switching I got from Mitchy.

All hell broke loose because Will was duly incensed by the severity of the punishment and wrote a stern letter to the Principal. The outcome of this being; the Principal decided that in future only he would do the caning when warranted and none of the staff could do so.

I appear to have done a lot of blokes a favour in saving them from Mitchy's swagger stick!

The aftermath of this was I gained something of a reputation amongst the Junior Dorm boys for being a tough bloke. It had all happened on only my third day at school. I thus became the holder of a questionable school record that would never be equalled or beaten.

The young larrikin was on a steep and painful learning curve!

31
Tom cop's a walloping!

THERE WAS A STANDARD DRESS CODE listed by the school that all had to follow. White cotton shirts and grey drill shorts, black stockings and black Bata "naughty-boy" shoes or black Army "amjacks" or boots. Even the girls wore the Bata naughty-boy shoes as well so I guess "unisex" was already in vogue.

The red and blue striped Baldwin tie, blue monogrammed peaked cap, school blazer and white pants completed the dress code for major functions or whenever we left the school premises. In addition to the school blazer final year students also had to have a grey cotton or woollen suit; the ultimate mark of growing up.

All this was packed into a black tin trunk as there were no such things as suitcases, along with a blanket and listed bed linen. My name and BBHS was painted stylishly on the top of the box in Will's workshop.

A long sausage canvas khaki kit bag carried the general gear; black army surplus leather boots with metal studs called am-jacks, cricket boots, a pair of white canvas and always smelly rubber-soled runners called keds, a hockey stick, polish tins, brushes and other personal stuff.

Spit and polish was the order of the day and heaven help a boy whose shoes were not gleaming black every morning. "Blanco" would be softened-up with water and a rag and applied lovingly to the cricket boots and keds ready for sports.

And yes, we all had canvas haversacks, the 1940's equivalent of the modern backpack for our schoolbooks. Once again, they were army surplus khaki backpacks complete with brass buckles that had to be shined with "Brasso".

In the early years, our head-gear consisted of a khaki pith helmet, called a topi. It was not popular, but wear it we did to avoid getting the dreaded sunstroke. I cannot remember anyone suffering from sunstroke so the topi helmet must have worked a treat! Well, that was the logic! Fortunately, grey canvas floppy hats eventually replaced the hated topi.

Over the years at school, the ultimate accolade was to be selected as a House Captain. Then, a beautiful red tassel would be added to one's school cap a treasured piece of adornment. A white silk scarf draped around the blazer and neck completed the dress of a young strutting peacock! House Captains were selected each year only from the boarders.

I was determined to become a House Captain one day but paid scant respect to the standards required to become one, and that was to stay out of trouble!

The first yarn to greet all newcomers to the Young Dorm was: "Watch out for the skull-ghost with fiery eyes which will appear in the mesh window tonight." Folklore had it that the seniors would bring a skull from the science lab and hold a lighted candle in it and howl like wolves. It never happened of course but you'd keep a watchful eye on the partition window until sleep claimed you. And of course, the story was duly embellished and passed on the next batch of new entrants the following year.

We slept in our houses on the third floor. We had iron beds with iron slats and coir mattresses and pillows that were hard as stone! But no one had any trouble sleeping. We strung our mosquito nets from the overhead wires like "tepees" the quicker to take down at reveille, fold under the pillow and make our beds. Every bed had to be made-up tidy to a certain standard. Everyone had a school issue of a blue cotton counterpane with a red border, a handy cover-up of an unmade bed that I often took a chance on. The Dorm Master would do a snap inspection and if caught we would have to strip the bed down completely and start again. This meant setting you back in a strict regime of time for the day meaning you could miss out on the morning snack of a cup of "dishwater coffee" and two butter biscuits; which in turn meant you had to go to PT on an empty stomach while somebody else on your table knocked off your biscuits.

While the Young Dorm had a small urinal on the 2nd floor, the Middle and Senior Dorm boys had to troop down one flight to the bog in the cold of winter. I can tell you what I often did and I was not alone mind you; I'd climb up on the window sill and let-fly through the iron bars. A warm stream would fall twenty feet to the ground below. Getting caught meant the cane.

The young larrikin still took risks!

Another luxury for the Young Dorm was hot showers. Once one graduated to the Middle and Senior Dorms it was cold showers suspended from the roof in rows. One queued up in houses and about twenty of us would hit the showers at a time all yelling our war cries as we jumped in and out of the shower to soap ourselves. It was aptly termed "the cat's lick" and being nude while having our showers never ever bothered us at all. In any event, the cold water reduced any boasting of the size of one's "pecker" to a uniform size of a shrivelled prune!

The Cantonment did get cold in the winter months and I suspect this fact once more raised my testicles to the soprano. The music master decided otherwise and alto I was in the school choir.

In addition to the mainstream sports there always seemed to be a season for extra-curricular "mini-games" which we played during recess and on weekends especially Sunday's. The competition was serious, tempers would flare and the odd punch-up would happen suddenly. These included the games with strange colloquial terms such as; tops, mud cricket, crucifixion (which was a painful bruising game with a tennis ball), flying kites, marbles, kicking the can, doms (played with metal balls a bit like petanque) and a few more long-forgotten games. The forbidden sports which nevertheless one played clandestinely included gilly-dandu, and "cops and robbers". That last game was banned in case one got hit in the eye because it involved a strong rubber band stretched on a home-made wooden pistol with a trigger release that zinged the rubber band viciously through the air like a bullet. Getting caught meant a switching, but a good "man" keeping KV (an oft used code for "keep vigilant") in all such devilment kept us away from the DM's eagle eye.

Suffice it to say we were never bored and on the contrary, we didn't have enough hours in the day.

Most of us somehow would get a nickname or a shortened form of our name. Sometimes, the nickname referred to an abnormal feature of the boy. There was "Batlugs" because he had larger than normal ears; "Snotty" because his nose was always running; "Cockeye" for a squint; "Buckey" for protruding teeth; "Bumbu Kutchee" for a skinny bloke, "Tops" for a fellow with a big head and "Jasper" for no reason at all; or was it because he had tight kinky hair and a huge smile. Jasper was just a happy go lucky bloke liked by all. And sometimes, a rather unusual surname could be quite embarrassing. Coultrip ended up as "Colypee" (which meant chook poo) and a master called Woodcock was promptly nicknamed "Splinterdick". But there was one bloke whose surname was Dikshit. Yes, Dikshit was his name and it's not a typo. There was no need to give the poor bloke a nickname, he was born with it. I was known "unfortunately" as Loo, and that stuck so much a few of the teachers ended up calling me Loo.

Jason, better known as Jase was a tough nugget of a boy and probably a year or two too old to still be in the young dorm. He was an orphan and we had quite a few orphans as boarders in the school. Perhaps, for this reason, he had an attitude. In short, he was a bit of a bully and was ready to start a fight if you so much as blinking looked at him. He started to pick on me as I was one of the new boys on the block and gaining a reputation of sorts for being tough. My new chums warned me not to take him on as I would come off second best. Anyway, after a few scuffles between us, the Young Dorm Matron came to hear about it and packed him off to the middle dorm.

There was another bloke who was in the same lower standard as all of us, but like Jase was a year or two older. His name was Hafez who used to stammer and was nicknamed "Awa-Awa". He took over from Jase and became a real pain and started throwing his weight around. Now, "Batlugs", despite his ears was a happy-go-lucky friendly bloke and certainly not feisty. Anyway, one evening as we were getting ready for our showers Batlugs and Awa-Awa started a real punch-up. All hell broke loose as I promptly waded in, not so much to save Batlugs from a bloodied nose but I saw my chance of two against one! In the melee of grunting, swearing, wrestling and punching; suddenly Batlugs let out an almighty howl of pain. Awa-Awa had latched his teeth onto one of Batlugs ears and gave it one heck of a bite.

Like Jase, Awa-Awa was transferred to the middle dorm and poor Batlugs wore a bandage for a week or so.

Strangely, over time Jason was cured of his feisty nature becoming a top bloke and a dashed good all-round fearless sportsman. Likewise, Hafez became an absolute master at the art of massage. At athletics or boxing, we little "champions" tried to emulate the feats of Jesse Owens and Joe Luis. This involved rubbing down the calf and arm muscles with coconut oil to improve our performance. Hafez was in constant demand!

Meanwhile, long since cured of my sore behind of the three cuts with the swagger stick; I found a way to completely perplex our benign and kind-hearted teacher Miss Aggie. I could whistle through my teeth and taught a few of my friends how to do it. While the class was in session I would start this soft annoying whistle. For a long time, she thought it was some strange phenomena resonating in the classroom until she got suspicious. Miss Aggie would stop and listen intently, then the poor old dear would start going down each row bending over toward each student to detect its source. I honestly wondered how she believed that the student would continue the soft whistle if she bent over near his head. Of course, as she was approaching me I would stop and another bloke would immediately take it up in another row. We drove her to distraction until we tired of the game much to her relief.

It was still an era of ink wells with blue and red ink in the ink wells on the teacher's desk. Since I was prone to not paying due attention in class my exercise-book had a lot of red crosses on the mistakes I had made. I took an intense dislike to red ink and in typical fashion boasted revenge on that vile red ink well. It was just an idle boast.

"I'm going to pee in that red ink well one day."

"Bet you won't Loo."

Now a bet could not be ignored. "Bet I will. I bet you your Sunday apple cake."

Now, a Sunday treat for tea was a cake and an apple or Japanese cake was the most prized one. Often, trading went on between us boys for such goodies. A prized cake could be traded for six butter biscuits.

One fine day when an opportunity presented itself I stole the red ink well emptied some of the contents on the ground outside and "peed" into it. For the next week or so, mine and everybody else's rule book had a distinct orange coloured cross instead of a bright red one; and I got three apple cakes!

What a disgusting young larrikin I was!

Each Saturday morning we queued up at the window of the school clerk known only to us boy's as "Bob Scratchit" for our weekly pocket money allowance. Money was scarce as hen's teeth so most or all received the standard four annas as juniors, around eight annas at about middle school and one rupee when in the two final years. This equal pocket money policy might also have been the school policy.

This had to stretch to cover the tuck shop for the whole week as well as the Saturday afternoon flicks. This was impossible for the larrikins amongst us so cadging was not uncommon. School ethics or customs have strange twists known only to the boys of the day. For example, it was not nice to be branded a cadger but it was perfectly okay to welcome a "wood-duck" into the fold so to speak. A wood-duck might have something to share, especially money if he came from an affluent family! To successfully cadge meant you had to find a friendly bloke "in the money".

Joe, the Tuck Shop man could also be relied upon to put our purchases on tick when times were tough. Joe was a lovely bloke and would ware pained expression when he had to say "no" to a boy whose tick had run out. Today's dieticians would cringe at the tuck shop fare on offer; jigs and jogs which was peanuts and jaggery, half-ripe mango or guava and cucumber slices all liberally coated with chilly-powder and salt, sesame seed toffee's, and the all-time favourite of every schoolboy of that era, "stick-jaw". I guess to balance all this unhealthy tucker, was the fact there was no such thing as a Coke, Fanta or any sweetened drink and above all, we were always physically active.

Just about this time and out of the firmament so to speak arrived Sabu as a school boarder. He maintained that was his real name. Sadly, he was not the same Sabu the "efalant" Boy, but a real-life one. Sabu McKay was a strapping young fellow much my senior, walked with a strange swagger, spoke with a slight twang and was instantly good in all the sports including boxing. Yet he was one of the friendliest blokes this side of the black stump. Everybody liked him. Scuttlebutt had it that Sabu was an orphan and his father was an American sailor in the

2nd WW. But he never chose to elaborate. Sabu never spoke of where he came from; only where he was going. You could bet I promptly made his acquaintance and told him all about "Sabu the Elephant Boy". I didn't have to, he knew all about him anyway.

"That's how I got my name Loo" he assured me.

I was ready to believe anything he said. "Really?Gosh, Sabu maybe you can be a movie star as well."

"Nah Loo I'm going to join the Navy as soon as I can."

Well, Sabu's all-round sporting prowess, unfortunately, did not match his academic performances and sadly the moment he reached the required age Sabu disappeared just as suddenly as he had come. Sabu never spoke of where he came from; only where he was going and he did join the Navy.

As our tucker was pretty Spartan there was nobody amongst the boarders who could be called fat, except one bloke. He was in the senior dorm and had already earned the nickname of "Busty". As you can imagine he hated it, even more, when one of us young idiots from the young dorm would dare to yell out Busty from a hidden location. Well, one fine Sunday while mucking around with the gang I yelled out: "Hey, has anybody seen Busty?"

For the life of me, I don't know how I missed him but he was right behind me. Grabbing me around the neck with his left arm, he busily belted me with his right fist. Self-preservation is instinctive in a boarding school. I somehow managed to kick him on the shin with the heel of my army surplus am-jacks and he promptly let go of me in a howl of pain at which point I bolted to safety. I ended up with a slightly swollen cheekbone and was pretty sore in the ribs for a week but poor Busty's shin was actually in worse shape. And to his bad luck, Hansie came to hear about it and roughed him up as well.

Now, Hansie was certainly not feisty but he did have as you know a temper if picked on too much. Hansie had what was known as a bit of a "chicken chest"; that is, the sternum of his rib cage stuck out. Anyway, another bloke kept having a go at Hansie and his chest to the point where they ended up in a real free for all in the second-floor dorm. While Hansie had the better of the other bloke by giving him a bloodied nose and a bung eye, the bloke managed to wrestle Hansie to the floor just near the dormitory stairs. The two of them came rolling down the flight of wooden steps and Hansie ended-up with a broken collar bone. That sorted out their differences and Hansie was left alone after going to the hospital and having his shoulder fixed.

Did he snitch on the other boy? The answer is no. It was just not the done thing unless the problem persisted, in which case the next option was to tell your House Captain and the matter would be settled by him. That was one of the unofficial responsibilities of being a House Captain, to protect anyone who asked for it.

Life was certainly tough in a boarding school but I cannot recall anyone of us being the worse for it. Things had a habit of sorting themselves out and to my knowledge, a weaker quiet boy never really suffered any persistent bullying.

The inter-house sports were fiercely contested; hockey, soccer, boxing, swimming, and athletics. It was a points system based on "Entries", "Finalists" and "Place getters". Many a young fellow would be lugged into the boxing ring by his house captain just to get the entry-points for one's house. Was that barbaric? No. It was well supervised and we only wore amateur gloves and the most harm caused would be a bloodied nose or black eye. The Ref would stop the fight pretty quick in the case of a mismatch or if someone was getting a hammering. But most importantly it gave us boys the confidence of self-defence.

The Cross Country Run, the school "marathon" event was more fun than a slog. This was a joy for the larrikins amongst us. It was genuine cross-country as you only hit the tarmac for the last half-mile to the school gates. There were no heats to this event; you simply required the ability to convince the Games Master that you could run the five miles and were a serious contender. If you managed to do so your name went on the list.

The course would be marked out with pennants, up-hill and down dale, across streams, along the bunds of the paddy fields, while Masters were posted along the route to check us off. At one point however the route passed temptingly close to a guava tope or orchard that was completely irresistible to some of us larrikins. So, with a combination of athletic sprinting, guile and calculated timing one could get amongst the guava trees, have a quick feed, fill the pockets, dodge irate farmers and re-join the race on the blind side of the Master on point duty. Needless to say, I never featured in the first twenty to finish the race but did have a good feed of stolen guavas. Getting caught of course would have earned us the dreaded "three or six of the best" for stealing! I managed to never get caught.

The years seemed to roll by fast. Hansie, who had problems keeping up with his class had to pass the big hurdle of the Middle School public examination and sadly stumbled. But the Principal, who had recognised Hansie was good with his hands used his influence to get him an apprenticeship with a leading metal turning and fitting company by the name of Barton's. Hansie was tickled pink and in his element and went and stayed with Granny Loots. I now got to be the last Loots in Baldwin's.

The growing larrikin would have to make it alone!

If truth is known, I always thought Hansie's chest deformity helped him cut through the water like the keel of a boat while swimming. He was not a sprinter but he was a superb long-distance swimmer, though he could still lap me easily in a fifty-yard pool.

Hansie boarded with the Matheson family and his friend was David Matheson. David once bet him just one rupee as a joke to swim across the Madras harbour. Hansie showed him a point way across the harbour on the opposite side and told him to wait there with his bicycle. I've no idea about the distance but the fact that ships, tugs and boats are moving about made such a swim a crazy, if not hazardous caper not to mention the water quality which would have been filthy. None of this deterred Hansie. He collected his blinking one rupee!I asked him about that caper long after and his only comment while giving me that crooked smile of his: "I went to four flicks with that rupee Scoot".

Little altered it seemed in Hansie's contented life; the companionship of his couple of mates, cycling in the countryside for miles, the flicks especially, swimming and when prosperous a big feed made him happy.

And that was Hansie!

32
Tom's school year's roll on!

BACK THEN FANCY RESTAURANTS were few and far between and definitely beyond the "pay grade" of us schoolboys. So, when we could afford it we joined the common herd at the cheap veg and sometimes non-veg restaurants. A vegetarian one was usually called a Bhavan and a non-veg one was self-importantly signed as a "Military Hotel".

The Bhavan's served cheap tucker and were quite basic without the trappings of fancy furniture and menus. It was all vegetarian. These restaurant's ranged from a small hole in the wall that could cram in a dozen blokes or so, to one that had an indoor hall plus outdoor garden seating and could handle even a hundred hungry patrons that would turn-over every hour or so for eighteen hours of the day. Bangalore was the only place in the world I reckon where you could legitimately order a "one by two" coffee or dosa; which was one coffee and one dosa split in two and shared by two blokes.

Bharat Café, at the bottom of Brigade Road, was a popular pit stop for us boarders so there would be quite a few blokes in a blue blazer with red piping, school tie and blue school cap and white trousers milling around in the Café garden. It was popular for three reasons. The first was it was very cheap and a "one by two" even cheaper. The second was that it was always well patronised with customers constantly trooping in and out of the gate and third; the outdoor garden eating area, with a fair bit of foliage was easily accessible to the Bharat Café gate.

A group of us "locusts" would descend on the Café about ten in the morning when it was really busy. After having a good scoff, when an opportunity presented three or four of the blokes would stay behind and pay their bills at the counter while the others would blend in with the crowd and vanish out the gate without paying. It was surely an act of a petty thief not to pay for the tucker. So did us 'Scarlet Pimpernels' feel guilt or remorseful? Sadly no, it was all just a big lark. Hunger was our constant companion and money was scarce as hen's teeth, so deplorably we never saw it as an act of thieving but just one more adventure to undertake occasionally.

Now with a full belly, we larrikins would head up Brigade Road toward South Parade to sus out what flick we wanted to see at the matinée show.

If Will heard I indulged in such a low act he would have skinned me alive and hung me from the rafters as he sometimes threatened to do, and God knows what punishment our Principal Andy would have meted out. Perish the thought!

Like old George I had a splice of the petty criminal lurking within that could be added to my long list of transgressions.

Granny Loots had moved into rooms with Aunty Bunny and with her went Christine who had gone back to being a day's scholar at the girl's school in her final year. Once a month I was able to spend the weekend with Granny. They were not only fun times with Chrissy but I would get a massive breakfast, lunch and dinner always cooked especially for her favourite grandson. When "his Lordship" was not "in residence" so to speak poor Chrissy had to be content with a far more ordinary fare. Granny Loots never changed. The boys came first in her life!

I was so much in favour Granny Loots would regularly make special eggplant sweet pickles, crystalized raw ginger and my absolute favourite, the Loots "secret" recipe Christmas pudding boiled in a small Quaker Oats tin. So, whenever a batch was ready poor Chrissy would have to bike about seven miles each way uphill and down dale to deliver these favourites of mine at School. This treat I always shared with my mates and it would vanish in an hour. Scoffing raw pickle straight from the jar defies imagination but there is no link between hungry young boys and any such niceties.

Now, Chrissy being a "girl" meant Granny Loots would not give her any money to hire a nice bicycle from the bike shop just up the street. No, she had to use a ladies bike Granny had in the shed that had seen better days. The tyres were almost bald, the wheels a bit wobbly because the spokes had never been trued or tightened, the chain so slack it would come off the main sprocket from time to time and the framework rusty, but worst of all, it didn't have a blinking saddle! So would you believe it? Chrissy rode that bike whilst constantly standing on the pedals. Now, this saddle-less bike always bothered me more than Chrissy. That bare tube where the saddle was fitted stuck up like a blinking constant phallic symbol of pain!

"Just watch out Chrissy don't you accidentally sit on the blinking thing. It could be awfully painful."

Back came her instant retort: "That would make you very happy wouldn't it?"

Ah well, I had tried and gave up.

Now Chrissy always maintained she made that tiresome trek on her saddle-less bike, arriving all flushed and perspiring only because she loved her "Coz" so much. I held a far more truculent view as was my nature. First I reckoned that Chrissy only came because she could escape for a few hours from the suffocating confinement to the house by Granny Loots. Secondly, by this time Chrissy was a very pretty teenager with a pair of "knockers" that would have made her the envy of every less endowed girl of her age. You see, she would get a heck of a lot of wolf-whistles from the boys whenever she rocked up and I was keen to see her leave soon after making the delivery. I reckon she knew this and would deliberately hang around like a persistent rent collector; lapping up the attention she was getting from the boys. I couldn't leave her alone or the boys would have descended on her like a pack of blinking wolves. So twice a month or so this embarrassing situation, for me that is, would happen.

"Okay Chrissy, thanks, you can go now."

She was a determined cuss. "No, I'm not. I didn't ride all this way just to hand your goodies over and then buzz off."

"Ah well, I'm hungry and want to get stuck into the grub with my mates. They'll be waiting."

"Okay, you can buzz off if you like."

The wretch knew I couldn't as I cast my eyes around the ever-growing hoard of "teenage wolves" grouped nearby who were ogling Chrissy's knockers and I was sure would be making lewd remarks about that dammed saddleless projection as well! No doubt the word was passed around as was the practice whenever a good looking girl came into the school. Why was I always on the back foot when it came to dealing with Chrissy? She blinking well knew I was feeling more self-conscious than a Nun squatting in a cabbage patch with her habit drawn above her knees! Desperate, I had to try another effective tack to get rid of her.

"I'll tell Gran you were flirting with the boys."

"You dammed sneak, you would wouldn't you?"

"I'm not a sneak."

"Yes, you are."

"I'm not."

"Well, Thomas you tell Granny if you like but whose going to bring you your grub?"

Hell's bells. I was trumped once more. She always got her way with me and hung around like a bad smell in a lift lapping up the wolf whistles while I looked around for a hole to climb into.

Finally, Chrissy did get a second-hand saddle from the Goodge or the second-hand market that was fitted up on her bike; but she was so used to riding the pedals she blinking lost her balance and fell off every time she tried to sit on it!

And that was my favourite Coz Chrissy.

And I was an ungrateful young larrikin!

She confessed much later she got to "scrape the cooking pot" for her share. If I was aware of this rank unfair treatment I didn't seem to care. Chrissy would never whinge. As far as she was concerned I was her favourite younger brother and she loved me dearly. Her only respite was when she would come home with me on holidays.

As time passed, I was entitled to an exeat every Saturday ostensibly to spend the day with my grandmother. I would hire a bicycle from a bicycle shop at the rate of one anna an hour to go and spend a few hours with Gran and Chrissy and have a thick feed for lunch. After this, I'd bluff Granny I had to return to school. She always asked how much the cycle hire was and I always doubled it and added an extra hour for good measure. With money jingling in my pocket, off I would whiz to join my mates for the afternoon flicks and money to spare for a peanut stick-jaw. It was aptly named stick jaw, as the brown unrefined cane sugar from which it was made would stick to your teeth and gums (like poo to a blanket) while dissolving slowly.

The young larrikins aptitude for deceit was limitless.

Now one would rightly conclude that I was a scoundrel without equal but even scoundrels like me had certain uncharacteristic scruples. For example, I always felt Aunty Bunny did not treat Granny Loots well enough even though she'd put her up in a wing of the same house. She was rich enough to keep a beautiful home with fine furniture, oil paintings and classy cutlery and crockery. Anyway, the first weekend I spent with Granny Loots she invited me to lunch with her. I was embarrassed that she did not include Granny and Chrissy but sent their lunch across separately. She was intelligent and asked me a lot of questions about school and boarding life. When I was leaving she offered me the bounty of one whole rupee. Now that was an entire month's pocket money in one hit, but rather than accept it graciously; guess what came out of my idiot's mouth?

"Give it to Granny Aunty Bun; she's the one that needs it!"

I was never invited back for lunch or offered a copper thereafter but I never left without saying hello and cheerio whenever I visited Gran.

Yep, even the young Loots's were a daft lot!

Baldwin's was a Methodist school, so aside from a short Chapel each weekday morning, on Sundays we were marched in our respective Houses for a morning and evening service at the Methodist church. I remember that the first time we were marched off to the Methodist Church I was a tad apprehensive wondering if I was in for a Pentecostal experience. It was quite sober in fact and even more interesting than the very limited Anglican experiences I had because there were plenty of jolly Hymns; you know tunes that could be sung with gusto.

The Church was "L" shaped and the Baldwin girls were separated in the other section of the "L". I discovered that the boys could exchange fond smiles, winks and sign language during the service with their girlfriends. Methinks that many of us became masters at this "Morse code" caper and scored zero in the Christian faith!

All was well until the annual arrival of the evangelist preacher J T Seamen's. JT played the trombone so the opening rendition of "Onward Christian Soldiers" rocked the plaster off of the ceiling, but that jubilation would quickly evaporate certainly for me. You see, JT was a fair dinkum evangelical firebrand preacher, with long fervent prayers and sermons filled with hell and damnation stalking those who didn't repent. Heck, I started to feel the long-forgotten heat of the "eternal frying pan" again! Mind you, there were none in the congregation jumping up, waving their hands and carrying on like daft people but a few loud "amen" could be heard from time to time.

JT's fervent and final exhortation to "repent" meant that one had to troop up to the altar rails after his sermon and there JT laid his hands on each one's head and prayed long and hard for the persons' soul. This took a long time and I got to thinking about the blokes amongst us who were quick to line up to "repent" and have their souls saved until I discovered their little caper. The boys and girls were making the "repentance" trip only because they were then led into the vestry and given a cup of milk and because it was dark outside they could slip away and have a bit of a pash with the girlfriend. I guess their souls were less important than a welcoming cup of milk on an always empty stomach, plus the reward of a cuddle in the dark! Alas, I cannot explain why but I never did make that "repentance trip" and missed out every year JT came around.

JT, who was American was also an old boy of Baldwin's during the early 1930s and endeared himself to us "fleetingly" (that is not while Bible thumping) when he mentioned that he knew Gentleman Gunboat Jack and had entertained him in his home for "Thanksgiving Day" dinner.

Now Gunboat Jack, a coloured American, was a legend amongst us young fellows as we often passed him on Brigade Road and would say a shy hello. He always responded with a big wide grin and a: "Hi there" with a wave of his hand. At that time he looked a sad pathetic figure, dreaming his dreams while sitting out in the sun on an old cane chair in front of Bosco's Pub with a big old Stetson on his head. But that never stopped us from regaling the yarns we had heard about him and passed down in school folklore: "Gunboat Jack is fearless; he rode the motorbike in the well of death" …"He was the greatest welterweight boxer in the world" … "He beat everybody in the world in America, Australia and India" ... "He was not scared to take on all comers" ... "He once beat the great Jersey Joe Walcott"; and so on.

Gentleman Gunboat Jack was not only a huge figure to us boys but a giant of the Cantonment scene. He deserves to be remembered.

However, the larger than life Gunboat Jack was not the only famous personality of the Cantonment scene; there was another who was the roving "society" newspaper reporter for the Deccan Herald.

Being smaller than Delhi, Calcutta or Bombay those big smoke dwellers tended to look "down" on Bangalore Cant as a backwoods country town in the Ozarks filled with unsophisticated hicks. However, because of its salubrious climate, it had a healthy population of well-heeled snobs who liked to get their names and photos in the Deccan Herald. To cater for the elite the Herald had a "society reporter" who covered the posh events. The name of the reporter in question was Roshin. Now the oft-told local story whether true or not is that Roshin, whether invited or not would ferret out and rock up at every christening, birthday, engagement, wedding or social event to gather material for her weekly society column complete with photos of course duly supplied by the hosts. So far so good, except Roshin, our intrepid reporter never went alone but always had her two younger sisters in tow. The three of them would happily enjoy the free drinks, the good food and if that was not enough would also fill the bags they carried with tucker before departing. They gained the reputation for gate crashing and helping themselves to loads of food and drinks, and none would dare stop them for fear of getting a damaging write-up by Roshin in the society column the next day.

Like Gunboat Jack, the three spinsters were also genuine "characters" of Bangalore Cant and some wit gave the three the unkind sobriquets of "Roshin, Motion and Pull the Chain"!

As we boys grew up and moved up the pecking order to the middle and senior dorm, perhaps a tiny bit of the testosterone developed apace and we started taking notice of the girls in our sister school; Baldwin Girls High. Making surreptitious contact was easy. First one had to get an autograph book with coloured pages. Then you wrote something flattering to the sweet young thing that had caught your eye, give it to a friendly day scholar courier who had a sister in the girl's school and wait anxiously for the return via the courier; all the while sweating on a favourable reply. Your heart rate soared if the response was favourable and conversely dropped to dangerously low levels if given the brush-off. Anyway, if successful you promptly boasted that Valerie or Janet or Edwina or the blond blue-eyed hotly pursued Pam or Hillary or June or whoever was now your "steady girlfriend" and if you got the brush- off you kept quiet about it. All the girls were beautiful to us, but as Mendel's law proved some were prettier than others. So obviously they got more autograph "proposals" than a Postie's bag and some blatantly gave us blokes a hard time. The less gallant amongst us, who had been given the flick promptly dubbed them as "flirts"; completely ignoring the fact that there were quite a few blokes who were flirts as well!

There were hazards in this caper too which was politely known as being "cut-out". Janet had light brown hair, blue eyes and was definitely on the "most wanted" list of many a hopeful. After a hot pursuit, I finally captured her "heart" and made the usual boasts. After getting on famously with her for barely two weeks my ego was crushed. My closest mate Austin took me aside and told me he had "cut me out". I could have killed him but being my best mate I grinned foolishly with a sinking heart and said; "ah well Aussie the best man wins I guess." And with that, the undeniably pretty Janet disappeared out of my dreams and into Aussie's arms. Now that surely has to qualify as the litmus test of "mateship"!

One of the unique aspects of our education was handicraft as an optional subject. Aside from using it as a lark because there was no exam attached we learnt to use the basic tools for woodwork and plastic work. There used to be a material called "Perspex" and we learnt to make stuff like combs, rings plus wooden toys and other knickknacks. The best work was collected by the Carpentry Tutor and was duly displayed and sold at the annual School fete. Before Hansie left to work at Barton's he was the school champion for making Perspex rings. He would polish them to a glass finish and using a piece of brightly coloured plastic from a toothbrush handle he would insert it into a groove on the ring to look like a highly polished gem. For a bit extra, he would put a bigger "gemstone" and emboss the initials of the girlfriend. The blighter did well out of this caper and made a handsome quid by quietly selling them off to the Lotharios as a gift of undying love to the girlfriend. Such a prized gift I was told could earn the bloke a cuddle and an amorous lingering pash. He refused to make me one though: "No point chasing girls Scoot" he admonished. If only I took his advice!

As a senior, we could visit the girls on a Saturday evening if no sport was on. So we scrubbed-up styled the hair into a Tony Curtis puff with copious dollops of Vaseline pomade and headed off to the girl's school. There were stone benches scattered under the trees in the school compound, some more secluded than others where one could hold hands, talk about favourite movies, boast about sporting prowess and steer clear about academic issues. In time one could steal a kiss, whisper sweet nothings or swear undying love; and maybe, just maybe, if she was willing to sneak behind the girl's dormitories for an amorous pash!

Hafez or Awa Awa of massaging fame had a bit of a stutter and was unfortunately also a tad dyslexic as well. Anyway, these minor impediments aside he had a fine personality and more importantly had money. Hafez's father owned champion racehorses and lived in a grand mansion on St Mark's Road not too far from our school. Why he was put in as a boarder I have no idea, perhaps his folks reckoned he would be "polished" up. Anyway, Hafez confided to us larrikins he didn't have a girlfriend so after a powwow we concocted a plan to get him one. After due diligence, we found a rather serious, yet charming young thing who'd never had a boyfriend! So we set about coaching Hafez.

First, we decided he needed the finest leather-bound autograph book money could buy. This was duly purchased for him at an inflated price and we kept the substantial change leftover as well. We then coached him to write a loving message; about how he had admired her for years and though he was shy he was seriously in love with her. It was duly despatched via a day scholar to the sweet, but a serious young lass. It worked a treat and Hafez got a sweet reply. That done, we set about coaching him on conversation and if he felt she was amenable ask her for a kiss. Scrubbed up and looking his best we headed one Saturday evening for the girl's school. Hafez was no fool, as on the way he stepped into a shop and bought a bag of lovely peppermint bulls-eyes for the new girlfriend and the blighter wouldn't give us any despite the help and coaching we had given him!

When the 6.00 PM bell was rung to quit the premises we Lotharios started to troupe out in dribs and drabs and I found Hafez waiting at the gate looking a bit forlorn.

"Hi Awa-Awa how did you go?"

"Awa-awa; not good man."

"Heck, why not?"

"I gives her the awa-awa bulls eyes man and she was so happy I said; how's about a gizz and she awa-awa got up and walked away man."

Poor Hafez, like I said he was a tad dyslexic and it let him down at the wrong moment. But in time, the damage was repaired and with a bit more coaching not to ask for a "gizz" too early in the piece Hafez was a regular at the girls' school on Saturday evenings.

We, boarders, were not without our real-life heroes and it mattered little whether Air Force Pilot Stan White was an "Old Baldwinian" or not, we simply adopted him as one since he was married to Andy's daughter Joan and their two young tackers were in our school. In schoolboy logic, therefore, he had to be an "Old Boy".

We had all heard and watched the MGM film-news of the marvellous invention of Jet Planes but never seen a real one until the Vampires came screaming overhead in the beautiful blue skies of Bangalore Cant. Fighter Jets they were, "faster than light," we said; which would have made Davey shudder had he heard such nonsense but there is never any correlation between pure science and the wild imagination of young boy's.

Enter jet fighter Pilot Sq. Leader Stan White an instant hero to us boys whenever he visited the school on his annual leave. He had the presence and personality of a movie hero especially in his Officers Uniform and with his Officers Peak Cap on at a rakish angle. Again, fact or fiction is immaterial as far as we were concerned he played the lead role in our "Jetplane experience".

Very early one morning dressed in blazers and caps we senior boarders lined up and marched the eight miles, a goodly distance it was, to the HAL airfield to see the Vampires in action. We lined-up in a prime position near the runway and watched mesmerized as three; or was it six? Vampires came screaming in low over the runway, did touchdowns and take-offs and low altitude fly-pasts. In our minds, the formation was always led by Stan White of course! What a thrill. What a show. We marched back "on-air" each trying to outdo the other in exaggerated stories of what the planes did and what we saw.

To cap-off, this grand experience was the constant rumour circulating that Stan was going to "dive bomb" Oldham Hall in his Jet, so his wife Joan who was staying at the time with her father Andy could wave out to him! For days every time we heard the Vampires overhead, we would crane our necks in anticipation; until one day, as we were all out in the schoolyard Stan did come screaming in very low overhead; "just missed the Clock Tower" (it was said) which of course is nonsense; but what a ripper. The sound was pure adrenalin pumping stuff. We all broke out into a spontaneous cheer.

33
The confessions of Tom!

OUR SCIENCE TEACHER was a PhD in Maths and Science who dedicated his life to teaching students in a Christian school, rather than accepting a professorship at a university of his choice. His name was Dr Devaputra, better known as "Davey". Now Davey was a brilliant maths and science's teacher but fortunately had a hopeless throwing arm. When he caught someone fooling around during the lesson he was apt to throw the blackboard duster at the miscreant. We all ducked when he let fly as the missile could go anywhere except near its intended mark.

I always sat at the back of the class by a window and one day he caught me fooling around. The blackboard duster sailed harmlessly over my head and with unerring accuracy went clean through the barred window. Despite ourselves, we all burst out laughing including Davey.

"It is your turn to fetch the duster, child," Davey said to me with a grin. He always had the habit of referring to us as "child" and never by name.

Despite my wayward ways, I loved science subjects and did very well in every exam and I could manage maths and geometry; but was a total dud when it came to Algebra and Trigonometry. I once put a crack in a prized beaker in the Physics lab while fooling around behind Davey's back and I knew discovery was inevitable so I owned up to the crime with a huge lie. I told him I had left the beaker half-filled with paraffin oil on the concrete benchtop. It cracked as a result of the resonance and vibration coming from the wooden stairway just alongside the science lab as the other class boys pounded up and down the stairs. His look said it all but his response cannot be forgotten.

"Child, I have never heard such a story before but I will accept it this once. Be careful next time. Beakers are very expensive and a gift from America."

There was a culture of many unwritten "codes" that governed many areas of boarding life. Nothing sinister or bullying about it, but it was there and sensible to follow. You simply learned to respect your seniors as you progressed through school or ended up with a bloodied nose or black eye. There was no such thing as rampant bullying. The odd bully existed for sure, but if it got out of hand the House Captain quickly stepped in or a group of boys would sort him out.

"Sneaking" on a fellow boarder was out of the question no matter how serious the prank; but if the situation warranted collective punishment or the threat of collective punishment by the DM or Principal, e.g. collective "gating" (that meant no exeats or going to the flicks or see the girlfriend on a Saturday); the perpetrators must own-up and take their punishment like men.

So the code was; you never let your mates carry the blame. To this day, I like to believe our Principal Andy was a most wonderful, wise and remarkable person. He long knew of this code. He understood its value in developing the best in young boys as long as it was healthy and stayed within the bounds of reason.

Somehow, I had the problem of getting into strife.

We were getting ready for house parade in the gym shed when a day scholar brought the news that King George VI had passed away. I was just near the Principal's office when I piped up loudly:

"Hip hip hooray, the King has passed away ... Let's have a holiday!"

I still cannot understand my stupidity, or maybe my behaviour proved beyond doubt there was only a very tenuous connection between my brain and my mouth. I can still picture Andy come out of his door onto the veranda and demand to know who that boy was who uttered those appalling words. Dead silence overcame the large crowd. His face was furious. I put my hand up as the guilty one and about three hundred pairs of eyes followed me through his office door and the three hundred pair of ears heard the swish and whack of the cane.

We got the holiday and I deservedly got three really hard ones on the backside. I ended up with a sore bottom and three hours of detention to remember it; during which I was ordered to read certain chapters from one of Shakespeare's plays. I'm not sure if it was Julius Caesar, Macbeth, or King Lear but blow me; though not quite the same as the King of England dying in his sleep due to some illness, here was the famous Bard merrily "bumping off" Kings in the chapters I read. In retrospect not a good choice of punishment under the circumstances!

"Gating" usually arose when a group of boys or a boy did something and there was a delay in owning up to the crime. There's also no doubt that young high spirited boys can sometimes be senselessly cruel.

Not too far down the road from us was a very poor run-down suburb of Anglo Indians. It was called Austin Town and a neighbouring town to Shoolay of a Loots abode. They had a micro-culture and accent of their own. Anyway, a Swiss company opened up a watch factory a couple of miles up the road and generously employed many of these girls from Austin Town on the assembly line. Each morning, a large group of them would have to pass by the entire half mile or so of our school wall and each evening, on their return run the gauntlet of some malicious teasing. Frankly, it was often insulting and cruel. The trick was to hoist ourselves up with our heads just above the wall and deliver the insults. I must confess that I was one of the idiots that sometimes participated.

Well, one evening one of the girls had probably had enough of this idiocy. Getting off her bike, she gave the boys a mouthful including a few choice words beginning with 'f's' and 'b's'. Fortunately, I was not among the miscreants that particular evening. She was so incensed that she led the whole blinking gang of about twenty girls on their bikes through the eastern main gate and congregated near the Principal's office. Andy had gone somewhere on school business as all hell broke loose. As the word got around more and more of the boys started gathering around them. In no time the still angry young woman had an audience of about a two hundred very amused boys lapping up her tirade because she was still letting off steam and pulling no punches.

The Duty Captain came at a run and tried to assert his authority and calm them down. They had no idea of the status of a House Duty Captain; after all, he looked just like any one of us. The black "Hippolyte" gave him a Joe Louis verbal knockout:

"You stay quiet man, or I'll slap your "f'n" face!"

That brought howls of laughter from the big audience at which point the Duty Master, Mr Ireland, better known as "Karavad" (which was a salted, smelly dried fish) arrived and took over. He was suited and booted, so our furious Hippolyte sort of half settled down, but since he didn't know what all the fuss was about Karavad made the fatal and disastrous mistake of asking her to tell him her complaint.

All hell broke loose once again, as this time he had all twenty screaming young Vishpala's complaining about the boys abusing and insulting them every day. By now he had lost control of the situation. Honestly, it was hard to keep serious since the look on his face as he confronted the angry girls was worth the price of a balcony movie ticket. I reckon all the girls were letting rip with the 'b's' and occasional 'f's' and he sort of went very pale.

Now Karavad had a strange nervous habit whereby he acted as if pulling up his pants every little while with his elbows. At that moment he was tugging at them so agitatedly and frequently as if they were ready to fall around his ankles! He twitched uncontrollably at every "f" thrown by the young women and they were frequent. He succeeded, at last, to calm them down and assured them that the miscreants would be punished and it would never happen again.

The justifiably aggrieved girls finally ran out of steam and quietened down, and the crowd of us boys made way for them to file through with their bikes.

What happened next might just have balanced the scales a little bit of our complete idiocy in delivering our daily insults to the girls. Perhaps there was the sudden recognition of their courage to stand up for themselves and take us on. I honestly believe this was our motive because we suddenly and spontaneously all started clapping them and a few loud calls of "sorry!" were delivered. The leader of the pack gave us a huge grin and waved as she rode off. They were left in peace forever after.

The incident was duly reported to Andy and for a long time the miscreants of the day didn't own-up nor would anybody snitch on them. However, with the weekend looming the threat of gating was issued by the Principal. Six or so of the boy's trooped in to get their medicine, which was "six of the best" or "three of the best", depending on the severity of the crime. That was Andy's famous expression of six or three cuts on the behind with the thin cane. In such cases, depending on one's status in the group or gang it was very wise to go last as by that time his arm was tiring a bit and it didn't hurt as much.

It was only through happenstance that I escaped the Austin Town caper, but like I said I found it hard to stay out of trouble for any length of time and the next time around that same eastern wall became my downfall. Our entire school grounds had been levelled out from a slope so that the public road on the eastern side was higher than our grounds and that's why we had to hoist ourselves up to look over the boundary wall.

On the weekends the village farmers would carry their bundles of produce on their heads past our school and sugarcane was a seasonal treat, usually unaffordable from the tuck shop. My meagre weekly pocket money never went far enough. Well, we would place a bloke on KV so we were not spotted by the DM on constant patrol and then we'd entice an innocent farmer to sell us a stick of sugarcane by hanging over the wall and holding up a coin. The poor weary farmer would place his bundle on the wall and hang onto it. This is when the distraction would start by pointing to this stick, and then another, and another, and another, until he relaxed his hold on the bundle and then four of us, in a well-coordinated attack would pounce and drag the bundle over the wall. Honestly, like the notorious piranhas, we would strip the sugarcane bundle and bolt with a cane each while the poor farmer would be yelping blue murder by the wall. Unfortunately, one of the gang ran straight into the blinking DM and the poor farmer got back most of his sticks of sugarcane.

Stealing sugarcane seemed to have lingered in the larrikin's blood!

The next day we trooped in to get "six of the best". Stealing was a serious offence. And yes, by now I had established myself enough to go in last. Perhaps that's the reason why Andy seemed to always remember caning me.

Since he had stayed with us in Belgaum he certainly knew Will and so each time this exchange would take place:

"I see it's you again Thomas? Your father would be very disappointed in you."

"Yes sir."

"When are you going to learn to stay out of trouble?"

"I'm trying hard, sir. Awfully sorry sir it won't happen again!"

"I seem to remember you saying the same thing the last time. All right, bend over and I hope this is the last time."

Sadly it wasn't; so I may as well confess to only the gravest examples of the larrikin acts I got up-to over the years and forget about the minor skirmishes that also merited the cane! Nevertheless, I will always hold to the truth that I deserved every one of them and had I been spared the rod I just might have ended up an uncontrolled hoodlum as an adult!

The earliest motorized bicycles were ordinary ones, fitted with an add-on motor and transmission to assist peddling up the steep hilly roads of Bangalore. Mr Ringrow, who was one of our masters, had one of these motorized bikes because school folklore had it that he had only one lung. Consequently, the poor man carried the nickname of "One-a-Lung". Boys can be callous sometimes. Harking back to Will's BSA days I had this uncontrollable urge to have a ride on it and one day found it parked and unattended near the music room. I promptly jumped on it, peddled away to get the motor started and went buzzing around and around the large playing field with the blokes chasing me and hollering away in excitement. The blinking idiot on KV duty failed to warn me in time and my caper ended up badly when "One-a-Lung" suddenly showed up.

I was once more in Andy's office.

"I see it's you again Thomas? Your father would be very disappointed in you."

"Yes sir."

"When are you going to learn to stay out of trouble?"

"I'm trying hard, sir. Awfully sorry sir it won't happen again!"

"I seem to remember you saying the same thing the last time. All right, bend over and I hope this is the last time."

This routine exchange with Andy remains imprinted on my brain. I got "three of the best", but it was worth it!

Now I guess every student at school has his pet subjects and others he hated. One of my pet hates was English grammar. I imagined I could speak English fluently, write composition and essay's, read Shakespeare and enjoyed it, and study the great poets and also enjoyed it and I also successfully participated in the Debating Society; but for the life of me, I could not get my head around grammar! Each year the English exams included grammar questions that carried ten or twenty marks out of a hundred. I would do the English Composition exam and score well despite never answering a single grammar question; until one day in a mid-term exam, one question paper was devoted purely to grammar. Rather than feel alarmed, I was angry as an unhinged hornet. I spent the entire hour laboriously copying every word of the question paper with one letter in blue ink and the next letter in red. To add insult to injury, I wrote down the following on the bottom of my answer paper:"Grammar is superfluous to the English language!"

I folded my answer paper, wrote my name in the prescribed area and handed it in.

Our English master at that time was a Mr Ince, a quiet, dignified and very likeable person. "Incey" called me to the staff room. "I know grammar is not your strong suit Tom, but what on earth drove you to this level?" He was referring to my intemperate "postscript".

"I don't know why sir, but I just have an intense dislike for the subject."

"Would you like me to tutor you? Remember, public exams also carry twenty marks for grammar."

"Thank you, sir, I'll try to do better."

"Well, I'm sorry Tom but I'm obliged to report any mark below ten and I could only give you five for neatness."

"Thank you, sir, I quite understand."

A day or two down the track I was once more in Andy's office.

"I see it's you again Thomas? Your father would be very disappointed in you."

"Yes sir."

"When are you going to learn to stay out of trouble?"

"I'm trying hard, sir. Awfully sorry sir it won't happen again!"

"I seem to remember you saying the same thing the last time. All right, bend over and I hope this is the last time."

I got "three of the best" and it was not for the fact that I hadn't answered a single question but for the reckless comment I had added below my answer paper. Besides, I received a severe dressing down by Andy to boot. After that incident, I honestly tried to learn a bit of English grammar without much success yet continued to score high marks in English composition.

I'm afraid my egocentric dislike for grammar pursued me even as I progressed to a higher class where my new very competent English teacher in school, George Brown, better known as "Geo", who's enunciation, punctuation, grammar and rounded vowels, was the epitome of the "King's English". Geo is probably long dead. He was a polio victim and moved around on crutches. Geo didn't like me, mind you with very good reason, after all a silver paper "spitball" thrown with deadly accuracy to whizz past his ear while his back was to the class and splat on the blackboard with a sickening thud was not quite the respectful thing to do. Own up I did, for that was the honourable thing to do in a boarding school and take my punishment which he called a "jhap". Now, I must explain that perhaps because of his dreadful affliction Geo had large spatula-like hands and fingers that could pick up a football between thumb and forefinger! As a consequence, the jhap delivered across the side of the head set Big Ben ringing in the ears for the rest of the boring class period.

There is another reason why Geo didn't take to my unruly ways (aside from chewing gum placed on his chair), and it is to do with the school debating society. The subject for debate was: "Are Leaders Born or Made" and our team had chosen Jesus as the example of a leader who was "made". I started my address with the stirring declaration: "Jesus Christ was a fraud". This was the early-fifties and such pronouncements were hardly the acceptable norm. I of course blithely thought my attention grabber was a brilliant manoeuvre in the debate. I was an idiot. It was more than an attention grabber it must have sounded more like pure blasphemy. A palpable shiver and a discernible rustle and shifting of positions went through the crowded school hall of more than three hundred fellow students and slowly travelled all the way back to the august group of the Principle and faculty sitting way down the back on a dais.

What forbidden threshold had I crossed? Had I indeed crossed the Rubicon? What would be my punishment, caning or even expulsion? None of these thoughts crossed my mind at the time. They should have. Instead, I dived headlong into a convoluted harangue to justify the "ice breaker" (correction "bombshell"). Christ was "made man", I argued and therefore subject to all the temptations and influences of society, good and bad, just like any other man. He had a temper too just like any other man after all He knocked seven bells out of the money changers, didn't he? And yet He rose above the common herd and crafted himself into a leadership role not only of His Disciples but also the common folk. A "made" leader without parallel, was achieved as "born of man and woman" that had a profound influence on the world!" Had I been a member of the Bible Study group; of which I was not, I might have been better informed as methinks I was skating on very thin ice.

Yet strangely I did not get the cane or receive any punishment at all and the only reason I could subscribe to my great escape from "Stalag Luft III" was because of Andy the Principal. He was a wise and intellectual person and possibly viewed my intemperate "comment" as relevant and acceptable in the bull-pit of a "debate". However, I don't think Geo ever forgave me for my impious outburst, he was deeply religious and so debate or no debate he ultimately had his revenge.

There were other serious offences I got away with as well. Some of the more affluent boarders would receive regular food parcels from home or arrive with goodies. This was kept in the Food Matron's care under lock and key. The fortunate boy was allowed in under supervision to enjoy his treats. One of my mates received a parcel and so got into the room to have a bite and bring us a small share. He reported he had seen a huge bottle of Horlicks on the shelf quite close to the door, so we put a plan in place to distract Mrs Yaull the Food Matron and he would nick in and out with the Horlicks. The plan worked a treat and the bottle was smuggled out and hidden in a locker. That night after lights out we went down to the second floor and gormandized on plain powdered Horlicks until we were damn near sick of it. We suffered no ill effects the following morning. The body metabolism of active and always hungry growing boys worked a treat. The owner of the Horlicks was tracked down and politely thanked for his "gift", as well as advised that reporting it as missing would not be a good idea!

Now, if that wasn't outright blackmail, I don't know what is! But, "three or six of the best" was not a pleasant option.

Oldham Hall had a clock tower that could be reached for servicing only with the aid of a ladder. Every so often, Luciano (school folklore had it that he had once been an Italian POW), the school maintenance man would lug his ladder up the stairs to our sleeping dorm to attend to the clock. A small louvered entrance door stood at the base of the tower. Once inside there a narrow passage and rickety steps that led up to a platform below the clock workings to carry out the servicing. In the huge face of the clock, there was a hinged look-out window probably used for setting the "hands" and cleaning its face. Up there you could look out for miles at the lights of Bangalore.

Without the ladder "climbing the clock tower" was a hazardous caper especially at night reserved only for the very brave or foolhardy larrikins amongst us boarders. Some climbed for the adventure and others just to go up there and share a fag.

I called on the help of an old friend and fellow boarder Ike Evans in just how we managed to climb to the entrance of the trap door. Ike who was two years my senior also had a generous splice of devilment in his character and, dare I say it, had a certain way with the girls! Ike belonged to that select group who could do a nightly bunk "the gentleman's way", that is, one Eugene Ellis managed to get the key to the large old fashioned lock to the senior dorm barred door and make an imprint of it in a cake of soap. After some trial and error, he cheekily fashioned one out of Perspex in the handicraft class. Work it did and his group would sally forth without any personal risk to the flicks, a loaf on Brigade Road and even visit their girls in the girl's school! I'm reliably told, getting close up and personal to the girls in their up-stairs dormitory did involve scaling a drainpipe and onto the single-story adjoining roof that conveniently aligned with their windows. Having a pash through barred windows was not my cup of tea but many of the earlier batches did indeed enjoy it! To be fair to Ivo he denies ever risking the climb and midnight pash through a barred window! I find it hard to believe him because he was definitely a boy for the girls. He did admit though that having bunked to a late-night flick instead of going back to the dorm to sleep they dossed down on the gym mattresses in the school pavilion and the following morning, bleary-eyed, re-joined the morning parade!

The rather risky caper of climbing up to and into the clock tower of Oldham Hall was bold, imaginative and downright stupid. The main tiled roof of Oldham Hall was supported by the "King Post" design made of sturdy angle iron spaced at regular intervals. From the main tie-beam, a network of steel wires was suspended to which we attached our mosquito nets. The cross wires could only be reached by standing on a bed or a window ledge. The trick was to swing up onto the cross wire and from there grab the tie-beam. It then involved scaling along the steep slant of the angle iron strut that was conveniently near the trap door. After that, it was a doddle, by comparison, to enter the clock tower and climb the rickety wooden ladder to the clock. The hinged door in the face of the clock creaked like blazes and sounded loud in the confined area but open it I did and stuck my head out to look at the wonderful sight of the Cantonment at night. From my lofty perch of about sixty feet, it appeared like a city of fireflies! The risk of "climbing the clock tower" was worth it, and such was the "Boarders' Code" this risky caper remained unknown to Andy and the Dorm Master.

Sometimes, the best-laid plans of a caper can go awry but still result in escape from dire punishment. Just behind Oldham Hall stood the Home for the Aged establishment run by Catholic Nuns and a six-foot wall divided the property on our side, but because of our ground levels, there was a drop to about seven feet on the other side. From our top floor dorm windows, we could look down into the old folk's home. Built-up against the wall was a big chook run and alongside it a smaller pigpen. The fowl run had a stout overhead mesh installed because of earlier forays by the boy's before us who'd knock off the chooks. The dear innocent Nuns who ran the home had always assumed it was rogues from town or the villages doing the dirty on them and not those "nice polite" school boarders next door!

We kept pondering how to get into the fowl run. It would require some implements to cut or prise the mesh off the metal framework we didn't have any such implement. Jason observed one day that the sow whose pen was unprotected from above had six healthy piglets and growing fast. He came up with the idea to steal a pigling at a conference of the larrikins.

"The chook pen is out of the question so why not knock off a pigling? It has a heck of a lot more meat than a fowl and a lot better taste too?"

What he said was true, but a squealing pigling?

"Don't be daft Jase a squealing pigling will wake the dead even in blinking Hosur cemetery." The very large Husur cemetery was a bit down the road of the Old Folks Home complex.

"No, seriously we can muffle it. You blokes can let me down over the wall one night. I'll grab the pigling, hand it up to you and then you haul me back over the wall."

The "brains trust" mulled over it for a week or more and decided it was worth a try. The plan included getting a cooperative day scholar to stand-by who would then bolt home around the corner from our school with the pigling to be cooked on the weekend by his mum for us. The dear lady would be led to believe that that we poor and hungry boarders had collectively saved our pocket money to buy the pigling. None of us considered how this day scholar would explain the piglings delivery late at night. But that would be his problem.

The spirit of adventure far outweighed the collective intelligence or cerebral capacity of four idiot brains!

The copy of the key to the dormitory that Ivo and his mates enjoyed was a well-held secret or the key was never passed down, so we lesser mortals had to take the dangerous ledge route euphemistically termed as "walking the ledge".

Oldham Hall, our main building and dormitory was a striking edifice built from stone blocks and crowned by the clock tower. A stone ledge about twelve inches wide ran all around the building below the windows of the second floor and top floor. Only the topmost floor had barred windows at the rear of the hall, while the lower floor did not. The top floor ledge was about a twenty-foot drop onto a concrete passageway behind the building and most of the eastern section. Earlier "adventurers or pirates" had carefully dislodged one of the bars on the rear window nearest the partition to the young dorm so it could be removed completely and they concealed their handy-work with brown clay. This was known only to those who knew what to look for.

To get out of the dorm at night after lights out and do a "bunk" to the flicks in the dark of night (or in this case knock off a pigling), meant removing the steel bar, then carefully walk along the narrow stone ledge while gripping window bars and the jutting support pillars between the windows, make our way all along a quarter of the length of Oldham Hall and the entire eastern face until we reached the corner of the building. There on the corner was a metal rainwater down-pipe which we had to scale down about twelve feet to land on the corrugated iron roof of the barbers shed that was level with the boundary wall. We could then hop down onto the Main Husur Road.

To ensure a firm non-slip foothold some of us wore rubber keds and some went barefoot, with their keds strung around their necks. "Walking the ledge", as it was termed, was about seventy feet of dare-devil stupidity or more likely a brain dead enterprise. Falling off that ledge meant death or at the very least serious injury and yet such thoughts were secondary to the adventure. What was it that drove us to this foolhardiness? The spirit of adventure or be part of a gang or to brag or was it so you wouldn't be labelled a "funk"? I know this, whenever we got back safely and slid through the window bar to land on the dorm floor, the adrenaline would be pumping and there was a palpable sense of relief. There was lots of soft giggling as well which might have been proof that we were all really scared.

One dark night the four of us walked the ledge, scaled down the drain pipe and then stole along the boundary wall (which by comparison was hardly a challenge) and perched above the pig pen behind the water tank. Several pairs of socks plus a length of rope nicked from the scout's room were carried with the idea of stuffing the socks into the pigling's gob and tying its snout tight so it couldn't squeal and to tie its legs as well. One bright spark had made enquires from heaven knows who but firmly assured us it would work so Jase was duly let down the seven feet into the pigpen. We could barely see him by starlight as he stealthily made his way to the small pig shed, and then pandemonium followed!

Jase failed to get a firm grip on the sleeping pigling's leg in his first grab and there he was now fearlessly chasing the squealing piglets around the small pen; diving and grabbing without success while a blinking two or three hundred pound angry sow was, in turn, chasing him with loud grunts. The hog must have been blind or couldn't see in the dark, or sure as there are no fleas on a dead cat Jase would have become pork meat if it got him! The adrenalin pumping in Jase's veins had also jammed his hearing as he completely ignored the danger behind him.

Fierce loud whispers were urging Jase to abort the mission as the squealing of six blinking piglets on a still night seemed louder than "Tchaikovsky's Classical Cannons" but the stubborn adrenalin drunken Jase kept diving and grasping in vain. Surely the permanent tenants of Husur Cemetery could hear the squealing piglets never mind those temporary residents still alive on this earth!

Lights first started to come on in a few of the old folk's rooms. Desperate whispered calls of; "Jase, Jase for God's sake quit and get out of there" were ignored. But the idiot wouldn't give up and then the old folk's long veranda light was switched on. That was still okay because the lights were pretty dim, the pigpen was still in shadow and the eyesight of the old folks had seen better days, but a cavalry of Nun's was now sure to follow!

"Jase, you idiot the lights are coming on, so get out now!" But Jason kept chasing and diving as if his blinking reputation or life depended on it. "If you don't get out of there we'll bloody well leave you behind."

Jase finally gave up the chase and we leaned over and hauled him up back onto the wall in time before the big sow could get him. He was breathing hard and despite that, couldn't smell himself. Jase was stinking to high Heaven of pig poo! Honestly, pig poo smells worse than a bucket of dead prawns left in the blazing hot sun!

We made our gateway just in time as the Nuns arrived with torches. We scurried back along the boundary wall while Hughes'ie the day scholar was not to be seen and had probably bolted on hearing the squealing. Up the drainpipe we went and clawed our way back along the ledge empty-handed. Jase had to come last because he was stinking so much and we thought the pig poo on him would make the pipe slippery. He didn't complain, but he had to sneak downstairs to the second floor and have a cat's lick to clean himself up and at least partially wash his clothes. We were dead to the world before poor Jase came to bed and we kept away from him for days. You have no idea how long the stench of pig poo can hang around in your nostrils until you experience it!

The Nun's once again blamed the village rogues and in time also sealed off the pig pen from above. Our caper may have deprived future generations of any such adventure!

The growing larrikin was still at it!

Jason had that rare quality of raw dogged courage, even in sports. He would stand over the stumps as the wicketkeeper to the Davis brothers who were fast. He would do this when he noticed a batsman batting out of the crease or just to upset a good opposing batsman. His reflexes were terrific but every so often a ball would thud into his body and yet he never flinched. There were times when his skin would be black and blue and yet he would do it again and again, with the same determination of diving after piglings.

And that was Jase!

34
Tom and Desiderata!

WHEN I WENT HOME ON ONE CHRISTMAS HOLIDAY Mahmood was not on the station platform with Dad to greet me and carry my kit bag home. There was a new man. It was suddenly a huge hole in my life. Mahmood, my faithful friend and minder on whose back and shoulders I rode a thousand times was gone. I had never noticed that he was growing old with the passing years. He was there from the very first time my memory became a subliminal confirmation of his presence in my life; and even before that he was with Will and Carrie for Hansie and Nanette. He had devoted his life to us and we were his family but it was time for him to go back to his village and tend to his actual family and small farm. While I was unpacking my gear Will came into the room and placed a small package wrapped in newspaper on the bed. "Mahmood left this for you with your mother Tom."

I picked up the package and knew instantly what it was. "It's his favourite Pathan knife Dad. When I was little he never ever allowed me to play with it no matter what a fuss I made."

"Well, I suspect you were his favourite and like a son to him so he didn't want to see you do yourself an injury."

Will left me alone as I removed the newspaper and quietly shed a tear. I was the son Mahmood never had.

At the start of a new term, every boy came back with some shaggy dog story or other that had occurred over the long Christmas holidays. One of the popular yarns was; "a brush with a mad dog", or "I saw a mad dog" or even the ultimate lie of; "I shot a mad dog". With what he shot it nobody would ask. That would expose him to being a "humiliated liar" and open the door for suffering the same fate yourself. It was a well-respected "liars protocol". To be fair stray dogs in the villages and even the cities are common and number in their millions so Newspaper articles on mad dogs were not uncommon and this was the source of the yarns.

Will with his profound knowledge of everything from bridges to bugouts and everything else in-between had long since alerted me on what to look for in a mad dog because of my penchant of visiting the local village. None of us had ever seen one until one evening while we were playing six a side practice match of hockey. News that a mad dog had entered the school precinct quickly spread, and with it wild claims of where it came from and who had seen it. Some claimed they had seen it come in from the Curley Street gate, others that it had come from the direction of Johnson Market and entered from the Husur Road gate. Stray dogs around Johnson Market were as thick as midges in a swamp on a warm evening and so it was the most likely source. Nevertheless, it came in from the eastern gate and had staggered its way along the entire length of Toussaint Hall; stopping every so often to sort of turn on itself to lick at its wobbly left hind leg and look back at the baying crowd of excited boys behind it. None wisely chose to come too close or to be in front of it.

The news reached us on the playing field and twelve brave souls, armed with hockey sticks rushed to the corner of Toussaint Hall; and stopped dead in our tracks some distance away in front of the dog. It looked disoriented, scrawny and pathetic and hardly capable of walking let alone attack us; but no one was game to go in and finish it off with our hockey sticks. While we were debating what we would do it turned on the corner and now started its painful advance toward us, its teeth bared and saliva or froth visible on its jowls; just as Will had told me. We marched backwards at the same agonized slow pace. It crossed in front of Andy's office then the gym shed slowly, as we kept backing away until it stepped right into the "long and high jump" sandpit. The poor suffering animal just stopped right there sort of bent on itself in half. It didn't seem to want to move out of the sandpit.

The Duty Master arrived now behind the huge gathering in the gym shed and ordered the whole lot to immediately return to the dormitory on the double. The brave armed hockey stick "Pretorian Guard" of twelve stood its ground now in surreal silence. The Duty Master now suddenly saw us and in some shock yelled at us to go around the other way, on the run, via the music room and the bog and back to the dormitory. As we rounded the corner the other side we saw Mitchey hurrying toward the assembly shed armed with his twelve bore shotgun. We slowed to a walk and by the time we reached Oldham Hall, we heard the loud boom of the shotgun.

We were confined to the dormitory while the clean-up was carried out and lime powder "broadcast" along the path it had travelled as well as the sandpit. The sandpit was placed out of bounds until the bloodied sand had been carted away and fresh sand replaced.

For a long time, the story of the mad dog was told and retold.

The mad dog incident had faded but my brush with irate dogs didn't; though it became a school joke thanks to our school doctor Major Mac. The "Vet" believed in curing every ailment from stomach ulcers to scabies with a blinking dose of Epsom salts.

We were playing a bit of practice soccer and Camo fell awkwardly in a tackle and broke his forearm. It was a horrible break and poor Camo's arm was almost bent in two. He kept yelping in pain. The Holms'ie the Games Master yelled to me to go at a run and fetch Major Mac. Off I bolted at a hundred miles an hour down Serpentine Street and Myrtle Lane to his house and banged on his front door. Instead of the Vet answering the door a pair of pink-pig-eyed blinking bull terriers came around the corner of his house at a dead run and straight at me. They meant serious business in my opinion and to my luck, there was a small guava tree near his front door and I climbed it faster than a bride whips off her nightie on her honeymoon.

At least, the larrikins earlier practice of scurrying up a tree came in handy!

Unfortunately, the tree wasn't very large and the two were keen to get their teeth into my ankles and kept leaping up like Masai warriors. I only had my keds on with rubber soles but managed to kick one in the snout. He snorted in pain like a hog and now started jumping higher to get at me. In between kicking and yelling loudly for the Vet, I managed to hold them off. He must have been in the bog or having his tea because he took his own sweet time coming out. The Vet finally came out of his front door and stood there puffing on a big cigar with his hands in his coat pockets, clearly enjoying the fact that I'd been treed by a couple of his blinking bull terriers ready to have a serious piece of me. Of course, he didn't call them off immediately. He just thought it all a huge joke. Honestly, some adults are strange!

I finally got my message through to him that Camo had broken his arm and he was required urgently.

"Okay, you can come on down Loo. They won't bite you."

"I'm not taking any chances, Sir. You lock them up and I'll come down."

He laughed uproariously without a thought of poor Camo, or me for that matter, but he finally did take them in and I bolted for his gate. I made it back to school and the still suffering Camo. By this time the school nurse, Mrs Martin had given him some aspirin and put his arm in a sling. The Vet didn't give Camo a pain killer or anything like that; he just packed him off to the hospital in the school van with the Duty Master.

To add insult to injury the Vet told the entire teaching faculty and anyone else who would listen about: "how Loo

Loots was treed like a monkey" by his blinking bull terriers!

Yep, some adults are certainly funny!

Sometime later the Inter-House Boxing was on and I had made it to the semi-final stage when I came up against a South-Paw. He was an "artist" and I was a brawler and thus I couldn't lay a glove on him as he kept ducking and weaving and scoring points with his punches. He wasn't hurting me much and my close mate Aussie Banks, who was a very good boxer and my corner seconds told me his first move instinctively was always to my left when I used my right.

"Just keep feinting with your right Loo and when he moves left again straight punch him with your left to his head."

Well, I did just that. I kept feinting with my right and jabbing him with straight lefts. It worked a treat until I figured I would throw a straight left as hard as I could and go in for the kill with my right. I lined him up and with all my weight threw a straight left while off balance. Instead of my left glove hitting him flush in the face it glanced off his shoulder and out popped my arm from my shoulder. I think my howl of pain had more effect on my opponent than my punches.

The Vet, who had to be present at all the fights hopped into the ring with alacrity and tried to pop my arm back into its socket. I don't know if he had any previous experience on how to do it but by golly, he wasn't having much luck and I was in agony. He kept yelling at me to stand still; but just how one did that while someone was mucking around with one's arm I didn't know. Finally, he succeeded and what relief. A couple of aspirin and a sling for three weeks was the treatment. I was lucky not to get the dreaded dose of Epsom salts!

We had some really good boxers and I'm glad I didn't bump into them in the ring because of different weights.

The Davis boys, all six of the Sims boys, Mickey Oliver and my closest friend Austin Banks were what we called scientific boxers. They had class while the rest of us were brawlers.

My shoulder healed and I was fine the following year and just managed to win my weight in the finals. Uncle Maurie and Uncle Bertie came to see the finals and at the finish of the bouts, with one eye all bunged up and a towel over the head I met with them. Maurice took out a five rupee note and held it out to me: "Here you are Thomas, well done." I was gobsmacked as five rupees was five weeks of my pocket money and in embarrassment, I mumbled that it was too much. "Take it, Tom, you beat the wog." That word was taboo and Will would never use it. I took the money anyway with a feeling of some guilt. Uncle Maurice was my hero after his amazing exploits in East Pakistan and it made me sad to hear him say that. The Loots, I'm afraid we're racist, at least some of us anyway!

But history has a nasty habit of repeating itself, this time around not with me but with my very good friend and "seconds" at the time, Austin. You wouldn't believe it but he threw his arm out just as I had and ended up in the same agonising situation. One would have thought the vet had gained sufficient experience from me but I reckon Aussie had an even harder time. Honestly, it took ages to get his shoulder arm back into the socket and since I was his "seconds" this time around I felt every moment of it.

We, boarders, came from far and wide, certainly from faraway places like Bombay, Hyderabad and Trivandrum way down the south of India, but just like the sudden appearance of Sabu McKay; a young boy arrived a very long way from Fiji. Fiji was some 11,000 miles away from Bangy and the other side of Australia. Crikey, it must have been an epic journey for a young lad. The Fijian boy was shy and quiet and in the rough and tumble of boarding life, I figured he needed a bit of friendship and "protection". As

I was much senior to him I tried to do just that. He gave me a colourful bush shirt as a "thank you" when I finished school with all the Fijian Islands printed on it.

The years as a boarder rolled on. The annual Sunday School Picnic was something to look forward to, something to remember and so deserves special mention because it was a genuine day of release for us boarders. This was the one occasion each year when both the girl and boy school boarders "came together" without MI5, CIA or ASIO supervision at Kings Farm! Aside from organised fun games, there was plenty of time to walk together around the farm property and when possible hold the girlfriend's hand and even get in a quick smooch. Lunch always consisted of a substantial serving of biriyani. We even got a cake and biscuits for tea. What a day. What wonderful memories of sweet young things and strutting young peacocks and as we marched back at dusk we would spin yarns of an amorous pash in the long grass of Kings Farm!

It was in my penultimate year at school when I was the instigator of a bunking caper and this time my luck seriously ran out.

The short spell of the Michaelmas holiday had come around and only the boarders who lived a short travelling distance away could go home for the ten-day break while the rest of us cooled our heels and counted our pennies to get to see a movie. Since it was never enough I decided to do a bunk one night with four of my closest mates to take in a late-night movie. A late-night movie was never really policed carefully by the theatre ushers, or maybe they didn't really care and one could either mingle with the sparse crowd and slip in, or, as in the case of the Rex Theatre, one could walk along the wall of the houses behind the theatre and climb in through the urinal transom window.

I reckon there was a "hex" on the caper from the very beginning as when "lights out" was called and we four crept to the window to "walk the ledge" four other blokes with the same idea rocked up. I brought up the rear as now the eight of us did that crazy walk along the Oldham Hall stone ledge once again toward the drainpipe by the barber's shed. As we got to the drainpipe a hand-drawn rickshaw was coming along the lonely Hosur Road which we unfortunately ignored. It stopped as the first and second then the third bloke slipped down the drainpipe onto the barbers shed and that's when we heard a voice from the rickshaw: "What on earth is happening here?"

We were all now fully exposed like rabbits in a headlight and any thoughts of turning back were futile. We were caught red-handed by some school well-wisher squatting in the blinking rickshaw. I whispered fiercely down the line. "Keep going chaps, we're done for anyway so we may as well enjoy the flick". This was brave, if not idiotic encouragement indeed!

And the blinking voice from the darkened hood of the rickshaw kept tallying the "escapees" shimmying down the drainpipe as if he was buying bananas: "Four, five, six, seven, eight" …. The ass was counting out aloud. If a brick had been handy I might have thrown it at the bloke in the rickshaw, instead, we scampered down the road at a hundred miles an hour laughing like drunken kookaburras.

Happy-go-lucky Jasper said; "there's a French movie on at the Rex rated "Adults Only" chaps so its bound to have some steamy scenes." That sounded good so we walked along the house wall behind the theatre in the dark, crawled through the urinal transom window and slipped inside. If the voice from the rickshaw hadn't been enough to signal disaster the almost empty blinking theatre certainly should have. Except for a few like-minded voyeurs in the cheap section down at the very front you could have fired a shotgun and hit nobody; and here were eight idiots sitting together in an almost empty superior class area.

The French movie droned on and on with English subtitles down the bottom and if there were any steamy scenes, they must have been reserved for the very ending. As the halfway interval approached an usher came through the curtain and sort of looked around, departed, then popped straight back in again. It looked very suspicious to me as I reckoned he had spotted the eight wood-ducks that hadn't been there at the start. I whispered down the line: "Let's get the heck out of here. The movie is rubbish anyway and I think the door usher is suspicious."

After a few dissenting "oohs and aahs" I decided enough was enough and headed for the urinal. Either the last bloke was reluctant or slow to leave but we suddenly heard a yelp of anguish from the direction of the urinal window. Hell's bells something had gone wrong! We scampered along the wall and hopped down onto the street. A quick head-count showed only seven of us had made it and Todiwalla hadn't. It must have been his yelp that we heard. We went all the way around the streets to the front of the Rex and waited in the almost empty car park hoping that Toddy would show. Show he did after a long wait and his "disguise" looked a bit the worse for wear. Now you'd think his welfare would be our primary concern; but no!

"Toddy, what the heck happened?"

"I was halfway out of the damn window when a couple of blighters dragged me back. They gave me a bit of a roughing up…"

"Never mind the roughing up. I hope you didn't tell them what school you were from."

"Nah, I wouldn't do that. I told them I was a day's scholar at Cottons and they were satisfied. They took my name and asked the names of you blokes and I just made them up."

"Good one pal; never let your mates and the old school down eh!"

A show of remarkable concern and respect for the "old school" considering we were dressed as clowns and doing a bunk! Moral, however, was low so we did a quick check of how much money we had between the lot of us and headed for the Imperial hotel. Six cups of hot chai and two fags were shared around. Despite the "buck me up", it was a bit of a forlorn group, without the usual banter and laughter that made its way back to school wondering what sort of reception awaited us.

Now one of the long-held inspirations when bunking for the flicks was to dress as much as possible as the local folk so we could sort of "blend" in. It was a daft idea because we must have looked like clowns. Anyway, we all usually dressed in our striped night suits, an old cotton coat or cardigan and a towel wrapped around our heads to appear like a turban. If Andy was going to cane us on the spot the night pants were going to offer precious little protection. Such thoughts certainly swirled around in my head, and just what he would think of our "fancy dress" didn't bear reflection.

There was a small side gate by the barber's shed known as the Staff Wicket Gate that was never locked and since we all knew our number was up, any thoughts of trying to re-enter un-noticed would prove useless. As we trooped through the gate Andy materialized in his woollen dressing-gown along with Mr Wright, the Dorm Master. Both had been sitting on chairs waiting for us by the barbers shed and heaven knows how long they had been waiting as it was now nearing midnight.

Andy's usually soft tones sounded ominously angry this night. "Are all of you present and accounted for?"

"Yes Sir."

"Very well Mr Wright will properly let you in and report to me in the office at 9:00 AM sharp tomorrow."

It was quite obvious the blinking "rickshaw night stalker" had gone in and reported what he had witnessed straight away.

"Yes Sir. Good night Sir." Andy didn't return our chorus of wishes I'm afraid.

Mr Wright was an affable and lovely man who had been a railway guard and was known to have a fine repertoire of good jokes he could tell. He had a special liking for me because he knew Will was on the Railway.

"I think you fellows have been very ill-disciplined Tom especially in taking such a terrible risk." Once again the "rickshaw night-stalker" must-have described our descent down the drainpipe from the third-floor ledge.

"Yes Sir, awfully sorry Sir."

"Well, you better show me how you got out tomorrow."

"Yes Sir. Goodnight Sir."

He wished us good night and I have a feeling he felt sorry for us in a way.

As it was the holidays and therefore no staff around Andy lined us up in the outer office. I guess we all expected him to be furiously angry, but instead, there was a strange calmness in his tone of voice. He delivered his message with quiet force giving us the dressing down of our lives; especially in explaining the risks we were taking and what terrible misfortune could have taken place if any one of us fell and killed ourselves; the terrible trauma we would have caused our parents in addition to us bringing our Alma Mater into disrepute.

For the life of me, I cannot explain this rationally but I shall try. First, his mention that we could have "killed ourselves" had we fallen suddenly brought back my Carrie's long-forgotten words to Will: "That son of yours will kill himself one day." Secondly, hanging on the wall behind Andy was a large framed print of Desiderata and while he was giving us his lecture in a steely tone I couldn't help reading the lines of Ehrmann's poem, even though I had read it many times before from the same print. At this perilous moment somehow the morally instructional words and direction for a code of life took on a special significance.

"Speak your truth quietly and clearly…"

Andy finished and I only half heard what he had said. Then he asked; "Now, whose hare-brained idea was it to do this?"

I answered without hesitation since it was true; "mine, Sir."

"I'm sorry to say I'm not surprised Thomas," but what Andy said next shook me to my very core. "Very well; since this stupid and dangerous idea was yours can you give me a reason?"

"We, I mean I, intend you no disrespect Sir. It was stupid I know but I guess it was just an adventure for us."

"And for how long and how many times has this adventure, as you call it, been going on?"

Now it was advisable to introduce a fib, despite Desiderata, before it got out of hand and others who sometimes bunked to the flicks were also involved. "This is my third-time Sir."

"I see. Who else has been involved in this dangerous enterprise you call adventure?"

"No one that I personally know or saw doing it, Sir."

"You mean you won't tell me isn't it?"

"Yes Sir. I'm sorry Sir but I cannot tell you if I didn't see them."

His grey eyes bored into mine but I didn't look away. He knew the long-held code of honour. What followed next left me momentarily gobsmacked. This was an Andy I had never come across in all the years. I can't explain why but I had a feeling he was trying to teach us something that would perhaps "reform us".

"Very well Thomas, since you appear to be the ring leader you can perhaps tell me what punishment should be meted out."

"Six of the best and one month's gating Sir." I said this without hesitation and I'm not sure how my fellow miscreants reacted at the time.

This time I went first and did get "six of the best". The other blighters got only "three of the best" and I guess that was fair enough. We also had one month to examine our navels and mourn our misfortune while all the blokes got exeats to go for a loaf and to the flicks. That was the hardest part.

I had to send Granny Loots a fib of a message that I was studying hard and so couldn't see her for that month. Chrissy had to work overtime bringing me my pickles, ginger and home-made boiled fruit pudding, lovingly made in a Quaker Oat tin! The wolf whistles from the boy's around got louder and louder with each trip and that was her reward!

The iron bar on the window was refixed and two more I didn't even know about were also found and fixed. But I knew in my heart that when the dust settled that those following would prise another bar loose and risk life and limb to "walk the ledge" again. Boarding school seemed to uncover the spirit of adventure in boys that triumphed despite the life-threatening danger and dire punishment.

As for me? I believe that was my last caning and for about the next year and a bit, I was a model of propriety.

In my penultimate year, I was selected by Andy to take over the School Banner from the out-going Senior Captain in the year-ending ceremony and take the oath on behalf of the school. That singular honour earmarked me to be the Senior Captain the following year. So in my final year I was the senior House Captain and had that cherished locker No.1 and my close mate Austin Banks locker No.2. The five House Captains were presented with their red tassels by

Andy and given a quiet lecture about upholding the School Motto and what was expected of our "position".

Owning a watch in school was an absolute rarity in that era particularly for a boarder. One morning there was a sudden commotion in the Middle Dorm while we were all getting washed and dressed to go down for breakfast. A boy's watch had been stolen. He had left his locker door open while washing with his watch temptingly visible on his locker shelf.

The Dorm Master ordered us to all "stand by our lockers" and the Captains to help him in a quick locker search. No luck as it was a cursory check at best as we had to keep the breakfast time. The Duty Master spoke to us at breakfast parade and sternly warned the culprit to own-up and see him with the watch. The warning was repeated at lunch parade. That night, after dinner grace the Principal addressed us very seriously on the issue of thieving and issued a final warning for the culprit to own up by the next morning.

Still, no result the next day and a notice was posted that all boarders were "gated" until such time the culprit owned-up and the watch returned. The situation was now at crisis level and something had to be done. The word was passed down the line, so to speak, to let me know if there was a "suspect" and believe me in a very short time I was told of a prime suspect. Let's call him Mac and while there was absolutely no evidence of it, Mac was "known" to knock off textbooks and to flog them. That evening Mac was roughly hauled before a group of us behind the scout's room that was usually a favourite "battleground" for free-for-all fights because of its seclusion. I told him to own-up or get a hiding. He swore innocence and got a sample of what was to come. He still yelped "innocent" and got another round of punches, this time harder and better directed. But still his protests of innocence; when on impulse I suddenly said to him: "Listen, Mac, if you own-up I give you my word I won't sneak on you to Andy". It worked a treat. With a look of relief, he took us back to his locker and there cunningly hanging by a black thread and secreted behind the shelf was the watch. I went to Andy's residence with the watch. He urged me strongly to tell him who the culprit was, but I simply said to him: "Sir, I gave him my word of honour that I wouldn't tell you if he owned-up."

He looked at me in stern silence for what seemed like an eternity. He admonished me about protecting thieves as it would only encourage them to do it again. I remembered his words and that night Mac received another "reminder" from me. I am pretty sure Andy would have noticed Mac's puffed-up lip, right cheek and eye at some point on his daily rounds or in the Chapel line-up in the Gym Shed and just might have wondered; "is this the miscreant to whom due punishment has been meted out?"

After this event boarders with watches had to hand them in to the office for safekeeping.

The scout's room and the secluded rear is the venue of a caper that went awry that happened sometime before my time and was part of the school folklore. At the northern end of our main sports field was a Mosque and within its grounds was a huge big jackfruit tree whose branches overhung our boundary wall. Jackfruit is very large and heavy with a very thick blunt spiny skin. There is an art in opening up a ripe jackfruit to get at the large fleshy yellow pods within because it gives off very sticky milk and the less ripe the jackfruit the more the sticky fluid. A very sharp knife and coconut oil to remove the goo is required. Some blokes were eyeballing a slowly ripening jackfruit the branch of which was quite near our wall and one night they did the "ledge walk" and hoisting themselves onto the shoulders of one of the blokes he got to the top of the high wall and onto the tree. The deed was done and "scouts honour" conveniently forgotten they hid the jackfruit under some tarps inside the scout's room so it would completely ripen. How it was not discovered defies imagination because it does have a strong smell and when opened up pongs like a dead dingo.

However, the story goes that one night after lights out they "walked the ledge" again opened up the scout's room and set to on the now ripe jackfruit. While enjoying their scoff they kept tossing the incriminating evidence of the large seed of the jackfruit over the wall and onto Curley Street. To their very bad luck, "Wessy" was walking back from somewhere just at that time and a big seed landed right on his head, or so the story goes. Nevertheless, he watched seeds flying over the wall for a time, figured out from where the missiles were coming from, collected his cane and made his way to the scout's room. No doubt the unfortunate blokes "dessert repast" would have been rather painful; plus Wessy docked them their pocket money as restitution to the Mosque.

Suffice it to say, that in my time jackfruits on the Mosque tree continued to flourish but this Adam refused to be tempted into plucking the forbidden fruit!

I was certainly not the sharpest tool in the shed when it came to having the best grades in the class, nevertheless, on graduation, I was selected to deliver the Valedictory Address and hand over the school banner. Because our hall wasn't big enough it was always held in the newly built Baldwin Girls School hall which seated about three hundred folk. It was filled to capacity and overflowing. I was chuffed.

The larrikin had somehow reformed his ways.

Despite these achievements there lingers one disappointment.

Aside from the "Cock House Cup" there were individual medals for outstanding achievers in sport and academic excellence. These were all chosen for by the school faculty and I was not a contender for any of them.

But there was one medal that was voted for by the student body and It was for the boy they held in highest esteem for character and leadership and frankly the one I prized most. Only a boarder could be voted for because logically they were under school supervision day and night. Leading up to the day of the vote, it was not uncommon for one's schoolmates to keep passing the word: "Don't forget to vote for X, Y or Z". This could well be deemed as canvassing but it was pretty harmless stuff and certainly happened every year. In any event, it was a secret ballot.

The vote was held after morning prayers in the Chapel. Andy would first address the student body and spell out the relevant criteria they should consider when making their choice; CHARACTER AND LEADERSHIP were the key elements. One ballot slip per student was handed out, on which one wrote their name, House and of course their choice for the medal. It was folded and passed to the end of the row where it was collected by the Masters.

School scuttle-butt had it that I was the front-runner for the Medal, though I thought my close mate Austin Banks would win it. The vote was cast that year as usual, however, at next Chapel instead of announcing the winner, Andy made the surprise announcement: "There will be a re-vote, the first in our history", or words to that effect but no reasons were given. Honestly, the announcement of a re-vote was a huge surprise to the student body and you can only imagine the stories concocted as to the reason. So it was conducted again and this time the worthy winner duly announced and applauded. It was not to be me or Austin. I must confess I was bitterly disappointed.

There is a strange sequel to this "event" that is best buried and forgotten. A year or so later while I was at College, a master in the school Ivor Hunter told me that I had won both the votes but a certain master had made a representation to Andy that I was instrumental in getting my mates to coerce students to vote for me and that was counter to the criteria of "character". So it was awarded to a boy who came second. It's certainly not his fault.

Well, as I said early in this story; "Geo would have his revenge"!

If one could present a model of the "perfect" Principal it would have to be Andy. Like his Danish forbears, he was tall, big made never raised his voice, always treated us fairly and had a huge personality. He never spoke "down" to you. Above all, he understood perfectly how to handle a large number of high-spirited boys during their growing years and no matter how naughty bring the very best out of us.

I should know, better than most as my "association" with Andy went beyond my eight school years as a boarder. While I attended university I stayed on as a "staff boarder" in the old school.

The larrikin had learned his lesson at last! Or had he?

PART FOUR
A chronicle of College capers!

BEN LAFFRA

35
Tilting at college!

A LONG-HELD TRADITION after completing our final year exams was that the Principal invited us all to tea in his home. The purpose was to discuss our future plans and impart advice.

My youthful dreams of becoming a fireman, a Spitfire Pilot, a Spy, a Cage of Death rider and a host of other careers had over the years solidified into my first love of joining the Army. My career plan was to join the Military Academy at Dehradun; easier said than done. I applied for and was selected to sit for the exam in General Knowledge, Maths and English. Unfortunately for me the Maths papers also included questions in Algebra, a subject I was a duffer at in school and all my dreams of becoming a Gentleman Cadet evaporated in the "virus" of Algebra! I was bitterly disappointed and even incensed. Fuming because I knew fellow students ahead and with me, who never showed any leadership qualities, didn't make the cut in the first or even second eleven in hockey, cricket or soccer, didn't compete in sports or swimming, couldn't tell their blinking left from the right leg in drills or marching and they sailed through to join the IMA in Dehradun!

While still hanging around in Bangy I met Bernie Caps who was ahead of me by a year or so and he too had failed the IMA exam, but still determined to join the forces he had joined the ranks in the Air Force. He told me that he could work his way up in the ranks and being in the forces he could apply for entry into the IMA. So unknown to Will I was off to the recruitment centre at the High Grounds Camp; sat for the rather simple exams, ran a short obstacle course and passed in a breeze.

Our group was loaded into a truck and despatched to the Military Hospital for the medicals. Oh dear; flying through the air like Spy Smasher proved to be my undoing.

My left knee was bent inwards over the limit like a "knock knee" and I now failed the medical. There I was, standing only in my jocks gobsmacked and incensed once again. The MO conducting the medicals in full Officers uniform was rotund and I figured couldn't run out of sight in a fog and he had the gall to fail me? So help me, like the ass I was, I promptly challenged him to do the obstacle course against me. Fuming, he threw me out of the room and I made my sorry way back in the truck; now with the sad realisation that even if I had passed the IMA exams I would have failed the medicals!

Having failed the IMA exam an equally disappointed Will asked me what I was going to do; adding: "you're not going to join the railways so get that out of your head." I announced, tongue in cheek, that I would like to go to University. I think he looked at me aghast as I was not a scholar having scraped through with a very undistinguished "third class".But Will, as was his way encouraged me to go ahead even though he would still have to continue to support me and pay all my college fees.

I thought I could stay with Granny Loots but Will wouldn't have a bar of it. He must have figured that I would play-up even more and so arranged with Andy for me to remain on as a staff boarder at the school. I roomed with the bachelor teachers who had a section reserved above Andy's home in Lincoln Hall. I shared a large long hall-like room with Ivan Oliver, a junior teacher at the school.

I entered the next phase of my somewhat questionable scholastic career at St Joseph's College; grappling with subjects like Rural Economics, Statistics, Economic Geography, Accounts Administration etc. before going on to Farm Fragmentation, Farm Inputs, Farm Gate Costs, Soil Sciences, Entomology, Plant Pathology, tractors and in the end shovelling even blinking chook poo and cow manure out of the trailer and then spreading it! While most had nice new rubber boots I went to Will's favourite place the Goodge and got myself a pair of second-hand rubber boots for a pittance; while some just rolled up their pants and went bare feet! Fieldwork had to be followed with a thorough scrubbing of the good old lifebuoy soap to get rid of the pong or no girl would come near us.

The first year especially had a lot of theory classes and I was often late to class. "Father Cauliflower" a nickname I had given Father Mascarenas, the campus Principal, would wait by the one entrance we all had to file through with his "donation" tin that had a narrow slit in the cover and jiggle it at the latecomers. Even the one anna donation was starting to tell on my meagre monthly income so off I went to Luciano the school handyman and convinced him to make me a stash of metal "coins". He did, complete with the scallops. He was an artist at his trade and it worked a treat as I craftily "palmed" the coin through the slot. I got away with the caper and I wonder what the good Priest thought each month when he opened up the tin! He just might have suspected me but he never said a word. He sort of liked me and didn't mind a bit of the larrikin spirit in the students. I'm afraid this was to be sorely tested.

I guess I was sort of growing up or at least I thought so. Anyway, I settled down to some serious study but the larrikin spirit seemed always to be just below the surface.

One of the college boys in his senior year had an old 5 HP Norton motorbike that I had my eye on. One fine day we had a long break between classes and my mate Pat and I were killing time in the canteen as usual and the Norton was parked in the cycle park nearby. I just couldn't resist it.

"Pat, fancy a ride on that bloke's bike?" Pat didn't need any further encouragement. With one quick kick start the lovely measured thump, thump, thump beat of the motor came to life. Pat hopped onto the pillion seat and off we roared out through the campus gates and went for a smashing joy ride. We went roaring down South Parade and around the girl's schools in-between. We were going flat chat along the long straight strip of South Parade when I tried to coax the bike into even greater speed and broke the throttle cable connection to the throttle. The bike was rolling to a halt with the motor ticking over but not to be deterred by this small inconvenience, I stuck the soldered end in my teeth and pulling back on the wire off we roared again. We were completely oblivious to time and when we returned to the college the bloke who owned the motorbike stood waiting.

Now, our college sports field near the canteen sat at a different level. The bloke shook his fist at me as we approached so I took off down the slope of the playing field and the ass started chasing me. The devil in my soul could not be contained. I deliberately slowed down and let him chase me around the field, then roared back up the mound to the top-level all this with the cable between my teeth. He soon ran out of puff after a couple of times so I gave up the game and duly parked his bike in the same spot. He came up after a bit and as you can imagine he was out of breath and bloody furious. He abused the hell out of the two of us and I was quite happy to cop his invective.

As he paused for breath I thought I should tell him how to cope with the broken throttle cable by putting the soldered end between his teeth.

This was too much for his already aggrieved soul as he literally exploded and in the process made one fatal mistake; he called me a "half-cast bastard". So help me, my reaction was instinctive and without thinking I clocked him one straight in the face, damaging his glasses and possibly his nose. Anyway, he was bleeding profusely. I'd been in many a scrap in school termed a "free for all"; that involved a lot of wrestling, kicking and a heck of a lot of misdirected punching; but never before or since, did I clock a bloke so perfectly. I took my handkerchief out of my pocket, that was weeks old and probably ponging and threw it on the saddle before walking off. I guess I must have felt sorry for him. With that out of the way Pat and I returned rather late to our next class.

The next morning Father "Cauliflower" sent for the two of us. Pat was understandably scared as hell and I got a bloody shock because when we went into the office as a police inspector was sitting there. I didn't think it was fair on my mate so the first thing I said was that Pat was not involved. The long and the short of the interview in the presence of the police bloke was that the bike owner had made a police complaint that I had stolen his bike and assaulted him as well.

This was really serious stuff. Aside from the cops I had visions of being expelled from college. I figured my only defence was to state the facts with a bit of a fib thrown in for the policeman. I said I had certainly borrowed the bike but in full view of everyone in the canteen and had brought it back, so I couldn't have "stolen" it. I also added I knew the owner well and had he not been in his class I would have asked his permission to borrow it. That was a fib because at best I had said "hello" to him a few times at most.

Cauliflower heard me out. "But why did you strike him Loots?"

"He first abused me Father and I didn't object to that because I deserved it but he insulted me by calling me a half-caste bastard. So I hit him without thinking."

Cauliflower, who was a dashed decent bloke, was quite taken aback when he heard that. He was quiet for a long time then asked Pat to confirm it; which he did and also added a bit to explain how much abuse we had both copped before I clocked him. It was then that the Principal pulled off the feat of the century. He quite innocently asked me: "Loots, do you know Mr R D Anderson the DIG of Police?"

I was gobsmacked. "Yes, Father I do. He was an old boy of my school and his three sons studied at Baldwin's during my time."

"Yes, I know. R D Anderson did his Law in St Josephs as well." After a pregnant pause once more and in perfect theatrical style Cauliflower asked me: "He is Anglo Indian like you isn't he?"

I was again gobsmacked. "Yes, Father."

"Very well, wait outside please." I didn't miss the Inspector sort of squirm a bit in his chair.

What Father Cauliflower had astutely done with his question was to signal to the lowly police inspector that the head honcho of the Police was an Anglo Indian and, by inference was being labelled with the racist slur of "half-caste". Wow! That was a "Churchillian" manoeuvre. A few minutes later he called me in and told me to return tomorrow morning with twenty rupees, ostensibly to repair the bloke's glasses and the motorbike throttle cable.

Case dismissed; except, where was I to get the princely sum of twenty rupees that was two months of my allowance?

I went back to the chummily and tried to borrow the money from Ivo. I must confess I asked him more in desperate hope than anything else, but it was worth a try.

"Better ask Andy friend."

"Yeh, but what story am I going to tell him? Twenty bucks is a heck of a lot of money." Anyway, I went to Andy and rather than tell him any fibs I gave him the truth.

"Just when are you going to learn to stay out of trouble Thomas?"

Shades of the past but this time, without the cane!

"Yes Sir awfully sorry, it won't happen again. I promise." I heard him sigh in exasperation.

Andy loaned me the money and I had to repay it by instalments out of my meagre monthly allowance.

After a couple of weeks, I approached the bloke who I had clocked and apologised. He just glared at me and I can't blame him.

I must confess my scholastic career was hardly off to a flying start. The release from the strict regime of boarding school discipline went to my head and I was off enjoying my freedom in parties and cheap booze.

Granny Loots said goodbye to her son Maurice as he and Chrissy left for the UK. I honestly missed Chrissy in more ways than one and felt a big hole in my life, plus I now had to pedal to Granny's to collect the goodies myself. Nanette returned to Bangalore to take Chrissy's place with Granny. She pursued her secretarial trade certificate course and on completion started working in Bangalore while staying with Gran.

Granny Loots received the surprise of her life when her daughter Kitty and her husband Fred returned to Bangalore and India after a long absence in Rhodesia. They bought a home just behind Aunt Bunny's and set about doing it up, converting the old carriage house at the rear into a "granny flat", after which Gran and Nanette moved in with them.

Uncle Fred was a bonzer bloke and a lovely person though definitely under the thumb of Kitty. He discovered to "our" mutual benefit that I could be his escape route. Whenever I visited he would innocently suggest we go for a ride. Off we would go on our bikes straight to Dewar's Pub, which was not too far away and relax in the old cane chairs while knocking back a few beers. Of course, he always paid and it never cost me a penny. Uncle Fred would then buy a pack of strong Egyptian Bakery peppermints; I would have a couple and he would scoff the rest to get rid of the beer smell on his breath as we deliberately took a long way home. It must have worked a treat because Aunty Kitty never latched on to our little caper.

I was a mercenary scoundrel as I now had access to two resources of largesse in one home. My visits became more frequent, much to the pleasure of Uncle Fred as we became regulars at Dewar's and I would sometimes bunk in overnight with Granny Loots and Nanette. Whenever I stayed overnight Kitty would ask me to dinner, but she obviously suffered the same affliction of Bunny that the both of them inherited from Granny Sarah Loots. It was bloody embarrassing but poor Nanette was never invited. Boys ruled supreme! Even in the morning's Kitty would step out of her rear kitchen door and call out: "Thomas come and have a cup of "caaw-feee". She always pronounced coffee in a drawn-out way which I used to quietly mimic to make Nanette laugh.

Well, if that wasn't strange enough about the Loots's I reckon Uncle Bertie of shikar fame took the chocolates! Now that his sister Kitty was there he would come to visit Granny more often than permitted before, but his wife had told him he could not enter her granny-flat. So Bertie would come to the gate and ring his bicycle bell and Granny Loots had to go and have a chat with him at the gate. When they finished and Gran returned to her granny flat Bert would go in through the gate and see Kitty and Fred in the very same compound.

Gosh, the Loots were indeed a daft lot!

Bert and his wife Nora lived in a house down Bangy East way with high walls and gate, with masses of fruit trees in the backyard and two huge German Shepherds. Nora used to teach at St Johns school and was afflicted with a visible patch of a birthmark on the side of her neck. Maybe because of that she remained unfriendly, aloof and distant. A greeting of "good morning Aunty" or "hello Auntie" as she cycled past never got a sideways glance!

Monkeys were plentiful in Bangalore and existed in plague proportions so Bertie's fruit trees proved an awful temptation. But, few monkeys survived the temptation.

Bertie was a crack shot with the small-bore rifle and would pick them off and feed them to his dogs. It's a gruesome but true tale. I often saw him exercising the dogs. He would be on his bike with them on long leashes pulling him along at speed uphill and down dale. The Cant had very few flat stretches of road, so one pedalled valiantly up each long never-ending slope and flew down to the bottom; giving one that inexplicable feeling that no matter which direction you took the upward slope of the roads was always longer than the downward.

Small in stature Bertie might be; but he was wiry, tough and muscled. I reckon he was well into his sixties and had seen me box at school when he asked me one day to feel his stomach muscles. They were hard as stone. He invited me to take a punch at it, then a second and a third. My blinking knuckles, hand and wrist were aching while he laughed: "Better get yourself fit sonny," he advised.

Bertie's and Norah's daughter Helen was a strikingly good-looking girl but even though a first cousin, had little to do with any of us Loots. Perhaps it was her mum's orders as well. Anyway, as fate would decree she met and fell in love with a Sikh who was a pilot. I guess they eloped and got married and she became a Sikh. With the bigoted racist Anglo Indian mores of the day she was "cast" out of her family. Poor girl, I saw her only once with her husband in a restaurant in Bangy and we recognised each other immediately. I don't know if she had any children. To my downright shame, I did not go across and speak to her.

As Will said, the Loots were indeed a funny lot! Perhaps he meant daft!

36
Nanette & Claude tie the knot!

TIME SEEMED TO PASS AT HIGH SPEED. Nanette met her beau in Claude and a courtship developed. Granny Loots promptly sent her son Will a postcard to that effect and he was on the next train to Bangalore to investigate. Knowing Will I thought better of being present when he bailed-up Claude and decided to disappear. Claude was given the third degree as to his intentions. He must have convinced Will his intentions were indeed honourable and the pair duly got engaged; and in time married at St John's, the very same church Will and Carrie had been married in. I was best-man for their wedding and I was the beneficiary of my first new wool suit for the wedding. In the past, they tended to be second-hand suits from the Goodge which was a colloquial term for the second-hand market. Nanette looked as pretty as a rose in bloom and as radiant as the morning sun on her special day.

Will was chuffed and had a few too many sherbets at the reception. He signalled me to escort him to the wedding couch, no less, confiding that his legs were giving away. Will was just not a drinker and a couple of pints were his limit. I'm ashamed to say I could easily out-drink him even as a teenager. I reckon that was the first and last time I saw Will "pickled", as was his expression for being tipsy. Carrie had no such problems and enjoyed the wedding so much she never got off the blinking dance floor.

Hansie showed up at the last minute for Nanette's wedding; he was in his element as Uncle Bob Kerr had got him a job working in the forest logging industry in Dandeli. He never caught up with Sabu of our childhood dreams but there were plenty of wild elephants around as well as trained tame ones that were used for logging. It was great to catch up with him after a long time and we had a long yarn.

The blighter told me he went swimming regularly in the river populated by crocs. I was horrified.

"Crikey Hansie, what a bloody daft idea; aren't you scared of the blinking crocs?" He just shrugged and gave me that same old crooked smile of his.

And that was Hansie!

As I was staying in my old school chummily, I scored all the duplicate wedding presents Nanette and Claude got. This included an electric iron and stove, a kettle and several pots and pans. The electric iron was a blessing because to save dhobi money my habit was to put my pants between newspapers under the mattress and sleep on them. They sort of looked pressed. Anyway, with the wedding largesse, we set up a "tea shop" in the chummily. Aside from Ivo three other mates made up the group; Charley Baldrey, who was in the Railways, Jeff Basith who didn't work but had some sort of family income on which he had to survive and Willy Wollen who worked in the textile industry and joined us off and on. They lived nearby in their own homes and contributed sugar, condensed milk and tea leaves. These were great times together.

Time seemed to fly at college and Will had a nose for what I was up-to. Since it was coming up to my public exams, he figured I should go and stay with Nanette and Claude. Nanette was expecting her first baby and that was the reason given for my temporary shift out of the chummily. Claude meanwhile had bought a little Austin Seven and I had fun teaching Nanette how to drive. Fun because she just couldn't get the hang of gradually releasing the clutch while pressing the accelerator. Fortunately, it was a tough little car and withstood the punishment of stalling until she finally got her left and right foot to coordinate.

Now that she got that part right, we had fun changing gears while the little car put-putted along in first gear. I reckon by the end of the month she was cooking on gas, but there were two things I could never teach Nanette. The first was to slow down going downhill. Nanette would flatten the accelerator and we would careen downhill at high speed. Hair-raising stuff at twenty-five miles an hour and since there were no centre lines on the road she used every inch of the entire width of the road as well, dodging bullock carts, rickshaws and cyclists by inches! She hotly denies this though. The second thing I couldn't get her to do was to drop a gear when going uphill instead of riding the clutch. I had horrible visions of a burnt-out clutch plate and an angry Claude. Nevertheless, she was getting adventurous and so off we went for a long drive to Ulsoor Lake. My fault I guess but of all things we ran out of fuel and then Nanette told me that this was the second time it had happened and almost in the same blinking area. Claude had taken her and their dogs for a drive to Ulsoor Lake and committed the same cardinal sin. Either that or the fuel gauge was malfunctioning.

Claude had to take a long walk to get some fuel but my rank impudence had not deserted me over time. We were stuck just opposite the army officers' mess. I waltzed up and announced that I had a very pregnant sister in the car and had run out of fuel. Believe me, the gallantry of the Indian army officers came to the fore. They downed their gin and tonic's and in two shakes of a duck's tail, the orders were issued and we ended up with a full tank of fuel plus two hefty Jawans to give us a push start to get the old Austin going once more! I think we laughed all the way home. It was a lovely incident with my sister and one to remember.

Behind Nanette and Claude's home sat a vacant paddock and an old Bangy practice was for glass pieces or shards to be embedded in the top masonry of the boundary wall ostensibly to keep the rogues out. They had a glorious but overgrown bougainvillea growing against the back wall. One fine day I took the trusty Bowie out and started hacking it back and like the larrikin I was reached over on tip-toe and threw the cut pieces over the wall into the vacant block. All went well until while in the act of throwing a heavy branch over the wall a thorn from the bougainvillea dug into the top of my arm and like an idiot, I pulled my arm down right onto a glass shard.

My forearm was bleeding like heck as I made my way through the rear kitchen passageway of their home toward the bathroom when I bumped into a very pregnant Nanette. She took one look at the bloodied handkerchief over my arm and the blood dripping from the knife and promptly fainted. I yelped for help from their servant, and honestly; if Claude was at home and rocked up to investigate my yelping he would have witnessed a bloodied knife, a pregnant woman also spattered liberally with blood and would have concluded I was a blinking murderer! Anyway, between the servant and myself we managed to revive her and put her to bed.

My brief stay with Nanette and Claude ended in the most awful tragedy imaginable for them. They lost their first baby boy at childbirth despite the best efforts of Dr Bamford. I can only imagine their grief and the effort required to rebuild their lives. But, rebuild it they did and over time, first Depp and then Jellicoe followed. Will and Carrie had two lovely grandchildren to spoil.

37
Tom at "High Noon"!

I GOT A STERN LECTURE FROM WILL that I had better buckle down in my studies as I had just scraped through my second-year public exam. I returned to the chummily and college life after my study sabbatical with Nanette and Claude and started to do better because I found the subjects more interesting. Things were looking up.

Ivan, better known as Ivo was my flatmate in the chummily. He was an old boy from Baldwin's who did his teacher's training and returned to teach at his alma mater. We hit it off instantly because we had one thing in common, we were constantly broke. I, because I was still dependent on Will for a monthly sum of ten rupees that had to cover my laundry, toiletries, college library fee, stationery and sundry other fees leaving very little for entertainment. Ivo did receive a far more substantial teacher's salary but he smoked like a train and had to buy a daily couple of packs of Charminar, better known as coffin nails. Besides he could not stay away from betting on the gee-gees and playing cards. So, roughly at the end of the third week of every month, he was stone broke.

We developed a solid friendship built on the rock of penury!

Ivo was a character you just couldn't get angry with. I reckon he stood five foot six in his socks and weighed in at 120 lbs wringing wet. I reckon that's what attracted him to horse racing. A little shorter and Ivo could have been a blinking jockey.

Betty Hughes, an old Baldwin Girls schoolgirl we both knew was getting married to an Air Force pilot. She was a sweet gorgeous girl and I imagine she felt sorry for Ivo and me so she invited us to her wedding. We had a smashing time with the girls, dancing, free grub and a truckload of powerful Services XXX 50 proof rum! Ivo and I were decidedly drunk when we quietly staggered up the creaking stairs to our chummily. We somehow changed into our pyjamas, put the lights out and collapsed into bed. As I put my head on the pillow my world started spinning erratically around a keg of XXX Rum. I was feeling queasy and fighting manfully not to barf and make a horrible mess that I would have to clean up if I didn't make it to the bathroom in time. These priorities were suddenly disrupted when I heard Ivo's despairing call from his bed close-by.

"Tom, Tom wake up for God's sake help me I'm paralysed."

I slurred a response: "Don't be an idiot. Go to sleep you're bloody drunk."

"No Loo I'm serious, I cannot move my legs."

The genuine tremor of fear in his voice sobered me up just a little bit. I wobbled out of bed, switched the lights on and lifted his mosquito net to check out his paralysis. Ivo was paralysed all right; paralytic bloody drunk in fact as he'd somehow managed to contort both his blinking legs into one leg of his pyjama pants and naturally couldn't move them! If anything the sheer idiocy of Ivo's "paralysis" seemed to get rid of my looming throw up and I burst out in drunken laughter.

It was a late-rising the following day with a shocking hangover and I reminded Ivo of his paralysis. He couldn't remember it. Even when I told the boys the story a few days later and they laughed with genuine mirth Ivo flatly denied it and insisted it was a story I had made up.

And that was my mate Ivo.

I had a different group of mates at college. Four of us became fast friends, principally because we were like-minded larrikins. But this sort of held a fascination for many a college student who came from rather well-heeled families. In short, they wanted to sort of engaging with and join us. Since the campus canteen was our regular hang-out this worked out rather well. As we were permanently broke we welcomed them as long as they paid the bill. Most came from strictly Brahmin vegetarian families but we soon had them converted to savoury omelettes and boiled egg curries. I kid you not they liked the clandestine diet change so much they took to it like starving dingoes and happily paid the bill. Life was sweet because my packed lunch box from the school was usually a sandwich and a banana.

We had just four girls in our college class who were discovering the "gender equality" notion and making a good fist of it as well so we decided to put it to the test. We all went-off to Crown Café played the jukebox, did a bit of jiving between the café tables and stuffed ourselves with savoury patties and cakes. When the bill arrived I said: "Traditionally the male always gallantly paid now with gender equality you can have the honour." That trick worked only once unfortunately and the girls gave us a wide berth after that despite several invitations to go jiving in Crown Cafe.

In the early period of my college years, the freedom from school-age boarding discipline again got me into strife. I played-up and had a great time. My testosterone levels were mounting far too rapidly for my own good and scholastic career. I just couldn't stay away from the girls.

One day I was ripping down Mosque Road on my bike on the way to see Granny Loots when I saw "her" for the first time and was instantly smitten by her figure, but then I was easily smitten by any pretty girl I saw. She wasn't pretty in the conventional sense but she had personality. I smiled at her and said hello as I was whizzing past. Her returning smile was certain. I threw out the anchors of my bicycle and did a swift U-turn to sidle up and make her acquaintance.

"Hello, again my name's Tom. Can I walk with you?"

She kept her gaze fixed to the ground while she sort of nodded and her luxuriant red hair bounced in unison. She was shy. I wasn't.

"What's your name?"

"Adrianne."

"It's a nice name, Adrianne." Her name rolled off my tongue smoothly. Flattery delivered even with disguised sincerity always works.

"Thanks."

We were nearing the general store where she was heading. I made a quick calculation of my always desperate financial position. I had enough for perhaps two ice-cream sticks but prudence intervened and with it a cunning idea. She bought what she had to for her mother and held shyly onto the paper bag. So I bought just one stick of ice-cream; a vanilla stick from the big Thermos containers in which ice-creams and sweet coloured ice-sticks were stored.

"Here. Take a lick and we'll share it. That way we'll come to know each other better and all our secrets will be shared." What a well-worn or corny fairy tale but she smiled timidly and we happily shared one ice-cream stick. I liked the look of her tongue and she certainly knew how to lick an ice-cream better than me. I walked her home and was not surprised when she stopped at the head of her street.

"I think I better go on alone from here in case my father sees me with a boy."

"That's okay. Can I see you again?" It was the beginning of one more delightful relationship and conveniently on the other side of town so as not to trample on the delicate toes of an existing one at my end of town.

If you have seen that 1955 memorable movie "Picnic" with William Holden and the sultry red-headed sex goddess Kim Novak you are bound to remember that erotically powerful dance scene of the freight train intruder and the belle of the town to the music of "Moonglow". I confess it was imprinted on my pubertal teen-age mind forever; as was the special sultry whistle William Holden used to signal her that he was waiting outside her house.

Adrianne quickly learnt the sound of that secret whistle from Picnic and would slip out of her house and hop onto the crossbar of my bicycle. Then I would manfully peddle up the steep slopes each time driven with optimism. The prospect of success each evening rested in our favourite trysting place, a park not too far from Ulsoor Lake. The place was verdant, green and teeming with delightfully clandestine vegetation, not that I was there to admire it.

A couple of months on and Venus had lost her shyness and found her tongue; yet, she did not misplace her determination to ward off my eagerly probing hands to touch her bare flesh. Still, I thought that I was making progress. But, this potential relationship so full of promise had its hazards. She was the belle of her end of town and had her admirers and I was the trespasser from the other side of town and the local boys were determined to protect their territorial rights.

I dropped her home at dusk at the top of her street, as the mores of the day required she couldn't be seen by watchful parents with attractive daughters. After we exchanged a lingering parting kiss, my eyes lingered on the quick-step of her departing figure too long to notice that someone was waiting behind me as the belle disappeared through the gate of her house. My delightful reverie of promise to come was shattered by a gruff no-nonsense voice behind me.

"You better not come back here again buddy or I'll knock your front teeth into the back of your gob."

There was not one, but three. The bruiser who had issued the dire warning of dislodging my teeth was rubbing his fists rather menacingly.

But, seriously, of all the things in my time of peril I noticed he needed a decent haircut! His hair was slicked back and plastered with Vaseline that showed on his up-turned collar like fireman's waste! I, who hated to have my hair cut as a tacker now sported a regular shorter crewcut in the style of "From Here to Eternity." Again, I once a grot who'd revelled in muddy clothes and dirty fingernails was now very conscious of being as neatly dressed as possible in my old clothes. Eight years of spit and polish as a boarder had knocked those bad habits out of me. The bruiser could have also done with a change of outfit as I could smell his sweat-stained clothes. His "BO" carried the scent of genuine menace!

Anyway, he would be difficult to manage in a brawl let alone three but to give in even before a fight would have been cowardice. Jack Johnson, my hero of old and Joe Louis my present hero would never have done that. I thought at least a bit of lip would save my bacon.

"Why not ask Adrianne who she prefers, you or me?" I thought that was rather clever. The bruiser didn't. He had a matchstick handy and whilst I helplessly looked on, he let the air out of my rear bicycle tyre. He meant business.

"Next time, you not only won't have any teeth but you'll need to buy two new tyres. Understand buddy? Now bugger off and don't come back." I did. He had since discarded the matchstick and produced a sharp little pen knife which he rubbed menacingly against the bike tyre so I figured discretion was the better part of valour!

I didn't have a bicycle pump so I started to half lug my bicycle so as not to damage the inner tube up-hill and down dale to a cycle shop. If the fool hadn't let the air out of my tyre I would have probably thrown in the towel on Adrianne; Joe Louis or no Joe Louis I valued my teeth higher than her! But about a mile later when I reached the tyre repair shop I was fuming and promised revenge and had worked out just how it could be done.

The bike fixed I made a beeline for my friend Charley's place. His diminutive sweet calm wife June answered the door. Charley was out on line and due back late that night. I was invited to drop by the next day around lunchtime and have a bite to eat as well as see him. A free home-cooked meal was always a welcome change even from the Baldwin School staff table.

Now my friend Charley a good decade and a bit older than me was one of the nicest unflustered blokes this side of the black stump. He could afford to be. He was built like the proverbial brick dunny. He stood over six foot in height and his shoulders, arms, chest and leg muscles were that of a born athlete. He had not lost his fireman's muscle despite now being a driver and had been both an athletics and boxing champion on the Railways. He just happened to be an old boy from the same school I attended, albeit long before me. What a friend to have eh?

He heard my story out patiently without comment as I sensibly left out the specifics of my attempted explorations of "Venus's" body in deference to June. Chas disappeared for about ten minutes after an excellent lunch of rather hot chicken curry and rice.

"Here you go, Tom. This should even it up a bit."

He handed me a pair of leather half gloves, thickly lined with felt that covered the upper part of the hand, fingers and over the knuckles. They were heavy, looked sweaty, well-used and very much leather knuckle dusters. "Heck, what's in them lead?"

"You guessed it in one, chum. A strip of lead stitched in-between the leather. I used to use them to punch the bag and harden my fist and knuckles. You weren't the worst boxer I'd seen when you were in school. A punch in the jaw or the ribs with that on Tom and the bloke will be out like a light."

"Uh um, I'm not so sure Chas. The boxing ring is one thing but three goons in a street fight might be different."

"Nah it isn't, any way you tell me what you want."

I had a much safer strategy worked out.

"If you have a couple of evening's free coming up we can go together. I reckon these goons hang out every evening at the café and store, up the street on Coles Road, and that's how they see me and Adrianne on the way to the park. They don't have bikes and so waited for me at the top of Robertson's where I drop her off. If you wait around the corner I'll just take her for a ride around the place for a bit, make sure they see me and then drop her off. I bet the buggers will be waiting and then the two of us can have some fun. How's that idea?"

Charley tossed the idea around in his mind while June looked more than a bit anxious; actually, she was frowning. He suddenly got up and came back with his roster book for the month. After looking through it he gave me three evenings he could spare.

On the evening of the day Charley picked me up and we headed for the other end of town. He waited at the spot just around the corner from where I usually dropped her off. I cruised down to Venus's street and made a few passes giving her the whistle from "Picnic." Out she came and walked quickly to the top of her street. She was breathless and not from walking. "You better be careful Tom. Some fellows are out to get you."

"Is that so? How do you know?"

"One of my girlfriends told me. They were boasting that they had scared you off already."

"Well, I'm here aren't I? So let's go."

"Tom, I don't want you to get beaten up because of me." She melted my heart further. She was concerned about me, poor girl. I loved her dearly, but I was a villain.

"Okay. Hop on darling and we won't go to the park. I'll just take you for a ride."

She hopped on and away we went careening around the streets and making sure I passed the Café several times. As soon as I spotted the three goons I gave them a huge grin, slowed down and leisurely made my way to her street corner. I didn't miss the sharp intake of her breath when we passed them. I rode past Charley and gave him a wink that they were probably on their way.

"You better go now. I saw them." She was sincere and ready to bolt for home. I loved her even more.

"Nah, don't worry. They're probably all vinegar and piss."

"Not Tony. I heard he's been in a few dance fights."

"Which one's Tony? Is he the one with the big Tony Curtis Vaseline puff in his hair and a grubby turned-up collar?"

She nodded and was now biting her under-lip as she kept looking toward the street corner.

"Oh my God, here they come. Quick, go now Tom."

Ah! I loved her more and more with each passing moment but wanted her to feel that I was a hero! My bike was already on its stand. Instead of the customary parting peck on the lips, I held the moment longer. Venus's lips felt cold when they were usually hot!

"Look, why don't you watch what happens from your gate?"

"Tom, please...!"

"Don't worry. Do as I say." She almost ran. It's quite amazing how much courage one has when he knows a friend standing by could clean up all three of the idiots in less than a minute.

The larrikin was still a dreadful braggart and a show-off!

I turned to face the three goons walking toward me; Tony with the Vaseline puff flanked by his two henchmen. I noticed the idiot still hadn't changed his clothes. Deep within me I guess resides a hidden sense of theatre for in my perceived time of peril my silly mind suddenly thought of that Western film classic "High Noon". The haunting melody of the Ballad of High Noon flitted across my mind. Grace Kelly in the shape of Adrianne now waited by her gate and I stood waiting like Gary Cooper in the middle of the street as Frank Miller and his two sidekicks walked menacingly ever closer toward me.

I do not know what fate awaits me
I only know I must be brave
And I must face a man who hates me
Or lie a coward, a craven coward
Or lie a coward in my grave.

I slipped my hand into my pocket and quietly pulled out Charley's "equaliser". My blinking hands trembled as I put the "loaded mits" on. Though my heart rate must have gone up a hundred per cent and my knees sort of shook I cocked a crooked grin at them in confidence because of Charley's presence. He had caught up with the three desperadoes and was now quietly and leisurely pedalling up behind them. They pulled up short and I thought, seemed a bit puzzled by my grin because I made sure Charley's equaliser was visible. Tony scowled his face a mask of pure anger. I reckon this was something he hadn't bargained for and couldn't back-off now and not appear a funk. I kept my eyes on him because I figured he would make the first move. They didn't even notice Charley park his bike just behind them.

"Hi, Tom need any help?" Charley quietly said.

Three heads swivelled one hundred and eighty degrees in remarkable unison; so fast I would have missed the gesture if I had blinked. At the sight of Charley, their body language resembled an ice-cream melting in the midday sun of the Sahara desert. What a moment to remember! My friend stood there, hands-on-hips towering over all four of us. The moment of mute submission was broken by his quiet voice. "All right, beat it now. If any of you buggers so much as look at my friend again, let alone touch him, I'll come after you. Now bugger off before I change my mind." It was a clear message from Charley that they would be in serious need of dental attention if they didn't listen.

I couldn't help but add as they took off: "Hey Tony, have a bath, will you. You smell like a camel." He didn't even glance around.

They needed no further encouragement to make a swift departure never to be seen again. I took Charley for a cold beer at Dewar's. He offered to pay but I owed him.

"You know Chas, Joe Louis flattened Max Schmeling in two minutes four seconds of the first round in their return fight. Those goons didn't last thirty seconds." Charley just smiled. We did a sweep past Venus's house and pedalled back toward our end of town.

"You remember that movie High Noon with Gary Cooper Chas?"

He looked down and sideways at me, brow furrowed at the question. "Yeah, it was a good one."

"Do you prefer Tex Ritter's version of the song or Frankie Laine's?"

"Tex Ritter's version Tom I sort of like his deep voice." I was sorely disappointed in my friend and rescuer of my choppers, Chas Baldrey. Frankie Laine was my favourite and I always thought he should have sung the background ballad to that movie.

I was shameless. Would you believe I pulled the same corny line about High Noon when I next met with Venus? To her undying credit, she preferred Frankie Laine's version of The Ballad of High Noon. Precious inches were gained the very next evening. She must have seen my heroic stand at "High Noon" from her gate (albeit in the evening) and I was permitted a delicious taste of bare skin of the upper anatomy, but only for a short time!

Unfortunately, I lost in the tactile quest with Adrianne. Venus was resolute in defence of any sustained forensic examination of her delightful anatomy and force was not my style. I believed in the adroit pursuit of the prize. The gentle, gradual melody of the "Adagio" of love must never be compromised. I might have won the battle with Venus but conceded that I had lost the war. Sadly, she did not have the longed-for compliant disposition of Boccaccio's Griselda!

My next public exams were approaching and I had three months to make up for the twelve months of neglect. Not entirely impressed with my results at university Will issued a dire warning in a post-card that started to ring incessantly in my ears: "If you don't buck your ideas up, Mister, you will be pulling rickshaws for a living and it will be your Aunt Bunny sitting in it, prodding you with the sharp tip of her umbrella."

As I had been witness to this dreadful behaviour many times I decided I had to move on and study harder.

I would have to leave the delightful Adrianne, with her pretty freckled face, the wide generous mouth and long tongue that tickled my tonsils; but when not so engaged would also wag incessantly. She had a head full of red hair and the body of a Venus that surely demanded further exploration but she could cross her shapely legs with vicelike ability. We were about seventeen and she was regrettably religious as well. Worse still, her father was a policeman! I gave up and Adrianne and I parted ways without a tear or a prayer!

It was in times like these that I felt life was unfair to prurient Lotharios!

However, I returned to a far more compliant relationship at my end of town and one that was less demanding on my time. June was an immaculate and sophisticated air hostie; more than a tad older than me but her age was of no consequence. Her looks were and "hostie's" were engaged for their looks. She was generous to a fault with her love and her purse. I paid for nothing. I couldn't. Her perfume alone would cost three months of my meagre allowance. But she was sweet and would always pass me the money surreptitiously under the restaurant table before the bill arrived so as not to embarrass me, or pass me the money quietly to pay for the tickets to the flicks. She would even invite me to keep the change, but, contrary to nature I had pride and never did. Rake I was; willing to sprinkle my favours liberally but not an out-and-out cad!

She who flew above the clouds transported me there becoming the first to leave her lipstick on more than my lips and collar. I swatted hard for my exams in-between her landings!

But, in time June with the exquisite perfume and unstinting largesse for a hard-up university student surprised me. She showed me her engagement ring one late evening. A Second Officer or something like that had proposed to her. I dabbed the tears from her eyes with one of the silk handkerchief's she had bought me and soothed her aching heart. The parting lingered that night for the last time as I wished her genuine happiness. She deserved it, for she was exceptionally sweet of nature.

I returned later that night to the chummily to find my mate Ivo lying despondently on his bed. He paid little attention to my tale of woe at losing June, who had saved me a lot of money. I gave up as Ivo continued to look glumly at the high ceiling.

"Okay, you're not listening to me so what's up?"

"I'm stone broke Loo and I dare not ask Andy for another advance on my salary."

I had forgotten it was the fourth week of the month and this conversation had taken place many times before. "Don't worry mate it's nothing new. We'll get by somehow. We have before you know."

"Not this time. It's bloody serious Loo. I can't get any more tic for fags at the shop and I even had to cadge a couple of fags off Mitchy. To add to it, that miserable sod Bamford sent a letter through his Secretary Kay to Andy that I hadn't yet paid for my hernia operation and he bailed me up in his office about it."

Now, to be fair Dr Bamford was a renowned Anglo Indian surgeon with his private nursing hospital. He operated; pardon the pun, on the Robin Hood principle where he charged the rich like a wounded bull to subsidise his services to the poor. Ivo's hernia bill would have been pretty small and the only reason he hadn't paid Dr Bamford's bill or the shop bill for his fag's was because of his gambling habits. Nevertheless, he was my mate and Ivo would certainly die if he didn't have his fags while Dr Bamford wouldn't die for the lack of it since he had the good sense not to smoke! Anyway, this was serious and all thoughts of losing June were instantly wiped from my mind. Now, if blinking Ivo gave up his gee-gees and cards he wouldn't be in this financial stew but it was useless bringing that discussion up again.

"We've got to find a way to augment "our" income Loo."

Now, the expression to "augment our income" was one of Ivo's favourite lines every month to which there never seemed to be a reasonable solution. The blighter was already using my soap, my toothpaste, my shaving cream and my Brylcreem! Nor was his expression of "we've" got to find a way lost on me either! How the heck could I augment my income since I was still getting pocket money to survive on? But, he was a mate and needed help.

"Look Ivo, why not take up tuition? There must be students in your class that need it?"

"I tried Loo. None of them fancy English and Geography tuition. They only want Maths."

He sounded doleful but I suspected he hadn't really tried hard enough to build up his tuition group as most other Masters did. "Heck Ivo, third or fourth standard maths shouldn't be that difficult?"

He looked at me balefully. Ivo was obviously hopeless at maths. We were in a bind so I thought a bit of levity would help. "Okay, desperate times demand desperate action. Why not stick-up the blinking Post Office? Now that should augment our income quick smart. I'll stand KV at the door while you do the job and you can count on Winsome the Postmistress not identifying us to the cops as the bandits. Be adventurous Ivo. Just think you're James Cagney as Al Capone"; and here I did a pantomime of speaking from the side of my mouth, and with my forefinger and thumb made the imitation of a pistol: 'Stick 'em up babe and hand over the loot!' That would scare the heck out of Winsome wouldn't it?"

"Come on Loo, for God's sake be serious and stop being a clown."

"Yeah, okay, okay. I was joking and just thought it would cheer you up." I was a bit flushed thanks to June's largesse. I never had to pay for the frequent brunches at Koshys, the booze for parties or the tickets to the flicks so I got on my bike and got Ivo four packs of his Charminar "coffin nails" so he wouldn't die before the week was out. There were ten fags to a pack and he finished five fags in five minutes. "At that rate Ivo you'll be out of blinking fags by tomorrow."

"Thanks Loo. I just had to make up for the day. I'll pay you back."

Anyway, Ivo survived the week and as luck would have it that weekend he actually won on his blinking gee-gees. It was probably the first and only time he did. Anyway, he repaid me and I think he paid a little bit back toward the hernia operation that got him off the hook temporarily. Ivo decided we ought to have a party. He bought a couple of bottles of the local rocket fuel known as Arrack, gutter Vada's and a big packet of hot gram. Jeff, Charley and even Willy rocked up with some home-cooked tucker and we had a great time.

The school holidays were due with which Ivo packed his bags and headed home to Hyderabad and I had a better chance to swat for the exams.

It was just about this time that Bill Hailey and his Comets captured the music world with "Rock Around the Clock". Every radio station was playing it, every live band in the Cant was playing it and every man and his dog was whistling, humming or singing it; but, nobody in Bangy knew the Rock and Roll steps because the movie had been released only in Bombay which was the capital of movies. It would take some time to reach sleepy Bangalore Cant.

Re-enter our hero, none other than my mate Ivo. He returned from holidays and announced he had gone to Bombay on a holiday and, despite the jam-packed theatre had gone to see the movie three times so he could learn to rock and roll.

"Come on Loo, I'll teach you the steps."

Like Will, I had two left feet when it came to dancing the fox-trot and couldn't do the waltz for nuts but rock and roll I learnt, or sort of learnt. We would sing, hum or whistle "Rock Around the Clock" as I practised the caper with Ivo. If truth be known I was just doing the "strong-arm" stuff and the nimble little Ivo did the blinking splits, the slide between my legs and every rock and roll step in the movie. We practised like heck and I reckon we became pretty good at it. Jeff, our mate also picked up the steps from Ivo so there were now three of us who knew the dance steps.

The Bowring Institute on St Mark's Road had a beautiful polished wooden dance floor and held a "jam session" every Sunday for the young folk. The entrance fees was a hefty one rupee but beg, borrow or steal, going to the jam sessions was a must. Aside from having a good time all the girls were there and believe me Bangy had the prettiest girls this side of the black stump! They always had a live band and dashed good ones at that. There were the Aces, Claude Thomas, The Rhythms and the evergreen Fred Hitchcock. There were several singers too who performed with the bands.

On the very, next Sunday Ivo and I hit the floor at the Bowring when the band struck-up "Rock Around the Clock". All the other dancers on the floor, who were doing something like a cross between the jitterbug and the jive suddenly realised we were doing the real rock and roll steps. Gradually the crowd on the floor stopped dancing and formed a huge circle around the two of us idiots and clapped to time. We were instant heroes and got a huge ovation. We probably hold the dubious record of being the first to do the rock and roll at a public dance in Bangalore Cant! One more dubious record to add to my school record of getting a caning in my third day at school! Fred Hitchcock, the bandleader was so impressed he invited us up onto the stage and Ivo gave the story of his Bombay trip. A few more impromptu exhibitions on the floor and we soon had the crowd following suit.

A decent education may not have been their strongest suit but Anglo Indians were very good dancers and singers. It was in their DNA.

Now, Jeff was not much taller than Ivo and even a bit skinnier. He was a regular with us to the Bowring and equally a hero in showing the girls the rock and roll steps. There was a bloke who was suspected of having a different sexual orientation. Jokes, innuendo and blatant whoppers surrounded him; that is until Jeff went to the toilet at the Bowring. He was alone in the urinal when this chap came up beside him and after a bit started feeling Jeff's arm.

"My, Jeff you do have muscular arms" he cooed. Poor Jeff's arm was hardly muscular but he took no offence until the chap let his hand wander down Jeff's back. "And what muscular buttocks you have Jeff" and he then squeezed Jeff's bum. At which point poor Jeff almost wet his pants as he fled the urinal. He returned to our table fuming like a cock sparrow and told us what had happened. To his chagrin, we all burst out laughing and forever after the teasing stuck to him: "My, Jeff, what muscular arms you have." He never lived it down.

I noticed "her" on the dance floor at the next rock and roll jam session at the Bowring Institute. She was dancing with a bloke and was dressed in the fashion of the day with a wide knee-high skirt. The skirt flew dangerously high in the "twist"; and I succumbed. She was slim and graceful and she had the most shapely legs and ankles that stretched all the way up Payneham Road to Paradise!

She legged her way into my heart instantly!

I made her acquaintance at the very next number and she smiled and agreed to dance with me. The bloke at the table scowled and the chaperone matron, also at the table did the same. I must have had a bit of a "reputation" as my radiant and ingratiating smile directed at the two of them as I took the damsel's arm did not alter the scowling by the bloke or the matron! All was well though as it turned out the bloke was her older brother and the matron her mother.

She was doing a secretarial course. Her name was Dianne with a double-barrelled surname. That should have warned me because I held the view that if the woman (in this case her mother), added her name when married she had an "attitude". But Dianne had me whenever she did the twist to Chubby Checker and to heck with her dragon mother. I was an absolute sucker for long shapely legs.

Once again I just managed to get through my College exam and only got my attendance record to do the exam because of a peculiar incident that took place earlier. The Government Colleges went on strike for some reason or other and invaded our campus, smashing a few glass windows to force us to go on strike. They invaded our class and the Economics lecturer, a wonderful and dignified old man decided to give the invading horde a stern dressing-down. They didn't take kindly to his rebuke and started throwing their chappals or slippers at the poor old bloke. Things were getting serious and to see the poor man being humiliated as he cowered on the dais trying to protect himself from the "missiles" was too much to bear. I gathered my three mates and we stormed our way through the crush while surreptitiously cracking a few ribs with the elbow and administering judicious kicks to the groin. Grabbing our lecturer, we forced our way back through the idiots toward the door and onto the veranda and escorted him to the safety of the library and bolted ourselves in until the cops arrived. Remembering this act of "heroism" the College Principal, Father "Cauliflower" very kindly signed my attendance record off.

We had a long break before the start of the new semester and I decided to spend a couple of weeks with the "new" girlfriend before going home to Carrie and Will in the bush. Pervez, one of my college mates produced a newspaper cutting calling for applications to do a Railway Exam at a place called Waltair. The attraction was not the job but the fact that the Railway would send you a free travel ticket and then pay you a "travelling and accommodation allowance" to attend the exam. The both of us applied but at the last minute Pervez backed out as his parents wouldn't let him go for the trip. I had no such restriction as Will was far away in the bush and he would have surely killed me if he knew about the caper.

The Railway sent me a third-class ticket (it must have been a humble position) plus the welcome allowance by money order to go the six hundred miles to Waltair for the exam. At Waltair I met the station superintendent, a Mr Bone who was an Anglo Indian and with a bit of native guile, I ended up not only with a free comfortable retiring room bed and bathroom at the station all to myself but also with an invitation to dinner at his home! He had two rather charming daughters which were an added and unforeseen bonus and I was a regular dinner guest.

My close friend Robert who had much earlier substantially advanced my knowledge in the "birds and the bees" while in Madras had a sister who I couldn't remember. Nevertheless, I now heard that his sister Cindy, who I sort of knew, was now working in the American Oil Refinery and staying at the convent. So off I went to renew my non-existent childhood acquaintance. She had lovely green eyes which I fell in love with immediately, so after a long yarn about old times in Perambur, I offered to take her out for an ice-cream. She was rather cool and gave me no encouragement. Fortunately, she politely declined to save me the two bob in my pocket. However, it was a remarkably propitious meeting.

I did the exam with no intention of joining the Railways; passed the exam with flying colours and collected the balance of their allowance which was quite a bit.

Since I was half-way to Calcutta and with a couple of bob in my pocket I convinced "Uncle Bone" to get me a free ride the six hundred miles to Calcutta! He not only did but also sent me in 1st Class style. He also gave me a note for the Station Superintendent of Howrah (who also happened to be an Anglo Indian) to do me a return trip to Waltair. So armed with that and the promise to stop-over on my return and spend a few days with the Bone family, off I went on my next adventure.

I'm sure Uncle Bone or his good wife must have thought I was a good sort and they did have two lovely daughters!

The Howrah "Uncle" was quite old and if he had any daughters they were probably married, but he was more than helpful. He told me staying in Howrah was dull and that there was much more life in the city. He contacted a friend in the YMCA and fixed me up with accommodation at a special rate.

The larrikin was becoming an expert in building relationships or at scrounging!

The Calcutta "Y" was an old three-story building and very central. I shared a room with another bloke who had a penchant for reading the Bible every night for ages. He asked me if I did as every bed-side locker had one. Sadly I was a total disappointment to him and didn't dare mention the fiasco of the debating society!

I accidentally discovered a thriving industry in an attached warehouse of recycling particularly old clothes, bottles and even papers that was run by the "Y". While they seemed to have regular workers, who were usually very poor people I figured I was poor enough and so asked the supervisor if I could do a bit of "picking". I suspect he thought it was a job below the dignity of an Anglo Indian and gave me a look of baffled surprise. Anyway, he agreed and I pitched in sometimes for a whole day and other times for half a day. So, for the next week and a bit, I picked papers, bottles and clothing, i.e. separating paper from cardboard, coloured glass from clear glass, dresses from men's clothing, good from bad, etc. The income paid for my breakfast at the "Y", a cheap street lunch snack and a street vendor dinner. I was happy as Larry and had quite a bit of money in the pocket to even go to the flicks.

Calcutta was definitely the big smoke compared to Bangalore, with its bustling night-life and I figured I'd get plenty of job opportunities as there were still a lot of British companies around. Added to that, my discerning eye did not miss the attractive sleekly dressed Anglo Indian secretaries that traipsed each day to work in hand-drawn rickshaws. Gosh, there must have been thousands of them! I had a great time loafing around, taking in the sights, seeing the latest flicks and boldly smiling or giving the attractive secretaries a low wolf whistle. Their fluttering eyelashes and smiling lipstick lips stayed with me as a promise for the future. But all good things must come to an end and I had to get back home before the next college year started.

"Uncle" at Howrah Station was as good as his word and I got on the Calcutta Madras mail train duly ensconced in the 1st Class. He even introduced me to the Chief Guard (an Anglo Indian of course) and told him to look after me. The Guard did as asked and even shared his dinner with me.

When the train stopped at Waltair I skulked around so I wouldn't be seen by Superintendent Uncle Bone or I would have had to stop over as promised. Honestly, I felt a bit of a cad because he and his wife had been so kind to me. Nevertheless, it was a pity I had run out of time as the elder of his two daughters was definitely a very attractive proposition and had shown friendly intentions over several dinners in their home where we "accidentally" touched feet under their table several times. It was promising but I had run out of time. As it was I would have to think up some pipe-dottle for Will of what I did in the Cantonment where I was supposed to be. Granny Loots would have sent him a postcard that I had not shown my face for over two weeks!

I still had my Railway issue third Class ticket and sadly had to "slum" the six hundred return miles from Waltair to Bangalore.

Now one of the perks of old boys of Baldwin's was that if you came on a visit to Bangalore you could stay in the chummily and have your food with the staff for a fee that was far cheaper than a hotel. "Batlugs" of yore who almost got his ear chewed-off had passed out from school and was working, or sort of working on his father's coffee plantation in Coorg. On the first occasion, he rocked-up on a motorbike and stayed in the chummily. He was not short of a quid because coffee planters were very well off. We had a great time for a week at his expense, saw every movie, plied the cafes frequented by girls, played games of snooker, drank beer and rode all over town on his motorbike like a couple of liberated jailbirds!

One of our favourite pranks was to tightly roll-up the Deccan Herald newspaper, tie a few pieces of string to keep it firm and it became a great "thwacking" device. Batlugs would slowly ride up behind a poor bloke walking along the road and from my position on the pillion; whack him on the behind. The shock was more than the pain and would elicit a cry of "ay-yo-baba" much to our amusement though not his I wager. We didn't spare the poor cop walking home at night either though the motorbike lights were turned off so he couldn't see the number plate. In addition to the yelp of surprise, a cop would yell abuse as we roared off at full throttle.

I once whacked a poor old Sadhu plodding up the hill, flowing beard, bare top and only a "lungout" or loin-cloth (the closest comparison being a skimpy bikini bottom), with his skinny bum exposed. He almost jumped out of his lungout in surprise when I whacked him and it must have hurt as well because he set about gesticulating and pronouncing dire curses on us. The curse hasn't come to pass as yet and may still do so for our tomfoolery!

The next time Batlugs came down, the blighter arrived in a Morris Minor. I spent another week enjoying his largesse which included driving his Morris; sans the motorbike prank and when he was leaving he suggested I go back with him. I didn't think twice about college attendance and I was off. Coorg is located in the Western Ghats that was a forested and mountainous area. While the Morris was groaning slowly up the hill in first gear on a narrow road flanked by the forest, a huge grey rock in the vegetation ahead caught my eye. Suddenly the "rock" started moving toward the narrow road.

"Batlugs, Batlugs take a look, that blinking rock is moving!"

"Where?" I pointed it out. "Bloody hell Loo it's a wild elephant and it's about to cross the road."

"What, a damn wild elephant? Let's get the hell out of here quick smart."

"I can't. I'm going as fast as this thing will go."

I figured the "moving rock" and the Morris were definitely on a collision course and so did Batlugs as he had stopped the car and decided to reverse the car downhill and away from the danger. A splendid idea I thought, but only briefly as he managed to stall the motor and the breaks were not too good either. In his panic he was trying to do several things at once; steer the car in reverse down the steep curving decline, press the brake, the accelerator, the clutch, restart the motor, grinding the gears, while we inexorably rolled backwards and perilously close to the edge. I managed to yank the handbrake hard and finally, we came to a stop. The elephant didn't even glance at us as it walked across the road about ten feet ahead and again disappeared into the jungle. We let out a collective "whoosh"!

Batlugs was still standing hard on the brake so we wouldn't roll back and now wasn't sure if he could re-start the car while doing so. I could well understand his predicament but not his suggestion. "Loo get out and find a rock and put it behind the back wheel so we don't roll backwards."

I wasn't keen at his suggestion at all not with a blinking big elephant hanging around. But, get out I did and was horrified to find the car was at a 45° angle across the narrow road and I reckoned, despite the thick vegetation, perilously close to the edge of a steep slope. There was no rock in sight and I certainly wasn't going to search for one, so I did the next best thing. I braced my legs low and pushed back against the car. I yelled out to Batlugs to take his foot off the break and restart the car. I figured that if I couldn't hold onto the car at least I wouldn't be in it if it rolled off the road.

Friend, or no friend the larrikin's instincts for self-preservation reigned supreme!

If nothing else the Morris Minor was reliable. She started, after a couple of whirrs of the starter motor and off we were again. Batlugs made me promise not to talk about our little episode as apparently, the car was his elder brother's which he had borrowed. I had a great few days on Morton's estate. Coorg is a beautiful area so there was plenty to see; aside from rum or gin in the evenings followed by good tucker.

I was dropped off in Mercara and caught a bus back to Bangy.

You won't believe it but the dangerous tradition of "walking the ledge" and bunking to a late-night movie, or just for a loaf had not died out despite the legacy we left about being caught, caned and gated for a month. One day, Mickey O who was repeating the final year whispered to me that he and a couple of the boarders who I knew well were going to do a bunk and would I like to accompany them.

"Hell Mick, you were in on that caper when we got caught why risk it again?"

"It's only for a loaf Loo and to have a smooch with Jenny." Mick was sweet on a very good looking girl who lived down the road near All Saints. I honestly tried to dissuade him but it appears somebody in the long past had started this "challenge" and left a legacy that just would not go away. To my shame and the still-active larrikin spirit lurking within, I finally agreed.

Carrie had given me a Burmese chequered sarong called a "lungi" that she had brought out from Burma as a young girl. It was to be my "disguise" with an old cardigan top and the usual towel. I stole down the creaky chummily wooden stairs and waited for them at the barber's shed. As we were larking down Museum Road I spied none other than Father Cauliflower walking toward the main St.

Josephs campus where all the Priests stayed. Dressed as I was I had the harebrained impulse to have some fun; and so pretending to be a kojja, I started to do this crazy sort of tempting dance around and around him while mouthing off some drivel in a sing-song voice. Poor Cauliflower, I reckon nothing like this had ever happened to him in his cloistered life and here he was, at night and on a poorly lit road being accosted by a kojja. He had a walking stick but did not attempt to whack me but just waved it around repeating: "get-away, get-away, get-away from me." Meanwhile, my accomplices had collapsed on the road laughing and then roared with laughter when I told them a little later that Cauliflower was my college Principal!

Ever after I always held the uncertainty that Father Cauliflower suspected it was me who was the culprit because a kojja would hardly know English in the first place and he might just have detected my voice. Yet, he never mentioned a word to me. Honestly, Father Mascarenes, like Andy was a remarkably good and kind man.

The larrikin spirit had not deserted me!

I managed to finish my college education, once again scraping through without any further incident. I sold Nanette's wedding presents without a second thought, had a burst up with my chummily mates, bid a teary and fond farewell to the girlfriend and headed for home.

Will heaved a huge sigh of relief and perhaps the furrows on his brow receded just a tiny bit. I now had a two bob college qualification and had to find a job. Thoughts of Calcutta came to mind. Without admitting I had already been there I told Will about it. He needed little convincing that job opportunities in Cal were far better than in Bangalore, even the snobbish Cantonment. His one clear command was not to join the Railways.

After a short break, Will got me a return First Class Pass to Calcutta gave me some money and wrote to Uncle

Bruce and Aunty Muriel to put me up as they now lived in Cal. He also gave me a gold ring and told me to always keep it as insurance and if I needed money to pawn it but never to sell it. That way I could always redeem it sometime.

The larrikin was now ready to finally spread his wings in the real world!

PART FIVE
Farcical yarns of job hunting!

BEN LAFFRA

38
Tom the artful dodger!

BANGALORE CANT WAS STILL a pensioner's paradise with a population of fewer than one million, including the cousin Bangalore City while Calcutta had a population of around five million. It was truly the "big smoke" metaphorically and in reality and it was smelly as well. But it was the centre of India's largest mercantile companies; headquarters of the tea and jute industry and boasted a thriving manufacturing and heavy industry base. I figured getting a job would be easy. It was not.

Uncle Bruce and Aunty Muriel had "rooms" in a central Calcutta suburb and I dossed in with them. I happily slept on the couch in their little lounge and although they were not very well-off they made me welcome as they had no children. Bruce made a sporadic living as an entertainer and even though his suits were second-hand (and probably from the "Y"), he was a snazzy dresser when he went to work complete with the bowler hat, which he called a "billycock" and spats. It was quite an event in the courtyard when Bruce climbed into the rickshaw to go to a gig as he graciously doffed his billycock to all the residents who may be present in the courtyard as the rickshaw-wallah whisked him away. It was a grand ritual to remember.

Calcutta still had a large expat European population working there in the British companies and one could find many posh restaurants, clubs and gymkhanas in Cal. Club life was very popular and the centre of entertainment for the well-heeled gentry, as well as for the up-country tea planters who came down to the city for a bit of R & R. Uncle Bruce was a professional entertainer in the clubs and the big old colonial hotels. He played the piano and entertained the audience in "sing-a-longs". With his rubbery face and a fag dangling from the corner of his lips he was a brilliant raconteur and teller of jokes. I don't know how he did it but by some sort of twist of his under lip, he could make the burning end of the fag pop backward into his mouth and out again. He didn't have much hair but by crinkling the skin on his scalp and forehead he could make the billycock bob up and down. He could bring the house down with a risqué joke that had the ladies blushing and fanning themselves with hand fans and the men roaring with laughter.

He was also a brilliant snooker, billiards and skittles player and would hang around in the club's billiard room during the day and wait for a "wood-duck" to show up who fancied himself as a good player. They would start playing for small bets and Bruce would deliberately lose and keep losing and paying up until he put up the money on a really big bet. And that's when he would deliver the sucker punch and clean-up the wood-duck. To be honest Uncle Bruce lived day-to-day on his wits and yet they looked after me as their own. Bruce was wise to life in the big smoke and his advice was invaluable.

Getting a job in Cal was not quite as straightforward and simple as I'd previously imagined. In short, responding to advertised positions in the newspaper or ringing the company for an interview never seemed to work. Besides, laboriously handwritten curriculum vitae and applications were time-consuming and hard yakka. I guess it was the usual case of not what you knew but who you knew, and I didn't know anybody until Bruce suggested: "cold calling" would be the best option. Calcutta was a city of commerce and manufacture and there were heaps of posh old administrative offices along the Strand, Connaught Circus and Chowringhee in the CBD. The city was still dominated by all the old English companies and all of them had expats still working in them.

He shared the daily paper, "The Calcutta Statesman" with the neighbour and from it, he figured out a way for me to go job hunting. Once a week, the Statesman had a very extensive sports section that regularly reported on and published the results of the golf, tennis, polo, cricket, swimming, snooker and other sports tournaments that were taking place in the sports clubs around Calcutta. The strange practice was for them to not only to publish the names of the participants but also the prestigious companies in which they worked.

Bingo! I would laboriously list the names and companies and Bruce would work out their addresses from the old phone book. I had a personal almanac of the who's who of Calcutta and didn't know any of them from Adam!

Armed with my list I set about job hunting. Getting around a big city meant catching a tram or bus and that was fun, if not crazy because I never bought a ticket as I had to save every penny. The trick on the tram was to sit or stand by the door and when the ticket conductor was getting near, chanting "ticket, ticket, ticket" while clicking his ticket-punch to a curious cadence, I'd hop off the moving tram. It was a risky business but I quickly learnt the art and would run and hop onto the next moving tram coming along to repeat the same trick.

However, the bus service that catered to the companies outside the CBD was a different kettle of fish. They were always overloaded and careened around faster than a blinking tram. So, here the swindle was to literally hang on outside the open rear door along with others. It was a skill to hang on by a finger-nail and one foot and hope like hell the bus didn't get too close to another vehicle when overtaking. When the ticket conductor managed to push his hand and head through the mass of sweaty bodies hanging on and clicked his punching tool, you yelled back that the money was in your right-hand hip pocket and you couldn't reach it and would pay when the bus next stopped. Mind you, I was not alone in this little caper as other hangers-on would come up with the same yarn in the local lingo. The ticket collectors never believed this of course so you hopped off at the next stop and you guessed it; the caper was repeated on the next bus coming along!

Aside from the risk of hopping off and on, one had to keep an eye out for the ticket inspectors who would stop the tram or bus and do a spot check. One fine day I hopped off the bus at a stop without a ticket as usual and the inspector was waiting. He collared me first and demanded to see my ticket and so I gave him a fib that I had thrown it away and he asked where. I pointed behind him toward the crowd waiting at the stop and when he turned around to look, I bolted. Since inspectors appear to be promoted to that august position based on their bulk he had no hope of catching me. The funny part of it was that a few more blokes who had also got off the bus also bolted in different directions. The poor bloke ended up being the butt of derisive laughter from those waiting at the bus stop. You see, the "locals" knew the ropes well. The inspector would usually pocket a few coppers bribe from those who didn't have a ticket and let them off, but I had shown them another way. Perhaps I started an innovative practice by bolting!

One more dubious "first" on my suspect CV!

It was hair-raising stuff and I can still see the poor khaki uniformed tram and bus conductors shaking their fists and swearing at me as the vehicle went on its way.

My one and only "best man's" suit was getting a daily hammering in the humidity of Calcutta and hair-raising tram and bus rides and must have looked daggy. Aunty Muriel was working overtime to at least give me a clean shirt each day. Cold calling meant I would have to present myself to the ubiquitous receptionist counter of a company chosen from my almanac and make my pitch. Honestly, every blinking receptionist cum secretary was one of those well dressed and utterly attractive Anglo Indian girls I had seen in their rickshaws going to work.

As it turned out, the biggest hurdle was to get around these receptionists. They would give me the third degree of: "Do you have an appointment?"... "What do you wish to see Mr so and so about?" ... "Sorry, he is in a very important meeting" ... "Sorry but you must make an appointment"... "Please leave your name and contact details with me" ... "No don't call us; we will contact you"; and a hundred other variations of the same theme. Believe you me, despite me turning on the charm those delightful and vigilant creatures would shield their bosses from unannounced interlopers seeking an appointment; with greater determination than they would to protect their virginity! Or so I imagined in angry frustration.

It was tough going, but flattery, persistence, guile, or a sob story of being a very long way from Bangalore Cant, or, on occasion sheer bloody audacity was required. I was not beyond offering to take them to the movies or buy them an ice-cream after work which I had no intention of doing since I was broke. One or other of the swindles usually worked though and so most of the times I would get to see the boss I wanted to see on my list. The boss-man was far easier to get on with than the "Boadicea's" manning the reception desk. Strangely, most or all appreciated my initiative of how I came to pluck their name and that of the company out of the Statesman and this became my "ice-breaker" to try and sell myself into a job.

One of the oddest (and most memorable) interviews from my almanac was a contact in Garden Reach Shipbuilders out of town. The location of the company was a huge rambling construction site with cranes and steel sections and chains all over the blinking place and unsurprisingly no pretty receptionist in sight.I finally tracked the contact down in a dusty old double story office building crammed full of junk and files and stuff and there I found him in a singlet (not a suit shirt and tie) wearing khaki shorts and sitting behind a big old table with a huge parrot perched nearby on an old telephone stand.

There was no air conditioning except for an old fan twirling away lazily from the ceiling. The parrot squawked a greeting and the bloke told it to "bloody shoot uup" in a broad Scottish accent and the blinking parrot returned the compliment! Anyway, instead of a flash secretary, he had a peon who made us Indian chai served in tin enamelled mugs. He was a big barrelled Scottish bloke, red from the heat with a matching red beard and sweating away profusely but he turned out to be the nicest bloke this side of the black stump.

We had a long chat about everything under the sun and I gathered he was some sort of deep-sea diver involved in salvage and looking over the hull of a ship. I cannot put into prose his thick Scottish accent but we got on okay. When I congratulated him on winning some swimming competition or other, he roared with laughter so that the dust fell from the ceiling and the damn parrot laughed as well!

"Oi that was easy laddie half the booogers canna swim!"

He wouldn't let me go and I was in no hurry to leave anyway. The peon served up a huge curried lunch brought in a tiffin carrier. It was the hottest blinking curry I had ever eaten up-to then.

"Noothing like a hot curry laddie it's the only way to enjoy one!" This he said with the sweat pouring off him like a harlot in church for the first time!

Mac didn't have a job for me but gave me a couple of names and addresses of contacts I could go and see. He also made me promise I would let him know how I was faring. We parted on the veranda and I can still picture him standing there in his khaki shorts and singlet waving goodbye: "Ye've the right gumption laddie, don't bluey dy giv' oup."

I had regaled him with my experiences of job hunting, smarming my way past the Reception girls, and the tram and bus jumping capers at which he laughed with a big belly laugh. He loved the life in India and seemed to be living in a world of his own, as happy as ever but he did know people.

This was a character that gave life a delightful meaning and he was hard to forget.

One of the contacts he gave me was to the Production Manager of Metal Box. He must have phoned him because the charming secretary needed no coaxing for me to get to see him. After the obligatory cup of tea and biscuits and a short interview, he took me down to the huge manufacturing shop floor and at the end of it offered me a job as a supervisor (or foreman?) in the plant after three months of training. The offer was a good one with pretty good money.

Now, still prevalent in the British companies of India was the system of the "covenanted hand" which was an archaic carryover from the British Raj. Covenanted hands were reserved usually only for Brits and carried with them a far superior pay structure at any level of employment. I had seen this in Will's case. While he certainly enjoyed the "perks" of his position left by the Brits he was nonetheless poorly paid. A Brit with half his brain earned probably twice as much as Will.

In the business world, anybody not employed as a covenanted hand had no hope of advancing up the management ladder either. So while the pay was good at Metal Box and it was a well-known and major manufacturing company, I figured I would forever be on the shop floor and I would never get a management position. I thanked him and asked if I could think it over for a few days. He agreed.

Uncle Bruce, wise to the ways of the big smoke had previously warned me that this was not sleepy old

Bangalore Cant and to watch out for the Calcutta pickpockets, especially when in a crowd at the bus and tram stops. I couldn't figure out why I would attract the attention of a pickpocket, considering that I could do with a bit of pick-pocketing myself!

One of the tricks of surviving in Cal on the cheap was to know where the cheap food areas were, generally well patronised by the locals who knew the ropes. I had no problem finding them. My usual lunch repast consisted of a clay pot of a thick sweet curd (famous in Cal), and a cup of "chai". The curd was cheap, filling and healthy. One day it was the usual lunch hour and the street and shops were crowded as I waited my turn. I felt somebody pushing against me from behind and at first, took no notice; but then I was sure I had felt a hand around my hip pocket. Since I didn't own a blinking wallet I reckon the bloke had started to feel around. I spun on my heel and grabbed his wrist and in that instant saw the guilt or fear in his face. I just said one word, "Chor" (which means thief) and all hell broke loose immediately. The bloke tried to get away but I had a firm grip on his wrist and that attracted the rest of the crowd. Every man and his dog started to whack the blazes out of the poor bugger with their "chappals" that seemed to be the favourite weapon in India. I guess they had all been victims, or potential victims of a pickpocket or knew somebody who had their pocket picked and wanted their ounce of flesh! Honestly, he got the hammering of his life with their chappals and I got a free extra pot of curd from the shop owner for catching him. I left the bleeding and dishevelled bloke in their hands and finished off my lunch.

Once you managed to smarm past those dazzling Receptionists one always got a cup of tea and a biscuit or a piece of cake at these impromptu interviews and that helped, too! On one occasion I waltzed into a big law firm without looking at the company name and business. I smarmed my way past the receptionist and got to see the contact on my list. After a bit of chit chat, he asked me at which law firm I had done my Articles or some legal words to that effect. My face said it all. Anyway, he had a huge laugh when I told him I had made a mistake and did not have a Law Degree. He did give me a few leads to some other companies and promised to phone them.

I had high expectations of getting a job in the tea or jute industry so I canvassed the blinking lot of them. The reception here proved far more encouraging because my qualifications suited to the agricultural industry. The tea planting industry was run in the main by Scottish companies and they had a reputation for advancing employees on merit, not on their lineage; but, as luck would have it they had already filled their positions and asked me to come back in six months with the promise that they would view my application favourably.

I next scored an offer of a job with the pharmaceutical company Glaxo Laboratories in their Sales Division, but once again not as a covenanted hand. Again, the money was very good so I asked the bloke what prospects I would have of becoming a covenanted hand considering I at least had a decent qualification. He was a bit evasive and said it could be considered at a future date. I guess I was either opinionated in the extreme or an unmitigated ass because I next asked him how many of his British expat assistant sales managers had attended university? I reckon a pomegranate red was the best description I could give of the colour on his face.

Not surprisingly I was shown the door, proving beyond doubt that there was no connection between my brain and mouth!

Meanwhile, I pawned the gold ring Will had given me. I was running out of money as at this point I'd gone through more than a month of seemingly fruitless searching.

The moment I stepped off the pavement, out of the humidity and the harsh sunlight and through the eight-foot-high teak doors and into the cool ornate reception area and laid eyes on her; I knew instinctively this delightful creature was different. I was seriously smitten by this "Boadicea" at first sight; meaning the mythical beauty of Boadicea of my fanciful imagination and not the real one; who had a terrifying appearance, with the glance of an eye most fierce and with red tresses hanging down to the hips.

This charming Boadicea did not have red hair but brown hair and didn't affect the popular permed hairstyle of the period for starters; instead, she sported a fashionable short hairstyle that suited her finely chiselled oval face, pert nose and chin. I don't know how to describe it, but very few women have that unique look; not sultry or sensuous (or fierce) but stimulating or challenging! A look at which brave men balk, weaker men fly and only the foolhardy try! It may be the expression in the face or the eyes that gives them this exciting look. I think in her case it was the dark almond-shaped eyes. The expression of face and eyes sort of said: "I don't think you are up to it chum; but if you are good enough come and get me!"

The clack of the Remington typewriter stopped as those challenging black eyes pinned me to the polished floor. I figured smooth charm or a sob story would be useless; attack had to be the strategy. I loved the challenge.

"Hello, I'm Tom Loots."

"Yes?" What the 'yes' in her tone and eyes meant was 'so what'?

"You don't know it yet but we are going to the movies together."

"Are we?"

"Uh, yep! Now I bet no one has told you that you look like Kim Novak." I allowed a dramatic pause. The reaction was a curious stare. "I'm right, aren't I? But seriously you do look like Kim" Did I detect a faint smile on her mouth?I had to seize the moment and continued brazenly. "I saw her in that classic movie Picnic and I can't get her out of my mind. Did you see it?" There was a slight tilt of the head which I took to be an affirmative nod.

"Remember that dance with William Holden?" Again, the half nod. "Holden was the wild reckless intruder who breezed into that small town riding on a freight train, just as I've done bursting in through that door and he won her heart during that dance."

Those beautiful dark eyes had turned from challenging to "friendly" or so I thought so I went in leading with my chin.

"I'm sure you are a beautiful dancer "Kim"; I am not, but if you can produce some magic and turn that typewriter into a gramophone and play "Moonglow" we can dance to it on this polished floor."

I figured flattery, coupled with the humble admission that I was hopeless at dancing was the coup de grâce!

"Now what exactly do you want after all that Mr Loots?" Wow, she was smiling. She had beautiful even white teeth and just a blemish of dimples on her cheeks. She was very, very attractive. The best I'd struck.

"First, I want to see your boss about a job. He won the golf tournament and he's bound to be in a good mood. Don't you reckon? Second, check out the weekend evening movie you want to see and I'll meet you at the theatre. Agree?"

"Which one of the two is more important?"

She was now in a teasing mood. I took it as progress so I produced a coin and with a flourish tossed it into the air. "It comes up heads so I'm taking Kim Novak to the movies."

"It's Rhoda."

"Okay. I'm taking Rhoda to the movies and to heck with seeing your boss; how's that?"

She got up laughing ."I better find out if Mr Laycock will see you." I watched her walk with the eye of the connoisseur; a swaying walk so determined in its purpose and so unconscious of its attraction; the light graceful walk of a dancer. She was tall enough, had a shapely figure to match the face and a delightful sway to the hips. Mr Laycock was no longer of consideration. He wasn't available anyway and I was fobbed off by the inner sanctum to meet one of his assistants. I got the impression he was not rapt with my short-circuited presence. It didn't matter. My mind was in fact preoccupied with Rhoda.

That, I must confess, was one of the most outrageous entrées I'd ever pulled off successfully though the interview was hardly a success.

Rhoda was still game when I finished the interview despite the outcome which I told her about. She did give me the bad news though that we would have to go to a Saturday matinee as her mother would never allow her to go to an evening show with a stranger. Well, frankly I was starved of female company a yearning that was exacerbated by seeing hordes of these blinking beauties with iron hearts and steel skirts!

If truth is known, there was a simple reason for the large numbers of very attractive Anglo Indian "single" girls in the cities such as Calcutta. Post-1947, there was a steady migrant stream of Anglo Indians, particularly to the UK and Canada. If the entire family did not migrate, then the boys were first packed off in preference leaving the girls behind. As a consequence, available girls far outnumbered eligible bachelors. To paraphrase the economist authors Levitt and Dubner, I call it "Luckonomics" since this Larrikin was the lucky beneficiary of the hidden side of the phenomenon by being in the right place at the right time!

Anyway, we decided on the movie and I got to the theatre and bought two tickets and to my blinking horror she rocked up with a chaperone; her younger sister! Had she been a mind reader she would have taken the same rickshaw straight back home! Nevertheless, I bought the third ticket and craftily waited around to go in last hoping we would be separated from the sister. I had a feeling she was onto my little caper and when we got into the dimly lit interior she told her sister to grab a seat, then we went into the next row behind and sat together. I whispered a "thanks" both to her and the gods!

She told me her mum had cooked dinner for me and invited me over. I agreed with alacrity. Things were looking up! We held hands throughout the movie and whispered a few sweet nothings. The following weekend the same caper was repeated, but this time little sister didn't need to be told where to sit. Methinks Rhoda had had a word in her ear.

I was right in my first assessment of Rhoda; I had met and overcome the challenge of "come and get me if you are good enough". I was good enough so progress was swift. I don't know what the picture was about so starting with holding hands and doing a bit of arm stroking, followed by some very awkward kissing since movie seats are designed for contortionists when it comes to an embrace. This was a case of "love at first sight". We went home by rick with the little sister following in another. During the trip though she had the presence of mind to redo her stylish make-up and used my grotty handkerchief to wipe her lippy off my face.

Once again dinner was great but the conversation was a bit stilted. This time her mother (I could see where Rhoda got her looks from) wanted to know all about me and my folks, from A to Z and to make matters worse I discovered her blinking father happened to be a senior sergeant in the Cal Police. Hells bells; shades of Adrianne! I should have known my luck. Nevertheless, I appeared to have won their confidence and Rhoda was now allowed to go out with me anytime without an "escort".

Anglo Indian girls, most probably because of the Indian heritage have very smooth fine-textured skin. Rhoda's was like velvet as we spent time in their backyard supposedly "taking in the garden".We "rickshaw-ed" and walked our way hand in hand around Park Street each evening, not daring to go into the flash clubs like Mocambo,Flury's, or The Nizam but happy to eat "Kati Kabab" on the pavement, or go home to her place for dinner.

Soon thereafter, her father suddenly started calling me "son". Now that word belonged to Will and included special affection, so I was not too sure about this liberty. Anyway, the mother compounded my uneasiness by announcing that her Harold had contacts in the Police and would arrange for me to meet his deputy superintendent. Now, a career in the police I didn't quite fancy. I wasn't sure how my ability to identify or know the difference between "Alternaria" and "malaria", or that "aphids" had no connection with "alpacas" or my knowledge of Mendel's law would help me identify, catch and prosecute criminals in the big smoke!

While I was getting on famously with the stunning Rhoda, her parents, or more precisely her mother was coming on too heavy for comfort and started making rather oblique suggestions of me moving in with them when I got a job: "so you and our Rhoda can save money for your future." I got the distinct and uncomfortable feeling that they were making plans for the two of us, and marrying Rhoda would be pretty much like marrying her family. I'm sure her mother meant well, but she was very pushy. I figured privately that maybe that's why such a gorgeous girl didn't have a boyfriend when I came along.

Rhoda's mother was horrified that I had turned down a job in such leading and high profile British companies like Metal Box and almost had apoplexy when I told her about Glaxo. "Honestly Thomas" she all but screeched "to get an opportunity of an interview, let alone a good job offer and then turn it down is unbelievable? How could you." The way she said "how could you" sounded more like "how dare you"! I couldn't bring myself to tell her that "her Harold" would never get past being a Senior Sergeant; while I had aspirations of being something more than a lifetime Foreman in a Factory or a rep with a briefcase full of medical samples plodding around the countryside. Cocky and misplaced though it might be, in my pea-nut brain I had the spirit of ambition.

Gosh, why were mothers so difficult? There was Dianne back in Bangalore Cant with shapely legs like that of a cabaret dancer and a "battle-axe" for a mother with a double-barrel surname, and now Rhoda's mother with only the sound of wedding bells ringing in her head! Crikey, we were just out of our teenage years and here she was hinting at marriage? Maybe she, like Granny Sarah Loots married as a teenager!

I think what finally scared me was a party at their place to which I was invited. I loved partying so was looking forward to it. I discovered it was a party mainly of their rellies and a few close friends. That was fine except that suddenly it transpired the party was thrown in my honour. I don't know if it's universal but Anglo Indians have a habit of really celebrating the relationship of young couples, or maybe it was the free-flowing grog. Whatever, elderly rellies and Rhoda's friends just took it for granted that the two of us were: "inseparable" … "so suited to each other" … "absolutely in love" and "so looking forward to our engagement". I also got the impression that her mother was extra attentive and Rhoda sort of very possessive.

Crikey, it was certainly a whirlwind courtship but engagement and wedding plans were a bit over the top. I did not share her mother's plans and did confide as delicately as possible to Rhoda that we were a bit too young to enter into a serious relationship and both of us needed time. I also told her that I was keen on getting a job in one of the Agricultural companies and if I did it would mean working somewhere in the bush. In any case, I was asked to return for a second interview with a tobacco company and was pretty sure I would get the job; so I put it to her kindly that in time if things worked out between us (without her parent's interference) would she be willing to live in the bush? Rhoda was evasive. The big city life and her attachment to her parents was something she was reluctant to part with easily. I confessed that living and working in Calcutta unless it was a job that suited me was not an option.

She was disappointed, perhaps even hurt and yet she showed admirable spirit and there was a teary farewell and promises to keep on Howrah station when I finally left.

We did correspond for a time and the last letter I had from Rhoda was that her mother and father had decided to go "home" to England! Frankly, she was a delightful Himalayan Rhododendron in perfect bloom that I sadly had to forfeit but I came to the conclusion that physical beauty and Rhoda was genuinely beautiful also had to be matched by "inner caring beauty" as well for a relationship to last.

Maybe the Lothario had learned something!

However, after a few more hilarious incidents while job hunting, persistence paid off and I finally got a job after a second interview in the agricultural division of a large Public Ltd. Company. It was the second-largest tobacco company in India and aside from tobacco the controlling Company also had jute interests. While it was a publicly listed company, the major shareholders were the Elias family who were Jews. I was employed within the management structure as a "Leaf Trainee". And, as luck would have it I would be working in the bush which I loved.

I rang Mac to tell him of my good fortune and he was genuinely pleased. "You watch out for those Jews laddie.

They're stingy boogers and tighter than a fish's bum with their mooney!"

Coming from a Scotsman I thought this excellent advice!

39
Tom's personal epilogue!

WILL FINALLY RETIRED from the Railway and settled down with Carrie in a tiny Anglo Indian pensioner's hamlet called Whitefield about fifteen miles from the Cantonment. I guess he didn't like city life either.

Remember the green-eyed aloof girl I met during my clandestine trip via Waltair to Calcutta who was the sister of my long-time mate Robert? Our paths crossed again many years later and this time I felt it was right.

We were engaged in Whitefield at Carrie and Will's home. Carrie very sweetly said to Cindy: "now you can have the problem, my dear."

My carefree past was to catch up briefly with me again. I took my fiancée Cindy to meet my old school Principal Andy. He welcomed us into his office, the very one in which I had felt his cane on my bum many a time. He graciously welcomed us with tea and biscuits. He expressed the pleasure that I was doing well in my profession, though not so pleased I worked in the tobacco industry even though I was involved in the agricultural division of the industry. The truth was he'd never approved of smoking. After a bit of chit-chat, Andy suddenly turned to Cindy.

"Do you know the man you plan to marry?" he asked. I guess she was more than a bit surprised and I was squirming in my chair.

"Well, my dear," he continued, "he was one of the most taxing students that ever passed through the portals of this school but he did have two redeeming characteristics; he was honest and had excellent leadership qualities." He proceeded to give her a few "uncomfortable" examples that he still remembered despite the passage of years but he never mentioned the canings!

If that wasn't enough to scare the living daylights out of Cindy a week or so later we were invited to an engagement party of one of the Bamford clan; of Dr Bamford surgeon fame. There, sitting amongst a large number of guests was none other than Father Mascarenas or "Cauliflower" from my college days.

I took Cindy across to introduce her and once more, after a bit of chit-chat, Cauliflower almost echoed Andy's blinking words: "I hope you know what you are getting into my dear because you will have a tiger by the tail for a husband!" He then very sweetly gave us a priestly blessing.

The years had rolled by with alarming speed. Nanette and Claude had immigrated to Australia with their two young children. Will sadly passed away much before his time though he lived long enough to see his wayward son do well in his chosen career. Carrie and Hansie continued to live in Whitefield. Hansie had married Celine, a nurse from KGF and was now working in the Aeronautical Industry of HAL.

The only Loots Clan left in the "spiritual home" of Bangalore Cant now consisted of just two; Aunty Bunny and Aunty Ivy. As they were pretty old and lonely, whenever I visited on work or holiday Cindy would take Carrie and the two aunts out on sightseeing trips or to the movies, coffee shops, shopping or visiting their friends etc. Cindy was the real instigator of these outings and took them out far more often than I did.

However, these small acts of kindness and the fact that she once wanted to adopt me must have impressed Aunty Bunny. In saying that, I am now definitely betraying a meanness of spirit but later events (I believe) were to prove me correct. One fine day Ivy, in hushed tones and with due respect for the occasion told me that Bunny desired to see me and Cindy "to formally discuss the future of her estate". Perhaps the seriousness of the occasion was more significant to Ivy than me as while driving to Bunny's home she was not whistling as was her habit. Perhaps I should have paid more attention to that or sought her advice.

It was very formal, tea in delicate china, biscuits and silver service!

Bunny duly "announced," her wish, which in short was to make her will in which she'd leave me her property with "most" of its contents plus "a bit of money" (as she termed it) and "most" of her jewellery to Cindy. I guess she wanted to give some of her jewellery and furniture to Ivy. What she wanted to leave me was very substantial. She had a beautiful home, well maintained and appointed and in a very good suburb of the Cantonment and I have no doubt her bank balance would not have been paltry.

I listened politely, thanked her for her generosity and then respectfully told her that I lacked for nothing. I explained I was doing very well as the Leaf or Divisional General Manager in the company, so would she please leave the "inheritance" to Hansie who was not doing very well? I added that I also had plans to immigrate to Australia. This was greeted with what must have been stony silence and yet my stupid sense of self-importance could not detect the change in her mood. Like a fool, I took it as acceptance of my wishes.

Hansie was a shy, kind and gentle person in total contrast to his larrikin brother and regularly visited both Bunny and Ivy since he was now staying with Carrie in Whitefield. To do this, he would have to cycle a return trip of 35 miles, up-hill and down-dale; something I figured she would have appreciated. We left after some small talk and continued to see her thereafter when on work trips or my annual holidays. The issue was never discussed again.

When Aunty Bunny finally "passed on" Hansie received not one brass razoo. Despite my good intentions, I did him no favours. I could have simply accepted her generosity and then done as I wished, but I had once more proved that the connection from my brain to my mouth was indeed tenuous. The folly of my actions remains forever on my conscience. However, I tried to atone for this mistake by making it clear to my now widowed mother before leaving for Australia that I gift my one-third share in Will's property to Hansie.

What happened to Bunny's money and property? Well, she left a tidy sum to the RSPCA, probably to protect the bulls from being flogged and the rest of it to Ivy who was the one remaining senior Loots sibling. Ivy was reasonably well-off herself. However, my stupid refusal in refusing Bunny's offer had an even more bizarre ending.

An old friend of Aunty Ivy's son Tony returned to Bangalore Cant to settle down and made Ivy's acquaintance. Family gossip has it that he successfully ingratiated himself with her. Sadly she contracted Alzheimer's disease and when she ultimately passed-away her estate went to this "stranger".

Hansie did not receive a brass razoo once again!

I guess Will was right; the Loots' were indeed a daft lot!

The times they were "a-changing" and after eighteen years of a very successful and rewarding career, I decided I wanted a fresh challenge in life and applied to migrate to Australia. We were accepted. Cindy and I left for Australia to start life afresh with a meagre USD 15.00 in my pocket (that's all the foreign exchange the Govt. of India permitted) and a rather soggy £20.00 of Her Majesty's paper note smuggled out in my shoe! A hairy caper at best and being hauled away by Indian cops at the worst never to see the shores of Australia!

We left many good and dear friends behind and made many good and dear friends down-under. Most importantly, we never looked back!

As for Cindy; well over fifty years on and she is still hanging on to the tiger's tail with remarkable tolerance!

"In memory of"

IN A REMOTE PART OF the sometimes hot and dusty plains of India, where during the summer months the "rohini" blows relentlessly, scorching the earth, the eyes and the skin; a time when gasping parched birds fall from the trees and baby squirrels from their hollows; there is a small town. At the crossing of four dusty roads in this town sits St. Johns Church, a quaint little stone church with a bell tower. It was built almost two centuries ago by the Brits. It is surrounded by a rustic stone wall that is crumbling with age, its dark hue matching the stone of the church. The entry is guarded by a creaky and sagging ornate wrought iron gate, and within this rustic boundary, one finds a tiny graveyard of six tombs amongst which lies one grave with a polished granite stone.

The graves are shaded by three giant and ancient Indian Lilac trees that seemingly stand as guardians of this lonely outpost. Nobody knows who planted them there but they are a fitting choice for this forlorn sanctuary.

In addition to the person's details on the polished granite gravestone are engraved the following words:

"Only the actions of the just
Smell sweet and blossom in their dust."

The last two lines are from James Shirley's poem, "The Glories of our Blood and State".

Those words were deliberately chosen for the inscription as a tribute to the man who has lain there for these years long past; a man who believed that justice was the most valuable trait the human race could have.

I knew him well. They called him Will.

END

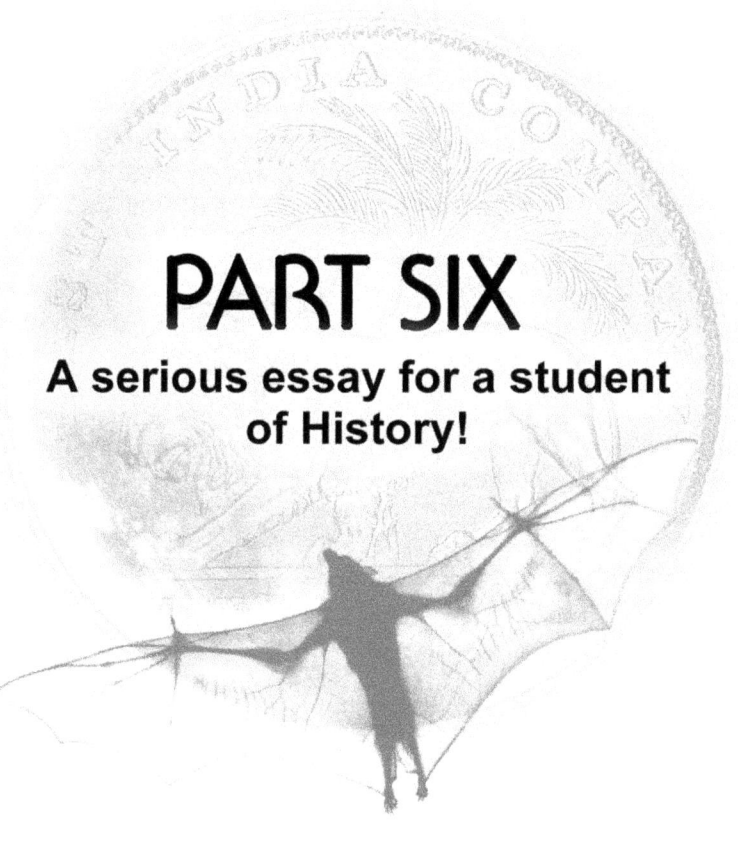

PART SIX
A serious essay for a student of History!

"THE LAST HUZZAH"
(i)

THIS WAS ONE MAN'S PUBLISHED POINT OF VIEW: "To all the complaining Indians, can you please tell me what the Mughal Muslim Sultanate of Delhi et al did for the common Indians? Apart from enjoying life, having a large harem and so on? What did the Hindu Rajas do for their Indian subjects? All of them leeched off the common Hindus. The British Empire in India was definitely not flawless but by far the most productive [for them and India] of all and by far the most humane, compared to the Mughals and the rajas. So before complaining about the British Empire in India, please read some history! - Apsara, London, 7/5/2012

No doubt his point of view would have caused a lot of angst amongst the Indian community; however, my task is to unpick three hundred and fifty years of absorbing the history and cram it into a few pages.

And while I'm about it; if there be a higher purpose to this essay, it is to raise an awareness of the origin of this 'species' specifically directed to the peoples of Australia and the Countries to which Anglo-Indians have migrated and indeed to the peoples of the subcontinent as well, so Anglo Indians may be seen both for their "historical worth" and valued as present-day citizens of society. For those Anglo Indians who wish to reflect, but not languish in the past, they have at the very least an interesting if not remarkable heritage.

Let me segue for a moment and share with you a rather astonishing piece of information. If you don't already know it, a new study of DNA has found that Indian people may have come to Australia around 4000 years ago, an event possibly linked to the first appearance of the dingo. "Australia was first populated around 40,000 years ago and it was once thought Aboriginal Australians had limited contact with the outside world until the arrival of Europeans. However, an international research team examining genotyping data from Aboriginal Australians, New Guineans, island Southeast Asians and Indians found an ancient association between Australia, New Guinea, and the Mamanwa group from the Philippines"

"We also detect a signal indicative of substantial gene flow between the Indian populations and Australia well before European contact, contrary to the prevailing view that there was no contact between Australia and the rest of the world. We estimate this gene flow to have occurred during the Holocene, 4,230 y ago. This is also approximately when changes in tool technology, food processing, and the dingo appear in the Australian archaeological record, suggesting that these may be related to the migration from India".

You can examine the research data on this site: http://www.pnas.org/content/110/5/1803.abstract

(ii)
About mixed races and a tribe called Anglo Indians!

PEOPLES OF MIXED RACES are to be found wherever European traders and conquerors ventured. Miscegenation and inter-racial marriages followed exploration and settlement down through the ages in the America's, Africa, Asia and Australia. Very few of them retained a separate identity for any length of time as miscegenation did not carry the recognition of a pristine provenance, or they disappeared into the milieu of the "host" population. The very earliest example was Alexander the Great who ventured into India in 325BC. Though the Greeks were the first Europeans to invade influence and leave their progeny in the Asian sub-continent, they faded away in the mists of time, to be absorbed by Persian and India's Dravidian culture dating back to 3,500BC.

This is a "historical" synopsis of a community of peoples whose roots go back to India, Pakistan, Burma and Ceylon officially termed in the 1911 census as "Anglo Indian" who migrated to the UK, Canada, Australia and to other parts of the world. That a tiny community can have a history of its own at all is unusual, but when it's both absorbing and colourful, it's worth the telling. Very few Anglo Indians would have a candid knowledge of their own history much less the peoples of the Countries they now live in.

The backdrop to the "story" is the highly advanced culture before and during the Mughal period and the British East India Company also termed The EIC or "John Company" that strode and often trampled its way across its canvas. Unexplored history is often revealing, sometimes confronting, even unpalatable to some, but always interesting.

Most nationalities can be clearly identified in their adoptive countries; for example Greeks, Italians, Germans, Brits, and Dutch etc. The Anglo Indians are not a race but a community of the Indian sub-continent and yet do not conform to the stereotype image of the indigenous Indian peoples. They look, dress, behave, speak differently and have Anglo-Saxon names. Add to this a mix of Portuguese, Dutch, English, French, several other lesser European nationalities, plus Indian, Burmese or Ceylonese and it becomes especially confusing to pick their origins even amongst themselves! So the oft-asked, but polite, question of an Anglo Indian is: "Excuse me, I detect an accent. Where are you from?" The answer to this question lies in the complexity of their 400 years of history; well before James Cooke arrived in Australia.

(iii)
The Portuguese and the Genesis of a mixed-race!

VASCO DA GAMA LANDED near Calicut in May 1498. The historical account of his reception by the Zamorin or Hindu ruler includes a remarkable description of the lavishness of his Court. "On the right side of the king stood a basin of gold, so large that a man might just encircle it with his arms: this contained the herbs. There were likewise many silver jugs. The canopy above the couch was all gilt".The Historian also confirms that the local peoples were far from impoverished. "The women of this country, as a rule, wear many jewels of gold round the neck, numerous bracelets on their arms, and rings set with precious stones on their toes"; and follows up with an interesting observation: "The city of Calicut is inhabited by Christians. They are of a tawny complexion. Some of them have big beards and long hair, whilst others clip their hair short or shave the head, merely allowing a tuft to remain on the crown as a sign that they are Christians. They also wear moustaches", confirming that either the Apostle Thomas Didaemus or the Syrian Merchant Thomas of Cana carried out these conversions about 1450 years before.

The "tawny complexion" in the historical account, however, remains a mystery, unless you accept the notion that the earlier Christian Missionaries indulged in a bit of nookie while carrying out their Pastoral duties!

Anyway, Pedro Cabral followed da Gama and established a permanent trading post at Cochin. However the scene shifts to Afonso de Albuquerque and the excellent harbour of Goa which was occupied by the Muslims. In two battles he overcame the Muslim army in November 1510. Goa was to be his naval base against the Ottoman Empire and to dominate and control the West Coast spice trade by establishing settlements at Galle, Colombo, Cochin, Calicut, Cannore, Bassein, Daman and Diu. Despite his fierce, almost piratical attitude, Albuquerque was a wise administrator. To retain his superior artillery power and the fighting core of his soldiers, he sanctioned the marriage of hundreds of his Portuguese soldiers to the "natives", mainly the widows of the slain Muslims. Albuquerque presided at their weddings and even gave them dowries. He established a Senate for Goa; abolished the cruel practice of "suttee"; entrusted the administration of justice and finance to Hindu locals, retained the customs and practices in the village communities; established schools to teach the children Portuguese and employed the locals in the trading 'factories' as clerks.

Under Albuquerque's policy, many of the girls of these marriages were sent to other Portuguese enclave's viz. Malacca, Sumatra and even Timor, to marry the Portuguese soldiers stationed there.

(iv)
Now to the Mughal dynasty!

THE NEXT STAGE BEGINS with the invasion and establishment in India of the great Mughal Empire that ruled most of central and northern India for almost 330 years. Of the seven principal Mughal Emperors only one, Arungzeb, was a religious despot.

The importance of the Mughal period in this story is: [1] They significantly advanced the already prosperous economy of India by opening sea lanes beyond Africa to the West. [2] This attracted the attention of Europeans to India which in turn led to the formation of the Anglo Indian community. [3] It also serves to expose the rapacious posture of the British that was to follow.

Under the Mughals, the Indian economy boomed. A standard monetary coinage, Persian architecture, books, poetry, roads, waterways, landscaped gardens flourished along with native Hindu culture. To place the wealth of the Mughal Empire in true context, it was estimated at 24.3% of the world economy throughout the Mughal reign. The pre-Colonial annual revenue was estimated at £17.5 million increasing to £100 million by 1770. Almost two centuries later the British economy was barely £16.0 million. Get the picture?

So, to the European travellers who came to the Delhi court of the Mughals; "the first impressions they received was of a gorgeous centre of power, filled with the panoply of state and supplied with all known luxuries. India had much to give Europe in the form of spices, silks, wines, precious metals and other oriental products". It must have dazzled the English seafarer Capt. William Hawkins who arrived in India about September 1600 to grasp the splendour of Emperor Jehingir's court, who was then the richest man in the world. By comparison, Hawkins's own Queen Elizabeth's London Court might well have appeared like that of a run-down London Borough, or slum when measured against the opulence of the Mughals.

Now attracted to the honey pot of Mughal India, ingenious European Traders soon followed the Portuguese example. The Dutch in 1595, establishing posts in Ceylon, Pulicat, Patna, Surat, Ahmedabad and Chinsurah; the English in 1600, the French in 1664 and the Danish and Austrian mission's in the 1720s. All came as merchant traders and were granted land by the Mughal's around the Coastal Ports to establish their 'trading factories'. This time, however, miscegenation resulted in a far more recognisable emergence of mixed-race communities in their respective areas of influence.

The Mughals welcomed the European artists, craftsman, writers and soldiers of fortune. Coming from every corner of Europe many stayed to marry local women. While 'multiculturalism' is a modern word, it was alive and well in India during the Mughal period. "It was almost as common for Westerners to take on the customs, and even the religions, of India, as the reverse". This period was symbolised by Sir David Ochterlony, the British EIC

Resident to Delhi. Also spread over India, were the not so public figure of the flamboyant Ochterlony; they were the likes of Kirkpatrick, Palmer, Gardner, Stuart, De Boigne, Polier, Fraser, Skinner and Job Charnock, the founder of Calcutta. All had married into Indian families.

This was an era when far-flung world colonies were often heterogeneous places. There was a blissful disregard of the boundaries and the narrow limitations of religion or ethnic difference. There was no clashing of European and Eastern cultures. Not yet anyway; that would follow. And so, finding themselves posted as soldiers or Residents to the far-flung Princely States of India (there were over 500 Independent States) the Europeans immersed themselves into the local culture, some to create following dynasties. It was perfectly common and normal to the Indian culture for them to also have several Bibis or concubines as well. But, Indian culture required these "White Nabobs" to care equally for and nurture his harem and the numerous offspring. This would suggest the offspring of many such liaisons were the real beginnings of the "Eurasian Community". Many of the children were strictly illegitimate yet all lived together in an amiable symbiotic relationship.

Many of these European's recognised that the hybrid nature of their offspring might be a disadvantage in the future, a "proper" education was required in the 'English' world. So the young boys, whose skin was suitably light were sent to England or France, or Holland for their education and military or commercial development, while most of the girls were usually raised locally. So indeed it should not be surprising that; "The wills of East India Company officials, now in the India Office library, clearly show that in the 1780s, more than one-third of the British men in India were leaving all their possessions to one or more Indian wives, or to Anglo Indian children; a degree of cross-cultural mixing which has never made it into the history books" ... "the India of the East India Company was an infinitely more culturally, racially and religiously mixed place than modern Britain can even dream of being".

However, this 'romantic' description of a mixed community applied to the "Upper-Class European" who had the status to intermarry with the "Upper Class" Hindu, Muslim or Sikh and should not obfuscate the fact that the many European "Lower Class" common soldiers and freelance mercenaries across India would have formed temporary relationships with the native women, leaving their progeny spread like illicit scattered seeds. These children were often taken from their mothers and placed in orphanages.

However, this harmonious West-East cross-culture of marrying Indian women started to decline from around the 1830s with the growth of the British 'Evangelists;' and all but disappeared by 1850 as you will see.

Now before we question or criticize the mores of the Indian culture, or indeed suffer the indignity of being an Anglo Indian or Burgher who historically "might" be of questionable lineage, remember promiscuity was the norm and strict sexual morality the "ab-norm", as perhaps it is in society from the late 20th century. For example, in 18th Century Queen Victoria's England, that model of absolute propriety, the rate of illegitimacy was so high it spawned the wretched practice of "Baby Farming" at 15 shillings a month. Nor would they have had the 'protection' of a culture of caring that was so well developed in the "Zennanas" of Her Majesty's Indian colony! This fact is a rather sobering reflection for those who believed in the absolute purity or 'blue blood' of their "Britishness".However, legitimate or otherwise this sets the exciting scene for the earliest generation of the 'Native Born' to place their imprint on history.

For centuries India was a fiercely divided conglomerate of over 500 Princely States often warring with each other. It was within these very Princely States that these early Anglo Indians made their mark as Soldiers of Fortune or in modern parlance, Mercenaries. Perhaps this was the finest phase of "Anglo Indian" History. Four of these mixed-race soldiers of fortune were to become legends in their lifetime. James Skinner (1775/1841), Henry Forster (1793/1862), Alexander Gardner and Hyder Young Hearsey. Other famous figures included General Joseph Barnsley of the Alwar Forces, General Jean Baptiste Filose of the Gwalior Army and several others in the Armies of Madhoji Scindia of the Mahrattas; and not forgetting the extraordinary influential Hyderabadi Banker William Palmer. They were all children of mixed marriages.

(v) The charismatic Eurasian mercenary James Skinner!

JAMES SKINNER DESERVES A SPECIAL SECTION, for though probably not atypical of the 'mixed-race community' he is symbolic of the egalitarian and tolerant society of the period. He was the eldest son of Hercules Skinner a Scotsman and his mother a Rajputani Princess. Though brought up a Christian of sorts, he had a harem of both Muslim and Hindu wives; fourteen of them mind you and essentially lived as a Mughal. Yet Skinner moved between the 'two worlds' of Eastern and European culture, in part as a result of his birth and a military career spent between serving the local Potentates and the British. He was a fair-minded person, for he not only built the beautiful St. James Church which still stands in Delhi, but also a Muslim Mosque and a Hindu Temple. His children were brought up as Christians, though some were to choose the Muslim faith.

However, it was Skinner's exploits as a soldier with the Marathas that gained him notoriety and wealth. He formed an irregular cavalry called "Skinners Horse". They were perhaps the earliest recognisable mercenaries who fought for a number of the Princely States. Picture them as charging into battle, a phalanx of cavalry in their distinctive red turbans, yellow shawls and black shields, sabres flashing, or deadly lance points glinting in the harsh light! It must have made them a fearful sight, for they were reputed to have never lost a battle. He was soon to gain the accolade of "Sikander Sahib"; an extraordinary title that had been accorded only once before to Alexander the Great.

Recognising his value as a leader and soldier, the C-in-C of the British East India Company Army wooed him for his services. He refused at first but was finally persuaded by Lord Lake on the condition that he would not fight against Sindia's Marathas he had served. Despite that agreement, later when war did break out between the Marathas and the British, Skinner and other Anglo Indian officers who refused to fight were dismissed; only to be re-engaged to fight again on behalf of the British. Despite this cycle of "on again; off again" treatment by the disloyal British, it was Skinners Horse that significantly enabled the East India Company to expand their territorial gains in India. For this service, he was decorated with the "Knight of the Order of the Bath".

The unfortunate flip side to this famed and charismatic leader was; though treated as an equal and celebrated for his exploits in the opulent Courts of the Indian Emperors, Kings and Princes of India; not so by the imperialistic hierarchy of the EIC. In Skinner's own words: "I imagined myself to be serving a people who had no prejudices against caste or colour. But I find myself mistaken." It was only much later that the British hierarchy accepted him and is captured in a generous letter by his friend Sir John Malcolm: "I do not mean to flatter when I say you are as good an Englishman as I know; but you are also a native irregular, half-born and fully bred; you armed them, understand their characters, enter into their prejudices; can encourage them without spoiling them; know what they can and, what is more important, what they cannot do. The superiority of your Corps [of troops] rests upon a foundation that no others have."

"Skinners Horse" survives to this day as a mechanized Cavalry Regiment of the Indian Army, and for a substantial part of its history, the Colonel of the Regiment was a descendant of Skinner. Gardner's Horse, founded by Col. William Linnaeus Gardner, almost parallels the exploits of Skinner though he was far more fortunate in his relationship with the British. Like Skinners Horse, Gardner's Cavalry Corps was also to serve gallantly during the 2nd WW and join Skinners Horse as a Mechanised Cavalry Regiment of Independent India's Army.

(vi) The British East India Company and the Eurasian tribe!

MUGHAL OFFICIALS PERMITTED the new carriers of India's considerable export trade to establish trading posts or factories in India along the coast; namely The British East India Company; Dutch East India Co., and the French East India Co. Concessions were also granted to the two lesser known nations of Denmark and Austria. While the others were more or less content to prosper their trading ventures, the British soon had visions of imperialism. Forgetting the hospitable and welcoming hand of the Mughal Emperors, the EIC gradually expanded their areas of influence. Cleverly noting the fractious nature of the numerous Indian Princelings, they set in place a colonising agenda of 'divide et Impera'. Enter the likes of Skinner, Gardner and others to further their aims!

Their stay was to last for almost 350 years and to change the face of India forever. It was the era of territorial expansionism and colonization. The superior musket, cannon shot and gunpowder was the force majeure of a different kind. But not all the British Residents within the EIC supported the rapacious policies of the Company, preferring persuasion and negotiation to achieve a balanced treaty with the Princely States rather than resort to threats and bullying. But alas they were too few of them and brute force was the standard they applied.

In time the EIC realised the resources of their armies were stretched. As late as 1880 there were barely 65,000 English troops, and 130,000 native troops in India and their loyalty was always a hidden concern since 1857. They needed a loyal second line of defence to protect the "Jewel in the Crown". So following the examples of Alexander the Great and Albuquerque, and with the precedent of intermarriage during the early Mughal period they now introduced a policy for British male soldiers to officially marry Indian women. "The Madras EIC granted a subsidy in 1687 for each child "christened" to an Indian mother and a European father". One can only speculate that this formal recognition, plus the princely largess of one "Pagoda", would have been most agreeable to the English Soldier recipients. Later British historians contested the rationale of these marriages as being merely a ploy to keep their troops out of mischief. Others claimed it was to protect and expand the Protestant religion from being overrun by the burgeoning Catholic Eurasian's. But, as events were to prove right up-to 1947 the Eurasian was arguably 'engineered' to expand and protect the territorial gains of their British masters.

However, as a point of differentiation from the pure-blooded Europeans and the Native Born, the EIC designated the offspring of these marriages "Statutory Natives of India"; but for the security of Empire purposes they were conveniently called "European British Subjects", so they were subject to a different set of laws.

Over a long period, the descendants of these marriages were to be termed variously as "Indo-Briton", "Country Born", "Native Born", "Eurasians", "Indo British", "Indian Colonials" and no doubt a few other less attractive and colourful colloquial terms as well! However, the term "Eurasian" is considered the most common description of this mixed "race". It was only in 1911 that they were officially termed "Anglo Indian".

So it is not surprising that the physical appearance of Anglo Indians varies widely in stature, features and the total spectrum of skin pigmentation. While the common factor was that they all mainly spoke English, their accents varied quite dramatically, reliant on where and how well they were educated. All of this much to the consternation of the peoples of the countries to which they were later to migrate … "Excuse me, where are you from?"

As is the case with mixed races the progeny was 'stronger' than their forebears; better able to cope with the rigours of climate, pests and diseases of the sub-continent. The women offspring of these early marriages, not only married within their Eurasian community but also in-turn inter-married with the British. Like sponges, they were to absorb the culture of the Indian as well as the 'habits' of their British rulers. Like "chameleons" they could blend with both societies, bridging the cultural gap between the indigenous peoples and the British.

Over time the Eurasians started to outnumber the British and the Community prospered up-to 1785. The more fortunate who were favoured by 'Mendel's Law' were sent to England for their education, some to merge into genteel English society and remain there. The most notable amongst these expatriate Eurasians who had blended into English society was Robert Banks Jenkinson [1770-1828], 2nd Earl of Liverpool and Britain's longest-serving Prime Minister. Most Eurasians however, returned to India to work as Civil Service employees or soldiers in the EIC.

Unfortunately for the Eurasian their very successes were to prove their undoing.

(vii)
Lord Cornwallis and a period of persecution of the Eurasian tribe!

TO COMPENSATE FOR THE IMPENDING LOSS of their American Colonies, the British policy turned to acquire a great Empire in India under the EIC. Denuding the riches of the sub-confinement to the benefit of Britain was the objective, and this foundation was laid by Wellesley between 1798 and 1805. He returned to England and was replaced by Lord Cornwallis.

It was Cornwallis's second term as Governor-General in India, but this time around he was fresh from a humiliating defeat and surrender at Yorktown to the American "Colonial" George Washington. Mentally scarred by this experience in an otherwise brilliant career, Cornwallis held all those who were not strictly blue blood British; to be "colonials and a lurking threat". Influenced by this imagined paranoia he was determined to put down and dilute the power of the Indian Colonials, i.e. the Eurasians to avoid a repeat of his American experience.

Fearing the burgeoning strength and influence of the Eurasians, he promulgated the first of three repressive orders between 1786 and 1795; depriving them of educating their children overseas, stripping them of their property and banished them from any areas of influence in the EIC. "These measures reduced the Anglo-Indian to political impotence and social degradation". Under Regulation VIII of 1813, they were even excluded from the British Legal System in India. "Thrown out of soldiering, the only profession to which they had been reared, there was nothing for them to transfer their services to Indian chiefs, and they were received with open arms. Others of them formed their own groups of irregular infantry and cavalry; while hundreds of Anglo Indian warriors won their spurs in the ranks of armies not belonging to the East India Company." Whatever the reasons it was an act of Imperial racism that was practised to break the Eurasians so they would not be the "lurking threat" that Cornwallis imagined.

But Cornwallis's repressive measures were perhaps the defining moment in the history of the 'Native Born'. Instead of being some form of human detritus, engineered by the Brits, Eurasians suddenly gained their own unique "Tribal Identity" or recognition, albeit due to the perfidious actions of Cornwallis. However, the EIC soon discovered they had lost a valuable fighting force and demanded the return of Eurasian led troops once again. Soldiers now serving with the Indian Princely States were forced to obey an official recall by the EIC, or be branded traitors. They obligingly returned to support them, and in doing so, clearly and indelibly marked themselves as aligned to British interests. Not surprisingly and true to the British characteristic of Imperialist duplicity, the Eurasians were once again discarded on the conclusion of the British military campaigns against the Marathas and Mysore's Tipu Sultan. In effect, the repression was to last for 40 years until 1833 when a petition presented by J W Ricketts resulted in the renewal of the EIC Charter and Cornwallis's repressions discarded. Section 87 of the Act now stated: "No native of the said territories, nor any natural-born subject of His Majesty resident therein, shall, by reason of his religion, place of birth, descent, colour, or any of them, be disabled from holding any place, office, or employment under the said Company".

(viii)

The British Raj in turmoil, the Eurasians and the 1857 – 1859 mutiny!

INCIDENTALLY, THE ROOT CAUSE of the mutiny was the aggressive Evangelical pursuit of the EIC toward the religious conversion of their Sepoys, and not the popular myth of the cow or pig fat coated cartridges supplied to them. That might well have been the excuse, but not the reason.

The 1857 'Mutiny' gained enormous support and momentum in the North Central and Eastern section of India, but none was forthcoming from the South. India remained too divided for the Mutiny to succeed against the British. This, plus the loyalty of the Sikh and Gurkha troops doomed the uprising from the start. The 'Mutiny' was to last for almost two years. It was a bitter, bloody and a cruel struggle in which countless civilians were to perish. However, now clearly identified as British supporters, isolated and exposed Eurasian civilians would have suffered dreadfully at the hands of the armed 'mutineers'. Numbers perished only to be counted as "European Subjects" killed and so justify the savage reprisals they in-turn inflicted on the Indian population. British subjects killed were barely 3900 approximately. There are no definitive numbers in English History of indigenous Indians killed. Estimates vary in numbers from hundreds of thousands to a million. During this conflict, however, there were clear instances of divided loyalties. Eurasian's and even a fewBritish, some of whom had become devout Muslims, actually fought on behalf of the "Mutineers"; and in one instance during the Delhi siege brother was pitted against brother, much to the disgust of their father Gen. Sir Abraham Roberts.

Despite its bloodied nature there were remarkable though isolated instances of devotion and loyalty. "It is due to some of them (sepoys) to state that they did not quit

Meerut before they had seen to a place of safety those officers whom they most respected. This remark applies especially to the men of the 11th N.I., who had gone most reluctantly into the movement. Before they left, two sipáhís of that regiment had escorted two ladies with their children to the carabineer barracks. They had then rejoined their comrades".

Equally, there was evidence of British Officers weeping when they found their previous Indian comrades butchered on the battlefields. Such is the tragedy of war.

Eurasians who distinguished themselves during this conflict were, Sir John Hersey who was Commander Bengal Army, Gen. Van Courtland of the Haryana Horse, along with telegraphists, W. Brandish and J W. Pilkington, who risked their lives to send an SOS. They remain immortalized in the Telegraph obelisk in Delhi. Battle Orders were awarded by Her Majesty to La Martiniere College in Lucknow, an Anglo Indian school, for the bravery of their Staff and Students.

Later Indian Historians referred to the Mutiny as "India's War of Independence". There is considerable merit to this interpretation, as 250 years of the rapacious EIC yoke would have been hard to bear for the indigenous peoples. However, the 'Mutiny' signalled a huge change in direction for India. Alarmed by the barbarous nature of the reprisals conducted by the EIC troops and the almost complete destruction of Delhi, their charter was revoked. The British Crown of Queen Victoria formally took over the Government of British India in 1858 from the East India Company. Relatively speaking, good Governance was to follow for the final 100 years of the "Raj" in India and a dramatic change in destinies for the 'Native Born' Eurasian.

(ix)

The "fishing fleet" and the changing economic & social norms that shaped Eurasian life!

DESPITE THE NEW CHARTER, the Cornwallis Repression Acts had long-lasting economic effects on the Eurasian's. They had been reduced to 2nd Class citizens economically and mentally. So almost a century later British Policy continued to restrict Eurasians to mostly subordinate or upper-subordinate positions. Few slipped through the net to gain senior positions in Government, the Services or in the mercantile arena. Though dispirited by the "Repression"; the vast majority were saved by the technology of Steam locomotion and telegraph communications that appeared in India around 1855. With it, two major changes were to overtake the 'Native Born'. The first was that they were guaranteed the subordinate positions in the strategic areas of Government. Their unquestioned loyalty was the key to British interests and so they dominated the middle infrastructure in the key strategic areas of Transport, Communications, Law and Order, Customs, Mining and Forestry.

The second change was "social" and far more psychologically profound. From an early period English maidens, spinsters and matrons sailed out to India in search of eligible bachelors amongst the British Civil Service or the Army. They were singularly unsuccessful. Picture the poor European girls, trussed up in suffocating corsets hoops and billowing petticoats, powdered and sweating in the stifling heat and humidity of Calcutta, Madras or Delhi. They had little appeal to "their" menfolk who had long become admirers of the cool diaphanous clothing and striking good looks of the Indian maiden. Most of the English maidens returned empty-handed, complaining that: "Englishmen in India all preferred Indian women to Europeans".

Even the autocratic, yet debauched Governor-General Richard Wellesley in a letter to his long-suffering wife Hyacinthe, described Calcutta European society thus: "the men are stupid, are coxcombs, are uneducated; the women are bitches, are badly dressed, are dull". The Company merchants meanwhile, were: "so vulgar, ignorant, rude, familiar and stupid as to be disgusting and intolerable; especially the ladies, not one of whom, by the bye, is even decently good looking" … "As for sex, one must have it in this climate". On Richard's later return to England in disgrace, his debauchery continued, prompting his brother Arthur Wellesley to write to the youngest William "I wish that Richard was castrated. It is lamentable to see talents and character and advantages such as he possesses thrown away upon whoring".

However, the opening of the Suez Canal now made it easier for the "Fishing Fleet" of European maidens, spinsters and matrons to re-storm their countrymen on the sub-continent. In time the 'Fleet' was to become the "Memsahibs" of the British social structure in India. No longer was it socially acceptable for the British male to marry an Indian or a Eurasian after all England was Victorian and they were now expected to fly the flag and live in India as proper representatives of the Queen. This new approach was amply supported by the arrogant Evangelists:"in perpetuating the Christian religion … for the ultimate civilization of the Natives".

Unfortunately, the 'invasion' of these rabid Christian Evangelists, many of whom were in far greater need of the religious ministrations they wished to impose on the "natives", because of their drunken ways and questionable morals; managed to destroy in 25 years the trust and goodwill that had existed between Christians and the Muslim and Hindu population.

With this new social order in place, it was now fashionable to look down on those who had "a touch of the tar". They knew naught of the refined and ancient culture of the Indian peoples', or of the contribution to the "Raj" by the Eurasians. The velvet skin, flashing black eyes and dusky good looks of the local women remained a competitive threat to their own matrimonial prospects. Sadly, racism had come to firmly replace the multiracial and largely tolerant society of the previous 200 or so years.

Nevertheless, now with guaranteed employment, the more ambitious Eurasians developed as Teachers, Nurses, Priests, Doctor's and of course always the Soldier; including "Boy Soldiers" from the likes of Lawrence Memorial Royal Military School. But in many cases, this was the exception rather than the rule. Too many did not seek education or do a trade and considered it below their Anglo Indian dignity to do a menial job. The women, on the other hand, did far better to qualify themselves with a trade and were often the bread-winners while the lazy husband stayed at home. "Males are charming, convivial, and stay at home, females are competent and efficient achievers".

Proof of this is during the War Years, the vast Army of India was staffed by an amazing 80% of Anglo Indian Nursing sisters (IMNS) and administrative Secretaries; numbers later to return to England as "War Brides". The guardians of the social morês and the power of the white English Memsahibs were ultimately swept aside by the brutality of the 2nd WW.

(x)
Anglo Indian culture and its heroes!

THE RAILWAY COLONY, Mines and the Military Cantonments developed as a microcosm of Anglo Indian society. The Indian continent now comprised the third-largest network of the railway in the world anchored by Anglo Indians in their every operation. All the colonies were exclusive enclaves of Anglo Indians. They populated them in numbers and developed their own social culture. The "European & Anglo Indian Railway Institutes" were the focal entertainment point. Dancing, parties, billiards, whist drives, bingo, picnics and sports fostered a spirit of conviviality and unity. They had an exceptional talent for music, concerts and plays; and it was from these nurseries of talent around India that produced the likes of Patience Cooper, Merle Oberon, Tony Brent, Engelbert Humperdinck, whose real name was Arnold Dorsey, Peter Sarstedt; and some claim even Sir Cliff Richards and Oscar winner Vivian Leigh, the Hollywood Actress in Gone With the Wind, to be of Anglo Indian lineage.

While they were very good all-round sportsmen Anglo Indians excelled in Hockey. The majority of players in India's Olympic teams of the '40s were Anglo Indians. They were to bring this talent to Australia and were at the forefront in the development of the AIS in Perth. The extraordinary talent of the Pearce family is exemplified in that they represented Australia at four Olympic's from Melbourne in 1956 to Mexico in 1968. Australia has since become the world powerhouse of the game, in both men and women's Hockey.

Perversely, the Railway and Mining Colonies had a downside. In reality, the Colony culture engendered mediocrity; a striking similarity to the Coalmine culture of Britain where sons aspired only to follow their fathers into the same occupations and never to venture beyond it. There was an aura of total apathy and little or no motivation to escape the dreadful cycle. They were often responsible positions in themselves but poorly paid and with little or no prospects to advance a career.

Religion played a significant part in their social structure. Every centre had an Anglican Church, favoured by the British Raj by land and cash grants, while the Catholic Church was usually dependent on overseas missions. Lesser Protestant denominations also sprung up.

The Catholics were far more rigid in Church discipline. A non-Catholic had to change their religion before they were allowed to inter-marry or suffer the dire consequence of ex-communication, purgatory and hell!

Remarkably, such a microscopic community has made such a positive imprint on History in India and around the world. At its peak, possibly around the year 1900, it is unlikely the Anglo Indian population would have exceeded much more than one million or 0.4% of the 1901 British India Census. Their real numbers will always remain a total mystery.

Every "tribe" takes pride in its heroes and its legends, from Abraham Lincoln to Nelson Mandela. Somehow these great people left their imprint on the world that the majority of us cannot emulate; but when 'heroes' surface from a small community there is something more tangible to the experience. This is but a tiny sample of outstanding Anglo Indian achievers with an Australian bias, and with apologies to those many, many more who also deserve inclusion:

- The enigmatic Catherine Noelle Worley (1762-1835) who went to France and there became the wife of Charles Maurice de Talleyrand-Périgord. He was chief adviser to Napoleon Bonaparte and French Ambassador extraordinaire.

- Novelist (The Animal Farm), Essayist, Journalist and Critic, George Orwell 1903-1950.

- Diana Hayden, Miss World 1997 and Bollywood actress.

- Closer to home (Australia): Col. William Light 1786 – 1839; surveyor and 'founder' of Adelaide City. His mother Martina was a descendant of Albuquerque's foresight.

- WW I & II: seven were awarded the VC and one a DSO, DFC & Bar and two Anglo Indian women medical personnel were awarded the George Cross.
- Olympics: India won five consecutive Olympic hockey gold medals where a majority of the players were Anglo-Indians.
- Australian Rules elite footballers: Daniel Kerr, Jordan McMahon, Clancee Pearce, Fred Pringle, Alex Silvagni. Andrew Embley, Trent Dennis-Lane, Hayden Crozier, Craig Jacotine, David Gallagher.
- Australian Test Cricketers: Rex Sellers, Dav Whatmore, Stuart Clarke, Ashton Agar andLisa Sthalekar who was Captain of the Australian Women's Test Team.
- Australian Matilda's: Golden girl Samantha Kerr; who also starred in the American Women's soccer league.
- Australian Decorations: Russell Jacob ADF [Conspicuous Service Cross], Peter Varghese OAM Diplomat; Philip Wollen OAM Philanthropist. Others have likewise shone in every field of endeavour including Politics, becoming Cabinet Ministers Robert Ray in the Hawke Govt. and State Members of their respective political persuasion.

However, it was in post-Independent India of 1947 where Anglo Indians stood tall especially in the Air Force. A significant number were decorated for acts of valour during the three Indo-Pakistan Wars and the Chinese invasion. Air Chief Marshal Dennis La Fontaine was Chief of the Air Force and Air Marshall Malcolm Dundas Wollen who also became Chairman of Hindustan Aeronautics Ltd. Eight others were to reach the status of Air Marshall.

In the Indian Army, at least six were to reach the rank of Lt. General. In the Navy, Admiral R. Pereira was Navy Chief.

It is quite an incredible achievement for a tiny community and a credit to independent India's pragmatic policy of its Armed Services; indeed a far cry from that of the treatment by the Brits for some three and a half centuries. Perhaps it was the mercenary soldiering in the 16th, 17th and 18th century's that implanted in their DNA the trait of being loyal and fearless. They were, are, and always will be loyal to the person's, organization or country that harbours, protects and pays them. Whatever the circumstance loyalty is one of their strongest suites.

And while this is a fine record of Anglo Indian achievers, were there also rogues, thugs and charlatans amongst them as well? Assuredly there must have been but they escaped notoriety and the scarce pages of a reliable Anglo Indian history.

(xi)
Directing education!

LED BY A DEDICATED BAND of educationists, Anglo Indians played a major role in English education in India. The High Schools were coveted as centres of discipline and learning excellence, patterned on the hallowed British Public School system.

While their schools stretched from the South of India to the Northern foothills of the Himalayas, generations of Anglo Indians failed to prosecute their advantage and pursue a University education, something that was to completely shut them out of advancing a reasonable career in developing India of the 1950s and '60s. Yet it was these very institutions that produced such world luminaries as Ruskin Bond, William Makepeace Thackeray, Benjamin Walker, George Orwell, Frank Anthony and the larger than life soldier, surgeon and politician Sir Henry Gidney; a onetime student of the same school of this obscure author.

The flaw in the otherwise excellent education curricula however comprised a 'corrupted' version of Indian History served up more like "Oliver's gruel"; or perhaps it was a deliberate attempt by historians to hide the fact that the British had raped the economy of India for over 350 years reducing it to the status of a 3rd World Country from its once preeminent position of a leading world economy in the 1600s. As a result, Anglo Indians and the British themselves, remain profoundly ignorant of India's rich and diverse cultural history. This arrogant posture is aptly summed-up by Thomas Macaulay who served in the G G's Council in India: "It is, I believe, no exaggeration to say that all the historical information which has been collected from all the books written in the Sanskrit language is less valuable than what may be found in the most paltry abridgement used at preparatory schools in England".

Obviously, the otherwise erudite Macaulay suffered a shocking ignorance of India's early civilization. "Consider the fact that Indian written history stretches back almost 4,000 years, to the civilization centres of the Indus Valley Culture at Harappa and Mohenjo-Daro.Britain, on the other hand, did not have an indigenous written language until the 9th century CE, almost 3,000 years after India".

However, Macaulay's attitude had an interesting if not sinister strategy behind it. It was a conscious policy to "exorcise" the Indian culture through schooling the indigenous population in the alien culture of the British via the education system. Persian and Sanskrit were expurgated from the education system and the "Official" language of India and replaced by English. "The curriculum followed classical British standards of the sort set by Oxford and

Cambridge and stressed English literature and European history".

Despite his concealed motives, Macaulay's strategy struck an immediate chord with the "Upper Class" community of India and was an outstanding success. "Thousands of elementary and secondary schools were opened though they usually had an all-male student body. Universities in Calcutta, Bombay, and Madras were established in 1857, just before the Rebellion. By 1890 some 60,000 Indians had matriculated, chiefly in the liberal arts or law. About a third entered public administration, and another third became lawyers. The result was a very well educated professional state bureaucracy. By 1887 of 21,000 mid-level civil service appointments, 45% were held by Hindus, 7% by Muslims, 19% by Eurasians, and 29% by Europeans". By 1911 the Universities and Colleges of higher education had expanded to 186 and kept increasing; so by 1939 it had doubled, and enrolments reached 145,000.

Generations of students were to earn the sobriquet of "Macaulay's Children" who would share in Governing India for the British. And many did. But contrary to his ideals of nurturing only loyal "Western Oriented Gentlemen"; there also grew amongst them the awakening of Indian Nationalism. Macaulay would assuredly have turned in his grave at what he would deem as disloyalty and betrayal by his "children"!

(xii)
The dark side of the British Raj!

THERE IS SOME CONSIDERABLE VALIDITY to this anonymous quip: "The sun never set on the British Empire because God could not trust Englishmen in the dark!"

Put simply, there will always be the debate on whether the British were "good" or "bad" for India. One suspects that the protagonists for the "good" often consider their reign over India as benign only in comparison to the rather tawdry Imperialism of the Spanish, Belgians, Dutch or French, not just in India, but in other parts of the world. Nevertheless, there were some genuine good legacies encapsulated below:

The Rule of Law that abolished Suttee; and the burying of lepers alive. They controlled female infanticide and eradicated the "thuggies" or vicious bandits. They created a system for the Princely States that could no longer be despotic Kingdoms. They certainly prospered architectural edifices, perhaps for their own comfort and prestige, but nevertheless a heritage legacy. They did build hospitals, establish the Indian Medical Association, saved many lives through the introduction of Small-Pox vaccination and did much to prevent the dreadful diseases of Malaria and Cholera.

There were two outstanding legacies though; the first of which was the introduction of English as a national language, though the policy behind it was questionable. The second was far more altruistic and that must be credited to the foresight of the remarkable Sir William Jones the eminent Jurist; and linguist (he mastered 28 languages) and orientalist. He established the Asiatic Society in Calcutta that preserved much of the manuscripts in the ancient languages of India between 1783 & 1794. He aspired to develop a means to foster collaborative international scientific and humanistic projects through the Society that would be unhindered by social, ethnic, religious and political barriers. "The society's library contains some 100,000 general volumes and its Sanskrit section has more than 27,000 books, manuscripts, prints, coins, and engravings". One wonders what his opinion of Macaulay would have been!

Many credit the British for the railways, introduction of electricity, a telephone system, Post & Telegraphs, forestry, mining, dams, hydroelectric power, canals and irrigation channels. So why not give the Brits the credit?

From a humble beginning of 21 miles of rail track between Bombay and Thane, the first train travelled on the 16th April 1853, by 1880 it had expanded to 9,000 miles. But here's the motive. The network radiated inwards from the three major port cities of Bombay, Calcutta and Madras, to carry India's production of cotton, indigo, jute, timber, wheat etc. etc. to "Mother England's" factories. The network burgeoned to over 40,000 miles by 1929 with the same aim, and at Independence, it was almost 60,000 miles of track. So was it built for the benefit of India's citizens? Hardly, as at the commencement of the 2nd WW 40% of the rolling stock, coaches and locomotives were dispatched to the Middle East to carry Troops and ammunition while the railway workshops were converted to producing armaments.

Dams and an enormous network of 71,000 miles of canals and channels were constructed not necessarily to feed or famine-proof India, but to produce the crops "Mother England" required, and of course, the railway carried it to the ports. And let's not forget one of the key reasons for the telegraphs and railways was for the rapid deployment of troops to the trouble spots of India.

Post-Independence India was to benefit from this inheritance of infrastructure, but it would be hard to argue that at the time of construction it was remotely beneficial to the indigenous population. The British in fact had the fond hope that the "Jewel in the Crown" would be theirs forever.

Despite this evidence, if there still be some who feel the British were good and kind masters, and indeed many individuals were, be ever mindful the overriding British Policy had an underlying ruthless economic agenda. "There were two incontrovertible economic benefits provided by India. It was a captive market for British goods and services, and served defence needs by maintaining a large standing army at no cost to the British taxpayer".

In 1901 the British Viceroy of India Lord Curzon summed it up succinctly: "As long as we rule India, we are the greatest power in the world. If we lose it we shall straightway drop to a third rate power". But that power and wealth came at an enormous cost. Over 35 million Indians died of famines caused by British misrule.

This economic agenda is best illustrated in how the British managed famines in India. India was no stranger to regional famines caused by monsoonal delays. Pre-British the Mughals and Marathas would introduce rationing to curtail black marketeering and transport food to the famine areas. Under the British: "In agriculture, the policy was to divert land from food production to the growing of exportable commodities such as indigo, hemp, cotton, tobacco, tea, coffee and opium". As a consequence of this policy, there were seven severe famines between 1770 and 1944 despite the dams and irrigation channels. "In the 1870s some 17 million or so Indians died in the Deccan and South India due to the "let them starve" policies encouraged by Lord Lytton and other British rulers. Indeed, whilst millions starved in 1876, the British held the biggest feast in human history in Delhi, the Delhi Durbar to celebrate Victoria becoming Empress, feeding 70,000 Britishers and Indian princelings for a week". Even the prestigious British Lancet estimated conservatively that 19 million Indians had died in Western India during the drought famine of the 1890s.

And did Imperialistic racism also play its dreadful part in the Bengal famine of 1943? Churchill was Britain's greatest wartime leader and yet he stated: "I hate Indians. They are a beastly people with a beastly religion. The famine was their own fault for breeding like rabbits." And so, while Australia offered food aid Churchill's War Cabinet refused to divert the ships necessary to carry it.

When the United States offered to use their ships to transport the food to India, once more his War Cabinet declined the aid. Between one and three million perished from starvation.

Author, Madhusree Mukerjee was not inclined to be charitable in her book "Churchill's Secret War" and squarely blames Churchill's racism for his refusal to intervene to save the starving millions; concluding: "Winston's racist hatred was due to his loving the empire in the way a jealous husband loves his trophy wife, he would rather destroy it than let it go". The evidence supports her condemnation.

An obfuscated version of the Bengal famines found its way into our history books, but not the tragic reasons behind what can only be described as a genuine holocaust presided over by the British.

(xiii)
The Anglo Indian diaspora and their identity dilemma!

THIS EXTRACT FROM THE BRITISH PARLIAMENT most aptly describes the Anglo Indian and more than a hint into their psyche: "Those who have been English educated, are entirely European in their habits and feelings, dress and language. They were more "Anglo" than "Indian".Their mother tongue was English, they were Catholic or Anglican and their customs and traditions were English. While most of them married within their own circle, many continued to marry expatriate Englishmen. Very few married Indians".

So despite a long history of being poorly treated by the English, and certainly better treated by the indigenous peoples of India, the facts distilled to the essence suggests that while their roots were in India the psychological "umbilical cord" of the Anglo Indian was firmly sutured to their European ancestry. "Mid-way between two cultural worlds, and under the peculiar conditions of their origin and socio-cultural development, Anglo-Indians could never get to know the West to which they aspired to belong, nor did they have emotional ties with India where they really belonged".

Few will admit it, but there was an overt denial of their maternal Indian lineage. Even those that remain behind in India and serve their country of birth with admirable loyalty will still say: "we are Anglo Indian" as if it's very emphasis possessed the pristine credence of a separate nationality. There remains a deliberate attempt to obfuscate their Maternal Indian lineage, perhaps developed over centuries. Nevertheless, at the least, it is a case of subliminal racism. The strange paradox, however, is that the vast majority of the peoples of India, especially in the rural areas, never saw the Anglo Indian as Indian but like the Iranian, Parsee or Armenian Community, some sort of foreigner! Despite their subliminal desire to be in all things very British, to put it kindly in real life: "Europeans said they were Indians with some European blood; Indians said they were Europeans with some Indian blood". Many struggled with this fragility of a twilight status.

(xiv)
The first migration; a little known fact!

THERE IS REASON TO BELIEVE that the following extract is erroneous. In 1852 the term Anglo Indian would have referred to the domiciled European who was Anglo-Saxon British but born in India. Again during that period, the "mixed race" was generally termed Eurasian, or Country Born, Native-Born or Indian Colonials.

"The earliest recorded suggestion of their immigration to Australia was made by the editor of The Eastern Times (an Anglo-Indian newspaper) on August 23rd 1851. At the time Australia was encouraging immigration and the Anglo-Indians were looking for greener pastures. According to Gilbert, some Anglo-Indians did migrate in 1852 and 1854, and T.G. Clarky, a Magistrate, confidently predicted that someday there would be unlimited demand for Anglo-Indians in Australia. An organisation called the South Australian Board of Advice and Correspondence for Anglo-Indian Colonisation was formed "to advise and assist Anglo-Indians desirous to settle in South Australia".

However, there are the following records that show there was indeed a migration policy, of sorts, by the NSW Government during that period to encourage the immigration of Anglo-Saxon Anglo-Indians. Interestingly the shipping records show that amongst them were Eurasians and Indian Labourers.

"A scheme for the employment of orphans from Madras and Bengal was adopted by the NSW Government in 1838. The first group of Indian orphans [7 boys] arrived on February 1841 on the "Sesostis", (probably the "Sesostris) with the passage paid by the East India Company's Marine Board. There were subsequent arrivals of other orphans, including girls entering domestic service".

The "orphans" were very likely Eurasian as the Orphanages in Madras were established precisely for the abandoned children of liaisons between the lower ranks of British soldiers and the native women.

"Sir William Burton, a former NSW Supreme Court Judge, and Puisne Judge in Madras from 1844 supported the emigration of young Indians to Sydney. He organised two groups of immigrants (mainly Anglo-Indians) from Madras. They arrived on the William Prowse 21 February 1853 and the Palmyra 8 November 1854".

"Under the Southern Cross" published in 1880 by Henry Cornish, includes a survey of the results of this scheme.

"The vessel 'William Prowse' left Madras on 12 December 1852 and made a slow trip to Sydney, Australia arriving there on 21 February 1853. Apart from the wealthier passengers, the vessel also carried 88 in Steerage. Included in Steerage were a number of Eurasian bounty immigrants who were part of a resettlement initiative by the East India Society".

The above extract from the shipping records provides the clearest evidence of the arrival in Australia of Eurasian's who were officially classified Anglo Indian only in 1911.

Interesting, isn't it?

(xv)
The final migration begins and the shock!

IMMEDIATELY AFTER WW II, vast numbers of Anglo Indians migrated mainly to the UK. This was the first post-war exodus and would have been made up of mainly ex-servicemen and women. The better favoured of "Mendel's Law" vanished; shed their Anglo Indian identity, or certainly tried to and melted sub-rosa into British society. "They lived in an unrealistic world and many of them escaped into a Walter Mitty-like 'white world' called England, where they imagined everything was plentiful and everyone was kind. It was 'home' in a sense which India could never be".

However, it was on the 15th August 1947 the world of "Anglo-India" truly vanished when India was granted its Independence. The British officially departed India. At a wild guess half a million Anglo Indians remained. They could not avoid the indulgence of introspection as they felt apprehensive and suddenly abandoned by the Brits. For many, there was the pain of the moment and the uncertainty of the future for them and their children. The subliminal fear of isolation haunted them and triggered the second major exodus. This time the exodus was not only to the UK but also to Australia, Canada, New Zealand and many other parts of the world. These were in the main "economic migrants" who generally had a poor education and no trade qualifications. In the 1950s and '60s, they had little prospect of competing with the better-qualified indigenous peoples of India who emerged as the preferred employees; and rightly so.

The Anglo Indian "birthright" to employment in the Railways, P&T, Customs, Police, Mining etc. had ended. The age of entitlement was over.

Racism, as defined by the Cambridge Dictionary, is: "an unreasonable dislike of people who have a different skin colour that results in the unfair treatment of members of different races". In real life racism is a "Hydra Headed Serpent"; to wit the British Class System; the Indian Caste system; Intermarriage of Catholic and Protestant; the fundamentalist Islamic Jihadist or simple colour prejudice.

It would be reasonable to say that the Anglo Indian community was the most colour prejudiced and racist "tribe" of India. Though the product of "miscere" themselves any intermarriage with the Indigenous Indian was unthinkable. The few that did so were completely ostracized by both family and community. They lived in a bizarre utopian belief that they were somehow superior to the indigenous peoples, even though they had suffered arrant racism for centuries by the British. It would be farcical if it wasn't serious; when even a black Anglo Indian would be contemptuous of a much lighter-skinned or even fair Indian. "Many of the prejudices of the British were adopted by the Anglo Indians towards the Indian people of dark complexion, thus creating rejection of the Anglo Indians by both British and Indian communities. Hence, they found themselves caught between the European attitude of superiority towards Indian and Anglo Indian and the Indian mistrust of them due to their aloofness and Western-oriented culture".

However, the Anglo Indian influx into these "new" countries was not entirely greeted with enthusiasm and many found to their horror they were now the subject of racism, completely forgetting that they were equally smitten with the same dreadful disease of racism while in India.

While this may be challenged by the experiences of others, there is little evidence that Anglo Indians were confronted by arrant prejudice in Australia, Canada, NZ and the USA. Why? Well, for example, Australians, in particular, may forgive, but will not forget British hierarchy attitudes during the 2nd WW, nor the vilification heaped on them by the War Historian Hastings; or Churchill's intemperate outburst that "Australians come from bad stock" in obvious reference to their convict and Irish history. Thus because of their own colonial past, these Countries had developed a less insular and more tolerant egalitarian society than "Mother England".

However, assimilation is always accompanied by degrees of difficulty, their fears of rejection a constant companion. They had to 'dig deep' to survive the indignity of being treated as foreigners. Today, however, the vast majority of Anglo Indian expatriates have embraced and welded into the culture of their chosen country though it is inevitable there will be exceptions.Unfortunately, there are still some, who bereft of intellect still live ferociously in the "twilight zone" of an identity dilemma, an identity that was equally obscure to them then, while living in India, as it is now. They remain permanent and confused malcontents, clinging to 'heritage' rather than committing themselves to a 'nationality' whether it be Australian, New Zealander, Canadian or British etc.

A much depleted Anglo Indian community remains in India, which has all but disappeared into the vast milieu of Indian life with the accelerated acceptance ofinter-communal marriage and the returning age of a multiracial society. Some might legitimately contend that this is a just and proper reversal to their colourful beginnings in history.

(xvi)
Living the lie and the future of the Anglo Indian diaspora

"THE COMMUNITY DISPERSED ALL OVER THE WORLD and for reasons ranging from shame, racism and discrimination to plain ignorance about their history, most Anglo Indians hid in closets".

It is impossible to determine how many Anglo Indians masqueraded as "Anglo Saxon" that blended (or tried to) into the countries to which they emigrated. One can safely assume that those who were better blest by Mendel's Law i.e. fair skinned would have done so to avoid any racism or perceived racism when seeking employment, or just to avoid the shame of having "a touch of the tar". Suffice it to say that many did so and lived the lie for the rest of their lives. They would, of course, seek to marry a local girl to buttress their social status. The Welsh accent is not entirely dissimilar to that of the Anglo Indian so again they would have posed as Welsh, perhaps sometimes adding that they had been born in India. A practised lie could in time become a subliminal truth. Nevertheless one ponders on the constant pressure to stay "on guard" and not let-slip the truth.

The interesting result of this life of deception was to be sometimes exposed by bumping into somebody they knew from India, one can only imagine the embarrassment or when they passed on and their progeny sometimes accidentally discovered the truth from hidden documents or papers. Below are some interesting examples.

William Dalrymple the celebrated British Historian and author of "White Mughals", "The Last Mughal", amongst many others, writes of his startling discovery."My relations suddenly became a lot more interesting, however, with the appearance in the story of a Muslim princess with the somewhat unexpected name of Mooti Begum Dalrymple, a woman whose name had certainly been rigorously removed from all the family records I had seen at home. Mooti turned out to be the daughter of the Nawab of the nearby port of Masulipatam, and was married to James Dalrymple".

Diana Marilyn Quick, famous as Julia in the British TV Series "Brideshead Revisited" and was once described by Sir Cecil Beaton, an equally celebrated Photographer, as "the most beautiful woman in the world", writes about her discovery in her touching memoir "A Tug on the Thread" ... "I had an intimation that there was something I didn't know," says Quick. "It was never discussed. My father was a very warm, gregarious, sociable person who had many interests. He lived his life very much in the present, full of activities and the next project. He had many hobbies. He was not given to retrospection. There are lots of things that I would have wanted to know about his life, that I suddenly couldn't ask. And my mother blocked any questions about it; she either didn't know, or she wasn't telling".

She had to spend ten years uncovering her father's 'lie'. This, of course, is why Quick calls her book "A Tug on the Thread". She came from a family steeped in denial and it is this denial that she has been playing out ever since. For the book, she traced her family history back to her great-grandfather, Christopher Quick, who enlisted in the army as a teenager and sailed to India in the early 1870s. He had a drinking problem and spent some time in jail. At the age of 32, he married an Anglo Indian woman; someone whose parentage included both English and Indian forebears. The couple had three Anglo Indian children, one of whom was Bertie the grandfather who ended up in Surrey but was never mentioned in Diana's house.

Even England's future King; Prince William apparently has Indian ancestry from his mother, Diana's side. "A geneticist at Edinburgh University has confirmed that DNA tests from members of his family have proved he has an Indian descendent on his mother's side. Six generations before him, Eliza Kewark, a housekeeper, had a relationship with one of his mother Princess Diana's ancestors, Thoedore Forbes, and bore him several children, including a daughter, Katherine, in 1812. Ms Kewark has, until now, always been thought to have been an Armenian living in India, where she met Theodore Forbes, a Scottish noble working for the East India Company which then ruled much of India. But DNA testing on saliva samples from William's relatives by Jim Wilson, a geneticist at the University of Edinburgh, have established beyond doubt that she was in fact an Indian".

Others who made the discovery are Alistair Charles McGowan the famous British comedian, Pete Best the Beatles drummer and Melanie Sykes, British TV Presenter and model.

The generations growing up in India before its Independence and through the 1960s are probably the last "traditional" Anglo Indians, so to speak. Some continue to retain, celebrate and enjoy their "tribalism"; but for a majority now abroad their connection to India is at best tenuous or fragile. Is there a "new" generation of Anglo Indians growing up abroad that are reconnecting with their roots? The answer is that at best they have a curiosity about their parent or grandparents lineage. Most have completely embraced their new country; having assimilated and forged new identities. In all probability, they do not want to cling to their Indian ancestry. And indeed, why should they?

(xvii)
The British disclaimer!

SADLY THE BRITISH failed to accord the Anglo Indian a rightful place in "their" version of the recounts and chronicles of India. They were simply a biological residue of British imperialism. No English historians; or none that I am aware of have documented or acknowledged the genuine contribution by Anglo Indians to the successes of the British Empire in India. If there be a parallel of such neglect it can be found in the meticulous account by Balbi of the Great Siege of Malta in 1565. He barely mentions the incredible exploits, bravery and loyalty of the native Maltese without whom Malta would assuredly have fallen to the Ottomans, as did Rhodes. His historical focus was on the exploits of the undoubtedly brave Knights of St. John. And so, without definitive documentation written during that period, as with the Maltese, folklore became the repository for early Anglo Indian history supported by fragmented records of their very existence.

The Anglo Indian identity emerging from the British rule in India will have lasted for some 400 years. Arguably there is nothing similar in the annals of mankind. Their forebears were a force to be reckoned with; they had their time in the sun and that sun is now setting! Perhaps, just like the Greeks of Alexander Anglo Indians will fade away in the mists of time; sâns any apology by Her Majesty's Government ... but remembered for their: *"Bonae timere"*; that is: "Fearless and loyal".

NB: For purposes of convenience and with a sincere apology the term "Anglo Indian" has been applied to embrace the Anglo Burmese of Burma, the Burghers of Ceylon, the Goan's and Luso's of Portuguese ancestry; and the Anglo Indian of India. Their histories are not entirely dissimilar.

Bibliography of reference sources:

❶ Australian Centre for Ancient DNA, Uni. SA. ❷Department of Evolutionary Genetics, Max Planck Institute for Evolutionary Anthropology.❸Ravenstein as transcribed by Chris Gage. ❹Maddison A. ❺Dalrymple W. ❻ Prof More S. ❼Hawes & Dennis Kincaid, British social life in India 1608-1937. ❽Haller D.L.❾Griffen C & other web sources.❿Weston C.⓫Gidney H. ⓬Gaikwad, V.R. in Younger C. ⓭Stark A. ⓮Malleson G.B. ⓯Wellesley Jane. ⓰Rev. C Buchanan.⓱Schermerhorn R. A. ⓲Szczepanski K. Asian History.⓳Studymode Essays.⓴Wikipedia on Macaulayism.

⓪BBC Archives.①British Gov. National Archives.②Eire Nua publication.③Gaikwad, V.R. ④Education and Science. ⑤Varma LB. & GilbertA. ⑥Suzanne Rickard, Lifelines from Calcutta, India, China, Australia Trade and Society, 1788-1850. ⑦Henry Cornish, Under the Southern Cross, Penguin Books, England, 1880. ⑧Crawford Alan. [India-L] Passengers "William Prowse" Madras to Sydney 1853.⑨Afsheen S. ⑩Minto, J.R. ⑪James S.P. Flinders University. ⑫Bhowmick N. ⑬Leith W. ⑭By Hannah Strange, agencies.

Also:
www.newworldencyclopedia.org/entry/Afonso_de_Albuquerque#First_Expedition.2C_1503-1504

www.britannica.com/EBchecked/topic/25052/Anglo-Indian#ref1167411

www.britishempire.co.uk/forces/armyunits/indiancavalry/skinners.htm

www.archive.org/stream/historyofbritish00kastrich/historyofbritish00kastrich_djvu.txt

About BEN LAFFRA

The author writes under the *nom de guerre* of Ben Laffra to honor his progenitor Nicholas Benjamin Laffra.

As a child of the 'British Raj' of India, he was born in its final turbulent decade. He studied, lived, and worked there after India's Independence; through the exciting and sometimes dangerous immediate afterglow as India dragged itself out of three hundred and fifty years of British rule. His Tertiary disciplines did not have the slightest relationship to a Literary Career; but he did have a passion for reading histories of wars and historical fiction because, in his own words, *"it injects that vital ingredient of realism into the narrative"*.

He admits to having enjoyed the adrenaline rush, the concealed menace, and the thrill of fear that was his companion on occasion. Those experiences paved the way to influence his novels.

He migrated to Australia in the 1970's, where he now lives with his wife in Adelaide.

He is the author of the historical novels *Gideon's Passage* and *Gideon's Credo*, also available from Optimus Maximus Publishing.

CHECK OUT THE OMP WEBSITE FOR
A COMPLETE LIST OF OUR TITLES

WWW.OPTIMUSMAXIMUSPUBLISHING.COM

BOOKS ARE AVAILABLE IN BOTH PRINT
AND ELECTRONIC FORMATS

The Optimus Maximus Publishing Shield Logo, the character of OPTIMA, and the name Optimus Maximus Publishing are registered trademarks of Optimus Maximus Publishing LLC. The OPTIMA character is also the intellectual property of Jeffrey Kosh Graphics.

Lightning Source UK Ltd.
Milton Keynes UK
UKHW021300071020
371168UK00010B/359